Chances Are

If you have a home computer with Internet access you may:

- request an item to be placed on hold.
- renew an item that is not overdue.
- view titles and due dates checked out on your card.
- view your own outstanding fines.

To view your patron record from your home computer click on Patchogue-Medford Library's homepage: www.pmlib.org

Also by Barbara Bretton
in Large Print:

Girls of Summer
Shore Lights
A Soft Place to Fall

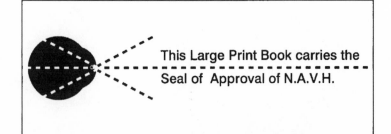

This Large Print Book carries the
Seal of Approval of N.A.V.H.

Chances Are

BARBARA BRETTON

WHEELER PUBLISHING

Published in 2005 by arrangement with The Berkley Publishing Group, a division of Penguin Group (USA) Inc.

Wheeler Large Print Softcover.

The text of this Large Print edition is unabridged.
Other aspects of the book may vary from the original edition.

Set in 16 pt. Plantin by Christina S. Huff.

Printed in the United States on permanent paper.

ISBN 1-58724-864-6 (lg. print : sc : alk. paper)

With love and thanks
to the three greatest sisters
this only child could possibly have:
Sandra Marton, Dallas Schulze,
and Bertrice Small.
How did I get so lucky?

As the Founder/CEO of NAVH, the only national health agency solely devoted to those who, although not totally blind, have an eye disease which could lead to serious visual impairment, I am pleased to recognize Thorndike Press* as one of the leading publishers in the large print field.

Founded in 1954 in San Francisco to prepare large print textbooks for partially seeing children, NAVH became the pioneer and standard setting agency in the preparation of large type.

Today, those publishers who meet our standards carry the prestigious "Seal of Approval" indicating high quality large print. We are delighted that Thorndike Press is one of the publishers whose titles meet these standards. We are also pleased to recognize the significant contribution Thorndike Press is making in this important and growing field.

Lorraine H. Marchi, L.H.D.
Founder/CEO
NAVH

* Thorndike Press encompasses the following imprints: Thorndike, Wheeler, Walker and Large Print Press.

Chapter One

Paradise Point, New Jersey

Three weeks to the day after Maddy Bainbridge announced her engagement to Aidan O'Malley, she found herself stripped and held hostage in the bridal department of the Short Hills Saks in front of her family, her future in-laws, and a PBS research assistant named Crystal whose tattoos were outnumbered only by her piercings.

Her mother had told her she was taking her out for lunch to celebrate the pending nuptials, a splashy, fun get-together with family and friends on hand to share the good news. She had set her taste buds for the amazing chicken burritos at Casa Mexicana in Spring Lake and was dismayed when they rolled right past the exit and kept on heading north. Visions of one of those terrible spa lunches — three lettuce leaves, a grape tomato, with a side of guilt — made her wish she'd stashed a bag of chips in her purse along with her daughter Hannah's current favorite Barbie.

As it turned out, a spa lunch would have been

a vast improvement over what her mother actually had in mind.

"Where is she taking my clothes?" Maddy protested as a fiercely groomed sales associate disappeared with her favorite cotton sweater and jeans.

"Don't worry," Rose DiFalco said to her daughter. "This is the only way we can be sure you won't make a run for it."

Her fashionable aunt Lucy turned her critical eye on Maddy's nearly naked form. "Does Aidan know about that underwear?" she asked, and the assembled aunts and cousins and future in-laws burst into laughter. Crystal, the research assistant, stood near the door trying very hard to be inconspicuous, which wasn't easy, given the scene from *Lord of the Rings* tattooed down the length of her right arm.

"Turn around," Maddy's cousin Gina ordered her. "I want to see if you have Monday embroidered on your butt."

The dream she'd been having lately — the one about being naked at Stop and Shop — suddenly seemed prophetic. How she had ended up standing on a carpeted pink pedestal in front of her nearest and dearest — and future in-laws — while wearing a pair of cotton bikini panties and a bra that predated the premiere of *Friends* was a question a Talmudic scholar couldn't unravel.

She was a grown woman. She had a child. She had a degree from an accredited university. She had figured out a way to balance work and romance with the equally demanding jobs of daughterhood and motherhood, but from the moment she said yes to Aidan, it seemed that control of her life had been handed over to a powerful force called The Wedding.

The questions were endless. How many bridesmaids? (Don't forget your cousins, Maddy.) Church or hotel? (Is there something wrong with The Candlelight?) Catered dinner or upscale buffet? (Why not ask Aunt Lucy to bake the cake?) Local band or big-city musicians? (You mean you're not going to ask your cousin Benny to sing at your wedding?) Long dress with a short train or short dress with a long train or maybe some combination nobody had even thought of yet. There were flowers and menus to consider, seating arrangements and engraved invitations to design, and whatever you do, don't even let them get started on hairstyles, makeup choices, and Brazilian bikini waxes for the blushing bride-to-be.

When Gina asked her if she was registered, it took Maddy a second to realize she was talking about wedding gifts and not the AKC.

Within moments of learning her daughter was planning to be married, Rose was on the phone to a multitude of sources, lining up auditions for bands, booking appointments to check out hotel ballrooms, and conferring with her sister Lucy about the all-important dress.

As a rule, Maddy was very happy to fly beneath her mother's radar, but as the days

9

passed, she began to feel like a guest at her own impending nuptials.

How come nobody ever told you that finding your soul mate was the easy part?

Falling in love with Aidan had been as natural as breathing. One moment she was moving through life, concentrating on being the best mother she could possibly be, and the next she was floating somewhere on cloud nine, madly in love and dreaming of a rose-covered cottage with a satellite dish. In her own mind she made the leap from courtship to marriage seamlessly, with maybe a few well-chosen words uttered in a small church while a handful of nearest and dearest dabbed at their eyes and toasted to their happiness.

Fat chance.

Her own clan hadn't the slightest idea how she was feeling. Between them, Grandma Fay's girls had walked down the aisle a total of sixteen times, which meant a total of sixteen engagement dinners, sixteen bridal showers, sixteen trips to the bridal department of every major store in the tristate area, and sixteen wedding receptions complete with laughter, music, and promises that this time it was going to last forever.

The trouble was, it never did last forever. In fact, on one memorable occasion, the marriage barely managed to last past the reception. When Aunt Toni grasped the knife to cut the pricey six-tier Weinstock wedding cake, you could hear the sound of three hundred wedding guests as they held their collective breath and prayed the groom didn't make any false moves.

She wondered if anyone would share that anecdote with Pete Lassiter, the historian/journalist currently gathering up tales of Paradise Point's past for a documentary on Jersey Shore towns. The second Lassiter heard that a DiFalco was planning to marry an O'Malley, his journalistic imagination shot into high gear, and he began to shape his narrative around the upcoming nuptials. The town's oldest families, whose establishments anchored the north and south ends of Paradise Point, were about to merge before man and God and a pair of PBS's best cameramen. Maddy had endured a series of preinterviews with Lassiter's underlings, long and exhaustive question-and-answer sessions that dug up details not even her own mother found very interesting. Aidan, not always the most cooperative man in town, made it halfway through his first interview before he called it quits in a fairly dramatic fashion.

"I'll bet that makes it into the documentary," she had teased him, laughing at his unprintable response. He had already sat for a preliminary interview at his old firehouse, held in place more by the memory of the brother he had lost than any desire to see his face on camera. She didn't blame him for not wanting to go through a lengthy retelling of the warehouse fire that had taken his brother's life almost three years ago.

Aidan had been cited for bravery for his own part in fighting that fire in a ceremony that was held in his hospital room a week after Billy's funeral, a fact she had to learn from his sister-in-law Claire.

The O'Malley and DiFalco families had both settled in Paradise Point in the early 1920s, immigrant families with nothing going for them but the fact that they had nothing left to lose. After decades of struggle, both families were finally beginning to reap the reward of over eighty years of backbreaking work. The town wasn't even a town back then, just a stretch of sand and hope with a couple of dilapidated Victorian houses facing the beach, a reminder of better days.

Under Aidan's guidance, O'Malley's Bar and Grill was taking giant steps into the twenty-first century and had posted its first profitable quarter in longer than anyone cared to remember.

But that success was nothing compared to the killing Maddy's mother Rose had made when she turned her own late mother Fay's rundown old boardinghouse into the most popular B and B on the East Coast. There had even been some talk of buying the B and B next door and upgrading it to meet The Candlelight's standards, but so far Rose hadn't made her move. Maddy knew it was only a matter of time. When it came to making money, her mother had the golden touch.

Out of all the DiFalco cousins, and they were legion, only Maddy had managed to reach her thirties without a divorce under her belt. "Don't look so smug," her cousin Gina had pointed out last week over nachos and margaritas at O'Malley's Grill. "That's only because you never married Tom. You were with him for six years before you two split — and that's longer than both my marriages put together — but let's face it, kid: he still walked out that door. If you ask me, I'd say you're upholding family tradition just fine."

Not something Maddy particularly wanted to hear, but since when had Gina — or any of her other relatives, for that matter — ever worried about anyone's sensibilities? Maddy loved them all dearly, but every now and then she was reminded why she had spent fifteen years living a continent away from their well-meaning observations. Maddy's one serious relationship had ended shortly after their daughter Hannah was born, and with it went her dreams of building a family with the man she had loved.

But then one day everything changed. Maddy left her old life in Seattle behind and brought Hannah home to Paradise Point, where she fell in love with Aidan O'Malley and, to her delight, the object of her affections returned the sentiment tenfold. Of all the surprises the fates might have had up their sleeves, that was the biggest one of all.

She glanced around the enormous dressing

room and did a quick head count. "Where's Hannah?" she asked Rose, trying to keep her tone even as visions of her five-year-old daughter running amok through row upon row of ten-thousand-dollar gowns made her knees knock.

Rose looked up from the book of fabric swatches she had been inspecting. "Kelly found her turning somersaults across a stack of bridesmaid dresses."

"Oh God —"

"She scooped Hannah up midroll and took her out for some ice cream."

Bless her future stepdaughter for always knowing the right thing to do.

"The bridesmaid dresses — ?" She steeled herself for the damage.

"Are fine," Rose said, her attention clearly divided between her daughter and a shimmering square of rum pink duchesse satin. "The child is full of high spirits. There's nothing to be concerned about."

A year ago Maddy wouldn't have been able to hold back the sharp retort, but times had changed. Now she counted to three before she opened her mouth.

"Did you see the price tags on those outfits? Hannah could somersault her way through a year's salary while I'm standing here in my underwear waiting for some snippy salesclerk to bring me a pile of —"

"And here we are," said the snippy salesclerk

14

as she sailed into their midst, arms piled high with gowns. "I brought three size eights and a ten . . . just in case."

Aunts Toni and Connie exchanged knowing looks. Maddy considered telling them she would choose padded hips over drooping jowls any day of the week but doubted anyone but Gina would see the humor in her remark.

Get me out of here, she silently pleaded to Gina as she stepped into a frilly white confection that seemed better suited to Scarlett O'Hara than a thirty-something Jersey girl.

Too late, Gina said with a grin and a shrug of her shoulders.

"We've all been through it, too," Aunt Lucy whispered in her ear as she helped button Maddy into the too-snug bodice. "The worst is almost over."

Sure it was. Try saying that when you were standing there in your underwear.

Rose, her usually practical and levelheaded mother, the woman who would be first in line to tell her it was time to cut a few calories, held up a narrow tube of ivory satin that looked like a ribbon of heavy cream. "This would look wonderful on you."

"On my right thigh maybe."

"Try it on."

"I don't think so."

"Madelyn, you can't judge a gown on the hanger."

"I can judge that one. It's too small."

"I'm sure it will fit."

"She's probably right, Rosie," Aunt Toni piped up. "Better you try it in a ten or twelve."

"Sleeveless?" Aunt Connie sounded dubious. "No woman should go sleeveless after thirty-five."

"I'm thirty-three," Maddy said, praying for a well-timed lightning bolt or a minor earthquake to put an end to this hideous scene.

"Be that as it may, if you're over size eight, don't show your arms," Aunt Connie barreled on. Her gaze zeroed in on Maddy's less-than-perfect upper arms like a pointer during duck season. "Case closed."

"Liposuction did wonders for your double chin, Connie," Aunt Lucy observed with a wicked smile. "Too bad Dr. Weinblatt also sucked out what was left of your brain."

Gina snickered loud enough to be heard in Pennsylvania while Denise and Pat quickly turned away so nobody could see them laughing. Lucy and Connie had been at war for as long as anyone could remember. Age had done little to diminish the sibling rivalry that had been simmering between them for more than sixty years.

Maddy caught sight of Aidan's sister-in-law Claire reflected in the huge dressing room mirror. Claire looked both amused and slightly embarrassed by the familial bickering, but at least she wasn't playing connect-the-dots with Maddy's stretch marks the way her blood kin were. Still, there was something disapproving

16

about Claire, something Maddy couldn't quite put her finger on but sensed through the wisecracks and laughter. Claire had seemed to like her well enough before she and Aidan announced their engagement, but the second Maddy showed up with a ring on her finger, Claire had turned noticeably chilly and, to Maddy's surprise, the coolness hurt.

It had to be hard for Claire to watch Aidan build a new family after all these years of being a single father, while she was still adjusting to life without her husband Billy. Aidan's firefighter brother had died in a blaze almost three years ago, leaving Claire alone with five children, a heavily mortgaged house, and a rundown bar on the blue-collar side of town.

Who could blame the woman if she found it tough to join in the preparations with a full heart? Still, Maddy found she missed the old wisecracking Claire. They hadn't been close, but at least the potential for friendship had been there.

Claire turned slightly, and their eyes met in the mirror. Maddy made a face, and Claire offered a sympathetic smile. It was the kind of smile you flashed at the woman in line behind you at the ATM. Impersonal. Easily forgotten. Still, it was better than the polar breeze Maddy had been feeling lately from her future, sort-of sister-in-law, and she was grateful.

Unfortunately, that was when she made the fatal mistake of sighing deeply, and the top button popped the loop and rocketed across the dressing room straight toward Aunt Toni.

Bull's-eye.

Toni slapped her hand over her right eye and let out a howl. "I've been shot!"

It would take more than a bolt of lightning or a minor earthquake to get Maddy out of this one with her dignity intact. "Aunt Toni, I'm so sorry. My — uh, my button popped."

Toni glared at Maddy from between splayed fingers. "I told you to try on the ten, didn't I?"

"Ma!" Gina's expression was downright murderous. "Can you give it a rest?"

"I think I need a doctor," Toni said, ignoring her daughter completely. "That button shot across the room like a bullet! It could've put out my eye."

"For God's sake, Ma." It was Denise's turn. "It didn't touch you. I saw it hit your ring and ricochet past you."

"My own daughters don't believe me." Toni turned to her sisters for support. "Is this the thanks I get for all I've done for them? I could've been killed, and they stand there telling me nothing happened."

Gina whipped out her cell phone and flipped it open. "You're right, Ma. You're lucky you weren't killed. In fact, it might have been attempted murder. I'll call the cops so you can file a report." She winked at Maddy. "Death by bridal button. It'll look good on the front page of the *Star-Ledger* tomorrow morning."

Toni huffed. She had had a lot of practice over the years and was a world-class huffer. "I don't know why we had to drive up to Short Hills anyway. We should've gone to the Bridal Barn in Freehold. They specialize in plus sizes."

"That's it," Rose said, flinging open the door to the enormous dressing area. "Everybody out!"

"You're throwing us out?" Toni looked horrified.

"What did I do?" Connie demanded. "I'm not the one who's calling the cops."

"Out!" Rose repeated. "Every single one of you."

Maddy gathered up her voluminous skirts and stepped down from her pedestal. "You don't have to tell me twice."

"Not you," Rose said, grabbing her firmly by the wrist. "The rest of you."

The aunts and cousins grumbled, but they knew Rose meant business. Crystal, the PBS research assistant, made a gallant attempt at standing up to Rose but quickly — and grudgingly — admitted defeat. Claire, however, looked profoundly grateful.

"My sisters are horses' asses," her mother said as she closed the door behind the extended DiFalco clan plus two. "If I ever doubted that fact, they proved it today."

"You won't get an argument from me."

"Buttons pop all the time."

"Sure they do," Maddy said dryly. Every time

19

you tried to squash a size-ten woman into a size-eight dress without a shoehorn.

"Don't make more of a popped button than the situation warrants."

Easy for you to say, Rosie. You're not the one whose cellulite was hanging out on display.

"I'm a size ten. I've been a ten all my life. Why pretend I'm an eight when I'm not? If I can live with it, why can't the rest of them?"

"Lucy was looking more for style than fit, Madelyn. They can take care of the fit once you've settled on a gown."

Maddy took a deep breath, and two more buttons clattered to the floor. There was no time like the present. "Ma, about the gown . . ."

Rose helped slide the fussy bodice off her daughter's shoulders. "Not your style at all. I completely agree."

Another deep breath. Thank God there were no more buttons to pop. "I'm not sure any of them is."

She stepped out of the gown. Rose, unnaturally calm, gathered it up and reached for the enormous padded hanger.

"You've only tried on one dress, Madelyn. I don't think you should lose hope quite so fast."

"Ma, this whole thing is moving a little too fast for me. I'm not sure a big wedding is what Aidan and I have in mind."

"Your wedding is only four months away." Rose fastened the dress to the hanger and suspended it from the rod in the corner. "Isn't it time you decided?"

Four months, three weeks, and eleven days. The unemployed accountant in her was keeping close track. "I thought we might just enjoy being engaged for a while longer before we start planning the wedding."

"I understand," Rose said, although it was clear to Maddy that she didn't, "but if you're serious about a late September wedding, we need to start planning right now."

"It's not even June yet, Ma. We have plenty of time."

"The best places book up years in advance. We're already operating at a disadvantage."

"Then we won't plan a big wedding." *Check and mate!* "We'll just have a small, intimate gathering."

She had to hand it to her mother. Rose didn't even blink. "A big wedding is every bride's dream." A beat pause. "Especially if the bride comes from a big family."

"The DiFalcos have seen more than their share of weddings. One more would only get lost in the shuffle."

"God knows we've given more than our share of wedding presents to your cousins. It's time we were on the receiving end."

A wiser woman might have retired to her corner to fight another day, but old habits die hard. Her mother's words reawakened her sleeping inner teenager, the same one who had made Rose's life as difficult as humanly possible a lifetime ago and enjoyed every minute of it.

"Aidan thinks we should elope."

This time Rose's expression shifted from surprise to shock and then from shock to outrage. "I hope this is your idea of a joke."

Oh God. Why did she say that? A hand grenade would have done less damage than those five words. "He — uh, he suggested we grab Kelly and Hannah and fly to Vegas." Next time she heard someone espouse total honesty, she would mention this hideous moment.

"I thought he was smarter than that."

She had been about to add that Aidan had probably been joking, but her mother's remark stung. "Actually, I think it's a very good idea. You'd save a lot of money, and I wouldn't have to stand around in my underwear while your sisters ridicule the size of my butt."

"Your aunts are the way they are. If I had a nickel for every insult they've sent my way, I'd own every B and B from here to Maine. You're entirely too thin-skinned, Madelyn. You always have been."

"Apparently my skin is the only thing about me that's too thin."

Rose quickly gave her the once-over. "Well, you have put on a few pounds since Christmas."

"Thanks," she snapped. "Nothing like words of comfort from the mother of the bride. Make sure you give my measurements to Crystal so she can use them in the documentary."

22

"I didn't say it was unbecoming. You're tall. You carry it well."

"Sure I do," said Maddy. "I guess I'm not supposed to notice that medieval corset the saleswoman brought in with her."

"Proper foundation garments can make or break a formal gown."

"I really don't need a lecture on girdles, Mother."

"I never said you needed a girdle. Bridal gowns require a certain type of underpinning. You either have boning sewn into your dress or you wear a merry widow. It's all part of the game."

"Maybe I don't want to play that game."

"It's one day of your life, Madelyn. It's about family."

"No, it isn't," she shot back. "It should be about Aidan and me. Nobody else."

Rose turned away, but not before Maddy saw the sheen of tears in her eyes. Her mother never cried. The only time she had seen Rose cry was that terrible day last year when they had rushed Hannah to the hospital and for a while it had seemed they were going to lose her. It had been a day of intense emotions. Anger. Guilt. Fear. And then the almost punishing sense of relief when Hannah came back to them.

"Ma," she said, swinging wildly between anger and guilt, "don't cry." She forced a laugh. She felt naked and vulnerable, standing there in her ratty cotton underwear. More like her

23

mother's child than the mother of a child of her own. "Get a shoehorn. I'll try to squeeze into that dress if it means that much."

"No need," said Rose as she turned back toward Maddy. The tears had been replaced by the familiar steely resolve that had sent her daughter running clear across the country immediately after high school. "It's almost one-thirty. I think everyone could use some lunch."

"But why don't we —"

"I'll get your clothes."

Maddy was trapped. Rose was already halfway out the door, and it was clear Maddy wasn't going to follow her in her bra and panties. The only thing she could do was wait until the snippy saleswoman relinquished her sweater and jeans to Rose, then join the rest of the clan for lunch.

Humble pie with a side of crow.

A DiFalco family favorite.

"I found a Priscilla of Boston with cap sleeves that would look wonderful on your daughter." The sales associate, whose discreet name tag read *Dianne,* pointed to an explosion of ivory satin and lace draped across a padded chaise longue. "And in a ten, no less. You have no idea how difficult it is to find anything suitable in double digits. We try very hard to accommodate the fuller-figured bride, but —" Her sigh of disappointment wasn't terribly convincing. "What can I say? Most of our customers maintain rigorous workout schedules, especially as the big day approaches."

Bitch.

"We're going to stop for the day," Rose said, managing a polite smile when what she really wanted to do was rip out the woman's artificial heart. "But thanks for all of your help."

"She only tried on one gown."

"That's right," Rose said pleasantly.

"You can't make a decision based on one gown."

"Of course you can't," Rose agreed. If there was one thing being an innkeeper had taught her, it was how to dissemble with the best of them. "That's why we're stopping for today and going out to lunch."

The woman's heavily Botoxed face approximated a human emotion. Amazing she could convey such disdain with so few moving parts.

"May I ask if she liked the Wang?" She flipped open a notebook and uncapped her pen. "I maintain a database of the prospective bride's preferences."

"That's wonderful," Rose said. "May I offer a suggestion?"

"Please do. I welcome input."

"Next time, try not to insult the prospective bride about the size on the label. Not very good for business, dear, and even worse for the young woman's confidence."

It wasn't the left hook she wanted to deliver, but that verbal jab to the chin implant was almost as satisfying. Rose had seen her daughter's face when talk turned to dress sizes and un-toned muscles, and she had wished profoundly that she had thought it through before ar-ranging this shopping trip from hell. It was one thing for Rose to gently criticize her daughter's expanding waistline or taste in clothes. It was something else again for anybody else to even think about it.

Rose was a lioness where Maddy and Hannah were concerned. The depth of her love had the capacity to terrify her. It made her vulnerable to life, to fate; and for a woman like Rose, that fed into her deepest fears. When she had first been diagnosed with breast cancer five years ago, her first thought had been for her daughter. She had stopped going to Mass a very long time ago, but the day before her surgery, she had found her-self in the last pew at Our Lady of Lourdes, praying not for herself but that her daughter would be spared a similar fate.

"My daughter's clothes," she demanded of the salesclerk, feeling an overwhelming desire to escape the perfumed excess of the salon.

Although it was clear there wouldn't be a sale — certainly not today — the salesclerk main-tained her professional poise in the face of a dis-appearing commission. Rose was impressed. "I'll bring them to her immediately."

Suddenly she saw her daughter the way the salesclerk never could. Her beautiful body, not the body of a girl any longer, but the body of a woman. A mother. The faintest silvery lines across her belly and breasts. The gentle softness that came with giving birth and nursing a child. Maddy had never been more beautiful or more vulnerable to the criticism of others.

And she should have known better than to expose her child to the scrutiny.

"I'll take them," she said, then waited while the salesclerk fetched the faded jeans and hand-knit sweater from some secret cubbyhole far away from the Wangs and Acras and Priscillas.

Lucy aimed an uplifted brow at Rose from the far end of the bridal salon while her other sisters scowled and turned away. It might as well have been fifty years ago when they were squabbling over a poodle skirt and the boy next door. They no longer fought over clothes or men — thank God for that — but everything else in the universe was fair game, most especially their children.

Of course they weren't children any longer. Except for Maddy, their daughters had been married and divorced and married again. They were already showing signs of outdoing their mothers in the marital sweepstakes, racking up numbers that would break your heart if you were foolish enough to think about it for too long. This would be Maddy's first trip down the aisle, and Rose wanted her day to be everything blessed and special that a wedding day could be. But, most of all, she wanted the marriage to be a good one, the kind that grew stronger, grew deeper, long after the wedding albums had been tucked away.

The salesclerk returned with Maddy's clothes. Rose thanked her, then slipped back into the private dressing room.

Maddy was slumped on the edge of the chaise longue in the corner, wedged in between a bolt of snow-blind white lace and a stack of design portfolios. She looked up at the sound of the door, then looked away when she saw it was Rose standing there with her sweater and jeans.

Rose handed her the clothes. "I figured you'd seen enough of our friend Dianne."

Maddy slipped the bright yellow cotton sweater over her head and tugged it on. "Thanks."

"We'll wait for you by the cars."

"Okay."

Rose hesitated in the doorway. "This shopping expedition wasn't a very good idea after all."

"Really?" said Maddy. "And here I've been having a swell time."

She wanted to apologize. The words "I'm sorry" balanced on the tip of her tongue, but she couldn't bring herself to utter them aloud. Did wanting the best for your only child require an apology? Was dreaming about a storybook wedding fit for a princess a crime against the nation?

"Don't take too long," she said instead.

"Bernino's stops serving at two, and it's a bit of a drive."

"Something to look forward to," Maddy mumbled as Rose closed the door behind her.

Sticks and stones can break your bones, but words will never harm you.

Whoever said that clearly never had children.

Chapter Two

It took every ounce of Claire Meehan O'Malley's self-control to keep from dropping to her knees in front of Rose DiFalco and kissing her cocktail ring. She had been about to fake a heart attack in order to get out of that toxic dressing room when Rose unceremoniously kicked their collective asses out, and not a moment too soon.

Claire had always believed her own family had the market cornered on dysfunctional behavior, but after seeing the DiFalcos up close and personal, she had to admit there was a new contender for the crown. Compared to the DiFalcos, both the Meehans and the O'Malleys were rank amateurs.

Those two old cows, Connie and Antoinette, looked like they were counting down the seconds to a brawl. Claire crossed paths with them a few times a week, and she always found herself whispering a prayer of thanks that she didn't have to look at either one of them over a breakfast table in the morning. No wonder their families were so screwed up. Generation after generation of DiFalco women continued to pick the wrong men with unerring accuracy.

Not that Claire was being judgmental. The cousins were a likable bunch — most of them, anyway — but their romantic escapades and mistakes were, in some cases, a matter of public record. Maddy's own history was decidedly less flamboyant, but even she hadn't escaped her family's unbroken run of bad luck in love.

Gina and Denise were whispering together near an arrangement of rhinestone-studded Manolo Blahniks that cost more than her monthly mortgage payment. Suddenly she glanced around her at the Vera Wang dresses, the Manolos, and caught the unmistakable smell of money in the air. What was she doing there? Saks wasn't her kind of store. She couldn't afford a pair of panty hose in this place, much less wedding party attire. Unless they somehow ended up outfitting the bridesmaids at Target, she would have to find a way to gracefully decline the privilege or tell her youngest that college was out of the question.

"I don't know who she thinks she is," Connie was saying, loudly enough for everyone in the store to hear. "She can't throw us out. She doesn't own the place."

"Take a look at my eye." Toni thrust her face in front of Claire. "Is there any blood?"

Neither one seemed the slightest bit disturbed

31

that the tattooed girl from PBS was frantically scribbling notes near a Badgley-Mischka.

Claire was about to say something uncharitable and possibly unforgivable when the dressing room door swung open, and Rose stalked out for a second time.

"Madelyn said she'll meet us in the parking garage, and then we'll go to Bernino's for lunch." She glanced around, mentally counting heads. "Kelly and Hannah aren't back yet?"

"I haven't seen them," Lucy said, a faint frown pleating her forehead above her nose. Connie and Toni turned their backs and ignored the entire conversation.

"Kelly was going to take Hannah for some ice cream," Rose said. "I wonder if —"

Opportunity didn't have to hit Claire O'Malley in the head twice.

"I'll find them," she said, "and meet you at the cars."

"I'll go with you," Lucy volunteered. "It's a big mall. This way we can spread out."

"It's not that big," she said to Lucy as soon as they ducked out of Saks.

"As long as they don't know that, I'm safe." She winked at Claire. "You think you're the only one who needed an escape hatch?"

They ducked around a display of enormous Hummers that looked like SUVs on steroids.

"We're not usually like this," Lucy said as they stopped to check out a map of the mall opposite Tiffany.

"Every family has a bad day," Claire said. It was easy to be magnanimous with Lucy, even when you didn't mean it.

"Actually we're on our best behavior." Her eyes twinkled up at Claire. "Hard to believe, isn't it?"

It was, but Claire kept that observation to herself. "My sisters and I once cleared the parking lot at Kmart with one of our fights."

"The one near Wildwood?"

"Nope," said Claire. "The big one up near A.C."

Lucy whistled low. "I'm impressed. I would think they'd pretty much seen it all up there."

"We put on quite a show," Claire said. "My sister Vicky had to wear a wig for a month afterward."

"I'm too much of a lady to ask for details," Lucy said, laughing, "but it sounds like we're all candidates for daytime television. Did you see the way our pierced friend has been taking notes? It terrifies me to think of what my sisters have told Peter Lassiter."

"Don't you meet him tonight?" Claire asked, trying to keep the judgmental tone from her voice. She hated Peter Lassiter and his entire crew, sticking their noses into places where they didn't belong, asking questions nobody in her right mind would even consider answering.

"Seven-fifteen," Lucy said. "He wants to see the scrapbooks from the dress shop I owned on Main Street."

"Now there's something worth reminiscing about," she said. "Bet you don't remember that I worked for you."

"Don't I? You were far and away the absolute worst salesgirl I ever had."

Claire winced. "My people skills needed a little work back then."

"You made my sister Rose look like Madeleine Albright."

"Did I ever thank you for helping me find a new job at the bakery?"

"Yes," Lucy said, "and so did my customers. Those were three of the longest days of my life."

Claire laughed. It wasn't an insult coming from Lucy. It was only the truth remembered with fondness. "Mine, too," she said. "My mother told me I had to earn the money for my prom gown or I couldn't go. I figured if I worked for you, I'd get a store discount. Nobody told me you needed a degree in abnormal psych to sell dresses."

"Why do you think I hid in the workroom with my sewing machine and my dress form? It was dangerous out there on the floor."

"The way I see it, I was lucky to make it through that third day alive."

"I hope I still gave you the discount."

"You did," Claire said. "And you even lent me a gorgeous pair of satin gloves to wear with it."

"At least that's one story I wouldn't mind ending up in the documentary," Lucy said with pretend relief. "Now, if I could bribe my sisters and a few of my ex-husbands to be kind, I could breathe easy again."

They chatted easily about the dress shop and Lucy's dressmaking skills as they approached the door of the ice cream shop. Huge hand-lettered signs adorned the windows, singing the praises of peppermint crunch, rocky road, and black cherry bonanza.

"Hand-packed cones with sprinkles," Claire said, barely disguising her longing. "Do you think we have time?"

"Honey, if you think I came all this way to leave without a strawberry cone, then you don't know me very well."

Too bad Lucy wasn't forty years younger. This was one DiFalco she would love to welcome into the family as Aidan's new wife.

"Vanilla, sugar cone, chocolate sprinkles," she said, fishing in her pocket for a few singles as they approached the counter.

Lucy waved off her money. "It's the least I can do after the horror show my sisters put on for you."

"I'll check the back room and the bathroom. You watch the door."

"Take your time," Lucy said with a wicked grin. "Wouldn't hurt the lot of them to cool their heels in the parking garage."

TJ's reminded Claire of Farrell's, an ice cream parlor that had been popular back when she and Billy first married. The cheerful ragtime music. The old-fashioned soda fountain decor complete with faux newspaper clippings pasted on the walls. The wait staff was dressed in billowy white shirts, black pants, and suspenders, and they exuded such all-American wholesomeness that she wouldn't have been at all surprised if they had been pasteurized, homogenized, and stamped with a freshness date.

She stood in the archway to the main dining room and scanned the crowd. It was the usual Monday mix of elderly shoppers gathering up their energy for the return trip home, a handful of teenage girls sharing a pair of hot fudge sundaes, young mothers with rambunctious toddlers and babies still in Snugglies or waiting in the womb.

Claire felt a pang as she looked at their ripe and burgeoning bellies. She had loved being pregnant. The entire experience had agreed with her. She felt better, ate better, slept better the five times she was pregnant than at any other time in her life. Her friends had complained about feeling sexless and ugly during their pregnancies, but not Claire. She had never felt juicier or more alive. Even Billy had noticed the difference and during those months their lovemaking took on a sweet wildness she still remembered.

Sometimes late at night when the bed seemed very wide and very empty, she took out those memories, dusted them off, and tried to call up a sense of how it had felt to be touched and held and almost loved.

They had tried hard to make it work, but the odds had been against them from the start. Maybe if they had been a little older, a little smarter, they might have realized that before it was too late, but in her most honest moments, Claire knew she would make the same choices all over again.

They hadn't had a storybook romance like Maddy and Aidan, one of those moonlight and magic experiences that made great fodder for TV shows, but it hadn't been all bad. They had built a family together, brought five beautiful children into the world together. Despite the anger, despite the disappointments, they had been together at the end. They had been a family, a real one, imperfect and loud but real and lasting. For many reasons, that was something she would never regret.

She didn't understand women like Maddy who moved away from home and made new lives for themselves far away from family and friends. The thought was as alien to Claire as life without soccer would be to her son Billy. You grew where you were planted. Sure, you made adjustments, a little more light, a little less water, maybe a judicious pruning every now and then, but you managed. You did it for your parents and for your kids, and as you grew older and a little wiser, you began to realize you did it for yourself as well.

When Maddy came back home with her tail between her legs, Claire couldn't help but wonder if that homecoming ever would have happened if Tom Lawler hadn't walked out on Maddy and Hannah. She was willing to bet her favorite earrings that Rose DiFalco's daughter would have stayed happily ensconced in some fancy penthouse in Seattle without a single thought for Paradise Point.

You're being a bitch, that small and annoying voice of clarity whispered into her ear. Her two middle girls, Willow and Courtney, joined the Army right out of high school in order to finance their college educations. How was that so very different from what Maddy had done? Sometimes the future ended up being somewhere — and with somebody — you would never know existed if you didn't take a chance.

One of the young mothers looked up and caught Claire's eye. They smiled at each other over the head of the woman's noisily nursing baby, one of those magical moments of connection between perfect strangers.

Cherish every single one of these moments, Claire wanted to tell her. *They'll be memories before you take your next breath.*

But she knew the woman would never believe her. She was young and she might even be happy and she had all the time in the world.

Just like Claire had believed a long, long time ago.

"I want my mommy." Hannah's stubborn little chin lurched forward in a way Kelly

O'Malley was quickly coming to recognize as trouble. "I don't want to be here anymore."

Kelly was smart. She was responsible. She went to Mass almost every Sunday. There was no way this could be happening. She held the door to the bathroom stall shut with her foot and wondered what she had done to tick off God so badly. There was no other reason she could come up with to explain how she had ended up puking her guts out in a john at TJ Sweet's while her future stepsister watched and probably took notes.

"I'm sorry, Hannah," she said, closing her eyes against a rising tide of dizziness. "I guess the ice cream didn't agree with me."

"Ice cream doesn't make people throw up," Hannah observed. "Ice cream makes you better."

"Well, this time ice cream —" She started to retch again but her stomach had long since parted company with its contents. Dry heaves were a nice change.

Hannah started to wail, big loud siren whoops of misery. If Kelly hadn't felt so horrible, she might have joined in. Of all the stupid times to get sick, this really had to be the worst. At least none of Maddy's scary aunts were here to see this. She could just imagine what they would have to say about it. She had no doubt that any time a female under fifty got queasy they started eyeing her waistline and whispering behind her back. The thought almost made her retch one more time, but she pulled in a deep breath and willed her stomach to calm down. It couldn't be. Absolutely positively impossible.

Almost impossible, a little voice whispered. The nuns had been right when they preached celibacy — if you didn't count the Virgin Mary — as the only perfect form of birth control. Condoms, the Pill, diaphragms, and coils and creams and foams — they all failed every now and then.

Funny how you could know something but not know it at the very same time. The statistics had been drummed into her head during sex ed over the years, those tiny little percentage point margins of error that could change your life forever, but you never thought they had anything to do with you or the way you felt every time he walked into a room and gave you that special smile.

Those things happened to somebody else, some anonymous girl out there who wasn't as smart or as careful as you were. Someone who didn't have a full scholarship to Columbia or a game plan for the rest of her life. Seth was going to Columbia, too, which made it so perfect that it almost scared her. They would be together for the four years it took to get their undergrad degrees, then they would marry, work on their M.A.'s and somewhere in the shadowy, golden future, they would finally start a family.

Hannah's wails turned into hiccups. The little girl looked up at her, eyes wide, and hiccuped again. Kelly couldn't help it. She started to giggle. The whole day had been surreal. Maddy's scary aunts. Her own aunt Claire looking like she wanted to make a break for it. Her future stepmother forced to stand there in her underwear. And now there she was, sitting on the bathroom floor at an ice cream parlor at snooty Short Hills Mall, watching Hannah go for the world hiccup record.

Hannah hiccuped one more time, then started giggling, too, and the next thing Kelly knew, the two of them were holding on to each other, laughing until their sides ached.

"I have to go," Hannah said when the laughter subsided. "Right now!"

"So go," Kelly said, starting to laugh again. "We're in the john!"

"No," said Hannah, that stubborn jaw beginning to wobble. "You can't be here when I go."

Kelly pulled herself to her feet and brushed off the back of her denim skirt. "Do you need any help?"

Hannah shook her head. "Go!"

"I'll be right outside," Kelly said, opening the door to the stall. "Shout out if you need me."

Hannah pushed the door closed behind her, and Kelly couldn't help grinning when she heard the little girl fumbling with the lock.

"Leave it unlocked, Hannah," she advised. "I'll make sure nobody comes in."

She held the door closed with her hand and rested her forehead against the cool painted sur-

41

face. At least the room wasn't spinning any longer. That was an improvement over the amusement park ride it had turned into a few seconds after she wolfed down some ice cream. The stuff should have a warning label on it. At least if you'd been starving yourself the last few weeks so you could wear that scrumptious strapless gown to the senior prom. That was probably the reason she had been sick. All that cold ice cream on an empty stomach would upset anyone's digestion.

And what about yesterday and the day before? You can't blame that on ice cream.

She heard the sound of paper rustling behind the door to the stall, followed by the snap of an elastic waist and mumbling. Hannah had recently turned five. Was that old enough to take care of things without help? She wished she could remember what had been within her abilities at that age, but it was so long ago that the details were a blur.

"Everything okay?" she called out.

Hannah's response was drowned out by the sound of the toilet flushing, which Kelly decided to take as a yes.

A minute later Hannah pulled at the door. Kelly let go, and the two of them trooped over to the wall of sinks, where Kelly lifted the child up so she could wash her hands.

"Soap," Hannah said, waving her fingers. "I need more."

Kelly gave the dispenser another push, and a

ribbon of golden soap settled in the palm of Hannah's hand.

"We'd better hurry," she said, holding Hannah once again so she could reach the stream of hot air from the hand-drying machine. "Your mom will be sending out a search party for us."

"I didn't eat my ice cream," Hannah pointed out with the relentless logic of a five-year-old. "It's still out there."

"It's probably melted. You can have ice cream with lunch."

She made it a point never to lie to a child. Kids might not be able to remember where they put their schoolbooks, but they never forgot it when an adult lied to them. They had to stop for lunch. There was no way they would drive all the way back down to Paradise Point on empty stomachs — not with her Aunt Claire in the group — and every restaurant in New Jersey offered ice cream for dessert.

Hannah tugged at her wrist. "I wanna go now."

She rinsed her face at the sink, then made Hannah laugh as she angled her face to catch a blast of air from the hand-drying machine.

"So this is where the party is." Aunt Claire popped up in the doorway, a curious expression on her face. "We were getting worried."

"Did you see my ice cream?" Hannah asked. "I didn't finish."

"You didn't? Wow! My girls always finished their ice cream." Aunt Claire's gaze traveled from Hannah to Kelly. "How come?"

43

No, Hannah, please don't!

"Kelly had to throw up, and she made me go with her."

Aunt Claire had a way of looking at you that made you feel like she knew what you were thinking before you thought it. As a little girl, she had seen her aunt turn that lethal look on her own kids many times, and it had always made her grateful she didn't have any deep, dark secrets to hide. She wished she could say the same thing now.

"Kel?" Her aunt could pack more into one word than anyone she had ever met.

"No big deal," she said. "The ice cream hit me funny."

Claire placed a palm against her forehead and looked deep into her eyes. Kelly wanted desperately to look away, but she couldn't. Her aunt's touch was as familiar to her as her own heartbeat. Claire had always been there, right at the center of Kelly's life for as long as she could remember. Claire's door had always been open to Kelly and her dad. There had always been a place for them at the table, even during those times when Claire's own family life was turned upside down.

That was a long time ago. Kelly loved her aunt with all her heart, but Claire would never understand. Not in a million years. But Maddy would. She found herself wishing it was Maddy's hand on her forehead, Maddy's soft voice asking if anything was wrong.

44

"You're okay?" her aunt persisted.

"Sure I am. Why wouldn't I be?"

Claire studied her for what seemed like for-ever, and she wished she could run into her arms the way she did when she was Hannah's age.

I'm scared, Aunt Claire . . . make it better . . . make it go away. . . .

Hannah elbowed her way between them and pulled on the hem of Claire's pale green cotton sweater. "Can we go now? Bathrooms smell funny."

Kelly took her future stepsister's hand in hers. "Come on," she said with a wink for her aunt. "I'm sure your grandma's plans for lunch in-clude ice cream."

"Why don't you come over for supper to-night," Claire said as she elbowed the door open for them. "We need to talk."

"I'd love to," Kelly lied, "but I have math club."

"Tomorrow then."

"I'm going over to Maddy's."

Oops. Wrong thing to say. Her aunt's face seemed to close in on itself every time she men-tioned Maddy's name.

"Then Saturday morning for breakfast."

"I really want to, Aunt Claire, but five of us in the senior class are being interviewed for the documentary Saturday morning. We're the sev-enty-fifth graduating class and —"

"You're going to make time next week, Kelly Ann. I want to know what's going on."

45

She leaned over and pressed a kiss to her aunt's cheek. "Did anyone ever tell you that you worry too much?"

"No," Claire said, ruffling her hair with a loving hand. "You're the first." She straightened the collar of Kelly's shirt. "Your father doesn't know how lucky he is."

It hurt to hear those words and know how wrong they were. She had always been the good girl, the achiever, the one you could count on to do the right thing. When her cousins were screwing up and getting in trouble, Kelly the Good was snagging straight *A*s and being voted class president. Her cousins had messy boy-friend troubles, occasional acne, and their fair share of fender benders and blown curfews, while Saint Kelly sailed along with the wind at her back.

The crazier things got in the O'Malley family, the greater the pressure Kelly felt to be perfect. Nobody asked her for perfection. Nobody had to. She had been hardwired that way from the start, in competition with some idealized view of herself that she couldn't possibly live up to. But that didn't keep her from trying. She liked the sense of order that came with following the rules. She liked making lists then checking off the items one by one as she completed them. She liked knowing her father and her aunt didn't have to worry that she was going to to-tally mess up her life by making some stupid, stupid, one-time-only mistake. . . .

Hannah was watching her closely, those big blue eyes of hers taking it all in, storing it away until she got home and could tell Rose and Maddy every single detail, beginning with the ice cream and ending up with Kelly hugging the porcelain receptacle.

Something to look forward to.

Chapter Three

Rose had reserved a table for fourteen in the main dining room at Bernino's, a steak and seafood restaurant situated atop one of North Jersey's many rolling hills. Maddy dawdled in the lobby, pretending to fuss with Hannah's shirt-sleeve until her aunts had claimed their seats at the far end of the table and she could situate herself and her little girl out of the line of fire at the opposite end.

Unfortunately, she would have had to find seats in Delaware to escape their notice.

"The girl's not eating her broccoli." Aunt Toni punctuated her statement with a wave of her well-loaded fork. "She's wasting good produce."

Aunt Connie nodded sagely. "I never let any of my children leave the table until they finished all of their vegetables."

"Which probably explains the rise in eating disorders in Paradise Point," Gina whispered in Maddy's ear.

"You're being rude, Gina." Toni glared at her

daughter across the table. "Tell everyone what you said to Madelyn."

Gina's smile was wickedly bland. "I was just telling Maddy about the time you and Father O'Donnell got stranded under the —"

The table erupted in raucous laughter. Toni pushed back her chair and made to leave in a self-righteous huff until Connie reminded her that they had driven there in her car, and she wasn't going anywhere before she had dessert.

"Make sure you pass that along to your boss," Lucy said to Crystal. "We'll end up on *Jerry Springer* instead of PBS."

Another burst of laughter from the assembled group, followed by a few comments that would make a seasoned sailor blush.

"Toni looks like she wants to crawl under the table and disappear," Maddy said to her cousin. "I almost feel sorry for her."

"She had it coming," Gina said, spearing a broccoli floret from Hannah's plate and popping it into her mouth. "The woman has a mouth on her that won't quit."

Gina reached for another floret, but Hannah covered her plate with her hands. The second Gina's fork withdrew, Hannah picked up the biggest piece of broccoli she could find and ate it with the same enthusiasm she usually reserved for ice cream sundaes.

"You're good," Maddy said. "That was an impressive display of maternal power."

"I've had more practice than you," Gina said

with a wink. "Just do what works and forget the rest."

Maddy caught Claire's eye across the table. Her future semi-sister-in-law was watching the two of them with an expression that was equal parts curiosity and — could it be? — dislike.

"What's her problem?" Gina mumbled behind her water glass. "At least we combed our hair before we went out."

"Gina!"

"I'm serious. Look at that face on her. I'd get a food taster if I were you, cuz."

"She's sitting next to Connie. Can you blame her?"

"That's not Connie she's glaring at, honey. She's aiming that stink eye right at you."

"You're imagining it."

"Am I?"

"Get over it, Claire," Gina murmured behind her linen napkin. "At least you didn't inherit the DiFalco thighs."

How were you supposed to instill in your child the value of good manners when you were teetering on the verge of a full-blown laughing jag? Thank God for Aunt Lucy, whose impeccable timing saved her from total humiliation.

"So, have you all heard what Olivia Westmore is planning for the old McClanahan cottage?" Lucy asked the table at large.

"I heard she's going to rent it to summer people," Pat volunteered from the other end of the table.

"God forbid." Aunt Connie crossed herself. "One thing we don't need is more summer people."

"Speak for yourself, Connie," Rose said. "Summer people are what brought our town back from the dead."

"Of course you like them," Connie shot back. "You make money off them at your inn. The rest of us have to deal with the messes they leave behind."

"What messes?" Claire broke in as Crystal scribbled away in her reporter's notebook. "I haven't heard of any trouble connected with summer people."

"That's because there hasn't been any." Lucy locked eyes with Connie until her younger sister finally glanced away. "Connie doesn't like Olivia because Olivia is dating one of her exes."

"Wait! Wait!" Crystal held up a hand. "Slow down! I can't keep up with you."

"You should carry a tape recorder," Kelly offered helpfully. "That way you won't miss anything."

Good thing the poor girl didn't look their way, because the looks Connie and Toni aimed her way would have killed a lesser human.

"If you're talking about Matthew," Connie said icily to Lucy, "that's ancient history. I couldn't care less who he dates."

"Good," said Rose, "because Olivia isn't dating him any longer. He was far too old for her. She's seeing the man who's funding the project for NJTV."

"Since when are you such an expert on Olivia Westmore?" Clearly Toni had been itching for a good fight all day, and now that she had one in her sights, she wasn't going to let it go. "You don't know her any better than we do."

"Actually, I do." Maddy had never seen her mother quite so gleeful at besting one of her sisters. "We've become very friendly since Olivia became vice-president of the Businesswomen's Association." She leaned in for the kill. "Did you know that Olivia's brother was featured in a documentary on the changing face of Eastern Europe last year? He's a very well-known photographer with PBS connections. They've been trying to bring him on board for our —"

"Oh damn!" Claire leaped to her feet. "I'm sorry! I tipped over my water glass."

One of the servers brought over a stack of napkins and quickly replaced the water. Claire, red-faced with embarrassment, reclaimed her seat.

Aunt Connie didn't want to hear about Olivia's semi-famous brother. "I don't know why they've been spending so much time interviewing her," Connie said with great indignation. "She wasn't born here. She doesn't know the first thing about our town's history."

"Her parents were born here," Rose said. "Not that it matters."

"She's part of the future," Denise jumped in.

"She's helping to shape the direction we're going in."

"Maybe they want her brother," cousin Fran offered. "If he's that good, he'll raise the show's profile."

"Weren't you listening?" Toni said to her daughter. "She's dating the producer. That's the reason."

Poor Crystal dropped her pen in surprise, then disappeared under the table to retrieve it. *Make a run for it,* Maddy thought. At least somebody had to get out of there alive.

"Better have your eyes checked, honey." It was Lucy's turn to join in. "When Olivia's around, those boys aren't thinking about history. They're thinking cleavage."

"If you're such good friends," Toni said to Rose, "then you can tell us what she's planning to do with the McClanahan cottage."

"I'd love to," Rose said. "She's opening a tea shop."

"What a great idea!" Maddy and Denise said simultaneously, then laughed.

"A tea shop?" Toni tried to scowl, but her most recent cosmetic surgery weakened the effect. "What do we need a tea shop for? You can buy tea bags at Super Fresh."

"Not that kind of tea shop," Claire said. "She's planning to serve a full English tea every afternoon."

Rose quickly covered her obvious surprise that Claire was in the loop right along with her.

"That's right. The shop will be called Cuppa, and she hopes to open it this summer."

"Who wants hot tea in the summer?" Maddy's cousin Pat asked. "She'd do better with an ice cream stand."

"I think it's a great idea," Maddy said. "Upscale, trendy but traditional. I think she's going to clean up."

"So do I," Rose agreed.

At least they were on the same side of one battle today.

"Just so long as it's not another salon," Gina observed. "More power to her."

"Which one is the McClanahan place?" Crystal asked as she reclaimed her seat. "Is it that old barn near the lake or —"

"It's the one on the corner of Shore Road and Paradise Point Drive," Claire said.

"With the red lacquer front door and the trellis of roses?"

"That's it."

"The place looks like a Hallmark card," Toni said. "It's sweet enough to make my teeth ache."

"Assuming you had any teeth of your own left to ache," Gina murmured, and Maddy kicked her under the table.

"So that's why all those workmen have been going in and out," Maddy's cousin Denise remarked. "Joe put in a bid for the plumbing, but it went to the Bielewski brothers."

"Those robbers." Connie dabbed butter on her slice of Italian bread. "You should see what they charged me to replace a hose on my washing machine."

You could hear Denise's jaw hit the floor clear on the other side of the table. "You called Bielewski instead of Joe, Aunt Connie? How could you do something like that!"

"Joe didn't wipe his feet last time he came by," Connie said with great indignation. "I had to follow him around with a spray bottle of Resolve."

"We're family."

"You're getting divorced."

"It's not final yet. The least you could have done was called."

"I didn't see you calling when they came to your house to film the kids getting ready for the dance recital. You called everyone else in the family except my grandchildren."

"Maybe if your grandkids had any talent, I —"

"Hey!" Franny called out from across the table. "My kids have more talent in their little fingers than your kids —"

Her family was off and running, insults flying across the table like rice at a wedding. Poor Kelly's eyes were popping, and Claire looked a tad too amused for Maddy's taste. After all, there were more than a few skeletons in the O'Malley closet, too. The only difference was, Maddy's skeletons were there at Bernino's having lunch with them.

She turned toward Rose, who nodded, then tapped her knife against her water glass.

"As charming as this discussion is," Rose said, "maybe we should table it for another time. I'm all for providing Mr. Lassiter and our Crystal here with colorful anecdotes for the documentary, but let's not get carried away. We're here to toast Maddy's upcoming wedding and to start making plans."

From the looks on her aunts' faces, you would think her mother had suggested a mass suicide into the salad bar.

Which, considering the way the day had unfolded so far, just might be an improvement.

"Tell me it's over," Gina said as they exited Bernino's parking lot two hours later. "Tell me it was all a bad dream."

"It's over," Maddy said, laughing, "but it wasn't a bad dream. It was our family."

Gina flipped on her directional and turned right at the traffic light. "You mean I'm not going to wake up and find out Harriet Nelson is my birth mother."

"Not unless DiFalco was her maiden name."

Gina sighed loudly. Her cousin usually had a high tolerance level for family chaos. It must have really been terrible if Gina had noticed it. "They were in rare form today."

"And you wonder why I ran away from home after high school."

"Hell, no. I wonder why you ever came back."

Bless Gina. She always understood.

"Thanks for drawing some of the fire in there.

It's nice to know somebody else in this family pisses off the aunts," Maddy said as they waved good-bye to Denise and Rose. "I was beginning to think I had that honor all to myself."

"Not as long as I'm still around."

Some of the afternoon's tension finally started to drain away, and Maddy leaned back in her seat and closed her eyes. "Did you know Rose and I fought in the dressing room after she threw everyone out?"

"Try telling me something the whole family doesn't know."

"You heard us?"

"We didn't have to. The seismic activity was a dead giveaway."

"I told her Aidan wanted us to elope."

"Get out!"

"He said we should grab Hannah and Kelly and elope to Vegas." She started to laugh. "Let Rose throw us a party when we got back and charge it to the PBS crew."

"Oh yeah," said Gina, starting to laugh, too. "I'm sure our Rosie would be up for that."

"It's not like I'm thinking of doing it or anything, but the second she told me to try on that strapless Band-Aid dress, I was looking to pick a fight with her."

"Bet you got our Rosie's blood pumping." Gina merged onto the highway behind Aunt Lucy's Buick. "So now what are you going to do?"

"Run away from home again."

"Not an option anymore. You're here to stay."

Maddy feigned a shiver. "A life sentence in Paradise Point."

"Within shouting distance of every single DiFalco relative on the planet."

"Stop the car," Maddy said. "I have a sudden urge to play in traffic."

Of all the cousins, Gina was the one who understood text and subtext. She always laughed where she was supposed to, but she saw beneath the black humor to the heart of the matter. There was more to Gina than her bawdy persona would lead you to believe. Maddy was one of the few people who was allowed to see the woman behind the laughter.

"I thought things were getting better for you and Rosie."

"They were," Maddy said, then corrected herself. "They are. We've both been trying hard to be more understanding, but I'd be lying if I didn't admit we've had some rough spots since Aidan and I got engaged."

"I thought she was crazy about him."

"She is. I think it's the wedding that's making us both crazy."

"Maybe not. Maybe it's the documentary that's fraying everyone's nerves. All this looking back isn't doing any of us any good."

Maddy looked closely at her cousin. "I thought you were enjoying the attention." Gina's salon stood to receive a fair bit of airtime when the documentary finally ran as part of a feature on the new wave of female entrepreneurs who were reshaping the old shore town.

"Dig deep enough, and you're bound to find something someone wanted to keep buried." Gina shook her head as if to brush away the idea. "I'd just as soon they kept the focus on your wedding."

"Thanks, pal," Maddy said. "I'll remember that. As it is, the house is sprouting bridal magazines, swatches of dress material, and if I hear one more word about caterers I swear I'll —"

"You've got the castle, the glass slipper, and Prince Charming, Cinderella. So what if there's a camera crew hiding behind the altar. You're not getting any sympathy here. You and Aidan might be South Jersey's Trista and Ryan."

"Bite your tongue."

"You love him, don't you?"

"Of course I do."

"And you want to marry him."

"I wouldn't have said yes if I didn't."

"So what's the problem? If there's one thing DiFalcos do well, it's plan a wedding. Why not sit back and enjoy it?"

"You think I'm being an ingrate, don't you?"

"Yep," said Gina as a carload of DiFalco sisters roared past them. "Rosie can be a pain in the ass, but she loves you. Besides, you're the only one of us who just might get it right the first time. You can't blame her for wanting to

make your wedding day something to remember."

"I think I'll remember it just fine without fifty
pounds of chopped liver and a champagne fountain."

"I don't know how to break it to you, but this
isn't about you."

"That's exactly what Rose said."

"Thanks," Gina said with an alarming roll
of her eyes. "I can feel the varicose veins
forming even as I speak. Still, you know I'm
right."

"She's not talking about a wedding, Gee.
She's talking about a circus."

"It's one day. Put up with it."

"I don't think I'm the big wedding type."

"Please don't tell me you were serious about
eloping to Vegas." Gina shuddered. "That's too
bleak a prospect, even for me."

"It could be fun. Especially if Fat Elvis per-
formed the ceremony."

"There's a charming thought for you."

"The kids might like it."

"The kids aren't supposed to go on the honeymoon with you."

"Does that mean you're up for baby-sitting?
You know how much Joey adores Hannah."

Gina ignored the question as she eased her
way around a slow-moving Cruiser. "You won't
get the big wedding checks from the aunts if you
don't give them a sit-down prime rib dinner and
a dance band."

"How big *are* those checks?" She pretended to rub her hands together in anticipation.

"Big enough to make up for a few snarky remarks."

"So you think I should sell out for a few lira."

"You might not believe me now, but by the time the day arrives, you'll understand. Fat Elvis might be fun, but he isn't family, and weddings are all about family."

"I've never heard you talk this way before. You sound downright DiFalco."

"Quote me, and I'll deny every single word. I have my reputation to consider."

"Rose and I might end up killing each other before I walk down the aisle." The thought of the PBS crew capturing it all on film was enough to make her queasy.

"Trust me, you'll bond."

"In prison," Maddy said, and they burst into laughter.

They fell silent for a few miles. Neither one of them had the chance to drive in silence very often. Gina had three children under ten, a trio of turbocharged live wires much like their mother. They were spending the afternoon at Upsweep, Gina's hair salon, being cared for in the mini–day care center Gina had established for employees and patrons in the rear section of the shop.

This was the first time Gina had left her youngest's side since he was released from the hospital three weeks ago. He had taken sick at his father's house up near Princeton, and Gina had parked her other two kids on her sister Denise's doorstep and raced up north to be with Joey.

"So how's Joey doing? I was kind of hoping you would bring him with you today."

Gina laughed. "Oh, there's a great idea: Joe and Hannah running wild in Saks."

"It does strike terror in the heart," Maddy agreed. "So how is he doing?" Gina had been uncharacteristically preoccupied since bringing Joey home, and details on the toddler's condition had been in short supply.

"We go back up to Princeton to see the doctor next week," Gina said, her gaze firmly on the road.

"Princeton? I thought you liked Dr. Jeanne."

"You'll have to ask the ex," Gina said. "He changed jobs, and the new HMO is being anal about where we go."

"That's not fair. Joey lives down here. You can't be expected to drive up to —"

"So what do you want from me?" Gina interrupted. "Maybe you have time to go bare knuckles with an HMO, but I don't."

They dropped back into silence, but it was a much less comfortable silence than before.

She shouldn't have pushed Gina about her choice of pediatricians. Her cousin had been under enormous strain since Joey's sudden hospitalization. You couldn't blame her for being short on patience. It was a situation Maddy understood quite well.

In early December Hannah had been briefly hospitalized for a violent allergic reaction to a cleaning fluid used to polish an old samovar, and she had been placed in a room next to Aidan's one-hundred-year-old grandmother Irene. The DiFalco and O'Malley families had been drawn together in both sorrow and thanksgiving as they said good-bye to the matriarch and celebrated the recovery of the child, and from that point on, Maddy swore she could feel the hand of fate drawing her and Aidan together.

Nothing in her life had ever been easier or felt more right. The chemistry between them was undeniable, but even more important, there was an emotional connection that seemed to grow deeper every time she saw him. Marriage would only make legal the vows they had already taken in their hearts.

She wasn't sure how much of this Hannah understood. She loved her Grandma Rose and Aunt Lucy, and if she wasn't too sure about her other aunts, they adored her enough to make up the difference. She loved her puppy Priscilla best of all, but Aidan was coming up fast on the outside. Aidan didn't want to take the place of her father, but when it came to raising daughters, he was a natural, and Hannah seemed to sense that.

His daughter was living proof. Kelly was everything a parent could want in a child, and Maddy thanked her lucky stars for bringing the perfect stepsister into her little girl's life. For all the talk you heard about how tough it was to raise a teenager, he had managed to bring up the perfect kid. Kelly was funny, smart, polite, charming, and talented. Her grades were top-notch. She was active in a dozen after-school clubs. She had great friends and a boyfriend even Aidan had to admit was a good kid.

Maddy should be walking on air. And she was. She really was. For the first time in her entire life, everything she had ever dreamed about was within reach. She was where she was meant to be, when she was meant to be there, with the people who meant the world to her, and with the man she loved.

Was it possible to let herself believe it might even last?

She had no troubles, no complaints, no reason for the sense of unease that had been growing ever since the documentary crew came to town and aimed their cameras at Maddy and Aidan and the upcoming wedding. But it was there just the same, and she couldn't make it go away, no matter how hard she tried.

She swiveled around in her seat and scanned the highway behind them. "I haven't seen Claire's car since we left the restaurant."

"I think she took the Parkway," Gina said. "We'll probably catch up with her when we get past Freehold."

"She is a good driver, isn't she?"

"NASCAR thinks so."

"Not funny." Even though it was, in a dark sort of way.

"She's gained a few pounds since she quit smoking."

"Why are we all so obsessed with weight? I think it looks good on her," Maddy said. Claire had one of those long, lanky frames that easily hid a small weight gain.

"Mmm," said Gina. "I keep wishing she'd come into Upsweep so we could do something about that Bonnie Raitt thing she has going on. Redheads do *not* gray gracefully."

"Gina —" Maddy searched for the right way to phrase what she wanted to say. "I — I'd really rather we didn't talk about Claire."

"Why not? She's about to become your sister-in-law. She'll be family. We always talk about family. It's a tradition."

"It's just that things haven't been all that warm and fuzzy between us since Aidan and I got engaged."

"You think that's what those snarky looks at lunch were all about? You're telling me she's jealous?"

"No! I didn't — well, maybe. But not of Aidan. I think she's jealous about Kelly."

"Oh boy! Now things are getting juicy. So you think the aging redhead is —"

"I don't want to do this, Gina. Let's change the subject."

"Why? Claire's as good a subject as any."

"Do I really have to spell it out?"

Gina's smile faded. "That was a long time ago, Maddy. Billy's dead."

"I still wish you hadn't told me," Maddy said, leaning her head against the passenger window. "Every time I look at Claire, I think of you and —"

"Would you rather think of me and Aidan?"

Nothing like the unvarnished truth to snap a woman back to reality. "No, but —"

"It was either tell you the truth or let you think I was sleeping with the man you were falling in love with. I don't see where I had a choice."

"Do you think she knows?"

Gina shook her head. "Not about me."

"But she knows Billy slept around?"

"Honey, the entire town knew Billy slept around. It wasn't exactly a secret."

"So how did you manage to keep it quiet about the two of you?"

"Are you implying I don't know how to keep my fucking mouth shut?" Gina, angry, was a sight to behold.

Maddy felt her cheeks redden. "Meaning I know this town. Like you said, there are very few secrets."

Gina opened her mouth to speak, but no words came out. The sight of her breezy, unflappable cousin brought to her knees by the memory of Billy O'Malley hit Maddy like a blow. Gina had loved Claire's husband, really loved him in a way she hadn't loved the fathers of her children, and that knowledge threw everything Maddy had believed about love and fidelity and the bonds of matrimony into chaos.

"I think it would have worked out," Gina said at last. "I think we would have ended up together."

Maddy had the feeling that even if Billy had lived, Gina would have ended up alone, but she held back the comment. She loved Gina. She didn't want to hurt her. But there were still parts of this puzzle she found difficult to accept.

"How can you stand around chatting with Claire, knowing that you wanted to steal her husband?"

"I like Claire."

"Obviously you didn't like her enough to keep your hands off her husband."

"If I remember right, he couldn't keep his hands off me."

Maddy's flush intensified. She could feel it creeping over her cheeks, down her throat, blossoming across her chest. "Listen, I'm sorry I said that. Why don't we just change the subject?"

"You know I'm not the first woman to have an affair with a married man."

Maddy knew the world wasn't a black-and-white enterprise. She was thirty-three years old. She had a child but not a husband. She had at least a nodding acquaintance with shades of gray. "Intellectually, I get it. Emotionally, it's another story."

"Billy and I were engaged once."

Good thing Maddy wasn't behind the wheel. She would have rocketed the car onto the shoulder in shock. "You're joking."

"It was right after I graduated high school. You were spending the summer at your dad's place in Oregon, while I was going up to New York to apprentice at Sassoon. Billy was a rookie at the fire department, so he couldn't follow me. He was afraid I'd have my head turned by one of those rich Wall Street types, so he staked his claim before I left." There was a softness to Gina's voice, a wistful quality she didn't often reveal.

"That means you were seeing him while you were still in school."

"On the sly," Gina acknowledged with a look in Maddy's direction. "I was marginal jail bait, after all."

"But you told me that it happened much later, after he and Claire were already married. You should have told me the truth when it was going on."

"Little Miss Innocent? You would've been the first to have me arrested."

"I would not." She grinned. "I would've had him arrested."

"Do you remember what you were like back then, Maddy? If you hadn't had a mouth on you, I would've figured you as a candidate for the convent."

"Somehow I don't think Rosie would've

agreed with you. She considered me quite the rebel."

"I love Aunt Rose, but she didn't know squat about rebels. She probably said a rosary every day thanking God I wasn't her kid."

When Gina was right, she was right. "So who did know about it?"

"His grandmother Irene. Denise. Aidan. We were planning to keep it secret until Christmas when he gave me a ring."

"And — ?"

"And I made a big mistake."

"Oh God, one of those Wall Street types?"

Gina nodded. "Greg had the Beemer, the weekend place in the Hamptons, the Armani suits, the whole nine yards. This Jersey girl's head did a one hundred and eighty. It only lasted long enough to break Billy's heart."

Billy drove up one weekend to surprise Gina and ended up being on the wrong end of the surprise when he caught Gina and Mr. Wall Street leaving her apartment hand in hand.

"Next time I saw Billy, he had a wife and a baby on the way."

"I never suspected."

"Nobody did," Gina said. "Claire's fiancé was killed in a car crash and before his body was cold, Claire and Billy showed up married and pregnant. I was old news by then."

"I'd forgotten all about Charles," Maddy said.

"The rest of the town didn't. Why do you think Billy's Grandma Irene hated Claire so much?"

69

"I never really thought about it."

"She knew the marriage was all wrong for both of them. She knew Claire's heart still belonged to Charles and Billy's heart —" She stopped abruptly. "You get the picture."

Maddy sighed. "I'm beginning to."

The story was a simple one, the kind that happened every day in a thousand different towns just like theirs. They had never really gotten over each other and, small towns being what they were, proximity worked its dangerous magic, and before either one of them could think of a good reason to back away from each other, they were lovers again.

"Being married to other people should've been a good reason," Maddy observed.

"It wasn't," Gina said.

"What about the kids?"

"People in love are selfish as hell, Maddy."

Maddy felt the way she had when she was a little girl, listening to her mother and aunts gossip about a neighbor. She grasped the intent of the words, but she didn't really understand.

"I always believed love made you more open and generous."

"Yeah, and the tooth fairy left a fifty under Toni's pillow when she was fitted for her new dentures."

They glided to a stop at the traffic light near the fancy town houses where Rose had lived before she moved into The Candlelight seven years ago.

"You hate me," Gina said. "I shouldn't have told you the whole story. I'm a good liar. You never would have known the difference."

"I love you," Maddy corrected her, "but I'd be the one lying if I said I liked the story."

"This is real life, cookie," Gina said as the light changed to green. "If you're looking for happily ever after, stick to romance novels, because happy endings are in short supply for the DiFalcos."

A prickle of alarm nipped at the back of Maddy's neck. "Is there something you're trying to tell me? Believe me, I know Aidan has some baggage." He had been widowed for almost sixteen years when he met Maddy. A lot of women had passed through his life. Maddy saw a fair number of them every day when she waited at the corner for the school bus.

She told herself that if he could welcome Hannah's father Tom into their extended family, she could accept the existence of ex-lovers, but there were times when her imagination went into overdrive, and she found herself speculating about every woman she bumped into.

"No, I'm not trying to tell you anything." Gina waved at Jim McDougall as he roared by in his pickup truck. "Just reminding you that weddings are wonderful, but marriage is something else again. Make sure you go into it with your eyes wide open."

"Meaning what?"

"Meaning I've seen the way you look at him, Maddy. You're head over heels for the guy, and that's terrific, but he's not a saint. You don't want any surprises."

"What do you mean by surprises?"

"I don't know," Gina said. "It's just with those journalists nosing around into everyone's business, you never know what they might turn up."

"What are they going to turn up that I don't already know?" Maddy countered. "Aidan had a sex life before I met him. That isn't news. Just as long as his sex life stops with me."

Gina burst into laughter. "Better rephrase that, cookie. I can't imagine Aidan's sex life stopping until he's six feet under. Better keep the reporter away from him, or the documentary will end up X-rated."

"Thanks for the advice." Just what the bride-to-be needed: relationship tips from a woman who had two divorces under her belt by the time she turned thirty. Gina meant well, but her heavy-handed warning had unsettled Maddy. "I think this whole town's gone nuts since they started filming those interviews."

"Listen, Mad, I'm sorry," Gina said as she pulled behind Lucy's car in The Candlelight parking lot. "Maybe it was all of those wedding dresses that got to me. Forget I said anything. Aidan's a good guy, and he loves you. You're going to have a great life together. Sooner or later one of us has to."

Chapter Four

Kelly asked to be dropped off at O'Malley's Grill where she had left her car that morning. Claire noted Owen's truck parked in the back next to Aidan's empty spot. Mel Perry's Saturn was angled to the left of the side door perilously close to the fender of his nemesis Fred DeTrano's gleaming Caddy. Some of the firefighters who had worked with Billy and Aidan were there, too, and she was glad she had an excuse to wave good-bye to her niece and keep going. She loved those guys, but there were times when the reverence they showed her as Billy's widow felt like a dead weight on her shoulders.

"Thanks for the lift, Aunt Claire," she said as she gathered up her stuff.

"Did you think I was going to have you hitch your way home from Short Hills?"

Kelly grinned and winked at Hannah, who was strapped securely in the backseat. "See you, guys."

"Kel, wait a second."

Kelly, who was ready to close the car door behind her, stopped and leaned back inside. "I know, I know. Remember to tell Tommy to fill out the work sheet before he closes out the register tonight."

She would skin the old goat alive if he forgot, but that wasn't what she wanted to say. "Tell me the truth, Kel: are you feeling okay?"

Kelly flashed one of her big, beautiful smiles, the kind that made her dimples even more pronounced. "I'm great."

Claire cupped her chin with her hand, remembering when those dimples had graced the face of a little girl. "Enough with the dieting, kiddo. You're perfect right now. Don't let all those damned fashion magazines tell you how to look."

"You sound like Daddy."

"Listen to him. He's a man. He knows what he's talking about."

"Yes, Aunt Claire," she said, with another wink for Hannah. "Anything you say, Aunt Claire."

"Go on with you," Claire said, laughing despite her concern. "And while you're at it, tell Tommy to fill out that work sheet or else."

Hannah, who had chattered nonstop all the way from Short Hills, fell silent the second Kelly closed the door behind her. Claire swiveled around in her seat and smiled at the little girl. Hannah looked very much like Kelly had at that age. Same coloring. Same bright

74

smile. The sight of the two girls whispering to each other during lunch had brought back a flurry of bittersweet memories of the early years when the kids were young and her biggest problem was what to make for supper. Kelly had been like one of her own. Younger than Kathleen, Courtney, and Willow, but older than Maire and Billy Jr., Aidan's daughter fit in perfectly. Kelly always had a place at Claire and Billy's dinner table, a bed to call her own when Aidan pulled nights at the firehouse.

Where her own kids had been troubled and occasionally difficult, Kelly was a dream. She sailed through childhood with a sunny smile on her face. When her girls were fire-spewing pre-pubescent monsters, Kelly barely managed an occasional flicker of flame. When her girls were out there cutting school and cadging cigarettes, Kelly was at band practice or studying for a history quiz.

It was a terrible thing to admit, but she had spent almost seventeen years praying Aidan wouldn't fall in love and remarry. Claire was the closest thing Kelly had to a mother, and she relished her position in the girl's life and didn't want to share her with anyone. Sometimes she even resented Aidan for doing such a wonderful job in bringing her up. He never backed away from the tough questions, the ones about sex and drugs that sent most parents scurrying for cover. He had been there for his daughter every single step of the way. The only time he had faltered was during those awful days after the accident that took Billy's life. Aidan had been gravely injured and hospitalized for months, and Kelly came to live with Claire and her cousins in a household so overcome with anger and grief that the only thing holding them together was the weight of their loss.

Kelly had stepped into the breach, taking care of details nobody had the heart to face, making sure the household retained a semblance of order in a world fallen into chaos. She had been there for Claire and her cousins as they struggled to accept their loss; she had been there for Aidan when he struggled to accept his new limitations. She maintained her grades and social life and still managed to hold down a part-time job.

Aidan's rehabilitation had been long and tough, and it had taken a toll on his daughter. Kelly had felt increasingly alienated from the father she adored and turned toward Claire for advice and consolation. Claire's own daughters had never asked for her opinion of their hairstyles or clothing choices, much less their lives, but Kelly was hungry to know what she thought, and Claire was equally hungry for the chance to share those thoughts.

She wasn't exactly sure when things began to change, but it was right around the time Maddy became a part of Aidan's life. There was a natural gravitational pull between Maddy and Kelly that couldn't be denied, even if it sometimes seemed to Claire that the attraction wasn't as mutual as Kelly might have hoped.

She told herself that it was a good thing that Kelly was so comfortable with Maddy, especially now that Maddy was going to join the family. Family life was tough enough in the best of times, and blended families had more than their fair share of adjustments to make right from the start. She should be elated that Aidan had fallen in love with such a terrific woman and over the moon that Kelly seemed to agree with his choice.

She wasn't.

Not even close.

But go figure. Aidan took one look at Maddy and fell in love, and from that moment on, Claire's life had been thrown into a tailspin.

"You're in a rut," Olivia had told her over lunch the other day. "You need to break out and try something new."

"You mean like tuna on rye instead of a burger?" she had asked.

Of course that wasn't at all what Olivia had meant. Olivia had been after her for ages to stop living like a married woman and start exploring the world beyond O'Malley's Bar and Grill, but so far Claire had rebuffed every attempt at matchmaking. Olivia knew her better than Claire cared to be known by anyone but her priest, and she sensed Claire's growing restlessness long before Claire herself had been able to put a name to it.

She had been parenting children since she was nineteen years old. Lunch money. Ironing shirts as they were running out the door to catch the school bus. Checking homework. Parent/teacher conferences. The gut-wrenching worry every time they were five minutes late. The joy when the one you thought was lost to you forever showed up at your front door. What would she do when it was just her and the dog and maybe her father, all alone in the house with nothing but memories?

Then again, maybe that was the problem. Memories. They were everywhere she looked. In the kitchen. In the bedroom. On the front porch. In front of the firehouse. Behind the wheel of her car. At the corner waiting for the school bus. And especially at O'Malley's. They had spent their honeymoon sleeping in the back room of the drafty old bar. Billy had loved that place almost as much as he loved the firehouse. He wasn't much of a businessman, but he had thrown his heart and soul into keeping the doors open and the prices down. She had often suspected that his bitch of a grandmother Irene occasionally kicked in guilt money of her own to keep the wolf from the door, but she had never been able to prove it. Not that it mattered. Somehow they had managed to keep the place going.

After Billy's death, the place had been a refuge for her. The familiar rituals of opening up the bar every morning, greeting Tommy or Owen as she headed into the kitchen to start

78

cooking for the lunch crowd — all of it sustained her. Aidan joined her in a partnership after he was back on his feet, and they had even managed to turn a small profit now and then.

But three years had passed since then. She was stronger now. She didn't see ghosts around every corner the way she had in those early months. Aidan had taken much of the daily grind off her shoulders and enabled her to cut back on her hours. They had hit a rough patch at O'Malley's, but the addition of an outdoor patio and a more upscale menu — both Rose DiFalco's suggestions — had greatly improved their bottom line.

Aidan had taken a second mortgage on his house, something Claire had strenuously objected to, but it looked like his gamble just might pay off. Sure, some of the old-timers worried it was going to turn into a singles bar with No Smoking signs and flowering plants, but so far they were holding the line between the generations.

O'Malley's was still O'Malley's but better, and she was glad of it. She loved Aidan. He had been to hell and back and deserved this happiness and more. She loved the regulars who had gathered around her like a human shield after Billy died and kept her from splitting apart from the sheer force of her grief. But it wasn't enough. Lately she had been finding it harder and harder to push herself through the front door and into the familiar yeasty, smoky haze of beer and cigarettes and settle into the comfortable old role of Feisty Claire, brave widow and mother of five.

She felt restless and edgy all the time these days, like a permanent case of PMS without the chocolate cure. The things that didn't get on her nerves bored her to tears. If anyone had ever told her that she would be a candidate for a midlife crisis, she would have laughed them right out of the room, but more and more she was beginning to wonder if anything short of a visit to see Dr. Phil was going to get her back on track. She yearned for something new, something different, something she had never seen or heard or experienced before, but damned if she knew what that something might be.

But she knew what it wasn't. The whole damn town was drowning in memories since the arrival of the NJTV reporter who was assigned to gather interviews about the history of Paradise Point. You couldn't take a step without tripping over a mossy story about the old days and the way it used to be. (The way it probably never was.) Endless tales about Billy and Aidan's grandmother Irene O'Malley and her husband Michael, ancient history about the bar's glory days when it was a restaurant worthy of a special trip down to the shore.

Irene's death last December had been reported in a surprising number of newspapers up and down the state. A centenarian with a sharp mind and amazingly accurate command of details, both social and political, was a rare find, and both historians and gerontology students had made it their business to interview Irene frequently during the last ten years of her life. One of those lengthy obituaries had snagged the interest of the state's public television programmers, and suddenly Paradise Point was at the center of production on a series featuring the rise, fall, and reemergence of Paradise Point.

The town library was stacked floor to ceiling with donations of scrapbooks, photo albums, old letters, and diaries found stashed away in attics and closets all around town. Locals compared notes every morning at Julie's Coffee Shop, trying to dazzle each other with outrageous tales about politics, family squabbles, hurricanes, nor'easters, and blizzards.

And the accident that took Billy's life and the lives of five other firefighters.

She couldn't escape it if she tried. The collapse of that warehouse roof three years ago had changed the town, brought them all closer together as they struggled to understand why God had let this tragedy happen. Paradise Point was a typical small town in that most of the residents. were second, third, and fourth generation, living in houses their grandparents had owned, going to the same school their parents had gone to, shopping the same markets, driving the same streets. Their lives were intertwined in ways Houdini couldn't unravel, and when Billy and his coworkers died, the whole town grieved.

Claire had watched it all through a bloodred haze of rage. Her anger burned through sorrow, through loss, ignited everything and everyone it came in contact with. She hated the pious prayers, the sympathy cards with the faded lilies and a cross, the pans of mac and cheese, pots of spaghetti sauce, the flowers that stank of death.

She hated the fact that after a marriage filled with second chances they had finally run out of time. She despised the fact that they thought they knew him, thought they understood who he really was, when they hadn't a clue. Her flawed, imperfect hero, the husband she had never managed to love the way she wanted to be loved herself.

A tiny cough erupted behind her, and Claire almost vaulted over the steering wheel in surprise. She had all but forgotten Hannah was strapped in the backseat, waiting to be delivered home. She turned around in her seat at the stoplight and smiled at the little girl, struck again by the resemblance to a young Kelly. Where had those precious years gone? Four of her brood were out there in the world, either in school or working, and this time next year Kelly would join them.

"Hannah, you're so good back there I almost forgot about you."

No response, just a thumb quickly inserted into a mouth that looked dangerously ready to cry.

"How would you like to go see the end of Billy's soccer game?"

Still no response. The thumb, however, was getting a workout.

She wasn't the mother of five for nothing. When it came to kids, you had to push your agenda with the zeal of a politician seeking re-election, or you'd end up living out the rest of your days at Chuck E. Cheese's.

"Did Billy tell you that Opal had kittens?"

Hannah nodded, eyes widening with interest.

"Would you like to see them?"

The thumb was ejected from her mouth with a pop. "Can I have one?"

Big mistake. Never mention puppies, kittens, or bunnies to a five-year-old. She regrouped. "They're too young to leave Opal yet, Hannah."

"Can I have one when they're big enough?"

"We'll have to ask your mom about that."

"She'll say yes."

"Well, your Grandma Rose has to agree, too."

Hannah's expression reminded Claire of how her kids looked when she served Brussels sprouts. "My grandpa has lots of cats," Hannah said. "Horses, too. He'll let me have a kitten even if Gramma Rose won't. I know he will."

So even Hannah had her issues with Rose. Oh, this had juicy possibilities. She could dine out on the gossip for six weeks and not even begin to wear out her welcome.

The thought of some of her own darker moments seeing the light of day brought her back to her senses. She couldn't do it. She wanted to, she was dying to find out everything, but she flat out couldn't ask. The thought of Denise or Pat grilling Billy Jr. for the scoop on the O'Malleys made her head spin. There were few things lower on the food chain than a thirty-nine-year-old woman who would pump a five-year-old child for gossip. No matter how juicy it might be.

"I have an idea," Claire said, as she made a left onto Main Street. "Why don't I take you home now?" Better to run from temptation than try to stare it down. She had learned that a long time ago.

"Okay," said Hannah. "I saw Grandpa Bill sleeping in Grandma's bed last week."

"I'll pretend I didn't hear that," Claire said.

"Grandpa Bill slept over with Grandma," Hannah repeated in a louder voice. "I saw them kissing in the kitchen."

"No, Hannah, I didn't mean I didn't hear you, I meant —" She forced herself to stop. Another five seconds, and she'd pull over to the curb and order the poor kid to spill her guts or Santa would skip Paradise Point this year.

Clearly it was time to get a life. She needed a new one, a better one, because the one she currently had belonged to somebody else, a woman who no longer existed.

Clearly the gods believed Rose had suffered enough during lunch with her sisters and they enabled her to escape Bernino's before any of

84

the aging DiFalco girls had the chance to ask for a ride home.

The car started on the first try. The lights were green from Bernino's to the parkway.

Even better, Olivia Westmore answered her cell phone on the first ring.

"I'm on my way home," Rose said. "Meet me at The Candlelight in an hour."

"I'm at work," Olivia protested. "I can't close up because you feel like gossiping."

"Be there," Rose said. "I promise it'll be worth your while." Fifty-eight minutes later she pulled into the parking lot behind The Candlelight and laughed when she saw Olivia perched on the back steps. She wore one of her trademark floaty skirts, the kind that automatically settled themselves into graceful lines around her legs. She had kicked off her Jimmy Choos and they sat at attention on the top step, gleaming expensively in the late afternoon sunshine. She was the picture of languid grace, a woman who clearly never had to work a day in her life.

All wrong, of course. Olivia owned Le Papier, the fancy stationery store in the heart of town that had suddenly become a shopping mecca for the men of Paradise Point. It had taken the women a little bit longer to warm up to the siren in their midst, but the quality of her wares — and her good nature — finally won them over, too.

"This better be good," Olivia said as Rose

walked toward her. "I left Sunny in charge and she still doesn't know vellum from construction paper."

"I'm so sorry, Liv, but I'm afraid I told them."

"Told them what?"

"That you're opening a tea shop."

"Is that all? And here I thought you told them about the night Simon and I —"

"Never," Rose said. "You swore me to secrecy."

"The tea shop is no secret. I filed the papers with the township. They're public record."

"But you haven't made an announcement. I shouldn't have said anything, but Toni and Connie were being such bitches that I couldn't hold back."

"Okay, so you told them. How did it go over?"

"Everyone who matters thought it was a brilliant idea."

"And Toni and Connie hated it."

"They despised it."

Olivia threw back her head and laughed. "That means it's going to be a smash hit!"

"That's pretty much what I thought, too." She met her friend's eyes. "If your offer still holds, I'm in."

"Of course the offer still holds. I'd love for us to be partners in the tea shop." Olivia extended her right hand. "Then it's a deal."

"There's one condition," Rose went on. "I'd like to offer the manager's position to Maddy."

"I thought she was working for you here at the Inn."

"She has been," Rose said carefully, noting the lack of enthusiasm in Olivia's tone, "but I think she needs a new challenge. Not everyone is cut out for innkeeping."

"Amen to that. Quite frankly, Rosie, I don't know how you stand sharing the bathroom with strangers."

"You sound like my daughter."

Olivia was quiet for a few moments. "What about that radio gig? Doesn't that take up a lot of her time?"

"Friday mornings," Rose said. "I see the radio show as built-in publicity for the new venture. She could do it from Cuppa if the station agrees."

A radio interview Rose had arranged back in December had generated a part-time gig for Maddy but not the career opportunity she had prayed would come her daughter's way. The local radio program paid her in free tickets to the Paradise Point Multiplex and ten percent off at O'Malley's Bar and Grill. The irony was not lost on either Rose or Maddy.

Olivia drummed her fingers on the step. "I had been thinking of bringing Claire O'Malley on board."

"As manager?" Rose didn't mean to sound quite so skeptical.

"She is the one who kept O'Malley's going before Aidan came on board."

"Not really," Rose said. "Jack Bernstein kept the wolf from the door and Tommy did all the ordering."

"A subjective evaluation?" Olivia asked.

"An accurate evaluation."

Olivia frowned. "We need someone with real experience to keep the books, take care of ordering —"

"Maddy can handle it," Rose said. "She was an accountant for years out in Seattle."

"There's a difference between bean counting and running a business," Olivia pointed out. "If you think Maddy is the best one to manage Cuppa, I'm willing to give her a try, but I have to admit I can't see her up front shmoozing with the crowd."

"I'm the first one to admit her people skills need work." It was the personal aspect of innkeeping that her daughter disliked so intensely. "I'm her mother but I do try to keep her away from the front desk."

They locked eyes.

"Are you thinking what I'm thinking?" Olivia asked. "Claire up front as hostess, Maddy in the back, keeping the whole thing running smoothly."

"They may say no." She wasn't at all convinced the two women were half as friendly as Maddy wanted her to believe. Working closely together might put a strain on their budding familial ties.

"We won't know until we ask."

"I'll talk to Maddy tonight," Rose said.

"Perfect," Olivia said. "We'll get to Claire's house early tomorrow night for poker and present it to her then."

"And what if they both say no?"

"They wouldn't dare."

"Not if we pay them enough."

Olivia's eyes widened. "You mean we have to pay them?"

It was the best laugh Rose had all day.

Chapter Five

"Five more minutes," Nina said as she crouched down next to the whirlpool. "We put you through a real workout this afternoon."

"I'm good to go," Aidan said, flexing his right ankle in the swirling warm water. He tried hard not to wince, but Nina could see right through him.

"Hurts?"

"Like hell. You sure I'm going in the right direction?" It seemed to him that he was in worse shape now than when he broke his ankle in that fall ten weeks ago.

"Two breaks on the same leg in three years," Nina said in the matter-of-fact tone he had come to know very well. A good physical therapist could make a crushed pelvis sound like a hangnail. "You can't expect to be one hundred percent."

"I'd settle for forty percent," he grunted as he shifted position slightly. "Right now I'd be lucky to push twenty."

"Since when are you such a pessimist?" she

90

said, giving him a playful sock in the left shoulder. "It's not like we haven't done this before. No reason to think we can't do it again."

"I've got a wedding coming up, Nina, and right now I'd have to ask the best man to dance with the bride for me."

"Have you set a date?" She asked it with just the right note of casual interest, but he wasn't fooled.

"September twenty-first, and it's starting to sound like the circus is coming to town." He tried to match her casual tone. "I tried to convince Maddy to catch a flight to Vegas and throw a party when we get back."

Nina groaned and rolled her eyes. "Great idea, sport. Bet Rose and company loved that."

"September twenty-first," he repeated, the attempt at laughter dying. "What do you think?"

"Four months plus a little," she said as much to herself as to him. "No crutches, but you'll still need a cane."

"No cane."

"I don't know, O'Malley," she said, meeting his eyes. "It's possible, but —"

"No cane," he repeated.

"Then we're going to have to work your ass even harder."

"Good."

"And I'll expect an invitation to the wedding."

"Play your cards right," he said, "and I might save you a dance."

She was still laughing as she headed toward the weights room to torture another patient.

He clocked another six minutes in the whirlpool, then hoisted himself out of the tub, swearing slightly when he lost his grip on the handrails and almost tumbled backward into the water. He understood how Mel Perry felt the time he fell off a barstool and needed help to get up off the floor. "Getting old's a bitch," he'd said with a shake of his graying head. "I used to deadlift hundred-pound bales of wire at the plant, and now I can't even haul my sorry ass up from the floor."

Aidan knew the feeling. Physical strength had always been a given with him, like chestnut hair and blue eyes. It wasn't something he thought about; it was simply a large part of who he was. Big. Strong. Immortal. Until the day he found out he wasn't any of those things.

Not that he thought much about the fire anymore. He had learned long ago when his wife Sandy died that the human heart could survive the greatest blows and keep on beating. There were many times when he wished that wasn't true, but as the months and years went by, the sharp pain of loss began to lose the jagged edges, until one day he woke up and realized he was almost happy again. Not happy the way he had been before she died, but happy in a new way.

He had tried to explain this to Claire not long after his brother Billy died, how one day she would wake up and she wouldn't feel like a stranger in her own body, in her own house, but it had been too soon and she had turned away from his words.

She had been married for sixteen or seventeen years when Billy died. She had given birth to five kids, built a life with the man. It wasn't like losing the family dog. You didn't go out and find yourself a new one to replace that empty spot in your heart. Sometimes that empty spot stayed empty while you struggled to rebuild what was left of your life around it.

Aidan was one of the lucky ones. After all those years of being alone, happiness found him. He hadn't been looking to fall in love. He liked the life he shared with his kid and would have been willing to go on living it for another few decades if Maddy Bainbridge hadn't come back to Paradise Point and captured his heart. She was funny, honest, loving, warm, sexy as hell, talented, smart, everything he ever wanted in a woman, in a partner. Everything he had always hoped his daughter would be.

And he loved her. When she wasn't with him, he was lonely. He wanted to see her first thing in the morning and last thing at night and all the hours in between. The last time he had felt anything close to this depth of feeling, he was seventeen years old and falling in love with Sandy. Love was easy when you were seventeen. You were all hormones and heart, Viagra packaged inside a Hallmark card.

And they would have made it for the long haul. He had never doubted it. If Sandy had lived — if God had shown them that kind of mercy — they would still be together today, watching their baby girl grow up into a beautiful and accomplished young woman. There would have been more kids, too. Another daughter. Maybe a son or two who would look up to him the way he had looked up to his father.

He tried to picture Sandy at almost forty, but it was impossible to project her beautiful nineteen-year-old self into the dark and murky future. She would always be nineteen to him, always be the way he had seen her on that last day with her blond hair scraped back into a high ponytail, her blue eyes sparkling with mischief as she grabbed the car keys and said she would be home in an hour with an anniversary surprise from Kutscher's Bakery on the other side of town.

Twenty minutes later, two cops were peeling him off the front step where he'd dropped when they told him his wife was dead.

Life was never what you figured it would be. Just when you thought you had it nailed, life pulled the rug out from under you, then laughed when you landed on your ass. He should have been an old married man by now. He'd been looking forward to growing old with Sandy, watching their kids grow up and leave the nest, waiting for the next generation of O'Malleys to be born.

Instead, he was a middle-aged single father, a

little bit worse for the wear, counting down the days until he married the woman he loved. He might look every single one of his thirty-six years, but inside he was eighteen again, filled with excitement, almost believing that this time life would look the other way and let a happy ending sneak by.

"Hey, O'Malley!" Fred DeTrano, a bar regular who was rehabbing a hip replacement, called out from the stairstepper. "Slow down. That pool's a safety hazard. You don't wanna slip, do you?"

They all worried about him like he was still the muscle-bound kid who had escaped Paradise Point on a football scholarship, only to return a year later as a twenty-year-old widower with a baby daughter and a future that looked every bit as bleak as the town's.

Grandma Irene had been caught in one of her own dramas, and the offer of a room in her small two-bedroom cottage had been extended only when he and Kelly were already settled in with Billy and Claire on the other side of town. He could still hear the sound of relief in his grandmother's voice when she realized she was off the hook.

Billy had always been the wild one, even though he was married with kids and a mortgage meant to keep a man humble. He loved Claire, but that didn't stop him from screwing around. Their house seemed to vibrate with secrets. The excuses. The late nights and early mornings that

Aidan struggled to explain away to his patient sister-in-law. He hated being part of Billy's other life. He didn't want to know that the woman chatting up Claire at the school bus stop had shared a bed with his brother the night before.

Claire deserved better. She was smart, opinionated, a great mother and wife. There were times when he wanted to cut through the layers of lies and spell it out for her, all the things she knew in her gut but refused to acknowledge, force her to see what was going on and make Billy choose. He tried once, late one night when they were closing up the bar together. Billy was supposed to close out on Fridays, but he said he had a Knights of Columbus meeting in Little Egg Harbor. Or maybe he said he was pulling an extra shift at the firehouse. Aidan couldn't keep track any longer, and neither could anyone else. He had stumbled over the first few words when Claire had fixed him with a look that stopped him cold. *I don't need you to tell me what I already know,* her look said. He never brought it up again.

He and Billy had been close as kids, and that closeness remained right up until the end. Still, he never had managed to find out what made Billy tick. He never found out what his brother worried about at night when the lights went out or where he wanted to be ten years, twenty years, into the future.

When you came down to it, the only thing he had really known for sure was that no matter what happened, no matter what shit came their way, they had each other's back. No matter what else happened, no matter who came in or out of your life, you took care of your own. It was as simple as that.

Ancient history, he thought, as he showered away the pain and grit of physical therapy. Billy had taken his secrets to the grave, and whatever Claire knew or didn't know didn't matter anymore.

Twenty minutes later he waved good-bye to Nina and pushed his way through the rear exit that led to the parking lot. He was an old hand at crutches by this time and knew to avoid the brick pathway in favor of the smooth asphalt surface on the other side of a narrow strip of well-manicured grass. The trick was to stay focused. Scan the ground for potential hazards and plot the simplest, safest course from point A to point B.

And, while you're at it, try not to fall on your ass.

"How did mothers survive before cell phones?" Maddy asked as she tossed her Nokia back into her tote bag.

"Smoke signals," Gina said. "That or carrier pigeons."

"It boggles the mind."

"So is the kidlet safely home?"

"She's playing Barbies out on the back porch with Priscilla."

"And Rosie?"

97

"I think Hannah put her in charge of Ken and the Dream House."

Gina laughed as they entered the Paradise Point town limits. "If anyone can whip the Dream House into shape, it's our Rosie."

"Remember the time she redecorated my Dream House?"

"You cried for a week," Gina said.

"I was the only kid in school with wainscoting."

Childhood was all about fitting in, being one of the crowd. If your friends were wearing green leggings, you wanted green leggings, too. It didn't matter if you hated them. It was all part of belonging to something bigger than your own small self.

"She meant well," Gina said. "She always did want you to have the best."

"I know," Maddy said on a sigh. "I'm praying it's not genetic. If you catch me installing wall-to-wall in Hannah's Dream House, you have my permission to kick me in the butt."

"You got it." They stopped at the traffic light at the corner of Bank and Main Street. "Isn't that Aidan's truck?" Gina gestured toward the parking lot behind Shore Fitness and Rehabilitation on the opposite corner.

Maddy twisted around in her seat to take a look. "It sure is." She could feel a goofy smile spreading across her face.

The light changed. Instead of turning right toward The Candlelight, Gina rolled across the intersection and stopped in front of the entrance to the parking lot.

"So go already," Gina said. "Seduce him in the back of that Jeep before he has a chance to close the door. You don't want today to be a total loss, do you?"

"But Rose expects me back in time for supper."

"Screw Rosie," Gina said cheerfully. "I'll tell her Aidan's bringing you home. Life is short, kiddo. Make the most of it while you can."

"I'll remember this when it's time to pick the matron of honor's dress," she said, kissing her cousin's cheek.

"You mean I won't look like Bo Peep on crack?"

"It's a promise."

His car was parked near the fence, but there was no sign of Aidan. She glanced at her watch. He usually finished around four, which meant she had just enough time to arrange herself seductively on the hood of his Jeep . . . or as seductively as possible for a size ten.

The air smelled faintly of early lilacs and sea spray. She had forgotten how beautiful the shore was in the spring. Her years in Seattle had dulled her memory of the magical transformation that happened every year when winter finally loosed its grip. Brilliant yellow forsythia lined walkways, vying for space with fuchsia and scarlet and baby-pink azaleas in full bloom. Buttery daffodils made room for tulips in red and yellow and orange. Their appearance was usually short-lived, which made the whole thing that much more magical.

She had just climbed up onto the hood when the back door to Nina's clinic opened, and she saw Aidan starting down the steps. The process had his full concentration. His head was down, eyes focused squarely on the ground beneath his feet. Late afternoon sun picked up the russet and gold lights in his thick, dark hair. He wore his usual uniform of boots, well-worn jeans, and an old long-sleeved cotton sweater that had probably been dark brown once upon a time but was now faded to the color of café au lait. Broad shoulders. Broad chest. Narrow waist. The classic lines of a man born to play football.

Strength seemed to radiate outward from him in waves, interrupted only by the slow, deliberate gait and the crutch he wielded like a weapon. Anger radiated outward, too. It had been his constant companion since the fall in February that had sent him back into surgery and long-term rehabilitation. He viewed his injury as a sign of weakness, something that diminished his worth, and it worried her that she hadn't been able to convince him of how wrong he was. Love was still new to them, its power still untested. That kind of trust would come with time.

Right now it was mostly about love. The romantic kind that made her heart beat fast every time she saw him, made her breath catch in her throat at the sound of his voice on the phone. Even the sight of his E-mail address — *fireguy@njshore.net* — in her in box was enough to make her head spin. She loved everything about him: the way he looked; the way he smelled; the taste of his mouth on hers; the solid, comforting weight of his body when he held her close. The way he listened to her when she talked and heard the words beneath the words.

Not that he was perfect. He had a temper. He could be as stubborn as her five-year-old daughter. He occasionally left the toilet seat up and had the alarming tendency to fall asleep in the middle of one of their late-night E-mail sessions, but he was a good man in every sense of that much-maligned phrase. She knew it wasn't fashionable to love a good man when bad boys were so much more fun, but she couldn't help it. She had learned from her father what a man should be. He had taught her that the strongest man was invariably the gentlest, that if a man couldn't show compassion to a child or an animal, he wasn't right for her.

The day she met Aidan for the first time, Priscilla had relieved herself on his shoe. She had stared in horror at the widening wet spot, expecting him to lash out and present her with a bill for a new pair of shoes. Turned out you could learn a lot about a man when he was standing there with a wet foot. He acted like poodles peed on him every day of the week, like it was no big deal. Silly as it sounded, that was the moment she started to fall in love with him.

The day's many annoyances fell away from her as she watched him navigate his way to the truck. Her embarrassment at Saks. The surge of anger toward her mother. The sense that everyone else's opinion, even Crystal the Tattooed Lady's, about how and when she married Aidan mattered more than hers. None of it mattered, not compared to the way she felt about him, about the future they wanted to build together, the blended family they would call their own.

"Hey," she said when he was just a few feet away.

He looked up, and she saw in his eyes everything she had always hoped to see reflected back at her. Joy. Wonder. Love in all its forms.

"Hey yourself," he said, tucking the crutch more firmly under his left arm. "How long've you been here?"

"Not very," she said, instantly understanding the subtext. He didn't want her to see him in what he perceived as a vulnerable situation. "We must have had our watches synchronized."

She slid off the hood of his Jeep, and he leaned against the driver's side fender and pulled her into his arms.

"How was the luncheon?" he asked after they had kissed.

"An afterthought," she said. "It was all a fake. Rose kidnapped me and dragged me to the Saks in Short Hills."

"For what?" Aidan looked as puzzled as she had been. "A forced march through the house-wares department?"

"Bridal gowns," she said, pausing for effect. "Hideous, fussy, overpriced bridal gowns I wouldn't wear on Halloween."

They kissed again, longer this time and deeper. Heat began to gather low in her belly and between her legs as she felt him growing hard against her.

"It gets worse," she said, wondering if maybe Gina had had the right idea after all. The backseat looked awfully inviting. "Toni and Connie were there, too." She paused. "And Claire."

"So she went after all?"

"Yes, and if looks could kill, I would've col-lapsed over my appetizer at Bernino's this after-noon. I swear she used to like me, Aidan. I don't know what's happened."

"Of course she likes you. It's your aunts she can't stand."

She told him about the dresses, the cracks about her weight, about standing there in her Kmart underwear in front of his sister-in-law, his daughter, and her relatives.

"Doesn't sound bad to me," he said, aiming one of those lazy, sexy smiles in her direction. "Wish I'd been there to see you in your bra and panties."

She tried to ignore the tingle of excitement his words awakened. "It was a nightmare. The salesclerk acted like she'd never seen a size ten in captivity before."

He said something wonderfully rude, designed to make her laugh.

"Don't go trying to cheer me up," she said, feeling cheered up despite herself. "I told Rose you wanted us to elope."

"Will I need a food taster next time I come over for dinner?"

"Might not be a bad idea."

"What did she say?"

"That she thought you were smarter than that."

"That's the best she could do?"

"She likes you," Maddy said, wishing she hadn't brought the whole thing up when kissing was so much more enjoyable. "She lets you get away with murder. If I had told her it was my idea, she probably would have had me arrested."

"I don't think eloping is against the law."

"Then you don't know my mother," she said and pulled his head down for another kiss. She could feel his heat through their clothes, and it took every ounce of self-control at her command to keep from pulling him into the Jeep and having her way with him. "Maybe we could —"

"A couple more weeks," he said, tracing the contours of her face with a gentle finger. "I don't want you to be disappointed."

"As if I could be," she whispered against his

mouth. "As if anything about you could disappoint me."

"The broken leg disappointed you."

"No," she corrected him, "it was the timing."

His groan of frustration said it all for both of them.

Ten weeks ago, the gods had miraculously arranged for them to have a free Friday night. The odds of that happening again any time soon were up there in the lunar and solar eclipse on the same day category.

They had been seeing each other for a little over a month at that point, and the attraction between them had reached the boiling point. There wasn't anyone in town who didn't know exactly what was going on. Passionate kisses at the door, stolen moments in the back room of the bar, whispered phone calls and incendiary E-mails in the heart of the night — all they needed was time and privacy to take the next step toward the future.

Maddy was discovering that taking a lover in her thirties was a very different experience. She was the mother of a small child now, a little girl who looked toward her for guidance in everything from brushing her teeth to understanding the difference between right and wrong.

The decisions she made no longer belonged to her alone; they created aftershocks, big and small, that had the potential to shake Hannah's world to its foundations. She had seen the chaos her aunts' endless stream of husbands and lovers had brought to her cousins' lives, and she would live the rest of her life alone before she did that to Hannah.

What she and Aidan had found together felt right. Beneath the wildly exciting electricity that sizzled between them, there was something deeper, something more profound than either had imagined possible. But she didn't want to make a mistake. Not every mistake turned out as wonderfully as Hannah.

They had talked about their future that night over dinner at a tiny inn near Spring Lake. They talked about their daughters, their parents, the partners they had loved and lost. They talked through the starter, the entrée, and through dessert, and they were still talking when they said good night to the small wait staff and started down the sidewalk toward the car. Countless stars spangled the winter night sky. Moonlight made the snowbanks sparkle. Disney couldn't have conjured up a scene more conducive to romance.

And they were ready. There had never been a couple more ready than they were. The looks they gave each other could have melted the polar ice caps. If they had fallen to the ground right then, right there in a snowbank, neither one would have felt the cold. Both had noticed a small hotel a few blocks away, the one with the Occupancy sign blinking in the window. The night was a gift, a blessing from the gods of love who occasionally took pity on couples in need of a break.

Unfortunately, the gods took their job literally, and a layer of black ice near the driver's-side door turned Maddy and Aidan's plans upside down. Aidan's right leg, the one he had fractured badly a few years earlier, sustained another compound fracture of the ankle which, in turn, required more surgery, more rehabilitation, and more frustration. Suddenly romance took a backseat to the grueling demands of physical therapy and pain on a newly blossoming love.

Now here they were, almost three months later, still waiting for the right time and the right place to come along so they could finally become lovers in every sense of the word. Whatever difficulties he perceived his broken leg would bring to their lovemaking could easily be overcome with a little imagination and a sense of humor.

However, Aidan was a proud man. He had been battling injuries for over three years now, and it was clear the experience had made him wary of appearing vulnerable in any way.

She understood all too well, because her own vulnerabilities were never far from the surface. The extra pounds that had settled around her waist and thighs. The stretch marks that silvered her belly. The fact that she was old enough to know that love didn't always last forever, that sometimes good people with the best intentions couldn't find a way to make it work, no matter how hard they tried, and it was always the children who paid the price.

That wasn't going to happen to Hannah or Kelly, not if she could help it. When she and Aidan married, they would marry for keeps.

"So how did you like the wedding gowns?" he asked as he edged the Jeep into traffic on Main Street.

"I didn't," she said. "I can't see buying a dress that costs more than a used car."

"I thought all women dreamed about wearing a long white gown and a veil." He waved thanks to Bob Heffernan from the auto body shop for letting him in. "The Princess Di thing."

"And you saw how that ended up," Maddy said. "I never dreamed about getting married. I was too busy planning how my Barbie and I were going to rule the world."

"Kelly was like that, too. She wrote inaugural addresses for Malibu Barbie."

"I wouldn't be surprised if she was writing an inaugural address for herself one day. You did a great job with her, Aidan."

"Not me," he said, deflecting the credit the way he always did. "All I ever had to do was point out the right road and watch her do the rest."

"I know that's not true. You're a wonderful father."

"She made it easy for me. If it hadn't been for Claire's help, I wouldn't have known my ass from my elbow."

There was no denying that Claire had been a rock for Aidan to lean on during the first few years of Kelly's life, but she knew who had done the real parenting.

"Hannah's lucky to have you in her life," she said. "And so am I."

He wasn't good with compliments. He didn't say anything, just stared straight ahead at the cars moving slowly up the main drag, but he was smiling, and she found herself smiling, too. He had already done the heavy lifting where Kelly was concerned and done it splendidly.

In a few weeks she would graduate high school as valedictorian of her class and then before they had a chance to take a deep breath, she would be off to school in Manhattan on a full scholarship, well on her way to the life of happiness and accomplishment she deserved.

In the midst of the chaos that came with planning a wedding, how wonderful to know there was one part of their lives that was perfect and likely to stay that way.

Chapter Six

There was one thing adults didn't tell you when they gave you the great facts-of-life speech. They told you about eggs and sperm, about fertilization and the division of cells. They told you about wombs and embryos, about missed periods and the nine months that followed, but the one thing you really needed to know you had to find out on your own.

The first time she and Seth had made love, Kelly knew instantly what no adult had ever been able to tell her. Sex changed everything. You couldn't pretend it never happened. You couldn't go back to the way you were before, not even if you wanted to. That decision changed you forever. The last whisper of childhood faded, and you were left all alone in the strange world adults called home.

She could barely look at her father for weeks afterward. Every time she did, she was torn between the fact that he was a sexual being — something too gross to contemplate — and the knowledge that she could never again be his innocent little girl. Those days were gone. The balance between them had been irrevocably altered, and he hadn't a clue. He talked to her the same way he had always talked to her, small talk about dinner, about Aunt Claire, about somebody at the bar, and he didn't even notice the difference. She kept her secret well, and he trusted her so implicitly that he didn't suspect a thing. Somehow that made her terribly sad, although she couldn't explain why, not even to her journal.

Her friends knew immediately. She walked into home room the morning after her first time, and Frannie flashed thumbs-up from across the room. By study hall, Rachel and Kimberly were begging for details Kelly suddenly realized she didn't want to share. Her friends were all on their second or third partners, happily experimenting, no strings attached.

Just like Kelly might have been if love hadn't entered the picture. Her friends were the ones who had played bride all the time, while Kelly holed up in her room with a chemistry set. Frannie and Kim had had their weddings planned from gown to party favors by the time they hit puberty. All they needed was a guy in a tux to come along, and their dreams would come true.

She wanted so much more than that. She wanted to go to school, get her degree, maybe go on to do graduate work, then travel before she was too old and settled to see the world.

And the best part of all was that Seth wanted the same things she wanted.

Her friends took chances and never got caught. Funny how something that used to worry her now made her feel a little better. She and Seth were always careful. They used condoms. They even kept an eye on the time of month, something nobody did anymore, not even the most devout Catholics. That was why she was so sure this couldn't be happening. There had to be some other reason for the way she had been feeling. Another reason why she had puked her brains out in the bathroom in front of — God help her — Hannah. Maybe she was getting some kind of nasty springtime flu. Or maybe it was food poisoning. Or maybe the stress of juggling schoolwork and her after-class clubs and her different jobs was taking a toll. It could be anything. It didn't have to be that she was pregnant.

She waited until her aunt made the left turn onto Bay Bridge Avenue, then jumped into her car. Five minutes later, she pulled into the parking lot behind the lake on the outskirts of town, where Seth was waiting for her in his brother's Honda.

"Missed you," he said as she slid into the passenger seat next to him.

"Good," she said after they had kissed hello. "I missed you, too."

"How long can you stay?"

She glanced at her watch, the one that had

been her mother's high school graduation present eighteen years ago. "Thirteen minutes." She sighed. "How about you?"

"Eight," he said. "I'm working two extra hours tonight." He pumped gas three nights a week.

"You work too hard."

"Yeah," he said with a grin. "So do you."

Kelly had grown up surrounded by love, but by the time her tenth birthday rolled around, she knew she would have to work hard to make her dreams come true. Firemen's kids didn't go to NYU or Columbia, not without a scholarship. And not without a healthy nest egg saved up from waiting tables, cleaning houses, and ringing up groceries.

"I'm not a rich kid like you," she said, teasing him. His family struggled as hard as hers did. "I have to."

"So do I," he said.

It was one of the many reasons why she loved him, had loved him for as long as she could remember. He worked hard for everything he had. Paper routes as a little kid. Shoveling sidewalks in the winter and mowing lawns in the summer. When he was fifteen, he discovered he had a talent for carpentry, and these days he made a fair chunk of change doing odd jobs for people like Olivia Westmore and Rose DiFalco. "He has real talent," Rose had commented just last week. "The work he did on the back porch was first rate."

You would have thought he'd won a Nobel prize the way her heart had swelled with pride. It felt good when someone complimented Seth, better even than when the compliments were aimed in her direction.

His hands slid along her shoulders and down her arms, and she shivered with longing. You couldn't turn back once you took the leap. Once you knew how it felt when skin met skin, once you understood what it meant to not know where you ended and he began — there was no way she could ever give that up. "Three minutes," she whispered against the familiar warmth of his mouth. "I wish —"

Suddenly she was afraid she was going to cry, and she pressed her face against his chest.

"Kel?" He placed a hand under her chin, but she refused to look up at him. "What's wrong?"

That was all it took. She couldn't control either her tears or the words that spilled out with them.

"How late are you?" he asked when she finally managed to pull herself together long enough to breathe. He looked shaken, but his embrace never faltered.

"Two days," she said, pulling a paper napkin from his glove box to wipe her eyes.

He balanced between hope and certainty. "You've been late before. Last year you were two weeks late because of the SATs."

"Last year we weren't sleeping together."

"It's not like we haven't been careful."

"Nothing's foolproof," she reminded him. "Things happen." She fixed him with a look. "I spent the morning throwing up."

"It was all that ice cream on an empty stomach."

"I only had two spoonfuls."

"You said you've been dieting."

"Dieting doesn't make you —"

"It's a false alarm," he said, pulling her close. "Everything will work out. Just wait and see."

"You really think so?"

He hesitated just a half-beat too long, and in that hesitation she heard the sound of her future rushing toward her, and it wasn't the future she had planned.

Billy Jr. was waiting for Claire at the edge of the soccer field with his best friend Ryan and Ryan's father.

"Sorry I'm late," Claire said while Billy gathered up his gear. "I stopped at Wawa for a gallon of milk and realized I didn't have any money, so I had to race over to the ATM and —"

"Don't worry about it, Claire." David Fenelli's dark brown eyes were warm behind his glasses. "Been there, done it myself."

Could a man be too nice? David radiated so much kindness and understanding that it was all Claire could do to keep from hitting him in the head with a soccer ball.

"Good practice?" she asked while Billy and Ryan snorted with laughter a few feet away.

"Billy had a great practice," David said with a nod toward her youngest. "Ryan had a little trouble, but he's making progress."

Ryan looked like he would rather be in the orthodontist's chair than standing there while two adults talked about him, and Claire's maternal heart went out to him.

"I've kept you long enough," Claire said, gesturing for Billy to get into the car. "Thanks for waiting."

David brushed her gratitude aside. "Listen," he said, watching as Billy fastened his seat belt, "we're planning to pick up pizza tonight. Why don't you join us?"

She hadn't seen it coming. The last time he asked her to go bowling with them her early warning system had noted the faint beads of sweat that popped out on his brow before he spoke, which gave her just long enough to make up a believable excuse.

"Pizza sounds great," she said, aware of the intense scrutiny coming from Billy and Ryan, "but —"

"I know," David said. "Mondays are tough. Maybe another time."

He really was too nice. No wonder his wife left him. Didn't he know nice guys ended up alone?

"I'd like that," she said. She hadn't meant to say that. She definitely hadn't expected to mean it.

David held her gaze a moment longer than

usual, and she felt her cheeks flood with heat. "I'm going to hold you to it, Claire."

She mumbled something incoherent in response, feeling more like a clumsy fourteen-year-old than a woman of forty.

"Your face is red," Billy observed as she slid behind the wheel. "Are you mad at Ryan's dad?"

"I'm not mad at anyone." She glanced at her reflection in the rearview mirror. Red didn't begin to describe it. She looked like she was about to spontaneously combust.

"Grandma's face used to get red all the time," Billy continued. "She said it was changes that did it."

"Menopause," Claire corrected, "and I'm too young for that."

Apparently that was too much information for her son, because he leaned forward and fiddled with the radio dial until he settled on WFAN, the all-sports station he loved, and Claire breathed an audible sigh of relief. She'd rather listen to a detailed analysis of the Mets' chances than face more questions.

Smooth, Claire. I'm surprised you didn't trip over your shoelaces when you walked back to the car. Fenelli must really be desperate.

"Turn up the volume," she said to Billy. "I want to hear what they say about plans for Old-Timers' Day."

Billy shot her a curious look but upped the volume so high she couldn't hear herself think.

Which, of course, was exactly the point.

Ten minutes later, she pulled into the driveway and cut the engine, mercifully ending a spirited on-air discussion of somebody named Marvelous Marv Throneberry.

Billy blinked like he was coming out of a trance and said, "You forgot to get Grandpa."

"Grandpa's home today," she said. "It's —" She rested her forehead against the steering wheel and groaned. "You're right. I forgot Grandpa." She looked over at her son. "Do you remember where he is today?"

Billy nodded. "The senior center."

She tossed him her cell phone. "Press number six, and tell Grandpa we're on our way."

She retraced the path back to town, made a left at the church, then whipped into the parking lot adjacent to the renovated barn that now served as a gathering place for Paradise Point's senior citizens. She pulled in between an aged Volvo and a spiffy new Mazda Miata with handicapped plates.

"Where did Grandpa say he'd meet us?"

"In front."

Her father had the annoying habit of running even later than she did. "Go in and tell him we're waiting."

Billy was out of the car like a shot, bounding across the sandy grass and into the center in the time it would have taken her to unbuckle her seat belt. Her father had been living with them for the last few months while he decided where he would settle, much to his grandson's delight.

Mike Meehan had been widowed for almost five years and had spent the last three of them making extended visits to his offspring while they tried to convince him he had to finally settle down someplace. Florida. California. Upstate New York. Minnesota. Nothing seemed right to him, not until he came to visit Claire in Paradise Point.

She was glad he had found his way back to his old hometown, but the past six months had been stressful to say the least. Mike was a robust seventy-five, a former fisherman with a powerful build and personality to match. He had an opinion about everything that went on in her house, from where she kept the tea bags to Billy's spelling tests to why she didn't buy out Aidan and run the bar herself.

And to make matters worse, he had a better social life than she did. Many of his old cronies were still alive and living in town or nearby, and just like the old days, Mike Meehan was at the center of the fun. The senior center had become the equivalent of a high school hangout, and Mike was the captain of the football team and class president all wrapped up in one geriatric package.

It made her biweekly poker party with the girls look pretty anemic.

"Took you long enough," her father said as he settled himself into the passenger seat. "Billy said you forgot your old man."

"Thanks, pal," she muttered to Billy's reflection in the rearview mirror. "I didn't exactly forget you, Dad. I just lost track of the days."

"You're — what? Forty? What the hell are you going to be like when you're my age?"

"Dead," she said. "You and the rest of the family will have worn me into an early grave."

He threw back his head and roared with laughter. "That's just what your mother would've said, God rest her soul. Said I had enough energy for five men and a midget."

"Dad!" She slipped easily into maternal reproach mode. "The politically correct term is little person."

"Little person? What the hell's a little person? We called 'em midgets when I was growing up, and they're midgets now. Scotty Henderson's brother was maybe three feet tall, and he'd break your kneecap if you tried to call him a little person."

"Dad." She added an extra note of sternness to her tone. "Times change. We have to be mindful of Billy and help him to be respectful of others."

"Who's being disrespectful? People are what they are. You can call a dog a cat, but it still lifts its leg to pee."

"Priscilla doesn't lift her leg," Billy piped up from the backseat. "Hannah says she just stands there and pees on her paws."

"Enough pee talk," Claire said. "All I'm saying is that if someone wants to be referred to as a small person, then that's what we should do."

"Next midget I see, I'm going to ask him what he wants to be called."

"You do that, Dad, but don't come crying to me if you end up with a busted kneecap."

Not for the first time, Claire found herself longing for a nice quiet secluded convent. Maybe that was what she should do. To hell with O'Malley's. She could open a convent for the Sisters of the Celibate Poor.

She pulled the car into the driveway for the second time in thirty minutes and shut off the engine.

"Eggs for supper," she announced as they trooped through the back door into the kitchen, "and I don't want to hear any complaints."

"Aw, Ma —"

"I'll make you a jelly omelet." She turned to her father, who was leaning against the door to the laundry room while he kicked off his shoes. "And don't start about your cholesterol. I'll make yours with Egg Beaters."

There were dogs to let out, cats to feed, laundry to start, eggs to scramble, nerves to unfrazzle. Too bad Billy was still at an impressionable age. She felt like saying screw the eggs and sitting out on the back step with a pack of cigarettes and a Bud Light, but she was trying to set a good example.

Her father whistled for the dogs, and she was almost trampled by the canine stampede as they converged from various points in the house and flung themselves out the door into the yard. Billy, with a little urging, popped the tops on a quartet of Fancy Feast and upended the contents onto four small white plates.

She was on her way upstairs to change into her usual uniform of jeans and T-shirt when the front doorbell rang.

David Fenelli stood on the top step with a schoolbook clutched in his right hand.

She fought down the urge to smooth down her hair.

"Sorry to interrupt your supper, Claire, but Billy left his spelling book in the backseat. Knowing how much our kids love homework, I figured I'd better get it over here."

"That's sweet of you, David. You didn't have to go out of your way. I would've come by to pick it up."

"If I'd known that, I would've told you to pick it up at Romano's over a pepperoni and mushroom."

"Who're you talking to out there?" her father bellowed from the kitchen. "If that's Barney, don't let him in. I'm not talking to that welsher!"

"It's not Barney," Claire hollered back. "It's Ryan's father."

"Ask him if he wants some eggs."

She met David's eyes. "You don't want eggs, do you?"

He shook his head. "No eggs."

"Thanks, Dad. They already ate." She lowered her volume. "He's not really my father," she said. "I found him wandering in front of the senior center and took pity on him."

"That's where I found mine, too. In fact, are you sure it's not the same guy?"

Some of the day's tensions mysteriously vanished as they laughed.

"Listen," he said, his gaze holding hers, "I don't want to keep you from your eggs."

"Seriously, if you and Ryan have room for some scrambled eggs and bacon, I'd —"

"I promised him pizza, but I wouldn't mind a rain check."

Say it, Claire. Go on. You know you want to. "I wouldn't mind one either." His eyes widened behind his glasses, and she felt that familiar heat rising once again to her cheeks. "I mean, maybe next time you and Ryan go for pizza, Billy and I could join you."

Fenelli really had a good smile, kind of loopy and ironic all at the same time. It wasn't a devastating smile or a sexy smile but still . . .

"Maybe next time Billy and Ryan could stay home, and we'll go for pizza."

"I'd like that." *You would? I didn't think you had it in you, Claire.*

They stood there staring at each other for what seemed like a semester or two. It took Ryan's plaintive wail of "Daaaaad!" wafting across the front yard to end the moment.

"See you at the bus stop," David said as he turned to leave.

"Thanks for bringing the book over."

"Maybe we can work in that pizza next week."

"Sounds great."

He smiled.

She smiled back.

He jogged across the lawn to his car.

She waved good-bye.

Okay, so it wasn't *Love Story*, but for Paradise Point, it wasn't half bad. Not bad at all.

Olivia Westmore, elegant owner of Le Papier, sat at Rose's kitchen table making notes on a beautiful pad of pale pink watermarked notepaper better suited for letters to the Queen of England.

"A fountain pen?" Rose couldn't help the note of incredulity that crept into her voice. "I didn't think anyone still used fountain pens."

"This is a 1950s-era Duofold," Olivia said proudly. "I usually keep it at home, but I was feeling reckless today."

"It probably cost more than your Jimmy Choos."

Olivia glanced down at her pricey footwear and shrugged. "And worth every penny."

"You really are a shameless hedonist, aren't you?"

"Damn right," Olivia said with a wicked smile. "Not much point to life if you don't enjoy the things around you."

"I know there's a flaw in your logic," Rose said as she pulled a container of boeuf bourguignonne from the freezer. "When I figure it out, I'll get back to you."

"Oh, don't play innocent," Olivia said, capping her pen and placing it on the tabletop. "I've seen those silky robes of yours and the bath oils. You're not a stranger to worldly pleasures, Rosie."

Rose didn't deny it. She loved fine wine, beautiful music, delicious food, soft and sumptuous fabrics that caressed her skin. It was those very inclinations that had helped her shape the fantasy world that The Candlelight Inn offered to her guests. Her eye for beauty combined with her head for business had turned her mother's tumbledown Victorian into a highly acclaimed moneymaker.

Now, if only the same thing would happen with Cuppa, she would be a very happy woman.

"So what did you come up with?" she asked Olivia, gesturing toward the pad of notes. "I'll need all the details I can get to make the presentation to Maddy."

"She's your daughter," Olivia said, "not your contracts attorney. Tell her it's a great opportunity, and she's the right one to manage it."

"She's also an accountant," Rose reminded her. "She'll want facts and figures."

Maddy was slightly fey and charmingly unpredictable, but like it or not, she had inherited her mother's business acumen. She would want to know cost projections, zoning laws, overhead.

Olivia read her the lists she had pulled together while Rose busied herself getting supper ready. Her mind, however, refused to focus on what her friend was saying. Her thoughts bounced from the way Maddy had looked surrounded by wedding gowns to the sound of Hannah's laughter in the backyard to how much she wanted them to stay in Paradise Point forever.

Rose wasn't fanciful by nature. That was one of the many differences between her and her daughter. Maddy had always been given to outrageous flights of fantasy that left Rose scratching her head in dismay. But when it came to her beloved Candlelight Inn, Rose could show her daughter a thing or two. The house wasn't just a house to Rose. It lived and breathed and had opinions, not all of which she shared. Every creaking board, every gleaming window, every single dust-free inch of the old Victorian wonder vibrated with a life — and a story — of its own.

On days when she was very lucky, her ex-husband Bill was there, too. He liked the little aerie on the third floor, the tower room with the antique iron bed and patchwork quilt. Twice last month she watched the sun rise over the ocean from that bed, head nestled against his graying chest, and thanked God for letting her live long enough to find her way back home to the first and only man she had ever loved.

Maddy seemed delighted that her parents had rekindled their love after so many years, while

Hannah, bless her heart, accepted it all as perfectly right and logical.

Maybe you had to be a little crazy to believe in love. Love didn't play by the rules. Love defied logic. It didn't come when you called or slink away when you were done with it. Love was occasionally fickle and sometimes, but not often enough, it was forever. Every time she looked into Bill Bainbridge's faded blue eyes, she felt the same sense of wonder she had felt forty years ago when he first asked her to marry him.

And she saw that same sense of wonder in Maddy's eyes when she looked at Aidan, as if her daughter couldn't quite believe her own good fortune. What a joy it was to see Maddy with a man who loved her the way she deserved to be loved. The sight of the two of them together made Rose's heart ache with happiness. There was a certain sweetness about them, a sense of completion that went beyond the sparks they generated every time their eyes met. The whole town agreed that Aidan O'Malley was as head-over-heels as any man they had ever seen in their lives. "Do you see the way he looks at our girl?" Lucy had asked with a sigh the other night. "I swear I could see the moon and the stars in his eyes."

Life flew by so fast. Maddy was still too young to understand just how quickly these precious days with Hannah and Aidan would disappear. One moment you were a young woman with a baby in your arms, and the next time you blinked, your mother was looking back at you from your mirror, and she was telling you that you were running out of time. Next month she would celebrate the fifth anniversary of her successful battle with breast cancer. Five years had come and gone since the doctor gave her the "all clear" — five years she wouldn't have had if God had decided differently. Five years that were lived with her daughter and granddaughter thousands of miles away, building memories that didn't include the people who loved them the most.

Maybe that was why she had this sudden, unexpected determination to give Maddy a wedding day to remember. She had missed the birth of her only grandchild, something she would always regret. Maddy had been deeply hurt by her absence, and the rift between them had grown wider and deeper as a result. Not even the truth, that she had been undergoing grueling chemotherapy treatments at the time and a cross-country trip would have been beyond her endurance, could explain away the fact that she hadn't been there when her baby gave birth to a baby of her own. She had waited too long to explain, and the years apart had already done their damage.

Sometimes she felt like she would always be playing catch-up where Maddy was concerned, struggling for the right thing to say and the right time to say it, but never quite succeeding. They had lost so many years to distance. Rose had seen to the emotional distance; by the time Maddy moved across the country to Seattle, she was only making it visible.

You couldn't build a lifetime of memories on a two-week visit every year, two weeks that usually ended in tears and recriminations. A wedding would be something they could share, a grand and beautiful event built upon a foundation of love and hope. The memories would be good ones, precious ones, that would weave their lives together indelibly in a way so far only genetics had been able to accomplish. Life was so painfully short. If they didn't start banking memories now, it would one day be too late.

"Rose." Olivia's voice cut into her thoughts. "You didn't hear a word I said, did you?"

"Not a single one," she admitted.

She put the saucepan on the stove and lit the burner beneath it. The sounds of Hannah's laughter and Priscilla's excited barking drifted toward her from the backyard. What a precious gift this time together had been.

"Second thoughts?" Olivia asked. "If you've changed your mind, we'll just shake hands and part as friends. We haven't signed any papers yet, Rose."

"No second thoughts," she said firmly. "I want to do this. It's a great opportunity, and I believe it will be a big success."

"But — ?"

"I don't think Maddy will go for it. We had a blow-up at Saks this afternoon about wedding dresses. She'll see this as just another attempt at trying to control her life."

"There are worse things."

"Working with Claire might be one of them."

"They're both big girls, Rosie. They'll reach an accommodation."

"They're going to be family. This might —"

"Don't micromanage. We'll supply the opportunity. They'll decide if they can handle it."

"Stay for supper," Rose urged. "Call Sunny and tell her to close up shop for the day. That way we can ask Maddy together."

"Ply her with Chardonnay and carbohydrates, and then go in for the kill."

"If you're here, she'll be more inclined to see it as a business deal, not some Machiavellian scheme to get her into a Vera Wang in front of six hundred of her nearest and dearest."

"You're not going to have one of those nasty *Mommy Dearest* spats, are you?"

Rose tossed a dish towel in her friend's direction. "Call Sunny," she ordered, "and I'll set another place for dinner."

And say a prayer to St. Jude, patron of impossible causes, while she was at it.

Chapter Seven

"Oh no," Maddy said as Aidan swung into the tiny parking lot behind The Candlelight. "Rose called in reinforcements."

Olivia Westmore's sleek Jaguar was parked next to Maddy's proud but battered Mustang. Rose and the chic owner of the only successful stationery store in Jersey Shore history had struck up a business friendship that had unexpectedly turned personal. They were an unlikely combination. Olivia was in her late thirties or early forties, statuesque and voluptuous, many times married. It was said her cleavage could shelter a family of five. She was flamboyant, wildly romantic, a woman with the heart of an earth mother hidden behind a high-maintenance exterior.

Rose, of course, was none of those things. Maddy's mother was a relentlessly practical woman. If she couldn't see it, touch it, or deposit it in her bank account, it didn't exist. She believed firmly in hard work and common sense, and that big boobs just got in the way.

Maddy definitely agreed with her on that last one.

"I don't think Liv is the type to take sides in family squabbles," Aidan said as he shifted into neutral.

"Oh, Rose is too sly for that. She probably invited Olivia over for supper and suggested she bring along her portfolio of wedding invitations for after-dinner entertainment." She brightened suddenly. "Why don't you come in with me?" she suggested. "If she can bring in reinforcements, so can I."

"Hell, no," he said, kissing her soundly. "Tommy has the night off, Claire doesn't do school nights anymore, and all of a sudden Leo says he wants quality time with his wife."

"That's what I get for falling in love with a barkeep."

"Say it again."

"Barkeep."

"The love part."

She grinned and pressed a kiss to the side of his neck. "For such a big guy, you're awfully sentimental."

"About you I am."

"You're sure I can't convince you to stay for supper?"

"Rosie and Olivia in the same room? I don't have the balls."

"That's pretty much what Dad said the last time he came to visit. He hid out on the dunes during poker night."

"Bill's a smart man. After we're married, I'll be out there with him."

They kissed again, then broke apart when Hannah popped out the kitchen door, with Priscilla right behind her, and somersaulted off the bottom step.

"That kid's going to be in the circus someday," Aidan said as Hannah launched herself into a saggy cartwheel. "Every time I look at her she's upside down."

"She somersaulted across a nest of Vera Wangs this morning. I saw what was left of my 401K going up in smoke."

"Vera Wangs?"

"You have a lot to learn, O'Malley. Vera Wang bridal gowns." She quoted him a price range.

"That's a down payment on a house."

"Now you see why I have to straighten Rosie out on this. I wouldn't spend that on a dress even if PBS was footing the bill."

Hannah held Priscilla up to the passenger-side window. The poodle lapped at the glass as Hannah dissolved in a giggling fit.

"Welcome back to age five," Maddy said as a river of puppy drool ran down the window. "Sure you want to go through it again?"

He winced as the drool made tracks through the road dust. "I can do it if you can."

They both came with daughters, family complications, a lifetime's worth of unruly, messy personal history that stuck to everything it touched like foam packing peanuts. Their eyes

133

met, and they started to laugh at the wonder and absurdity of finding love in the midst of real life. Hannah, thinking they were laughing at her antics, got even sillier on the other side of the car door. When she tried to balance Priscilla on her head, Maddy knew it was time to stop being Aidan's fiancée and go back to being Hannah's mother.

Hannah was bouncing off the walls with energy, a sure sign Rose had indulged her with some of Aunt Lucy's famous oatmeal cookies — on top of ice cream at lunch, no less.

Aidan waited while she scooped up Priscilla with one arm and took Hannah's hand. He waved good-bye to the both of them, then carefully backed out of the tiny parking lot while Hannah waved one of the poodle's paws at him in farewell.

"Gramma's friend is here," Hannah said after Aidan's truck disappeared around the corner. "The one that smells good."

"Olivia always smells good," Maddy said. Maybe that was why almost every man in town followed her around like she was the Pied Piper of Paradise Point.

"Priscilla ate her shoe."

Maddy's stomach knotted. Olivia wore Jimmy Choos with an occasional flirtation with Manolo Blahniks. Didn't her mother know anyone who shopped at Payless?

"Pris didn't really eat her shoe, did she?"

"She bit it," Hannah said, watching as

134

Priscilla sniffed around the rosebushes near the beach steps. "Gramma told her she was bad, but 'Livia said she was just being a dog."

Maddy made a mental note to stop by the stationery store and buy something she couldn't afford. "Is Olivia staying for supper?"

"Gramma said she had to. She needed the sport."

Sport? "Do you mean 'support,' honey?"

Hannah shrugged her shoulders and did an impromptu somersault.

"Oh, what the heck." Maddy knelt down on the sandy grass, ignored whatever might be slithering or crawling nearby, and pushed off into her own sloppy but enthusiastic somersault.

Hannah whooped with excitement. Priscilla yipped and poked Maddy in the side with her wet nose. There was nothing like encouragement to make a woman go for the gold. Three somersaults later, she was busted.

"Very cute," Olivia said, as she stepped out onto the back porch with Rose close behind. "Do you do any other tricks?"

Maddy was torn between mild embarrassment and amusement. "I sit up and beg for crème brûlée."

Olivia threw back her head and laughed. She had one of those full-throated laughs men would lay down their lives for. "Honey, I'd roll over and play dead for a good crème brûlée."

"Are you staying for supper?" Maddy asked as

she brushed grass, sand, and unmentionables off her clothes.

"Sunny can't figure out how to set the alarm at the store. I'll be back after I lock up." She looked at Rose. "I'll see if I can get hold of Stan or Larry while I'm there."

The wink Olivia gave her before she left made her mother look like a guilty schoolgirl. Was Olivia planning a threesome with the town's favorite CPA and contracts attorney? The idea almost pushed her into helpless laughter.

"What was that all about?" Maddy asked as she and Rose followed Hannah and Priscilla into the house. "What do you need Stan and Larry for?"

Rose busied herself with the salad greens, which lay drying in a metal colander suspended over the sink. "Olivia and I are going into business together."

"You're going into business with Liv?" Maddy plucked a grape tomato from its nest of paper towels. "What? Rental property?" Her mother had been a successful real estate saleswoman for three decades and had developed a sixth sense for undervalued property with potential.

"No rental property."

"You're not thinking of buying another B and B, are you?" Visions of the wedding gift from hell danced before her eyes. The thought of living the rest of her life with strangers gargling in her upstairs bathroom made her downright dizzy with trepidation.

"Such enthusiasm." Rose reached for the bottle of balsamic vinegar on the ledge. "I promise one B and B is more than enough for one woman. Now, would you go into the pantry and fetch me a bottle of extra virgin for the salad, please?"

"I don't need the fancy stuff," Maddy said. "Wesson oil's okay with me."

"Don't ever say that around the paying customers! The Candlelight has a reputation to consider."

Maddy wasn't sure if her mother was chastising her, being funny, or telling the truth. Rose had a caustic sense of humor, honed during years of battle with her sisters, and it occasionally drew a few drops of blood.

"Was that a dig or an observation?"

"An observation," Rose said. "I'm not being sarcastic, just literal."

"Considering everything that happened this afternoon, I figured I should ask before I went off the deep end."

Rose's sigh was long and low. "I'm sorry about today, honey. I don't know what I was thinking. I know you hate surprises."

"Yeah, especially ones that involve standing around in my underwear." If she had had a little warning, she could have gone out and purchased something a bit more presentable than her very basic cotton. Like a burka.

"You hate to shop. Your aunts can be horses' hindquarters. Your cousins could talk the ears

137

off Mount Rushmore. I can't for the life of me figure out why I thought that was such a good idea."

Her mother looked so unexpectedly contrite that Maddy exhaled for the first time since the salesclerk ran off with her clothes earlier that afternoon. "I'm sorry I overreacted about the dresses."

Her mother's left brow arched just enough to make itself known. "You're half DiFalco. It's in your blood."

"There's a frightening thought for you," Maddy said. "I've been engaged to Aidan for less than a month, and the wedding has already made me crazy. I don't know how anyone could survive doing this more than once in a lifetime."

"And God willing, you'll never know."

"I can't believe the price of this stuff," Maddy said as she walked back into the kitchen a few minutes later with the olive oil. "It's liquid gold. You should —"

She stopped when she realized her mother was plating the meal.

"We're not waiting for Olivia?"

"She called. She's not coming. There was an emergency at the store."

"A stationery store emergency? Did someone run out of gummed address labels or Magic Markers?"

Her mother laughed. "You should excuse the expression, but it's a wedding invitation emergency. The poor woman has to hand-address three hundred of them and deliver the lot up to Brielle by nine in the morning."

"Another good reason to elope." And a reason to be glad she had never learned the art of calligraphy.

"Madelyn —"

"I'm joking, Ma. You really didn't expect me to ignore a straight line like that, did you?"

"Call Hannah," Rose said, still smiling to Maddy's amazement. "Supper's getting cold."

Five minutes later they were seated at the kitchen table, ready to dive in. The place smelled heavenly. Boeuf bourguignonne. A loaf of crusty bread, wrapped loosely in a red and white checked tea towel. A crisp green salad laced with the pricey olive oil and fancy vinegar and sprinkled with fresh herbs in season.

This wasn't exactly the average Monday night supper chez DiFalco. She hadn't spent the last thirty-three years as a daughter for nothing. Rose was about to launch a full frontal assault designed to capture Maddy's heart and mind, but it would take more than a wine-laced supper to convince her she wanted the wedding of her mother's dreams.

"You really have to stop plying her with cookies and pastries," Maddy said as Hannah pecked at her salad. "She was bouncing off the walls when I got home."

"I know," Rose said with uncharacteristic sheepishness. "Grandma Fay used to slip you big wedges of cheesecake when she thought I wasn't looking, and I would read her the riot act. Now here I am showering Hannah with tiramisu and trifle."

"So when do the hordes descend upon us?" Maddy asked as she took a second helping of stew from the serving tureen.

"The cameraman will be back up from Cape May around ten A.M.," Rose said, refilling Hannah's water glass. "Peter Lassiter hopes to make it here by lunchtime."

"Doesn't sound too bad," Maddy lied.

"He's bringing cameramen, sound people, and a research assistant with him."

"The one with all the tattoos?"

"And the pierced tongue." Rose shuddered. "I don't know where to look when she talks to me. All I can see is that thing clattering around inside her mouth."

"I almost had my nose pierced when I first moved to Seattle."

"Please tell me you're joking."

"I came this close, but Dad found out and threatened to send me —" She stopped. "Maybe this isn't such a funny anecdote after all."

"He threatened to send you back here, didn't he?"

Maddy felt like a worm for even broaching the topic. "I'm sorry. I should've thought before I spoke."

"No revisionist history at this table," Rose

140

said. "That's the way things were between us, honey, but that doesn't mean that's the way they'll always be."

"Hannah."

The little girl looked up at Maddy.

"No tongue piercings, okay?"

Hannah nodded and went back to slipping pieces of tomato to Priscilla under the table.

"And good luck to you," Rose said, lifting her glass of water in salute. "Would that motherhood was that simple."

"At least I tried," Maddy said. "Ten years from now I'll need all the reassurance I can get."

"So, you remember what you were like at fifteen."

"Vividly."

"And do you plan on sharing any of the more quotable incidents with Peter Lassiter?"

"Not even if they try to woo me with Godiva and double-cheese pizzas."

Rose opened her mouth, then closed it quickly.

"You're thinking about my waistline, right?" Maddy asked.

"I was thinking about your cholesterol."

They looked at each other and started to laugh, much to Hannah's puzzlement.

"What's funny?" she asked.

"Your grandma," Maddy said.

"Yes," Rose said, leaning over to retrieve a lettuce leaf from the floor near Hannah's feet.

"Your grandma is a very funny — what are all those tomatoes doing under the table, Hannah?"

"Priscilla likes 'matoes," Hannah said, calmly poking through her salad.

Maddy darted under the table and scooped up the mess with a napkin. "Sorry," she said to her mother. "We'll have the 'don't feed the dog at the table' talk again tonight. At least the camera crew wasn't here to see it."

"I think they're more interested in watching us plan your wedding than in our dinner table."

"Well, I hate to disappoint them but —"

Rose raised her hand. "Why don't we just enjoy our supper and table the wedding discussions for later?"

"Don't have to ask me twice," Maddy said, raising her own water glass in salute. "Here's to our last hours of freedom before the hordes arrive."

There was nothing she hated more than a crowd of strangers, all dressed in jammies and bathrobes, marching past her bedroom door at all hours in search of a vacant bathroom. No matter how long she lived at The Candlelight, she would never adjust to bumping into a retired bank president, clad in jockey shorts and a faded Sticky Fingers T-shirt, brushing his teeth in the wrong bathroom.

Her mother, however, thrived on the commotion. "All the more reason for us to get an early start tomorrow. Lucy said she'll be here after early Mass to start baking, but you can sleep in until six-thirty. And Kelly comes in tomorrow, so she'll pick up some of the slack for you."

"I didn't ask for anyone to pick up the slack for me."

"I didn't say you did, Madelyn, but I did hope you'd be pleased to hear it. I know running an inn isn't your cup of tea, and this gives you the chance to join the poker game at Claire's."

She was pleased, ecstatic to be precise, but she had hoped her feelings were a little less transparent. She offered her mother a verbal olive branch. "I'll make sure all the rooms are ready before I answer Web site E-mails tonight."

Rose opened her mouth to say something, but Hannah beat her to it.

"Kelly threw up today."

Both women turned toward the little girl.

"What was that, honey?" Rose asked her granddaughter.

"Kelly threw up her ice cream at the mall."

Rose and Maddy locked eyes over Hannah's head.

"Did she tell you that?" Maddy asked cautiously. Her daughter's imagination was swiftly becoming the stuff of family legend. Normally she encouraged flights of fancy, but not this time.

"I saw her. It was all white and —"

"That's enough, Hannah." Rose pushed her plate aside. "We can figure out the rest."

"Can I go play with Priscilla?" Hannah asked.

"In the family room," Maddy said automatically. "We're having company tomorrow."

Hannah made a face, then scampered away. Clearly she was her mother's daughter when it came to paying guests.

Maddy turned to Rose. "What's going on with Kelly? She didn't look sick to me."

"It's probably nothing more than Hannah said. She ate some ice cream and it disagreed with her."

"The girl has Aidan's cast-iron stomach. I've seen her eat her weight in jalapeño peppers and not blink an eye."

"You don't think she's — ?" Rose diplomatically chose to let Maddy finish the sentence herself.

"Pregnant?" A shudder rippled through Maddy. "She's too smart and too ambitious." She crossed her fingers, wished on a star, murmured a prayer. "I can't imagine Kelly getting herself into that situation."

"It happened to you," Rose pointed out as she began gathering up their dinner plates.

"I had the flu," Maddy said. "I missed a pill and —"

"You conceived Hannah," Rose said as she elbowed the kitchen door open and held it for Maddy. "That's my point, honey. Things happen, no matter how smart a woman is. Sometimes nature finds a way."

144

"Don't say it!" Maddy practically stumbled into the kitchen. "Don't even think it! She's only seventeen."

"Are you going to mention this to Aidan?" Rose scraped the dinner plates, then handed them to Maddy for the dishwasher.

"Mention that my daughter says she saw his daughter throw up this afternoon? There's a great conversation starter for you. What if Hannah's stretching the truth?" She added dishwasher liquid to the machine and pressed the start button. "Kelly would never forgive me, and I wouldn't blame her."

"Then maybe you should speak to Kelly herself." Rose dried her hands on a pale yellow dish towel, then reached for the coffee mugs on the ledge near the window. "Find out exactly what happened."

"It isn't any of my business, Ma. It's Kelly's."

"You're going to be her stepmother. What she does is very much your business."

"She's done fine up until now without any help from me."

"Aidan's a great father," Rose agreed. "He's done a terrific job with Kelly. But maybe she could use a woman to talk to."

"She has Claire." Everyone knew Claire's door had been open to Kelly from the day she was born. If Kelly needed to turn to a woman for advice, why on earth would she seek out Maddy when she had her aunt eager to help?

"Claire has five kids of her own to worry

145

about," Rose said. "Besides, she certainly didn't do all that well with her first, did she?"

"Kelly's like her sixth child," Maddy pointed out. "And since you brought it up, Kathleen is pulling straight *A*s at Drew. Whatever problems she had, they're all in the past."

"Be that as it may, we can't deny Claire dropped the ball somewhere along the line. Drug problems in teens usually have their roots in family conflict, and God knows the O'Malleys know conflict."

"Thanks, Dr. Phil, but since when are you an expert on family relations? I don't think the DiFalcos are exactly the poster family for harmonious relationships."

"You don't need a Ph.D. to see which way the wind is blowing."

"Billy was still alive when Kathleen had her problems. What was he doing when this was going on? Why should Claire shoulder all of the blame?"

"You were away a long time, honey. A lot went on in this town during the fifteen years you were living in Seattle."

"I know Billy O'Malley wasn't exactly father of the year." Or husband of the year, for that matter. "Seems to me he could have spent a little more time at home instead of —" She barely managed to bite off the words *screwing my cousin behind his wife's back.*

Rose watched her carefully, as if debating exactly what Maddy knew and what she wanted her to know. Clearly they were both aware that Maddy would soon be part of the family they were discussing and that her loyalties would be necessarily divided.

"I vote that we change the subject," Maddy said with a slightly self-conscious laugh. "How about something less controversial —" she paused for effect "— like planning my wedding?"

Rose had the good grace to smile at her awkward attempt at extricating them from another discussion that was bound to end in raised voices and hurt feelings.

"You think I've gone overboard, don't you?" her mother asked.

"Renting a hotel ballroom does seem excessive to me."

"We have a big family. I would hold a reception here, but we would have to severely limit the guest list, and that would cause a lot of hurt feelings."

Maddy gestured toward the beach. "Lots of space for everyone down there."

"And I suppose you'd want a keg party and a clambake afterwards?"

"I'd compromise on champagne and lobster if you insisted."

Rose chuckled as she pumped two shots of espresso into Maddy's coffee mug then added the heated, frothy milk. "Cinnamon?"

"And some chocolate shavings. If I'm going to diet hell, I might as well enjoy the trip."

Maddy grabbed a fistful of almond biscotti dipped in bittersweet chocolate and followed her mother out onto the back porch. The yard, the trees, the beach were all bathed in the soft blue of dusk. Maddy shivered in the late spring chill and cupped her hands around the mug of her mother's perfect cappuccino. Hannah's laughter floated toward them, followed by Priscilla's soft yipping, and for a second she knew perfect contentment.

"I wish —" She stopped and shook her head. She didn't want to break the spell.

Rose laughed softly. "That you could stop time."

Maddy started in surprise. "How did you know?" She and Rose loved each other, but they were rarely in emotional synch.

"Because I felt the same way when you were growing up. I wished I could wrap you up in cotton wool and keep you safe from harm forever."

"I never knew you felt that way."

"You weren't supposed to. My job wasn't to hold on to you, it was to learn how to let go." Another wistful laugh. "Obviously that was one part of mothering I excelled at."

"I was never sure if you were relieved when I left or angry."

"Relieved, angry, hurt, lonely, sad — it took me a long while to accept the fact that you had really chosen to build a life so far away from your family."

"Dad is my family, too," she pointed out gently. Her father and his late wife Irma had opened their hearts and their home to her.

She saw herself at seventeen, filled with emotions she couldn't identify much less know how to handle. She had wanted to break free of her mother's shadow, to leave the paralyzing boredom of home behind and strike out on her own. Choosing a college out west had been the greatest act of rebellion her family had seen since Grandma Fay got herself tattooed three months shy of her eightieth birthday.

"I know he is," Rose said, "and I'm glad you had those years with them. That was the one thing that made it easier to let you go."

"But I came back home again."

"Yes, and it took you long enough." There was no sarcasm in her words, none of the bitterness that had marked their conversations just one year ago. Just an openness and vulnerability that Maddy had never heard before.

Slowly, slowly she was starting to understand. The thought of Hannah, her beloved little Hannah, aching to be anywhere Maddy wasn't made her want to weep.

It might be two steps backward for every three tentative steps forward, but those steps added up. Piece by painful piece, they were stripping themselves of their armor, revealing the tender flesh beneath. It wasn't easy and it wasn't fun, but the rewards were incalculable.

The trees rustled as sparrows and mourning

doves settled in for the night while one lone blue jay wheeled overhead on his way back to the nest. A car moved slowly down Main Street, the controlled rumble from its engine an odd counterpoint to the deep, restless sound of the ocean. Music spilled from an open window somewhere down the block. Those were the sounds of home.

She used to dream the sound of the Atlantic during her years in Seattle; that sound memory was her lullaby.

Rose shifted position just a tiny bit, and Maddy willed herself to relax as she leaned against her mother's shoulder. They had spent almost thirty-three years as mother and daughter, and yet she could still count on the fingers of one hand the times when the other's physical presence had been enough to provide comfort.

"Listen," Rose whispered.

"The ocean?"

"Shh! There . . . !" Her mother, her practical, no-nonsense mother, sounded enchanted.

Maddy closed her eyes as Hannah's voice, singing a song about Priscilla and her adventures as a sea captain, wrapped itself around her heart and around her mother's as well.

"She's just like you were," Rose said. "I used to stand in the hallway and listen to you telling stories to your stuffed animals. I've often regretted that I didn't write some of them down."

"I thought you hated it when I made up stories." When she and Hannah first moved back, Rose had worried incessantly about her granddaughter's overactive imagination, an unpleasant reminder of past differences. "Why didn't you ever tell me this?"

"I was afraid you would end up one of those girls who lived their lives searching for Prince Charming. I wanted you to be able to face whatever the world threw at you without disappearing into some rosy fantasy world. I wanted you to be strong."

"You can be strong and have an imagination."

"I know that now," Rose admitted, "but the world was a different place thirty years ago. I wanted to make sure you were prepared to make your own way."

"Oh, I was prepared. I got the degree. I got the job. And then I got the ax." Not at all the scenario of her mother's dreams. Or her own, for that matter.

"The company you worked for went out of business. You can hardly be blamed for that."

"Want to know a secret?" Maddy asked as darkness tucked itself around them. "The day they let me go was one of the happiest days of my life. I felt like I'd been let out of prison."

"I would have been terrified in your shoes," Rose said. "That steady income was my security blanket. Lucy wanted me to quit and go into business with her at the dress shop, but the thought of losing my regular paycheck was more than I could handle."

"I probably should have felt the same way," Maddy said, "but I was so excited that I would be able to pursue voice-over work that I think my brain shut down." The terror came later when she looked at her bank balance and Hannah's growing needs.

"That took guts," Rose said, and Maddy steeled herself for the sting behind the words, but the sting never came. "I always regretted not joining Lucia when she wanted to open a second dress shop down in Cape May."

"I haven't exactly been a rousing success on the radio." Her weekly on-location show had been nicely received, but the New York and Philly markets weren't exactly beating down her door. She was Paradise Point's favorite local show. Unfortunately, she was also their only local show.

"You're following your heart," Rose said. "It took me almost sixty years to finally realize how important that is."

"And it only took me thirty-three to realize you can't feed your baby on a diet of nothing but dreams. There's a real world out there, and it's not going to go away."

"I've never heard you talk that way before."

"It doesn't mean I'm giving up my dreams," Maddy warned. "I'm just rearranging them."

"I wouldn't want you to give up anything."

"Aidan isn't rich. I see how hard he works to keep O'Malley's on track. We have Kelly and Hannah to worry about, and we hope to have children together. You can't make that happen on dreams alone." She sounded like she was trying to convince herself rather than explain a concept to Rose.

"I think I can help."

"I don't want your money."

"I'm not offering you any. What I'm offering you is a future."

"I'm not cut out for innkeeping."

"I've noticed," Rose said evenly. "We all have. That's why I want to talk to you about managing Cuppa."

Her mother talked, and she listened.

". . . ready to open by July fourth . . . neither one of us has time or energy to . . . a future in . . . part ownership down the line then maybe . . ."

Was this the way lottery winners felt when they heard their numbers being read on television? She felt light-headed, and for a moment she was afraid she was about to hyperventilate with excitement. The more her mother told her about the idea, the more she liked what she heard. She would ostensibly still be working for Rose but with a degree of autonomy impossible at The Candlelight.

She would be the one responsible for charting a course for the tea shop, setting goals, digging roots deeper into Paradise Point soil. The venture would play to her strengths and call upon her to bolster her weaknesses. Both her practical and her creative sides would be called into play, and the idea of building a successful business in the town she had run away from all those years ago was irresistible.

". . . the details from Olivia . . . she has all of the financial data . . . the architectural specs . . . you'll want to go over all of it before you —"

"Yes."

Rose stopped midsentence. "You haven't spoken to Olivia yet. She's the one with all of the —"

"I've heard enough to know I want to do it."

"This is a big decision, Madelyn. It requires some thought, some research. You can't —"

"I can do this, Ma." She tried to ratchet down her enthusiasm, but it was impossible. "With you and Olivia handling the decor, it sounds like a piece of cake."

They discussed the interior setup, permits, and staffing needs.

"I wish I could steal Aunt Lucy away from you," Maddy said. "Her scones are to die for."

"And she belongs to The Candlelight," Rose said, laughing. "Olivia wants to speak with Claire about signing on."

"I knew there must be a catch somewhere."

Rose's left brow arched. "Claire is a problem?"

Time to regroup. "You know what I mean. Claire has a job. She's co-owner of O'Malley's."

Rose considered her for a moment before she spoke. "Olivia thinks Claire is ready for a change. We plan to speak with her tomorrow night before the poker game."

It all sounded a little vague to Maddy, like they wanted Claire to function as a combination hostess/pastry chef. Nobody in her right mind would take on two demanding jobs for one salary.

"I don't know what Aidan's going to say about this." She tried to keep her tone neutral and was surprised to discover how hard that was to do. "He and Claire have worked together for a long time."

Rose regarded her carefully. It was clear her mother found neutrality every bit as difficult as her daughter did. "Do you think there will be a problem?"

"I have no idea."

"You don't look terribly pleased at the thought of working with Claire."

"I like Claire just fine, but I don't think I'm at the top of her hit parade."

"You had a disagreement?"

"No disagreement. It's just that —" She searched for a way to explain a feeling that had only begun to take shape. "I don't know. I always thought she was fond of me, but lately she's been a little chilly." She met her mother's eyes. "Actually, it's ever since Aidan and I announced our engagement."

"She's jealous of your relationship with Aidan. That's understandable." Aidan had been her mainstay since Billy's death.

Maddy laughed. "Actually, I think she's jealous of my relationship with Kelly."

"I didn't know you had a relationship with Kelly."

"What's that supposed to mean?"

"I didn't realize you spent so much time with Kelly that Claire would feel threatened."

"I didn't say she feels threatened. All I know is that ever since we got engaged, there's been a definite icy wind blowing my way."

"So you'd rather not work with her."

"Given my choice, probably not. Besides, I don't see how she can handle the baking and serve as hostess."

"That had occurred to me, as well, but until we're on our feet we might have to double up on things."

"I don't know," Maddy said. "It all sounds kind of sketchy to me."

"You're not afraid of hard work. You never have been. It's Claire, isn't it."

Maddy didn't deny it. "She's going to be family, but this just might be too much togetherness for both of us."

"Do you want me to tell Olivia to ask someone else?"

She was tempted. Very tempted. But she was also her mother's daughter, and the DiFalco business sense won out. "No," she said at last. "I think Claire would bring in a lot of business."

Claire's life was woven into the tapestry of Paradise Point in a way Maddy's would never be. The town had watched Claire grow up, marry, have babies, bury a husband. She was one of theirs, and they would support anything she set her mind to.

"The timing could be better," Rose said. "Opening a new store and planning a wedding — that's a lot on your plate."

"Maybe we could have the reception at Cuppa," Maddy suggested then grinned when her mother burst into laughter. "Think of the publicity. Every public television junkie in the contiguous forty-eight would know our name."

Rose gave her shoulder a squeeze. "You'll have to take it up with management."

"Thank you for giving me this chance," she said, her voice betraying far too much emotion for her liking. "I won't let you down."

"As if you could."

Rose's hand still rested on Maddy's shoulder. She liked the feel of her mother's hand, its warmth and its weight. A year ago she would have moved just beyond her mother's reach, but tonight she moved a little bit closer.

"That gown was really terrible," Rose said with a soft laugh. "What was that saleswoman thinking?"

"She was probably thinking of her commission," Maddy said. "I wish we were closer to the same size. I would have loved to wear your wedding gown."

"It's yours if you really mean it." How vulnerable her mother looked, how defenseless.

"I'm eight inches taller than you are. I'm not

sure even Aunt Lucy and her magic sewing machine could find a fix for that."

Even Rose had to admit she was right.

"If I can't wear your gown, do you think maybe you and Aunt Lucy would —" She didn't get to finish her sentence because her mother, her reserved and undemonstrative mother, threw her arms around her and hugged her like she would never let her go.

"You'll be the most beautiful bride in the world," Rose promised, her voice breaking with emotion. "We'll make you a dress fit for a princess."

A beautiful dress of creamy satin with pearls and crystals embroidered on the bodice and spangling the frothy skirt and fashioned to fit her the way she really was, not the way somebody else wanted her to be.

A train that swished and whispered behind her like a fawning courtier. Shoes that glittered like Cinderella's glass slippers.

And maybe, just maybe, a tiny, discreet tiara.

"I don't want anything extravagant," Maddy said as her resolve began to crumble before her mother's enthusiasm. "Just something simple and —"

"Leave it to us," Rose said, eyes brimming over with happy tears. "We'll make sure you have a wedding to remember."

Suddenly she saw herself walking down the aisle, a glittering, twinkling vision in satin and crystal, her absolute gorgeousness blinding everyone who dared to look at her. Everyone but Aidan, who fell to his knees and thanked God for bringing this Jersey goddess into his life.

Ten bridesmaids, all of them DiFalcos or O'Malleys. Gina as matron of honor. Kelly and Claire and Billy Jr. would all play a part. Aidan's friends from the firehouse would be groomsmen, tall and handsome in rented tuxes with creases so sharp you could cut your finger on them. Jack Bernstein as best man, his kind, dark eyes alight with happiness. And Hannah! Oh, Hannah would be the flower girl who —

She blinked her eyes, trying to force the ridiculous images from her head, but they refused to budge. Waves of emotion washed over her, love and regret, hope and happiness. She and her mother had missed so much. She hadn't been there when Rose went through cancer surgery and its aftermath. Rose hadn't been with her when she gave birth to Hannah. She hadn't been there to hold Rose's hand. Rose hadn't been there to hear Hannah's first cry. No amount of wishing, no degree of regret could change the mistakes of the past. But it didn't have to stay that way.

Maybe Gina had the right idea after all. The marriage would belong to her and Aidan, but maybe weddings really did belong to your family. Maybe Rose needed to stage a fairy-tale wedding to show Maddy how much she loved her, and maybe Maddy needed to accept the gift for the same reasons.

"Crystals and pearls?" she asked.

Rose smiled the smile of a woman who knew she was on the verge of victory. "Thousands of them."

"Thousands?"

"If that's what you want."

And suddenly it was. She wanted crystals and pearls and yards of satin and handmade lace and blue garters and boutonnieres and flower girls strewing rose petals in her path and a ring bearer and a train so long it needed its own zip code. She wanted her family all around her, even the ones she didn't like, and she wanted Aidan's family, too. She wanted all of their friends, all of their neighbors, everyone who liked them or loved them or simply wished them well to be there to share their happiness, to mark the day, the moment, as sacred and special, the day she and Aidan and Kelly and Hannah became a family.

"I have an inner bride!" Maddy said with an embarrassed laugh. "Who knew?"

"I did," her mother said. "I knew it all the time."

Chapter Eight

On the other side of town, a nightly ritual was under way.

"Teeth brushed?" Claire asked as Billy Jr. dived under the covers.

"Yep."

"Did you floss?"

"Yeah."

"Pick the towels up off the bathroom floor?"

"Uh-huh."

"Say your prayers?"

"I forgot."

"Well, come on then. We'll do it together."

She sat next to him and took his hand as he closed his eyes and launched into the nightly litany of names.

"God bless Mom, Kathleen, Courtney, Willow, and Maire. God bless Grampa Mike and Uncle Aidan and Kelly. God bless . . ." He named every dog, cat, hamster, goldfish, and gerbil that had ever lived in or visited their house, and as he counted down the creatures, Claire felt the familiar tightening in her chest. ". . . and God bless

Gramma Irene and God bless Daddy in heaven."

He opened his eyes and gave her one of those smiles that never failed to turn her heart to melted sugar. God help them all, eight years old, and already he showed signs of exhibiting his late father's considerable Irish charm. He was her baby, her last child, the one whose arrival had almost made her believe God actually had a plan in mind when he brought Billy O'Malley into her life all those years ago, a sweet consolation for a heart that had come close to breaking more times than she would ever try to count.

"Can I read some more Harry Potter?"

"It's almost nine, Billy boy. Lights out."

"Just five minutes, Ma, pleeeeeeeeeeeeeeeeeease."

One look from those huge dark blue eyes and she caved immediately. Her daughters claimed she spoiled her only son rotten, and she couldn't deny it. She had been strict to the point of harshness with her four girls, trying desperately to bring order into her chaotic family life, and the results had been mixed at best. Billy had access to a part of her heart she had hidden away for safekeeping during his father's lifetime, and sadly it had taken his death to release it.

"Five minutes," she said with mock sternness, "then lights out." She bent over and kissed him on his forehead, trying to ignore the way he quickly wiped it away with the back of his still-babyish hand. "Promise?"

"I promise."

"You're on the honor system, pal, so you'd better be good."

He reached for the enormous Harry Potter on his nightstand and disappeared into life at Hogwarts.

She paused in the doorway. "Billy."

He looked up, finger pressed to his place in the book. "Yeah, Ma?"

"I love you."

"Maaa!" he protested. His face crinkled into comical lines. "Don't say that where my friends could hear."

"Cross my heart."

He grinned at her, then looked back down at his book. For an instant she saw him a few years into the future, with the soft roundness of childhood only a memory. He was growing up so fast. Growing away from her the way he was supposed to. Still, her heart ached at the signs of distance swelling between them. Billy was her fifth child. You would think she'd be used to it by now, but the thought of seeing her youngest strike out on his own made her feel like crying, and he hadn't even reached puberty yet. Her mother used to say that was why God made teenagers: so parents would be happy when their young finally left the nest. By the time he had his driver's license, she would be counting the hours until he started college.

Maybe.

She sidestepped Fritzie, oldest of their four cats, who was sprawled full length in the middle of the hallway. The enormous Maine coon had the unfortunate habit of blocking hallways, doorways, and steps with her girth and refusing to move.

"If I didn't know better, I'd swear you were looking to collect on the insurance." She bent down and scratched the lazy feline behind the left ear and was rewarded with a halfhearted purr that could easily be mistaken for gastric distress. One day some unsuspecting human was going to trip over Fritzie's bulk and end up in traction.

She was debating the wisdom of installing a night light in the back hall when she heard her father's voice rumbling from the kitchen. When the man wasn't playing cards with his friends, he was keeping the phone lines humming. Talk about golden years. Seventy-five years old, and he had a better social life than she did.

"Dad, I swear you're worse than my girls ever were," she said as she stepped into the kitchen. "We're going to have to —" She stopped in the doorway. "Aidan!"

"Surprise." Her brother-in-law raised his cup of coffee in salute. "The kid left his catcher's mitt in the back of my truck yesterday. I was going to drop it off and run, but Mike and I started shooting the breeze and —"

"Too bad we had eggs for supper," her father said. "No leftovers."

"Aidan knows how to cook, Dad," she said with an eye roll for Aidan. "He does most of the cooking at O'Malley's."

"Any meat loaf left from last night?" Her father shoved his chair back from the table and headed toward the fridge. "Nothing better than a meat loaf sandwich."

Claire poured herself a cup of coffee and sat down opposite Aidan. "Don't you have a bar to run?"

"Owen's watching things. Kelly's car wouldn't start, so I drove over to the school to give her a jump."

Claire looked up at the wall clock over the sink and frowned. "What was she doing at school at this hour?"

"Band practice."

Claire opened her mouth, thought twice, then took a sip of coffee.

"What?" Aidan asked, frowning in her direction.

"Nothing."

"You've got something to say, so say it."

"I don't have anything to say."

"I know there's meat loaf in here," her father muttered at the fridge. "Where the hell did I see it?"

"You think I should've left her there to figure her own way out of the problem."

"I didn't say that."

"So what are you saying?"

They had known each other too long and far too well to play games.

She put down her cup. "Since when does band practice run so late?"

"It didn't," he said. "It ended on time, but she sat there a half hour, trying to start the car before she called me."

"See?" Claire wished she could punctuate her words with one of those wonderful cigarette gestures that had seen her through her twenties and thirties. "There's my answer."

"Yeah, well, now I want an answer." For a basically nice guy, he could look pretty damn intimidating when he had a mind to. "Is there something I should know?"

"She's seventeen, isn't she?" Claire said with a sharp laugh. "Believe me, there's plenty you should know."

"Anything in particular?"

"Don't ask me, Brother-in-Law. Ask her."

"You should do what Lilly does." Her father swung the refrigerator door closed. "She marks those little Tupperware things with peel-off labels so you know what you got in there."

With that he wheeled and disappeared down the hall.

"Dad, watch out for Fr—"

"Jesus Mary and Joseph! Somebody hang a light over this cat, will you?"

The bathroom door slammed shut. She slumped over her coffee cup and wondered what it would be like to live a life without constant domestic chaos.

"Who's Lilly?" Aidan asked, ignoring the fact that her bangs were in her coffee cup.

"Do I have to be in intensive care to get a little

166

sympathy around here?" she muttered as she sat up straight. "Lilly Fairstein. Dad's new girl-friend."

"I thought he was seeing that widow over up in Tom's River."

"He caught her two-timing him with a retired butcher. He's been seeing Lilly for almost a month. Apparently she's South Jersey's answer to Martha Stewart." Lilly's Helpful Hints, courtesy of Mike Meehan, were starting to drive her up the wall.

"You don't like her."

"She irons newspapers before she reads them."

"So she's neat."

"She's psychotic. I think she irons Dad's jockey shorts."

Aidan's eyes were twinkling with amusement. "He's getting more action than either one of us."

"Dead people get more action than I do," she shot back, and then his words sank in. "Wait a minute! What do you mean, he gets more action than you do?"

He shrugged. "Nothing. That man's a rock star at the senior center."

"That's not what you said. You said, 'He's getting more action than either one of us.' What did you mean? You're engaged to Maddy. You two should be burning up the sheets."

"Figure of speech, kid. Don't go thinking you're onto a news flash."

He sounded relaxed, mildly amused even, but

she wasn't buying it. Was Maddy secretly a Rules Girl, holding out for the wedding vows? It seemed strange, considering the fact that she had lived with Hannah's father for years without marriage, but stranger things had happened. Besides, wasn't it always the girl who played hard to get who got the final rose on *The Bachelor*?

"I'd better move." Aidan pushed his chair away from the table and stood up. "Mark said he'd close tonight. I figure I'll swing by the bar on my way home and make sure he's okay."

"Just don't let him hit the alarm again," Claire said with a groan. "I swear the entire Paradise Point police department showed up last time."

"Yeah," said Aidan with a chuckle. "Both squad cars and the chief."

He reached for the crutch leaning against the wall. It was a bit of a stretch for him, and she noted the way he winced as he shifted the weight from his left leg to his right, then back again. She could easily have brought the crutch to him, but you didn't try to help an O'Malley. Not if you wanted to live another day. An O'Malley man would rather fall flat on his face than ask for help from anyone. She wondered if Maddy had figured that out yet or if that would be one of those little postwedding surprises nobody ever tells you about.

If not, Rose's daughter would find out soon enough.

She followed him to the front door, trying hard not to notice that the limp he had worked so hard these last two years to overcome was more pronounced than ever.

He opened the door, then turned to her. "You're being straight with me about Kel, aren't you?"

"I don't know if there's anything wrong or not. I'm just saying you should make a point of talking with her." She had never pulled her punches with him before. "Sooner rather than later."

"Based on — ?"

"She didn't seem to be feeling too great this afternoon. I asked her what was wrong, and she brushed me off."

"She's stretched too thin. I told her to drop one of her jobs, but she's stubborn."

"Gee," said Claire, "I wonder where she gets that from."

The crutch was wedged under his right arm, but he gathered her to him with his left and hugged her close. They weren't touchy-feely as a rule, and the hug surprised her. His chest was broad and muscular, more so now than a few years ago. His prolonged physical therapy had turned his already impressive proportions into something downright unnerving. God, how long had it been since she had been held by a man? He smelled so good, of soap and faintly of sweat and leather, that she closed her eyes and just let herself drink in the sensation of being close to another human being who didn't share her genetic code.

But he shared Billy's. It was there in the powerful chest, the silky chestnut hair, the way his eyes crinkled when he laughed. If she closed her eyes, she could almost imagine it was Billy who held her close. She felt that way sometimes behind the bar. Aidan would turn his head a certain way or laugh at one of Mel Perry's jokes, and for a second time would stand still and it would be Billy standing there near the ancient cash register with that slightly lopsided grin that all of the O'Malley men possessed.

She didn't need to squirrel away old ticket stubs and Valentine's Day cards in order to keep Billy's memory alive. She couldn't escape him if she tried. He was in every story told at O'Malley's, every Guinness pulled, every woman who looked away when Claire walked into the room.

"Get going," she said, pushing him gently away. "Mark needs a steady eye on him."

"I thought he was doing pretty well," Aidan said, repositioning his crutch.

"Better," Claire said, "but not well. Not yet. He still freaks every time he has to pull a draft, and considering we're an Irish bar, that could become a real problem."

"I'll give him a refresher course after we close up." He met her eyes. "Anything I should tell Kelly?"

"Just that I hope she's feeling better."

"That's it?"

"That's it."

He leaned down and pecked her on the cheek. "I'm glad you went with Maddy today."

"You don't say no to Rose DiFalco."

"Sure you do," he said. "You just don't say it twice."

"Rose DiFalco, mother-in-law." Claire pretended to shiver. "Be afraid. Be very afraid."

He grinned good-naturedly. It was no secret that he had grown very fond of Maddy's mother. "She's a force of nature."

"I hope her daughter's good enough for you," she said fiercely as she straightened the collar of his shirt. "If Maddy doesn't treat you right, she'll be answering to me."

"You worry too much."

"Your daughter told me that already today."

"Who knows? You might find yourself setting up house with David Fenelli one day and dealing with his —"

"Aidan!" She smacked him on the arm. "Where the *hell* did you get that idea?"

God, that wicked twinkle in his eyes reminded her so much of Billy. "I saw Fenelli in the school parking lot. He was there to pick up Will after freshman wrestling."

"What did he say?" Damn her Irish genes. She could feel her face burning with embarrassment.

"He asked if you were seeing anyone."

"He did what!?"

"You heard me. He wanted to know if you were seeing anyone seriously."

"And what did you say?"

"I told him to ask you."

She exhaled loudly. "Right answer."

"Then I asked him why he wanted to know."

Wrong question. "And he said — ?"

"That he'd asked you out for pizza, and you said yes." Now his wicked grin matched the wicked twinkle in his eyes. "I asked if Potsy and the Fonz were going to tag along."

She belted him in the shoulder again. "Jackass."

"Hey!" He rubbed his arm. "Since when can't you take a joke, Red?"

"We're going to take Ryan and Billy out for pizza one day. That's it. Don't go reading more into it, or I'll kill you."

He put an arm around her shoulders and gave her a squeeze. "No crime in moving on," he said softly. "We all do, sooner or later."

A violent surge of emotion crashed over her, a powerful mix of anger and regret and yearning so intense she couldn't speak. God, please don't let her cry. Not in front of Aidan. She hated weakness, hated seeming needy and helpless, even if she was both of those things and more in ways not even the people who loved her best ever suspected. Maybe she was more O'Malley than she had realized.

It took a few moments, but she managed to

172

gather up all of those unruly emotions and beat them into submission.

"Don't you have a bar to run, O'Malley?" The old Claire took over, the sarcastic, funny sister-in-law who wouldn't know sentiment if it bit her in the ass.

"Throwing me out?"

"You got it, pal."

He chucked her gently under the chin, then called out a loud good-bye to her father, who grunted something in return. He made his way down the front steps and toward his truck. She waited until he had crossed the driveway before she turned off the porch light and closed the door.

Her father was standing at the kitchen end of the hallway.

"Aidan says good-bye," she said as she lowered the hall light. "And thanks for the stories."

"He's a good guy. Got a real good head on his shoulders. I like what he's done to O'Malley's. His grandfather would be proud of the place." He nodded his head. "No doubt about it: Rosie D.'s girl got lucky."

Claire moved a plate from the sink to the dishwasher. "I don't think anyone in town thought he'd ever marry again." Much less marry a DiFalco.

"You missed the boat," her father said, lowering himself onto a chair. "Sometimes I think you married the wrong brother."

173

Funny thing, Pop, she thought as she poured herself another cup of coffee. *Sometimes so do I.*

Aidan exhaled loudly in relief when he pulled into the driveway behind Kelly's car. It wasn't that he had expected her to be anywhere else but home, but Claire's suggestion that something wasn't quite right had unnerved him. Maybe more than he had been willing to admit until this moment.

He let himself into the house and tossed his keys on the desk in the hallway. "You down here, Kel?"

She wasn't in the kitchen. He checked the den in the back of the house and the living room. No dice. He called out her name. No answer. His heart began to thud painfully against his ribs as he climbed the stairs. Her door was closed, but a puddle of light seeped through the crack, and he heard the faint thudding beat of music he no longer understood.

"Kel." His voice was low. "I'm home."

No response. He could feel the gathering rush of adrenaline in his bloodstream.

He tapped on the door. "Kel," he repeated. "I'm home. Just want to make sure everything's all right."

Okay, so she didn't feel like talking. No crime in that. She could be so engrossed in what she was doing that she didn't hear him. Or maybe she had conked out over one of her schoolbooks

174

and was dead to the world. It wasn't like that hadn't happened before.

He made it halfway down the hall to his room when Claire and her goddamn worried expression came back to him, and he wheeled and made his way back to her door.

"Kel, open up." He knocked twice. "We need to talk."

He was about to do something he hadn't done since she was ten years old and open the door without her okay, when the door swung open, and he looked down into the yawning face of his only child.

"I'm asleep," she said, looking like she was about to fall over into a heap. "Can't it wait until tomorrow?"

Considering the fact that he didn't know what the hell he wanted to talk to her about, it could wait until next year. He cupped her face with his hand and tilted her chin up until she met his eyes. "Is everything okay, Kel?"

She bit back a yawn and struggled to appear wide awake. "Sure it is," she said. "Why wouldn't it be?"

Damned if he knew but, looking at his daughter, he started to think Claire might be onto something.

"Go back to bed," he said, fighting back a rush of bittersweet longing for the days when a hug and a bedtime story were enough to slay the world's dragons. "It's late."

She looked at him with the same speculative

expression she had developed as a toddler exploring her ever-expanding world, a blend of intelligence and curiosity that he had never seen before or since on another child.

"I love you, Dad," she said then disappeared behind her bedroom door.

He stood quietly in the hallway for a few moments as memories came out of hiding, crowding into the small space, vying for attention. It all went by so fast. Too fast. He was closer now to the end than he was to the beginning, and that celestial clock was ticking away, counting down his days.

He blinked once — he must have because how else could he have missed it? — and Kelly turned into a woman with secrets of her own. He turned away for a second, and Billy was gone and Grandma Irene, too. So many things left unsaid. So many things he should have done before it was too late.

He had seen something in Maddy's eyes this afternoon, a look of puzzlement mixed with hurt that he still felt in his gut. He knew life didn't always play fair. It didn't send up warning signals before it knocked you to your knees. Maybe she really meant it when she said she didn't give a damn about the cast on his leg or the fact that he couldn't sweep her up into his arms and carry her to bed or that sometimes it hurt so fucking much he woke up in a sweat, hanging on to the edge of the bed and praying to die.

Then again, maybe she didn't.

A man didn't want the woman he loved to see him as anything less than a man. He wanted to be bigger than life in her eyes, strong and brave the way he had felt when he was eighteen and ready to take on the world. The trouble was, he wasn't eighteen any longer. He knew the world could kick his ass any time it wanted to, and there was nothing he could do to stop it. He would never be the man he was before the warehouse accident. Hell, he would never be the man he had been before he slipped on the ice in February.

She knew that, knew it all, and she claimed she wanted him anyway. Bruised, battered, down but not out. Not yet. Not as long as they had each other.

He glanced at his watch. A little after ten. Rose stayed up late. He had her private number. Once he had things worked out with his future mother-in-law, he would get on the Web and make reservations. Then, after he stopped back at the bar to make sure Mark could handle things on his own, he would swing by The Candlelight and sweep the woman he loved off her feet.

Metaphorically speaking.

Rose tapped on Maddy's door just before midnight. "Aidan's on the phone," she said, peeking inside. "He wants to talk to you."

Maddy, who had been playing Super Collapse

II on her laptop while downloading some files, leaped up from bed. "Why didn't he call me directly?"

Rose grinned and gestured toward the laptop. "You're on-line, right?"

"Oh damn!" She had forgotten she was using the dial-up while their high-speed connection was awaiting repair. "The office phone?"

"My phone." Rose handed over her tiny cell phone with a wink. "Good thing I charged it up after supper."

Maddy impulsively pressed a kiss to her mother's cheek. "Thanks! I'll recharge when I'm done."

Rose patted her on the shoulder. "I'm counting on that," she said, then disappeared back down the hall to her own suite of rooms.

"You were supposed to E-mail me," Maddy said, curling back up in the middle of her bed. "I've been waiting for you to show up on-line."

"I have a better idea," he said. "Look out your window."

Chapter Nine

Aidan was waiting for her at the foot of the driveway. She ran barefoot across the damp lawn and straight into his arms.

Her body melted into his in the soft darkness. His crutch was tucked under his right arm, but it didn't stop him from gathering her close, enveloping her in his warmth and strength.

Oh God, this man knew how to hug. He could win awards in hugging. Olympic gold medals in full-body, every-sense-on-red-alert hugging. She buried her nose against his chest and breathed in the deeply comforting, deeply erotic smell of his skin. She had never known a woman could get drunk on the smell of a man's skin, that she could crave it like a drug more powerful than anything the poppy had to offer.

"So what's going on?" she asked as they walked up the driveway to the back porch. "You're not in the habit of dropping by at midnight."

"If we didn't both have daughters at home, I'd be here every night."

"If we didn't both have daughters at home, I'd never let you leave."

"Maybe we should move up the wedding date," he suggested as they settled down on the top step. She sat as close to him as the laws of physics would allow.

"That would solve a few problems."

"Like I'm not in enough trouble with Rosie for suggesting we elope."

"You're not in trouble anymore." She leaned over and kissed his stubbly chin. "I caved."

"Right," he said, "and then she called the queen and asked if we could borrow the palace for the wedding."

"I'm not joking. I totally caved."

"You mean we're going for the big enchilada?"

"Yep," she said with a sheepish grin. "I said yes to the flower girl, the ring bearer, grooms-men, bridesmaids, rehearsal dinners, bachelor parties, bridal showers, the whole nine yards."

"What happened? A few hours ago you were dead set against it."

"I don't know," she said. "We were sitting out here on the porch after supper, and the next thing I knew, I was asking her if she and Lucy would make my wedding dress."

He pretended to examine the porch very carefully.

"Aidan! What are you doing?" she asked as he bent down to peer under the top step.

"I want to make sure it's safe to sit here. If I

start saying I'm a Giants fan, call in an exorcist."

She laughed softly. "She was so touched, Aidan —" Her voice broke unexpectedly, and she drew in a deep breath to cover up. "Her eyes filled with tears when I asked her. Can you imagine that? Our Rosie getting all mushy over a wedding gown."

"When it comes to you and Hannah, Rosie's a soft touch. She'd give you the moon if you'd let her."

"I'm just beginning to realize that."

"About time."

"What's wrong with this picture?" she asked in mock indignation. "You're not supposed to take my mother's side." He chuckled, and she pressed her face against his shoulder and smiled. "You'll be sorry when you see how much there is to do between now and September. She's going to run us ragged."

"We'll have the rest of our lives," he said. "We can give Rosie one day to call her own."

Your heart really could swell with love. She could feel it filling her chest, crowding out her lungs, making it almost impossible to breathe. Thirty-three years old, and she had never experienced anything even close to the way he made her feel just sitting next to her on the back porch.

"Tuxedos. Rehearsal dinners. Guest lists. All the things you hate."

"I'll get over it."

"Maybe you will," she said, "but will I?"

"You forgot the most important part of the wedding."

"Fittings. Shower. Bachelor party. Rehearsal. Ceremony. Reception. What else is there?"

"The honeymoon."

In an instant they were in each other's arms again. She opened her mouth to his, gasping at the touch of his tongue against hers, his taste, his warmth. Sweetly familiar, still new enough to be strange.

She whispered in his ear and heard his breath catch hard in response. "I thought you'd like that."

And then he said something, and she moved against him, on fire.

"So when are you going to ask me why I'm here making out on the back porch with you in the middle of the night?"

She brought his hand to her lips. "Why question a good thing?"

"You made me think this afternoon."

She leaned slightly away from him so she could see his eyes. He looked slightly uncertain, surprisingly vulnerable. "About anything in particular?"

"I was thinking that this isn't the most romantic engagement on record."

"Maybe not," she admitted, "but it's ours, and I wouldn't trade it for anything."

"Not even for a night at that little inn we saw at Spring Lake?"

"You mean the one we were heading for when you —"

"Fell on my ass and screwed everything up."

"I wasn't going to put it that way." She leaned over and kissed him. "The night we got serious."

"The night I was going to make love to you until the sun came up."

A voluptuous shiver rolled up her spine, a delicious tingle of anticipation and desire. "Yes," she said. "That's the night I was talking about."

"Saturday." He kissed the palm of her right hand, then folded her fingers around the warmth. "Just us."

"Say that again."

"Just us. Champagne. Dinner. No snow. No kids. No relatives. No friends. No phones. No poodles."

"Why — I mean, how . . . oh, I don't know what I mean! This is so wonderful! I can't believe — of course I'll have to clear it with Rosie," she said, mind spinning with details. "Make sure Hannah is —"

"Done," he said. "I took care of everything."

He had spoken to her mother, made sure Hannah would be taken care of, that Priscilla would be fine, that Kelly could stay there if she wanted to.

"You really did think of everything." She didn't have to explain her love for Hannah or her concern for her little girl's welfare. She didn't have to feel apologetic or made vulnerable by her sense of responsibility. He understood from the inside out.

"After seventeen years, you get pretty good at it."

"Does that mean it gets easier?" She was five years into parenthood, and there were still times when she felt like she was barely treading water.

"No," he said. "You just learn how to worry better."

For one fleeting instant she thought about mentioning what Hannah had said about Kelly, but the moment passed as quickly as it came, swept away by the night's excitement.

"I have some big news, too," she said. "Do you know the old McClanahan place that Olivia's renovating down near Paradise Point Drive?"

"I heard she's turning it into some kind of fancy cookie shop."

"An English tea shop," Maddy corrected him, "and Rose has decided to go in on it with her."

He whistled low. "When the hell did that happen?"

"Sometime late this afternoon. That's why Liv was there when you dropped me off."

"It's not like either one of them needs a business partner. Far as I can tell, they're both cleaning up."

"Liv said that cutting Rose in on the deal would free up some capital so she could expand her store."

"Who the hell would think anyone needed a

bigger stationery store?" He looked at her by the glow of the porch light. "So what's the attraction for Rose besides world domination?"

She laughed, then covered her mouth to muffle the sound. "She wants me to manage it. I'll be in charge. I'll be the one who'll hire wait staff, set prices, keep the books." Her enthusiasm was leaping ahead of her words, and she had to stop for breath. "Who knows? Maybe I'll even be able to buy them out one day if things go well enough."

"Yeah, and in the meantime you'd be working directly for your mother."

"She'll be a silent partner." This time he was the one who laughed out loud. "Shh! It's after midnight, Aidan. You'll wake the neighborhood."

"Your mother has never been a silent anything in her life, Maddy. You know how I feel about Rosie, but you two don't exactly have a great track record. What makes you think this will be any different?"

"Because it's not her show, it's Olivia's. I mean, she bought the place, hired designers, has been overseeing the renovations. It's her idea, her baby. It's just a business deal for my mother."

"Not if you're involved."

"I think I can handle myself."

"Are you sure? You two have come a long way in the last few months. Do you want to risk it for a tea shop?"

"I thought you'd be happy for me."

"I am, if this is what you want." He met her eyes. "I thought you were hoping the radio gig would lead to something."

"So far it hasn't led me to anything but a discount at the dry cleaners."

"And free lunches at O'Malley's."

She grinned. "I could get those without the radio gig."

"Pretty sure of yourself."

"Yes," she said, "and it feels good."

"What about the inn?"

"I'll continue doing the bookkeeping, but I think Rosie is counting the days until she can put some space between me and the paying customers. Besides, once we marry, I wouldn't be around to help out at all hours, would I?"

"You think you'll be any happier running a tea shop?"

"Do you have any better ideas?" she countered. "I'll have a fair degree of autonomy. I won't have to commute. The hours are reasonable, so I'll be able to be with Hannah. Claire will be there to deal with the public. And —"

"Whoa! Back it up a little."

"Oh God." She buried her face in her hands. "Forget I said anything. They haven't even asked Claire yet."

"Asked her what?"

"Aidan, I don't think I'm supposed to be talking about this with anyone right now." Of course, he wasn't just anyone. He was the man she loved. The man she was going to marry. She wanted desperately to share it all with her fiancé, but she wasn't too sure Claire's brother-in-law needed to know everything.

"Claire works at O'Malley's," he said in a tone of voice she hadn't heard before and hoped she wouldn't hear again any time soon. "She owns half of the place. Why the hell would they think she's looking for something else?"

"I have no idea."

"Has she said anything to you?"

If only she had kept her big mouth shut. "Aidan, Claire and I are friendly, but we aren't friends."

"You play poker together."

"With six other women. We play cards. We don't exchange confidences. To be honest, I'm not even sure she likes me." She tried to make out his expression, but his eyes were unreadable. "Are you afraid she might say yes?"

"Never happen," he said. "She's family. O'Malley's belongs to her as much as it belongs to me."

"I can't ask my mother and Olivia not to offer the job to her." A weird thought occurred to her. "You and Claire were never — ?"

He shook his head. "She's like a sister to me. Billy was the only O'Malley man for her."

She leaned closer, lacing her fingers through his. "Good, because I've staked my claim on the only O'Malley man for me."

He wasn't about to be sidetracked. "I

wouldn't have made it through the first two years after Sandy died if Claire hadn't stepped in and taught me what I needed to know." Maddy knew all about how Claire and Billy had opened their hearts and home to Aidan and Kelly after his wife died. Clearly it was the kind of debt that could never adequately be repaid. "She was always worried about making sure Kel did her homework and took her vitamins — all the mother things she wasn't sure I was bright enough to handle." He said it with a deep affection that took the sting from the words. "Speaking of which, Claire seemed to think something was off with Kelly today. You were with her. How did she seem to you?"

"In what way?" Her casual tone hid her great unease over the direction the conversation had taken. It was clear where this was going, but she prayed she would be able to sidestep the issue. *You might as well tell him what Hannah said. This is the perfect opening.*

"I don't know. Claire thought Kelly wasn't feeling that great today, but she went off on a tangent about work and school and being seventeen — you know Claire when she gets wound up."

"We *all* know Claire when she gets wound up," Maddy said with a laugh she hoped would deflect further questions. *Coward.*

"I thought Kel looked okay today. How about you?"

It was a direct question, and she wouldn't lie

to him. Not about this or anything else. "I think she's been looking a little tired lately, Aidan, and a little drawn." Careful, cautious, but honest. She owed their future that much.

"She's been on this damn diet for the prom. I thought she was too smart to fall for all of that magazine hype, but she's been living on lettuce leaves and protein."

"There isn't a woman alive who doesn't fall for at least some of that hype." Maddy's stomach clenched. *Go on, Maddy. Tell him. She's his daughter. He has the right to know.* "Could she have an eating disorder?"

"I haven't noticed anything."

"She's at school all day. You're at work most evenings. It would be easy to miss."

"Wouldn't she be skin and bones if she was into that?"

"There are degrees of illness," Maddy said cautiously. "I'm really no expert, Aidan. You need to speak to Kelly about it."

They fell silent and just sat there, fingers entwined, letting the night wash over them until Maddy stifled a yawn.

"You're dead on your feet," he said. "I'd better get moving."

They stood up, and she walked him to his car. "Call me when you get home."

"It's three minutes away."

"Humor me."

"I'll E-mail you before I go to sleep."

"If that's the best you can do."

189

"It's the best I can do."

He bent down to kiss her, and she yawned again.

"I'm sorry! I —"

He caught her midsentence, turning words into promises only she could hear.

"One hundred twenty-nine days," she said as he shifted into reverse.

He glanced at the glowing blue face of his watch. "One hundred twenty-eight."

"I can't wait until Saturday."

He motioned for her to lean closer and murmured something so intimate, so deeply erotic that she began to tremble and continued to long after he left.

Marriage wasn't all hearts and flowers. At least that was what she had been told, even if the romantic in her couldn't help delighting in the fact that a few fragrant rose petals had just dropped in her path. So far they had managed to navigate family stresses, the scare with Hannah last year, and Aidan's broken ankle with good humor and the very real sense that they were in this together. As much as she had cared for Hannah's father and knew he cared for her, she had never had the feeling that they were partners on the same team.

It was different with Aidan. She knew he was on her side. She had known it from the beginning, known it in the way she recognized the sound of her own breathing in the heart of the night. In the blink of an eye, a mutual chemical attraction took a sharp turn into something deeper, more powerful, more profound than she had ever dreamed possible.

The word for it was love. The kind that grew stronger with time, the kind that lasted.

This sense of unease that had been haunting her for the last month or so was only temporary, a by-product of Aidan's fall on the ice and the roadblock it had placed in the way of their romance. Maybe once they finally had the time and the place to be alone together, to express with their bodies all the things they had tried to express with words alone — maybe then she could let herself believe their story would end happily.

By eight A.M., the news was all over town that Rose DiFalco and Olivia Westmore had decided to go into business together. Maddy had been bombarded with questions at the school bus stop, and she had felt extremely uncomfortable when Claire and Billy Jr. joined them. As a teenager she had told more than her share of fibs and downright lies, but it was a practice she tried to avoid as an adult. Claire looked surprised but only mildly curious about the details, and Maddy was glad to escape back to The Candlelight, where she only had to deal with Rose's and Lucy's detailed questions about The Wedding Dress.

"Next time I'll call you right away," Rose said into the phone as she aimed an eye roll at

Maddy and Lucy. "I'm sorry you had to find out about it from Mrs. Anselmo at the deli, Toni. That was unforgivable of me."

Maddy and her aunt managed to suppress their laughter until Rose hung up the receiver.

"Menopause has not been kind to that woman," Lucy said as she eased a tray of apple turnovers from the oven and carried them over to the counter. "God help us when the doctor finally takes her off Premarin. She'll be unbearable."

"She *is* unbearable." Maddy drizzled glaze over the warm turnovers. "No wonder Charlie only managed to make it through six months before he filed for divorce."

"He even gave her the Saab," Lucy said. "That's how badly he wanted out."

"He loved that car," Rose said. "I used to see him in the driveway on Sunday afternoons, polishing every last inch of her with an old cashmere sweater."

"So when do you start working at Cuppa?" Lucy wiped her hands on a clean tea towel, then punched down a bowl of risen bread dough.

Maddy glanced toward Rose. "I don't have a clue."

Rose looked positively sheepish. "This all happened so fast yesterday I never thought to ask Olivia. We'll need to all sit down and figure this out."

"She's opening in July, isn't she?" Lucy asked

as she lightly rained flour on the slab of marble she used to knead dough.

"The holiday weekend," Rose said, "which doesn't give us much time to get things sorted out."

Maddy groaned and leaned against the work counter. "I think I'm beginning to understand what stage fright is all about." In less than two months they would be opening the doors of Cuppa to hordes of summer revelers. What on earth had possessed her to say she could handle the undertaking? She must have taken temporary leave of her senses.

"Have you spoken to Claire yet?" she asked.

"Olivia wanted to drop by this morning, but we decided to get to her house early for poker night and speak with her then."

"I have something to tell you," she said to Rose, "and you're not going to like it."

"Want me to leave?" Lucy asked.

Maddy shook her head. "You can stay."

"Thank God," her aunt breathed. "I'm too old to be eavesdropping at the door."

"I slipped," she said, "and told Aidan you were going to ask Claire to work for you."

Rose exhaled sharply. "I hope you asked him not to speak with Claire before we do."

"He understands that," Maddy said. "What he doesn't understand is why you think she would be interested in the first place."

"Neither do I," Lucy said as she rhythmically worked the dough with her capable hands. "She owns half of O'Malley's, doesn't she? She's a fixture there. Why would she start working for somebody else?"

"My thoughts exactly," Rose said. "This is Olivia's idea. She seems to think Claire is in need of a change."

"But why Claire?" Maddy didn't bother to hide her curiosity. "What does she bring to the mix that somebody else doesn't?"

Lucy looked at her across the work counter. "You don't like each other?"

"Maddy likes her just fine," Rose said. "It's Claire who doesn't care for Maddy."

"We're not close," Maddy equivocated.

"I thought you two were becoming good friends," Lucy persisted. "I would see the two of you chatting up a storm at the school bus stop every morning on my way home from Mass. You looked like great pals."

"It's the engagement," Rose offered.

"Of course." Lucy began to shape the loaf on the baking tray. "Classic situation. She's been mothering Aidan and Kelly for almost twenty years. She's not going to be too happy with Maddy taking her place."

"Maybe she just doesn't like me," Maddy said. "Did you ever think of that?"

Lucy popped the bread into the oven and set the timer. "Life is never that simple, honey. There's always more to people than meets the eye." She reached for another towel-covered bowl of risen dough.

"It's all Olivia," Rose said. "She's very fond of Claire. Apparently they met years ago down in Florida when their parents lived in the same condo development."

"Talk about an odd couple," Lucy said, punching down a loaf of rye. "They don't seem all that close on poker night. I don't remember them exchanging more than a few sentences last time."

"That makes me feel better," Maddy said. "At least I'm not the only one she barely speaks to."

"Go figure," Rose said with a shrug. "All I know is what I've been told by Olivia."

"Aidan doesn't think she'll say yes." Maddy hoped to slip this tidbit in among the conjecture about Claire and Olivia's friendship.

No such luck. Rose picked up on it immediately and arched a brow in her direction. "Really?"

"Family means everything to her," Maddy said. "He doesn't think she would ever stop working at O'Malley's."

"Neither do I," Lucy said, clearly enjoying the mother-daughter byplay. "For one thing, it's her last tie to her husband."

"The woman has five children to support, Lucia." Rose favored her older sister with a sharp look. "I would think those ties are stronger than anything she could find at a bar and grill. Let's not romanticize pulling drafts."

"Just my opinion." Lucy rarely took Rose's bait, a trait which Maddy admired inordinately.

"Who knows what means the most to any one of us."

"Well," said Rose, as the phone rang again, "we'll find out tonight, won't we?"

Chapter Ten

Claire was filling two dozen wooden bowls with smoked almonds and salted peanuts when Peter Lassiter walked into the bar. Tall, skinny, with pale wire-framed glasses that looked like they were floating in the middle of his painfully privileged face. He was hard to miss in this crowd of old salts, ex-cops, and off-duty firefighters.

The guy had become a fixture in town over the last few weeks, interviewing everyone and her brother about Paradise Point. They said he was an up-and-coming star in New Jersey public television, destined to be the new Ken Burns. Lassiter had already interviewed a group of seniors at the community center, and her father was so taken with him that he had just about given the guy his social security number and the key to his safe-deposit box by the time it was over.

Great, she thought as he made his approach, stopping to shake hands with some of the old-timers he'd met previously. You would think he was running for mayor the way he greeted everyone. *And now you're going to start haunting O'Malley's.* The place was lousy with town history. The wall of photos near the pool table would keep him busy for a week.

He didn't look much older than her Kathleen, maybe twenty-eight or twenty-nine, with one of those big trust-funded smiles that probably cost more than her house. She had spent a lifetime watching his type spin through O'Malley's on their way to somewhere better. That alone was reason enough to dislike him.

He turned that smile on her. "Mrs. O'Malley?"

She could play barroom tough guy with the best of them. "Who's asking?"

He extended his right hand. (His soft-as-a-baby's-butt right hand.) "Peter Lassiter from NJTV. You haven't been answering my E-mails."

"Sure I have," she said, surprised by the firmness of his grip. "Not answering *was* my answer."

Tiny patches of color bloomed on the apples of his cheeks. So Mr. Ivy League was feeling uncomfortable. This was too easy, like shooting fish in a barrel. She should be ashamed of herself.

"I tried phoning you," he said. She had to admire his tenacity in the face of utter rejection. "I left three messages with Tommy."

"Speak to Aidan," she said. "He makes all the PR decisions around here. I'm sure he'd set you up with some scrapbooks and answer your questions."

"I'd like to arrange to interview you."

"Sorry, Mr. Lassiter, but I don't have any interesting anecdotes for you about growing up in a bar and grill. I'm an O'Malley by marriage, not birth."

"I would like very much to talk to you about your husband and his considerable impact on this town. I've spent a fair bit of time with your friends and neighbors, and they are unanimous in their praise for your husband's bravery on the job."

She met his eyes, and the look in hers made him take a step backward. "No."

"I've talked with two of the other widows —"

"What part of *no* don't you understand, Mr. Lassiter?"

"Your husband was a hero. Everyone said so. He went back into that building and —"

He was still talking. She knew he was. She heard sound emanating from somewhere near him, but nothing made sense through the thick red haze of rage that enveloped her. She could have killed him with her bare hands, just reached across the counter and wrapped her fingers around that skinny throat, pressed her thumbs into his windpipe, and gleefully watched him die.

"Is something wrong, Claire?"

The haze of red parted slightly, and she saw David Fenelli standing next to the reporter.

Lassiter extended his hand. "Peter Lassiter, NJTV. I'm here to —"

David ignored his hand. "I know who you are, Lassiter, and I believe Mrs. O'Malley said she doesn't want to be interviewed about the accident."

Lassiter's smile was steady as he regarded David. "And you are — ?"

"A friend of Mrs. O'Malley's who thinks it's time you moved on to your next appointment."

"I believe I'll wait until I hear that from Mrs. O'Malley herself."

Bless David for showing up when he did, giving her just enough space to regain her composure. "If you want a draft, I'd be happy to pull one for you. Beyond that, you're wasting your time."

"Please think about it." Lassiter's expression wasn't quite as open and easy as it had been a few moments earlier. He looked uncomfortable but not defeated. "Why should you let someone else tell your husband's story when you can tell it best yourself?" He flashed his expensive smile one more time. "I'll be in touch."

David turned and watched until the front door swung shut behind Lassiter's ass.

"Bastard," he muttered, followed by a quick, "Sorry. I just don't like the guy."

"Join the club," she said, pushing her hair off her forehead with the back of her forearm. "You might have saved me from a murder rap."

"We're in the minority," David said, glancing around the room. "The rest of them are in his fan club."

"My father is ready to adopt the guy," Claire said. "Go figure."

"Talk is seductive," David said. "Especially when there's someone to listen."

Which was one of the many reasons why she was standing clear of the project.

"I know being nosy is his job," David said as she pushed a cup of coffee toward him then waved away his money, "but the guy goes too far." He emptied three packets of sugar into his coffee, then slugged it down in two gulps. "Would you believe he wanted to talk to me about Jill?"

Her mouth dropped open in surprise. "Get out! How would he even know about Jill?"

"Small town, big mouths," he said, and she laughed despite herself. "If he really wanted to know the history of the town, he'd search the Hall of Records. What they want is a social history that'll get them some ratings, and that means juicy family stories."

"No wonder they're spending so much time with the DiFalco sisters," she said, and it was his turn to laugh. "What did you tell him when he asked about Jill?"

"I told him to go fuck himself and hung up," he said, this time with no apology. "Like I'm going to sit down and tell a stranger my wife took off with my best friend. Bad enough everyone in town knows it."

"And they told him, didn't they?"

"Right down to her flight number," he said

with more regret than bitterness. He pushed aside his empty cup and looked her in the eyes. "Keep your guard up, Claire. He's digging around the firehouse, looking for a hook to hang his story on. You've come too far to be pulled back down again for the sake of a TV show."

She wasn't a fool. She knew exactly what he was saying. Billy might be three years gone, but the aftershocks still had the power to knock her flat. The thought of his many indiscretions being resurrected for public consumption infuriated her.

She made to refill David's cup, but he placed his hand across the top to stop her. "Believe me, if he's looking for a story, he's not going to get one from me."

He had beautiful eyes, a deep, warm hazel with flecks of gold and navy. She had known him for years and never noticed until today. "That guy can charm military secrets out of the Pentagon. I don't get it, but I've seen him do it."

She put the pot of regular down on the warmer behind her. "Thanks for the heads-up," she said as she wiped up a drop of coffee from the sleek surface of the bar. "I'll make a few calls later."

"Do it," he said. "Promise?"

She started to make a joke, her usual wiseass default position, but the look in his eyes stopped her in her tracks. "Promise," she said, crossing her heart with big, theatrical gestures.

"I better go," he said. "Jason's waiting in the car. I'm taking him for another interview at Penn."

"I thought he got his acceptance a while ago."

David shrugged. "A follow-up, they say, but who knows. He's sweating bullets, poor kid."

"Good luck," she said. "Penn's a big deal. They'd be lucky to have him."

"I'll call you about that pizza."

"Great," she said, smiling at him. To her surprise, she almost meant it.

They said good-bye, and he threaded his way through the crowded bar toward the exit. There was nothing special about him. He wasn't the best-looking guy in the room or the tallest or the best built. He was reasonably attractive, reasonably intelligent, mildly funny when he wanted to be, and genuinely nice. You wouldn't notice him in a crowd until he smiled, and then only if you had a fondness for loopy, lopsided smiles that didn't originate in the office of some fancy dentist. Flip to *nice guy* in the dictionary, and there was bound to be a photo of David Fenelli, surrounded by his kids, his ex, and a golden retriever, all posed fetchingly next to the requisite minivan.

There was nothing dangerous about him. Nothing exciting. He wasn't like Billy at all, the kind of guy who made a woman's heart slam hard against her rib cage when he walked into a room. He was just a nice guy from the neighborhood who happened to like kids and pizza.

She turned around and found herself face-to-face with Tommy, their main bartender.

"Don't say it," she warned, jabbing a forefinger into his soft swell of a belly. "Don't even think it."

"I wasn't thinking anything," he said, eyes wide in mock innocence. "My mind's a blank."

"Don't go reading anything into what you saw." She should be awarded a medal for sidestepping that straight line he had offered her.

"I didn't see anything."

"Then why the hell are you looking at me like that?"

His grin stretched from one side of his face to the other. "You have spinach between your teeth."

Barney Kurkowski finished loading the last bucket of Aidan's world-class ten-alarm firehouse chili into the back of his Ford Explorer and closed the lid with a satisfying thunk. "They're asking for your lamb stew again," the veteran firefighter said to Aidan as he squinted into the bright late morning sunlight. "Why don't you stop by the firehouse one day and give Hank a few pointers. Do us a favor and steer him away from creamed chicken."

"I learned a hell of a long time ago you don't give Hank Ulrich pointers about anything, Barn. Not unless you want to go home without a few of your teeth."

"He's mellowing," Barney said, shielding his

eyes with the back of his hand. "Al and Steve stuck one of those relaxation tapes in his locker last month. I think he's been listening to it."

"I partnered Hank for five years," Aidan reminded his old friend. "It's gonna take a hell of a lot more than a relaxation tape to cool that guy off." Hank was one of those hot-wired types who went through life believing the world was out to get him, and in his case, he was probably right at least half the time.

"Lamb stew might do it," Barney suggested with a grin.

"Next week," Aidan said. "And I'll toss in a pot roast."

"Don't let Sara hear you mention pot roast. My cholesterol's up again, and she's on the warpath."

"Sorry, buddy. I don't do tofu."

"Just wait until September," Barney warned with a twinkle in his eyes. "You'll walk down the aisle a single carnivore, but you'll walk back up a married vegetarian."

Aidan was still laughing when Barney gunned his engine and headed back to the station. Back when Aidan fought fires for a living, he had acquired the title of Best Firehouse Cook in the Garden State for specialties like his Irish stew and pot roast with potato pancakes, and he had maintained that link with his old coworkers by supplying them with a few tons of food every week or two. He knew they could drop by O'Malley's any time they wanted a bowl of stew or plate piled high with pot roast, but that wouldn't be the same. You needed the smell of lye soap, motor oil, and damp rubber boots mixed with the sounds of rowdy male laughter and a game blaring from the radio in the corner — special ingredients that only another firefighter knew how to appreciate.

Maybe someday he would have the balls to go back into the firehouse again and take a look at the plaque they had attached to Billy's old locker.

Then again, maybe not.

He glanced at his battered Timex and muttered an Anglo-Saxon expression that was nearly as old as his watch. Already pushing noon, and he still hadn't managed to haul his sorry ass in to work. Claire and Tommy opened up today, but he liked to get in by eleven at the latest, as much for himself as for the business. After the warehouse accident he had learned how easy it was to let go, to let the days slip away one by one until the weeks and months were nothing but a blur of nothingness. He missed the old routines, the discipline required in his old job, and had tried to move some of it into his new life.

He needed to go back into the house, grab his car keys, his wallet, and his files, then get moving before the rest of the day got away from him.

Kelly looked up from the cup of hot tea she was nursing when he entered the kitchen. Her

wavy blond hair was pulled back in a messy ponytail, and there were dark smudges under her
big blue eyes. She wore the sweatpants/T-shirt
combination she always wore when she felt
lousy, and she was hunched over the mug like it
was a life-giving hearth fire in the middle of a
blizzard.

"You're not going to school today?" Aidan
asked as he grabbed his car keys from the top of
the microwave.

"I couldn't sleep," she said, cupping her
hands around the cup.

"I thought I heard you wandering around last
night." He gathered up a sheaf of papers from
the shelf near the door and stuffed them into a
large brown envelope marked *File*.

"Sorry if I kept you up."

"You didn't," he said. "I couldn't sleep, either." His late-night visit to Maddy had left him
frustrated, agitated, lonely for the sound of her
voice, the touch of her hand, for all the things he
had been dreaming of since the day he met her.

Kelly took a sip of tea, then put the cup back
down.

"You're shivering," he said. "Better put on a
sweater."

"I'm okay."

He placed the palm of his hand against her
forehead, the way he had done a thousand times
over the last seventeen years. "You don't have a
fever."

She pulled away from him. "I said I'm fine."

She wasn't. That much was clear. But no sane parent argued semantics with a teenager.

"So what is it?"

"Nothing."

"A cold?"

She shook her head.

"Something wrong at school?"

She made a face.

"Everything okay with Columbia and the scholarship?"

"Everything's fine."

"Did you and Seth —"

"No!" She swung around in her chair and looked up at him with reproachful eyes. "Sorry to disappoint you."

This was an old argument he didn't feel like revisiting. He liked Seth, and she knew it. What he didn't like was how serious things were. She knew that, too. "If it isn't school and it isn't Seth, then what is it?"

She pushed back from the table, then ran from the room in a frenzy of sobs designed to break the hardest heart, leaving Aidan standing there wondering where the hell he'd gone wrong.

Definition of an optimist: the parent of a teenager who actually believed his kid would tell him what was wrong.

He wanted to do what he had always done when she was unhappy: scoop her up into his arms and hold her tight until he had absorbed all of her sadness and made her world right again. When was the last time he had had that magic? He couldn't remember. One day she's your little girl, and the next thing you know, she's a secretive, lovely young woman whose face comes alive at the sight of a boy who was still in diapers the day before yesterday, and all you can do is step back and watch it all happen.

No matter how much he sometimes wanted to, he couldn't turn back the clock. The little girl he had shielded from harm was only a memory, and in her place was a beautiful stranger who lived a life beyond these four walls that he would never fully know. He had done his job well. She didn't need him anymore. In another few months she would walk out that door and into a whole new world that didn't have room for him.

That was the way it should be. The way it was supposed to be. Kids grew up. They moved on. They went to school. They started careers. They married and had kids of their own, and the whole process started all over again. This was part of the cycle of life, the wheel spinning slowly, gathering speed as the years went on, until it was nothing but a blur of shapes and color and dreams.

He had a choice. He could march down the hall, rap on her door, and demand an explanation for the restless night, the teary eyes, the refusal to go to school. He was her father. She was still a minor. He had the right to some answers.

Or he could take a deep breath and give her a little room. Clearly whatever it was, wasn't life-threatening. She didn't have a fever. There were no broken bones. Kids like Kelly were under a hell of a lot of pressure to succeed. When a lot was expected of you, a lot was taken. Nobody worked harder or achieved more than his daughter. If she needed a day to get off the treadmill and rest, she could have it.

She had earned that and more.

Kelly lay facedown on her bed, listening for her father's footsteps. There was no way he would ever in a million years let her get away with running out of the room like that. Not without an explanation. She hadn't meant to go running out of the room like that, but lately it seemed she was doing a lot of things she didn't mean to do. Give him two or three more minutes, and he was bound to knock on her door, determined to find out what was wrong. She longed for him to demand some answers, force her to tell him what was really going on, and at the same time she prayed he would leave her alone.

How could she tell him she thought she was pregnant? It would kill him. All these years he had tried to impress upon her the importance of setting goals, of education, trying to make sure she understood that sometimes you had to choose between what seemed right at the moment and what was right for the long haul.

The distinction had seemed murky at best when she was younger, a vague litany of dos and don'ts that sounded more like a Sunday school sermon than anything that could help her in the real world.

Well, now she got it.

It wasn't like she and Seth had taken foolish chances, because they hadn't. They always used protection.

And they loved each other. Shouldn't that count for something? She wasn't screwing around with every guy who came along. If there really was a God up there watching over everyone, how could he let her end up in such a mess?

Look what happened to Maddy. Nobody's safe. Maddy was in her thirties, a grown woman who had been living with a man old enough to be her father, and that didn't stop that one lone sperm from zeroing in on its target. If it could happen to someone as smart and experienced as Maddy . . .

She waited, barely breathing, for her father to knock on her door. All her life she had taken her problems to him, and he had always managed to make things better. Okay, so maybe things hadn't been so great after the accident, but she knew he was there for her, and that meant the world.

He knew she wasn't a little girl any longer. That was why he was so hard on Seth all the time, making him uncomfortable every chance he got. She understood that. It was all part of letting go. But now here she was with the biggest problem of her life, and the one person who could help her was the one person she couldn't tell.

And she couldn't even think about going to Aunt Claire with this. Her aunt was suspicious and judgmental by nature. Who could blame her? Uncle Billy hadn't exactly made life easy for her, and Kathleen's problems had really pushed her over the edge. There were times when Kelly felt like her aunt had cameras hidden all around town, aimed at all the secret spots she and Seth claimed as their own.

She wondered what it would be like if her mother were still alive. She had been told a million times that she looked just like her, and that always made her feel glad and a little strange at the same time. Over the years she had heard stories about how funny her mom was, how easygoing and happy she always was. She'd heard Tommy Kennedy at the bar say how much Maddy reminded him of her mom, how she made her father laugh the same way nobody but her mother had ever been able to do.

Maybe Maddy would understand how she felt. It couldn't have been easy to find out she was pregnant with Hannah, not when Hannah's father was so dead set against having another child. Maddy must have gone through the same thing Kelly was going through right now, waking up each morning with just one thought

212

on her mind. *Please, God, please let me see that bright red stain . . . please . . .*

So far there had been nothing. Day after day of nothing.

Maddy wouldn't look at her with eyes filled with pain and disappointment if she told her she was late. She wouldn't turn icy with anger or act like the world was coming to an end. Maddy didn't have seventeen years of hope lying on Kelly's shoulders like a dead weight. She would understand. She would know what to do and how to do it. Maddy didn't expect her to be perfect, the way her aunt Claire and everyone else did.

She lay there for what seemed like forever, waiting for her father to knock on her door, but the only thing she heard was the sound of the garage door followed by the rumble of his engine as he backed down the driveway.

She started to cry again, and then, when she had no more tears left inside her, she closed her eyes and slept.

Chapter Eleven

The tenth biweekly meeting of the only ladies' floating poker game in Paradise Point history was set to begin in less than an hour. Five of the most opinionated, gossip-prone, interesting women in town were about to converge on Claire's house, and she hadn't even managed to stow the empty pizza boxes or play Hide the Dust Bunnies. In fact, she was wondering if she had time to rent a backhoe to shovel out the living room when Billy Jr. appeared in the doorway.

"Grandpa wants to know if he can watch TV in his jockey shorts tonight."

She wondered if Rose DiFalco had ever fielded a question like that.

"Only if he locks the door to his room and swears he won't set foot into the hallway until the party's over." The last time it was her turn to host the poker party, he had treated Olivia to a sight that had almost sent her elegant friend into intensive and prolonged therapy.

"That's just what Grandpa said you'd say."

"Your grandpa is a very smart man," Claire said, unable to hold back a smile.

"What if he has to pee?" Billy asked, his dark blue eyes twinkling with mischief. "What if —"

"I get the drift," she said as she gathered up the huge stack of *People*, *In Style*, and Spider-man comics that covered the coffee table. It hadn't taken her father long to figure out that Billy was his best ally when it came to getting what he wanted from his overworked, over-stressed, middle-aged daughter. "Why don't you both watch TV in my room? If Grandpa needs the bathroom, he can use mine."

"Can Bruno watch TV in your room, too?"

"Only if you make sure Fluffy doesn't start a fight with him." Bruno, a sixty-pound bulldog with socialization problems, was the latest addition to their family. Fluffy was a six-pound calico cat who ruled their domestic universe by virtue of longevity and divine right.

"Cool! I'm gonna go tell Grandpa."

Her youngest had two speeds: supersonic and warp drive, and he was halfway down the hall before she could remind him that the entire menagerie needed feeding and watering and walking.

She tossed the magazines into a recycling bag and snagged one of Maire's Mickey Mouse slippers from under the end table, a souvenir from — could it be Christmas? Maire had flown home from school in Ireland on her Aunt Frankie's frequent flyer miles and brought with

215

her the chaos only a sixteen-year-old girl knew how to create.

There had been a time when the thought of inviting someone like Olivia or Rose or the other members of their poker game into her home would have been laughable. "Five kids!" she would say with a roll of her eyes meant to convey unleashed chaos, and everyone would laugh and nod their heads in instant understanding.

It was an easy out, a way to keep the hum of gossip to a tolerable volume without inviting more. Her kids' birthday parties were held at the local bowling alley or down on the beach or maybe even at Great Adventure, someplace fun and impersonal. A place where she wouldn't be wondering if the woman smoking a Marlboro in her kitchen had spent yesterday afternoon in bed with her husband.

She had seen the looks, heard the whispers that grew louder over the years. She would have to be deaf, dumb, and blind to avoid them. *Poor Claire. How humiliating. Doesn't she have any pride?*

How many times had she asked herself the same thing? You run in to the supermarket to pick up a gallon of milk and end up wondering if the new girl on register six was your husband's latest conquest. Or how about the time you popped into the insurance office and found yourself face-to-face with the blond-haired office manager, and your imagination raced into overdrive. And then there was the owner of the pet shop, or maybe that sweet-faced kindergarten teacher, the one with the big weepy blue eyes.

No regrets. That was what she had told herself on a daily basis. Nobody had ever said it would be perfect between them, but for a little while it had been close to heaven. He had been her knight in shining armor, riding in on a white charger, offering her sanctuary when she had nowhere else to turn.

It had taken Claire a long time to make peace with the life she had been handed. She had spent most of the last three years since Billy's death looking for someone, something, to blame for the bad luck, the wrong turns, the fierce, nuclear rage that pushed the people she loved most far beyond the reach of her arms. She had blamed her parents, blamed her siblings, blamed her in-laws, blamed her husband who had died a hero's death before they had the chance to make things right one last time.

The O'Malleys always said that if it wasn't for bad luck, they would have no luck at all, and in the years she had been part of the family, she had come to understand the truth of that statement. She and Billy hadn't planned a life together. They barely knew each other when they exchanged their vows. Both of their hearts belonged to others, but fate had had other plans for them.

Before she drew her next breath, she was

twenty years down the road with five children, a mortgage, and a heart that had been broken more times than she wanted to count, in more ways than she could have imagined possible and still keep on beating.

She was nineteen when they met. She and Charles were newly engaged, and love had made her impervious to his best pal Billy's considerable charms. The truth was, even Billy had faded into the background next to her fiancé. Most men did. The fact that they both thought Charles hung the moon made them instant friends.

It was, of course, too good to last. Charles was killed in a traffic accident two months before they were going to be married, and his death devastated both Claire and Billy O'Malley. They loved Charles more than anyone else in the world ever could. He was the sun they revolved around, grateful for his light and warmth. Raw and aching with grief, Claire and Billy turned to each other for comfort, and that shared grief wove a powerful, if illusory, bond between them.

When she found out she was six weeks pregnant with Charles's baby, Billy asked her to marry him, and she accepted. Years later she wondered if it was their finest moment or the beginning of a tragedy that was still being written.

But once the play was in motion, there was no turning back. Claire needed someone to lean on, and Billy needed a family. They had been too young, too filled with emotion to know what they were doing. They had come together at the wrong time, for all the wrong reasons, even if those reasons had seemed pure and noble. And maybe they had been. She wanted to believe that.

There had been a lot of talk when she and Billy returned to Paradise Point as a married couple. The gossips had had a field day with their sudden marriage in the aftermath of Charles's tragic death, and much of that gossip had to do with the paternity of the child she was carrying. But as the weeks and months passed, Charles vanished from the town's radar screen, and the unexpected union of Claire Meehan and Billy O'Malley was no longer the number-one topic of conversation and conjecture.

When Kathleen was born, everyone said she was the image of Billy, and the two of them fell into a silent conspiracy that was much easier than the truth. But they had never been able to fool his grandmother Irene. The day she and Billy came home from Maryland with the rings and the marriage license and the belly bump, Irene had turned her cold heart against Claire.

At first Claire had tried to work her way back into what passed for the old woman's affections, but when Kathleen was born to the sound of her great-grandmother's indifference, she hardened her own heart in response. If Billy could look past Kathleen's paternity, why couldn't Irene do the same thing?

Billy loved the blue-eyed little girl like one of his own. Claire saw that clearly when three more daughters arrived in quick Catholic succession, and their fate was sealed. They were a family.

In the second decade of their marriage she made the decision that changed the course of her life. Everyone in town thought she had taken the kids down to Florida to see her parents, but the truth was she had left Billy for good. It was an impulsive decision, but then her life had been a series of impulsive decisions.

She had been waiting for the traffic light to change at the corner of Main Street where it intersected with Church, drumming her fingers on the steering wheel while she tried to figure out what she would make for dinner that night, when her gaze happened to land on Patty Hansen's living room window.

You don't expect to see your husband making out with the Brownie troop leader at ten o'clock on a Tuesday morning artfully framed by her Laura Ashley curtains and drapes.

Claire was on the road to Florida by late afternoon, determined to start a new life that didn't include sharing her husband with anyone who didn't also share his DNA. Her parents were curious, but for once they didn't ask too many questions. Mike and Margaret had an active social life that kept them busy, something for which Claire was intensely grateful. Besides, they had spent the first sixty-something years of their life in Paradise Point. They knew what was going on.

The kids missed their daddy, but she made sure they quickly settled into their new routine. The trick was to keep them busy so they wouldn't ask too many questions. She couldn't handle questions at the moment, especially not questions about why they were in Florida and Billy was still in New Jersey. Claire drove them to the beach, took them to Parrot Jungle, and one day while they were frolicking in the community pool, she fell in love.

She had been floating through her days, trying hard not to think too much, enjoying the occasional lazy afternoon with the daughter of her parents' next-door neighbors, a flamboyant thirty-something-year-old woman named Olivia Flynn, who was waiting out her second divorce in three years. The Flynns were New Jersey émigrés same as the Meehans, and the two families got on well together.

Olivia was the star attraction of Del Mar Vista, Phase II, and the male residents congregated around her, eager for whatever crumb of attention she might toss their way. Claire, who had never inspired slavish male devotion, stood back in awe and enjoyed the show.

Olivia had come to town to arrange a golden wedding anniversary party for her parents. Her younger brother Corin, a photographer, was off somewhere in Europe, but he had promised to make it home in time for the big day. It had been two years since Corin had been back in the States, much to his father's loud disapproval. Brendan Flynn was a retired Teamster. The fact that his only son made his living snapping photos of worthless celebrities at opening nights and other sideshows infuriated him. No matter how many times Olivia tried to explain to Brendan that Corin did much more than snap photos of Tom Cruise and Russell Crowe partying in Cannes, it simply didn't sink in. The work Corin had done in Bosnia had won international acclaim, but you wouldn't know it to hear Brendan talk.

Claire had been expecting a male version of Olivia, and in many ways she wasn't disappointed. Corin Flynn carried the same kind of high-energy-force field as his sister, a powerful magnetism that drew people to him. He shared her dark good looks, her sly sense of humor, but where Olivia saw life as an endless party, Corin knew it was anything but.

He lived anywhere and everywhere. He only owned what he could stuff into a backpack. He made his way through the world as an observer, capturing what he could with his camera, then moving on. There was an almost palpable sense of reckless danger about him that Claire found irresistible. She always had. Looking back, it all seemed sadly inevitable.

Night after night the three of them sat out on

the lanai and talked as the moon rose high in the sky. They talked about life, about family, about sex and politics and religion. Neither one noticed when Olivia began to say good night earlier and earlier. Everyone noticed when they began to stay out later and later. Corin told Claire about the wife he had loved and lost to another man. She told him about Billy, things she had never shared with anyone on earth. They told each other their secret dreams, their deepest fears.

And they fell in love.

Love was a terrible thing when it came to a married woman with four children. The emotions it awoke inside Claire were as terrifying as they were exciting. This was how it felt to be happy. This was how it felt to be desired. This was how it felt to wake up in the morning with every single one of your senses alive with wonder.

This was everything she had tried for years not to think about, not to want, not to believe existed beyond the pages of a romance novel or on the screen at her local multiplex. She tried desperately to hide her feelings, but it was like trying to lure the genie back into the bottle before she granted your third wish.

Happiness was the one secret she couldn't keep, no matter how hard she tried. His parents saw it on their faces. Her parents heard it in her voice, her laughter. Even her kids knew something was different, although they were still too young to be able to put a name to it.

To this day she didn't know who told Billy, but one afternoon she was sitting by the community pool when she heard Kathleen cry out, "Daddy's here!" and she looked up and saw Billy walking toward her. He looked cocky and unsure at the same time, her swaggering husband wearing his vulnerability on his sleeve.

This was a Billy O'Malley she had never met, a man she didn't know, hadn't imagined existed. She watched as the kids scrambled from the pool and ran toward him, wrapping him in wet chlorine hugs that left huge splotches on his jeans and T-shirt. Maire and Courtney clung to him like baby monkeys. Willow clutched his arm and sobbed, while Kathleen, always the least predictable of her brood, gazed up at him shyly, no doubt seeing the same handsome young knight in shining armor her mother had seen in him all those years ago.

Billy met her eyes over the heads of their children, and for an instant she saw that handsome young knight, too, and she was lost. They were family. Not even love could compete with that.

She had tried clumsily to explain it to Corin, but he couldn't hear her over the powerful rush of love and anger that rose up between them, wiping out everything but the fact that she was leaving.

Ten months after she returned to Paradise

Point, Billy Jr. was born, and there was no more looking back at what might have been. Corin was relegated to a secret, hidden part of her heart where he had stayed until Olivia moved to Paradise Point, and the possibility of seeing him again became all too real.

"Mom, can Grandpa and I have some of those cookies on the kitchen counter?" Billy was back, this time with Fluffy draped across his shoulders like a feline boa.

"No," she said, noticing a horrifying cobweb dangling from the far corner of the living room ceiling. She doubted if Rose DiFalco had ever seen anything like that in her life. "The cookies and cake are for my party."

"I just want one," he said, "and it doesn't even have to be chocolate."

"I said no. Those cookies are reserved for women over the age of twenty-one."

"That's not fair! They won't even eat them. Even the skinny ones are always on diets."

"I'll save you the leftovers. You can take a few to school in your lunch bag tomorrow."

"That's not the same."

She aimed some spray cleaner in the general direction of the cobwebs, then wondered why she had ever thought wet dust would be easier to eliminate than dry dust.

"You and Grandpa had pizza tonight," she said. "You love pizza."

"Pizza's not dessert."

Oh, he was her son, no doubt about it. Billy

Sr. used to say she was the only woman on earth who would turn down filet mignon and shrimp cocktail for a bag of Oreos.

"I think I saw a few ice cream sandwiches in the freezer," she said. "That's better than girly cookies, wouldn't you say?"

He gave her one of those smiles that were his father all over again and tore off full speed for the kitchen.

She quickly ran the vacuum cleaner over the carpet, then wiped fingerprints from the coffee table with the sleeve of her sweater. The pets were all accounted for, and with a little luck Billy and her father wouldn't turn her bedroom into a locker room. Now all she had to do was set up the card table, start the coffee, change into a pair of jeans that didn't have peanut butter and jelly stains on the back pocket, and she would be ready.

The doorbell rang as she was setting out the coffee cups on the sideboard. She glanced up at the clock. Nobody would dare show up a half hour early on Claire's night. Not if they valued their lives.

"Go away," she said as Olivia and Rose marched right past her and headed for the living room. "The card table isn't set up, I need to change my jeans, and —"

"Sit down," Olivia ordered, pointing toward the recliner near the window.

"I don't have time to sit down. I'm expecting company."

Rose at least got the joke, but Olivia walked right over it.

"We have something to ask you," Olivia announced.

"Ask me standing up." She turned around and pointed at her rear end. "Billy's PBJ."

"Honey, I want you to sit down."

Olivia spread a magazine over the cushion of the recliner, and Claire went light-headed with fear. "Is something wrong? Oh, God, it's not one of my girls, is it?" With two of them in the Army, worry was woven into the fabric of every single waking moment.

"I told you she would think that," Rose said to Olivia. "That's always a mother's first reaction."

"Your girls are fine." Olivia sounded bewildered, but then she had never mothered anything more than a series of Yorkshire terriers. "We're here to talk about you."

"About your future," Rose said, taking a seat on the sofa opposite her.

"And ours." Olivia perched on the arm of the sofa next to Rose.

"We have a future together?"

"We could have," Rose said.

"Please tell me you're not talking about sex."

"What we're talking about is better than sex," Rose said.

"Damn right." Olivia leaned toward her and whispered, "We're talking pastry . . . English breakfast tea . . . chocolates . . ."

"Oh God," Claire said. "Not those scary chocolates in the shape of —"

Olivia had one of those full-bodied laughs that women had been taught from childhood to tone down into a more ladylike chuckle. "Did you ever —" It was one of Olivia's more remarkable anecdotes.

"If I did," Rose said, "I'd take it to my grave."

Claire was equally amazed. "I wouldn't have thought there was enough chocolate in the state of New Jersey for that."

Olivia winked. "Philip was nothing if not resourceful."

"Be that as it may," Rose said, "we're not here to talk about Philip."

"Rosie's right." Olivia switched back into business mode, a transformation that never ceased to amaze Claire. Who would have guessed that behind all that cleavage beat the heart of a top-notch businesswoman? "You know about the tea shop I'm opening."

Claire nodded, eyes darting from Olivia to Rose as she tried to connect the dots. "Cuppa," she said cautiously, wondering what in the world any of this had to do with her.

Olivia continued. "Yesterday Rose and I reached an agreement that will make her co-owner."

Some women not only had all the money in town, they had all the luck as well. Talk about a sure thing. The charming McClanahan cottage, with its stone facade, red enamel door, and rose-covered trellis. A fragile china pot filled with fragrant Earl Grey. A platter heaped high with warm scones dripping with sweet butter or maybe delicate madeleines or tiny tarts bursting with vanilla-laced custard and topped with cherries and grapes glistening with sugar. And — no doubt about it — a cash register bulging with receipts as a line of customers snaked its way down Shore Road all the way to the library.

Separately both Olivia and Rose were formidable women. Together they just might be unstoppable.

"Wow," she said as the picture sank into her brain. "You two are going to rake in the bucks."

"We think so, too," said Olivia, "but we need you to make it work."

"I have an extra ten bucks. Would that make me a silent partner?"

"You misunderstand," Rose said. "We don't want your money. We want you."

"Me?" Her bark of laughter made her cringe. "I pull drafts at O'Malley's, ladies, for a group of old men, sports nuts, and slumming yuppies. If you're looking for a waitress for your fancy tea shop, you'd better —"

"We want you to be front and center," Olivia interrupted. "Both Rosie and I have our other businesses to run. We know you're the one who kept O'Malley's afloat on a day-to-day basis before Aidan came aboard full-time, and we also know you're the one responsible for those sinful macadamia chunk cookies."

"We're asking a lot from you," Rose said. "In the beginning, you might be doing some of the baking, acting as hostess, welcoming customers, making sure they're happy, overseeing the small waitstaff."

"You'll be well-compensated." Olivia quoted a figure that made Claire's eyes pop.

"And we'd be willing to consider a partnership if things work out."

"I'm already a partner at O'Malley's," she reminded them. "Twenty hours on a slow week, forty in high season." And O'Malley's was family, a fact she wasn't likely to forget.

"And you're barely scraping by. Tell me most of the proceeds aren't being plowed back into the expansion Aidan's been working on."

"Olivia," Rose said in a tone that would cause a normal person to rethink her position before uttering one more syllable. "That's none of our business."

Claire considered planting a big, wet kiss on Rose's forehead, but it would take more than Rose's indignation to stop Olivia when she was on a mission.

"She needs a change," Olivia said to Rose. "She told me herself."

"And she's sitting right here," Claire snapped. "If you have something to say, say it to me, Liv."

Olivia could be unnervingly direct when she put her mind to it. "As long as you're a fixture at O'Malley's, you'll never be able to move on with your life. You'll be stuck in time and place until Aidan closes the doors and retires to Florida with Maddy and their seventeen grandchildren. Don't you ever wonder what else is out there?"

For a second Claire thought she was going to choke on regret. It tightened her chest and filled her throat like thick, black smoke from a two-alarm fire. Olivia fought dirty. She always had. A friend wasn't supposed to take your truths and shine a light on them for all to see. A friend didn't fashion your dreams into something tangible, something so close you could reach out and grab it if you only had the guts.

"Why don't you think about it overnight," Rose suggested, clearly uncomfortable with the battle going on between Claire and Olivia. "You're bound to have a lot of questions. We can all meet tomorrow and —"

"I have a better idea," Olivia broke in, speaking directly to Claire. "Why don't you decide now. You know what you want to do, and you know the excuses for why you won't do it. O'Malley's . . . Billy . . . the four other children who don't even live here anymore . . . take your pick."

Olivia had given her the perfect out. Sure it was sarcastic and meant to inflame, but it was a way out just the same. Olivia was already in a snit, so that wasn't an issue, and Rose would simply be relieved to see this discussion come to an end.

"So what will it be?" Olivia prodded. "You

can save us all a lot of trouble and just say no right now, and we'll ask someone else."

Suddenly Claire had her answer, and it wasn't what anyone, least of all Claire herself, expected. "You'll find someone else over my dead body."

Come to think of it, once she told Aidan, it just might come to that.

Chapter Twelve

Crystal skidded into the kitchen like Priscilla on a rainy day and stopped just shy of Maddy.

"Peter has a problem!" she announced, and Maddy swore she could see cartoon dialogue balloons swelling over the younger woman's head.

"Another one?" *Uh-oh. Wrong thing to say.* This wasn't your ordinary garden-variety pain-in-the-neck guest. This one took notes. Maddy forced a smile and tried valiantly not to notice the quintuple piercing marching around the young woman's left nostril. "What can I do for him?" *This time.*

"You don't have high-speed access," Crystal said in a tone of voice usually reserved for the reporting of UFO sightings. "How can we transmit files without high-speed access?"

Count to ten, Maddy, and maybe she'll disappear.

"You're welcome to use my dial-up connection in the office." Her jaws ached from all the fake smiling she had been doing since the PBS crew checked in that morning.

"Dial-up? Pete's gonna freak."

"Tell Pete to consider it a reenactment of The Candlelight's original Victorian charm."

Crystal considered her for a moment. "Good one," she said, "but I don't think he'll buy it."

"I'm afraid he'll have to. Our high-speed access went down last week, and the technician won't be out to fix it until Friday."

"Where's the office?"

Maddy dried her hands on one of Rose's fancy dish towels, then led the girl down the back hall toward the office. She popped the phone cord out of the computer and stretched it across the top of the desk. "Primitive," she said, "but effective."

The girl eyed it the way Maddy might eye a rampaging garden snake. "I'm not sure . . ."

"I'm sorry, but it's the best we can do," Maddy said. "Your other choice is to wait for the library to open tomorrow morning and log on down there. Now, if there isn't anything else . . ."

"We'd love a pot of that great coffee and maybe some of those cookies you had out this afternoon. You can set it up right here on the desk."

Count to twenty this time, Maddy, and remember assault and battery is punishable by law. "There's an assortment of snacks available in the parlor. I'll make sure there's a fresh pot of coffee waiting for you in there." She would be damned if they dribbled Kona roast onto her keyboard; not on her watch.

Crystal thanked her, then raced off to relay the information to the rest of the crew.

Kelly was standing at the counter grinding coffee beans when Maddy returned to the kitchen.

"I thought you weren't coming in tonight," Maddy said, sidestepping Priscilla, who was lurking near the doorway. She bent down to give the puppy a quick cuddle. "Rose said you weren't feeling well."

"I think I had one of those twenty-four-hour bugs. I started feeling better this afternoon, so I figured I might as well." She poured more beans into the hopper. "I thought you'd be at Aunt Claire's poker party."

"I will be as soon as Rose gets home."

"I can take care of things for you if you want to go now," Kelly offered. "I know Hannah's bedtime drill."

"You're a doll," Maddy said, as she washed her hands at the sink. "I'd take you up on it except our PBS pals just put in a special request for —" She registered the coffee grinder and the bag of beans. "Are you psychic?"

"Lucky guess." Kelly grinned. "I see them drinking pots of the stuff at Julie's every day."

Maddy reached into the cupboard for the large cream pitcher and the matching sugar bowl. "They're going to be setting up shop in my office tonight. They need an Internet connection, and the high-speed isn't working."

"Your office?" Kelly shouted over the racket

of beans being ground into submission. "Poor you."

"Is it just me, or are they extremely annoying?"

Kelly turned off the grinder. "It's not you, and they are extremely annoying." She measured four scoops of ground beans into the filter basket, then switched on the machine. The room instantly came alive with the rich, unmistakable aroma of brewing coffee.

"Have they interviewed you yet?" Kelly asked.

"Two prelims," Maddy said, stifling a yawn. "I think I'm scheduled for the comprehensive interview sometime next week."

"How'd you like it?"

"It's a little scary," Maddy said. "You go in thinking you know exactly what you're going to say — and what you're not going to say — and suddenly you're spilling your guts. I was actually disappointed when we ran out of time." She had said far more about her relationship with Rose than she had ever intended. So much so that the Witness Protection Program was beginning to sound good.

"That *is* scary," Kelly said. "They'll know every secret in town by the time they finish."

"For four generations back. God only knows what juicy tidbits my aunts have served up."

"I saw stacks and stacks of printouts in Crystal's room when I went in to turn down the bed. Grandma Irene's was on top."

"Did you peek?" Maddy grinned. Aidan's

daughter was the last person on earth who would ever peek.

"I thought about it," Kelly said with an embarrassed shrug of her slender shoulders. "I caught myself just in time."

Being so wonderfully predictable wasn't always a bad thing. Kelly was proof of that. People expected the best from her, and she always delivered.

"Aidan told me they had pulled every interview she ever gave to the press and it totaled over three hundred pages of clips. They could do the whole Paradise Point segment on Irene alone and have enough information left over for two sequels."

"Grandma would've loved this," Kelly said. "She knew everything there was to know about Paradise Point."

"She put this town on the map." Irene O'Malley had been one of the first successful female restaurant owners in the state, and as time went by, O'Malley's became one of the most popular establishments on the shore.

"Dad never paid much attention to Grandma's stories. I guess he'd heard them all so many times they stopped meaning anything to him, but I always listened. It was like she was sharing something special with me, a part of herself I'd never see any other way."

Maddy was twice Kelly's age and, if she was lucky, half as perceptive.

"I wish I'd paid more attention to my

Grandma Fay's stories. I used to zone out every time I heard the words, 'Now, back in my day . . .' " What she wouldn't give to introduce Hannah to Grandma Fay. "Did you know my grandmother cooked for FDR once right here at The Candlelight?"

Kelly's eyes widened with interest. "Back when it was a boardinghouse?"

Maddy nodded. "Rose has the clippings upstairs in a box of stuff she's been gathering for Lassiter. Apparently FDR came through here during the 1932 presidential campaign and stopped to visit with the locals."

"Wow," Kelly said. "If these walls could talk."

Maddy faked a violent shudder. "If these walls could talk, I'd be on my way back to Seattle. Rosie and I fought a lot of battles in this house. I think my old room still echoes with some of them."

"The PBS crew is really wired about the wedding." Kelly wiped out the grinder with a damp cloth, then dried it carefully. "You'd think nobody in town had ever gotten married before."

"Tommy Kennedy told me some of those smart alecks at O'Malley's are taking odds on whether or not your dad and I make it to our first anniversary." She stifled another yawn. "I told him to put fifty on *you bet we will* for me."

Kelly grinned. "Crystal did another pre-interview with me last week, and all she could talk about was how many times your aunts and cousins have been married. Your family is legendary."

"You'd think our last name was Gabor."

Kelly frowned. "Who?"

Nothing like an outdated celebrity reference to remind you of the passage of time. "Ancient Hollywood history, Kel. Hand me the cream, would you please?"

Kelly pulled a new quart of half-and-half from the fridge and handed it to Maddy. "Crystal and the others are all so skinny. I can't believe they use cream."

How long would it be before Hannah started worrying about calories and cellulite? The thought of what lay ahead made Maddy terribly sad. She had spent much of her own life trying to diet and exercise herself into someone else's ideal of beauty and would trade five years of her life for the chance to save Hannah from the same fate.

"I wish you'd seen them at lunch. You would've thought they were coming off a five-day fast."

"I wish I could eat like that and stay so thin."

"You've lost a little weight lately, haven't you?" Maddy said carefully.

Kelly beamed an enormous smile at her. "You can see it?"

Maddy nodded. "Don't lose any more," she cautioned. "Don't get too thin."

"There's such a thing as too thin?"

"Did you take a close look at Crystal? You can count her ribs through her T-shirt."

"So?"

"So you're beautiful exactly the way you are. Don't mess with perfection."

"You sound like my father." She rolled her eyes. "He's always telling me to stop dieting."

"Listen to the man. He knows what he's talking about."

Crystal popped up in the doorway, and Maddy and Kelly both jumped in guilty surprise.

"Do you think we could have some popcorn?" Crystal asked. "Cheese popcorn if you have it. Ray the camerman's not into refined sugar. Thanks!" She disappeared back down the hallway to Maddy's office.

Kelly rolled her eyes in mock dismay. "I'd put a padlock on the fridge tonight if I were you."

"The heck with the fridge," Maddy said with a guilty laugh. "I'd like to put a padlock on the front door."

"Better not let Mrs. DiFalco hear you say that."

"I know. That was very uninnkeeperish of me."

"I hear you're not going to be an innkeeper much longer," Kelly said as she arranged cups and saucers on an enormous wooden tray.

"What?"

"I heard you're going to manage that tea shop Ms. Westmore's opening up."

Maddy looked up from pouring cream into the pitchers. "Where did you hear that?"

Kelly's cheeks turned red. "I wasn't eavesdropping," she said. "At least, not exactly. I dropped something off in Aunt Claire's mailbox on my way here, and Mrs. DiFalco was there and she —"

"Talks kind of loud," she said. "I warned her about it. One day we won't have any family secrets left."

Kelly leaned against the kitchen counter and fiddled with the fringed end of the dish towel. "Is Aunt Claire really going to leave O'Malley's?"

Danger. Reduce speed.

"I don't know, Kel. Rose and Olivia are talking to her about it right now." And taking an awfully long time, come to think about it. Her mother was supposed to be home by seven to watch Hannah and the inn so Maddy could claim her seat at the poker table.

"Does my dad know?"

Proceed with caution. Black ice ahead.

"I told him last night, then swore him to secrecy. Rose wasn't too thrilled with me. It was supposed to be hush-hush until they spoke with your aunt."

"Are you excited about running a tea shop?"

"Yes, I am." At last! Her first genuine smile of the day. "They're going to put me in the back where I can't upset the paying customers. It's a match made in heaven."

"What about your radio show? I thought —"

"So did I," Maddy said, "but it doesn't look like my big break is going to happen anytime soon."

"But you love the radio program. You can't quit."

"Who said anything about quitting? I can broadcast from Cuppa. It's only once a week. Rose and Olivia think it will be great publicity for the shop."

"You can't give up on your dreams," Kelly said with surprising force. "Just because something unexpected comes your way doesn't mean you stop reaching for the things you really want."

"I'm not giving up my dreams, Kel, but I'm not independently wealthy, and neither is your dad. I have to think about the future — Hannah's future in particular — and this was too good an opportunity to let slip by."

"I thought Hannah's father was rich."

"Tom is very comfortable," she said carefully, "and he has provided well for Hannah, but that has nothing to do with me or my responsibilities."

"You lived with him for a long time, didn't you?"

Where was Crystal the Tattooed Wonder when you needed her? "We split a few months after Hannah was born."

Kelly looked down, but not before Maddy saw the look in her eyes. She thought she was

242

pregnant. Any woman who had ever been late knew that look of fear and wonderment in the girl's eyes.

"Would you have married Hannah's father?" The question broke what was quickly becoming an uncomfortable silence. "I mean, if he had wanted children."

"Tom already had children," Maddy was quick to point out. "Grown children and grand-children. He felt he was too old and settled in his ways to start again."

"So you decided to do it on your own."

"There was no decision involved," Maddy said simply. "I wanted Hannah from the second I knew she was on her way."

"So you never thought about —"

"Not having her? No, I never did." She had been one of the lucky ones, old enough and set-tled enough to be able to embrace motherhood as a wonderful, if unexpected, adventure. Even Tom's decision to split with her, as devastating as it had been, hadn't caused her to rethink her position. The one thing she had been sure of was that she wanted the baby.

"Do you ever wish things had been different?"

"For a long time I did. I kept wishing Tom would change his mind and Hannah could have her daddy with her every single day, but it wasn't in the cards." She glanced at the engage-ment ring on her finger and smiled. "Now I wouldn't change a thing."

Kelly nodded thoughtfully, and Maddy wondered what was going through her head. How on earth did you explain your first real love to the daughter of the man you were going to marry? How did you explain to a fiercely intelligent, deeply romantic young woman that even though life didn't always work out quite the way you thought it would, it mostly worked out exactly the way it should if you gave it time?

When you were seventeen you believed love conquered everything. By the time you were thirty-three, you had learned that love conquered everything but itself. Only time could do that.

Claire would probably have had a better, more maternal answer. One that managed to be truthful and tactful at the same time, an answer perfectly tailored for the delicate sensibilities of a seventeen-year-old heart. They were only a few years apart in age, but the difference in parental experience was wide.

The coffee machine pinged to let them know it had finished brewing, and Maddy quickly poured the hot liquid into two insulated carafes while Kelly continued fidgeting with the fringe on the dish towel. Clearly she had something on her mind, a prospect that filled Maddy with apprehension. It could be as simple as wanting to make sure Maddy was good enough for Aidan or, as she suspected, as complicated as an unexpected pregnancy, and it was obvious that her answers were being considered very carefully.

I'm not ready for this, Maddy thought as Kelly

worried the fringe. Hannah was barely five. She had counted on a good eight or nine years before the questions started turning dicey. This was like being thrown into the deep end of the pool in the middle of the night when all you knew how to do was the dead man's float. She was terrified of saying too much or too little or not the right things. This sudden leap toward intimacy had her off balance and feeling very uncertain of exactly what was expected of her role as a quasi-friend/future stepmother.

She was grateful for the distraction when Crystal popped up in the doorway one more time and asked if there was any cheesecake left over from dinner and asked if maybe they could add a platter of sandwiches while they were at it.

"Can you spell *expense account?*" Maddy grumbled as soon as the girl was out of earshot. "Maybe we should just send them down to —" She stopped abruptly. "Kelly, what's wrong?"

The words had barely left her mouth when Aidan's daughter sagged against the sink and would have hit the floor if Maddy hadn't grabbed her by the shoulders and managed to lead her safely to a chair.

"I'm okay." Kelly's voice was so breathy and low Maddy had to strain to hear her words. "Just let me . . . sit a second —"

"You're white as a sheet, honey. Put your head between your knees."

"No . . . I'm —"

Maddy placed a gentle hand on the back of

the girl's neck and encouraged her to bend low from the waist. "Breathe deeply," she said in as soothing a tone as she could manage. "Nice and easy . . . that's good . . . deep, slow breaths . . . okay . . . better, much better . . . now sit here and let me get you some water."

Kelly forced a laugh. "I don't need water."

"Maybe not," said Maddy as she dashed to the sink, "but I do."

She wasn't joking. The sight of Kelly's face drained of color had almost buckled her knees. The last time she had seen anything like that was in her own mirror during the first trimester she was carrying Hannah.

Get a grip, she warned herself as she filled a cobalt-blue glass with cool water. People got woozy and light-headed every day of the week, and pregnancy wasn't the only reason it happened. Low blood sugar. Fatigue. Whatever ridiculous diet she was currently following. There were a million reasons that didn't end up in a maternity ward nine months later.

"Here, honey." She pressed the glass of water into Kelly's hands. "Take a small sip."

She cupped the girl's silky head as she drank, aware once again of the physical similarities between Aidan's daughter and her own Hannah. The distance between five and seventeen had never seemed shorter or more fraught with peril.

Kelly did as she was told. It seemed odd to see the normally self-possessed young woman in such a vulnerable situation, and Maddy's maternal heart ached to fold her into a hug that probably would have embarrassed both of them equally. They didn't have that sort of relationship. Not even close, not yet. Maddy was Aidan's fiancée. Kelly was his daughter. How those two realities would merge — or not — remained to be seen.

"Thanks." Kelly handed her the empty glass. "You were right."

"Too bad my mother isn't around to hear that." She put the glass down on the table and crouched down in front of the girl. "So what happened?"

"I — I think I'm coming down with something."

"Hannah told me you weren't feeling too well yesterday."

Kelly's cheeks burned red with either guilt or embarrassment. She looked down at her hands and said nothing.

"Maybe I should call your father."

"No!"

"Your aunt Claire would —"

"Really. I'm fine." She smiled up at Maddy, but it wasn't terribly convincing. "I just need some more water."

"I realize we don't know each other very well yet, Kelly, but if you want to talk, I'm happy to listen." *Please don't tell me anything important, honey. Don't make me have to choose between your secrets and your father's trust.*

The words hung in the air between them, balanced on the fragile threads of promise that were slowly beginning to bind their families together.

"I'm okay," Kelly said. "Really. It's probably just my allergies or something."

You don't believe that, Kelly, any more than I do.

But, oh God, how much they both wanted to.

She looked so young, so vulnerable, as she met Maddy's eyes. So terribly frightened. *Just let me hide a little longer,* her look said. *I need some more time to think.*

Maddy was almost ashamed of the powerful rush of relief that washed over her when Kelly stood up and smoothed the front of her T-shirt. "Want me to take the coffee in to them?"

"I'll do it," Maddy said, picturing a disaster if the young woman grew light-headed again. "I want to make sure they don't change any settings on my computer."

Kelly's familiar saucy grin, a trifle subdued but welcome, reappeared. "Better make sure they don't find any E-mails from my father!"

Maddy quickly hoisted the tray and bolted for the door. "Now I know how Paris Hilton must have felt."

Kelly's laughter followed her down the hall.

You're a coward, Maddy, a small voice whispered in her ear, and she couldn't deny it. Short of putting her fingers in her ears and humming really loud, she had done everything in her power to keep Kelly from unburdening herself.

Funny how relief could feel a whole lot like shame.

Funny and very sad.

Claire stared hard at a pair of fives while the other women waited. Maybe if she stared hard enough and long enough, they would turn into a full house. This was the same methodology she had used when she was fourteen and believed she could think herself into a C-cup bra when she was clearly born for the A team. It hadn't worked then, and it was unlikely to work now.

"For God's sake, Claire," Olivia chided in exasperation. "If you're going to fold, then fold. This is penny ante poker, girl, not high stakes."

"I'll see you," Claire said at last, "and raise you ten." Nothing like embarrassment to prod a woman into doing something irreversibly stupid.

"Too rich for my blood." Gina placed her cards down on the table. "I'm out."

Maddy considered her from across the table. She had one of those open, friendly faces you saw in magazines and television commercials. Too bad she also had one of the best poker faces Claire had ever encountered. Her future quasi-sister-in-law could be planning a coup d'etat or tomorrow's dinner behind that smile. It was anyone's guess.

Claire still wasn't sure if Maddy was pleased they would be working together at Cuppa or shared her misgivings. They had spoken briefly in the kitchen before the game started, made the right kind of nicey-nice noises, stopping just short of air kisses. They had even made plans to meet tomorrow to take a look around Cuppa, but she wasn't fooled. There was an alpha and a beta in every relationship, and Maddy was the lead sled dog. Neither one of them owned even one of Cuppa's tea bags, but it was patently clear Maddy was the woman in the driver's seat. Claire had no doubt that all Maddy had to do was say the word, and Rose would see to it that the hostess job went to someone else.

And why not? That was one of the perks that came with being Rose DiFalco's daughter. Some women were born lucky, and Maddy Bainbridge was one of them. When Rose died, Maddy would inherit The Candlelight, the Miata, the bank accounts, and everything else her Midas mother had accumulated over the years. Maddy would be able to buy Cuppa out-right without even dipping into the principal. No wonder she was smiling.

"I don't think you have anything," Maddy said, still smiling at her from across the card table.

Claire, whose own poker face needed improvement, smiled back. "Interesting," she said.

"In fact," Maddy continued, still smiling, "I think you're bluffing."

"Are you in?" she asked.

Maddy's ongoing smile gave nothing away.

She could have been holding a royal flush or worse cards than Claire.

"I'll see you," she said at last, "and raise you five."

As the song said, you had to know when to hold 'em and when to fold 'em. This was definitely time to fold them, but Claire was like Bruno when he had one of Billy's socks clamped between his teeth. Nothing short of the Jaws of Life would break her free of that table.

"I call," Maddy said, her smile glowing a little less brightly. "What do you have, Claire?"

"Not one damn thing," she said, spreading her cards out for the others to see.

"Now why on earth did you do that?" Olivia demanded. "Didn't you know we'd catch you speeding with cards like that?"

"It wasn't my night," she said with a shrug. "It happens."

"Not to you," Lucy DiFalco chimed in. "You usually wipe the floor with the rest of us."

"Hey!" Maddy protested with a laugh. "Isn't it possible my superior card-playing skills factored into this at least a little bit?"

"No!" they all responded in unison. Maddy was known as the "fish" of the group, the one who could be counted upon to lose a tidy sum of money to the rest of them.

"If I had my way, I'd pay Rosie to stay home and send you to all the games," Gina said, ducking a playful whack from her cousin. "I can count on winning at least a few hands if you're around."

"Who deals?" Olivia asked the table.

"I'm out," Lucy said, barely stifling a yawn. "I'm not as young as you girls. I need my sleep."

"Right," said Olivia with a playful wink. "Like we're not supposed to know your new beau is waiting in the driveway for you."

"In a vintage Austin-Healey, no less," Maddy said. "The man knows his cars."

"And his women," Lucy said. "He likes his wine, his autos, and his women well-aged." She winked at them. "Bless his heart."

Gina pushed back her chair and stood up. "Where is he?" she demanded. "I have to meet this paragon of virtue."

Claire pushed away a few uncharitable thoughts about Gina.

Olivia gathered up her coins and dumped them into a silk-lined velvet pouch. "My place next time," she announced as they carried used plates and cups into the kitchen.

Watching Olivia clear a table was like watching Queen Elizabeth II pull latrine duty. You didn't dare blink because you knew it was a sight you'd never see again.

"Please," Claire said, taking the plates from her friend's hand. "This is too painful. You wouldn't know how to wash a dish if your life depended on it."

"And that's why the goddess made dishwashers," Olivia said with cheerful disregard for the legions of mortals without modern conveniences.

"I'm with her," Gina said, adding her cup and saucer to the pile on the counter. "If it doesn't use electricity, I don't want to know about it."

"No wonder New Jersey is synonymous with protecting the environment," Maddy drawled to a chorus of catcalls. "I'm sorry, but it's done a whole lot better out west."

"And how many coffee beans died for your sins out there in Seattle?" Claire asked as she squeezed detergent into the little cup.

"I'm going cold turkey as of now," Maddy declared, arranging the cups on the top shelf of the dishwasher. "In honor of Cuppa, I'm switching to tea."

"No offense, Liv," Gina said, "but only an act of Congress could get me to give up my morning coffee."

"None taken," Olivia said, tucking a lock of sleek chocolate brown hair behind her left ear. "Maddy's just being a loyal store manager."

Claire couldn't help it, but the look of utter shock on Gina's face was very satisfying.

"Gina, don't tell me you didn't know," she said as casually as she could manage. "Maddy's going to manage Liv's place, and I'm going to serve as hostess and occasional baker. I thought everyone had heard by now." Okay, so maybe that last sentence was a bit much, but her willpower was weak.

Gina swung around to face her cousin. "So when the hell did this happen?" she demanded.

Claire caught Lucy's eye and grinned at the look of sheer enjoyment on the older woman's face. *You and me both, Lucy,* she thought. Although probably for very different reasons.

"You mean something escaped your gossip radar?" Maddy said with a laugh. "Claire and I are going to be running Cuppa for Liv and Rosie."

Slack-jawed shock wasn't a good look for Gina, Claire noted with satisfaction.

"Wait! Wait!" Gina sounded completely befuddled. "Rosie? What does she have to do with any of this?"

"You really are out of the loop, cuz," Maddy said.

Gina was clearly annoyed to find herself in the position of being the last one to know, and she peppered Olivia and Maddy with questions about the new business arrangements, totally ignoring Claire, who watched with a combination of annoyance and bemusement. She was glad when Billy bounded into the kitchen in search of some more cookies. She was even glad to see Bruno right behind him.

"What are you doing still up?" Claire said, ruffling her son's thick, dark hair. Any day now she would lose that maternal privilege to the surly bonds of adolescence. "Grandpa was supposed to make sure you were in bed by ten."

"Grandpa's asleep." He managed to put up

with her fussing for a record-breaking thirty seconds before he ducked just beyond her reach. "Can I have two more cookies?" Oh, that smile . . . she was still waiting for the day she could look at that smile and not feel her heart break just a little bit more.

"To bed with you."

"Ma, please, just two more, then I'll brush my teeth."

"One more and then — Bruno!" She grabbed for the dog's collar before he knocked poor Lucy to the floor with his enthusiasm.

Olivia, noticing the commotion, turned away from Gina and Maddy and smiled down at Billy. Her son had a major crush on Olivia. He did his best to hide his affections, but his flaming red cheeks were a dead giveaway.

"So how did your book report turn out, Billy?" Olivia never condescended to children. She always talked to them like they were adults in slightly smaller packaging.

"Fine," he mumbled, looking down at his bare feet.

"Did you end up using that papyrus scroll you designed in my workshop?"

"Yeah." One word, torn from the depths of his soul. The torment of unrequited love was writ large on his freckled face. The poor kid was torn between wanting to run for the safety of his bedroom and basking in Olivia's attentions for a decade or two.

Poor kid. She didn't have the heart to tell him

that this was one thing time couldn't cure. Love was fatal, no matter when it found you.

"Will you bring it into the store one day and show me the finished product?" Olivia asked. "I'd like to see how it turned out. Maybe we could display it on the samples board, if you wouldn't mind."

He beamed with sheer, undiluted joy but managed only to mumble an awkward "Okay" before he grabbed one of the leftover chocolate macadamia nut cookies and fled the scene in a blur of energy and nascent testosterone.

"He's a man of few words," Claire said wryly as Bruno tore after his master.

"You realize he's going to be a heartbreaker in a few years, don't you?" Olivia teased. "The quiet ones always are."

"Stop by someday around suppertime," Claire said. "You'll be praying for silence before you finish your salad."

"Oh, wait!" Maddy reached for her enormous tote bag, which was slung over the back of one of the kitchen chairs. "I have the print-outs of those pictures I took of the kids at the Easter egg hunt last month."

"Took you long enough," Gina said. "I figured we'd get to see them by the Fourth of July."

Maddy whipped a folder out of her tote bag and removed a sheaf of glossy photo papers. "I'm no Scavullo," she said, "but you can't take a bad picture of those kids." She sifted through the pictures. "Okay, Gina, here's your tribe and one of the whole group together . . . Claire, here you go . . . there's even one of Kathleen."

Olivia and Lucy crowded around as Gina and Claire examined the pictures.

"I'm impressed," Gina said. "Not a bad picture in the bunch. I even like the one of my mother and me."

Claire's eyes went all misty at the sight of the eldest of her four daughters standing with her at the foot of the church steps, smiling broadly for Maddy's camera. God, how much she missed her kids. "She looks so grown-up," she said, trying very hard not to burst into tears in front of everyone. "Wasn't it yesterday they were all running across the yard, looking for Easter eggs?"

"Oh come on, Mommy," Olivia said with a gentle poke in the ribs. "They'll be moving back in with you before you know it."

Maddy laughed out loud. "Let my story be a warning to you, Claire. Sooner or later, we all run home to Mother."

If Mother has a four-star B and B on the ocean . . .

"I love this one of Billy with Gina's kids." Olivia leaned closer to inspect the photo. "Look at those freckled faces! He and little Joey could be brothers!"

Chapter Thirteen

"Was it something I said?" Olivia asked as the last car backed down the driveway, then disappeared up the street. "I meant it as a compliment. They're adorable children. What on earth happened?"

Claire considered her clueless friend. "I can't believe you've lived here this long and you never heard about Gina and Billy." She recited the condensed version, the one minus all of the pain, anger, and humiliation.

Olivia sank down onto a chair. "I had no idea. I knew your husband slept around, but Gina —" She looked up at Claire with open curiosity. "And you let the bitch into your house?"

Claire poured them each a large mug of coffee, then sat down opposite Olivia. "He fucked half the women in town, Liv. I'd have nobody left to talk to if I start getting picky."

"So is Joe Billy's son?"

The question stung much more than Claire had expected it would. It was one she had asked

258

herself many times since her husband died, and each time she came back with the same answer. The connection between Billy and Gina had been a strong one. She couldn't deny that. It might even have been the real thing.

But she was the one he married. The one he always came back to. The mother of his children. His wife. His partner. His widow.

"No," she said then more clearly, "no, he isn't. They ended it for good a couple of years before Billy died."

"You say it so easily."

"I've had a lot of practice." *Be careful where you tread, Olivia. This is my family you're talking about.*

Olivia fell silent as she stared into her coffee cup.

"Forget it," Claire said after awhile, her flash of anger subsiding. "You can sit here all night, and you'll still never understand."

"Do you?"

"Sometimes."

Olivia arched a brow. "And the rest of the time?"

Claire laughed softly. "The rest of the time I think I must have been crazy."

"I thought after you came back here things got better."

"They did for a while. When we found out we were expecting Billy Jr. —" She shook her head. "I know it sounds corny as hell, but those were the best nine months of my life." They had been happy together, really happy, and the whole family had benefited. "The girls used to rush into our room every morning at the crack of dawn and fling themselves into bed with us and we'd all cuddle and talk about what we were going to do that day. They loved to press their ears against my belly and listen for the baby." She laughed softly. "I never knew exactly what they expected to hear but . . ." Her voice drifted away into memory.

"This is probably a hell of a time to give you this." Olivia reached into the soft leather purse resting next to her mug of tea and withdrew a small white envelope with a foreign stamp in the upper right-hand corner. She placed it face-down on the table. "Remember what I said to you when you told me you were going back up to New Jersey with Billy?"

"That was a long time ago, Liv." Almost nine years. A lifetime. "It's ancient history."

Olivia leaned forward, attention riveted to Claire. "I said to be very sure you knew what you were doing, because you and Corin would never get a second chance if you went back to Billy."

The muscles in Claire's jaw tightened. She could almost hear her molars grinding into dust. "I remember."

"He turned down this documentary because he didn't want to —"

"I know why he turned it down," Claire broke in. "You already told me."

"I mean, he's my brother, and he's never even seen my house or my store. He's stayed away from Paradise Point out of respect for your feelings."

So that was what he had told his sister. "I thought he stayed away because he was in Afghanistan."

"I told you that, too?"

"No," she said. "I saw his name mentioned in an article."

"You Googled him."

"I wouldn't Google God if He had a Web site." She pretended to yawn behind her hand. "Is this going someplace, Liv, because —"

"Here you go, Mrs. O'Malley." Claire slid the envelope across the table to Claire. "Guess who's coming to dinner."

Claire was still sitting at the kitchen table hours later, when her father came down for breakfast.

"Late night or early morning?" he asked as he pulled a container of orange juice from the fridge.

"I'm so tired I don't know," she said, yawning. "God, how I wish I still smoked."

"No, you don't," Mike Meehan said, pouring her a glass of juice. He set it down on the table in front of her. "Paper come yet?"

"I'm too tired to check."

"We'll wait until Billy gets up and send him out to look."

261

Claire managed to stifle another yawn. "Sounds like a plan."

"Poker game ran pretty late last night. I heard Livvy out here until all hours."

"Sorry if we kept you up, Pop. I thought we were being quiet."

"Did you clean up again? I always said you were born holding an inside straight."

"I lost," she said, shaking her head in disbelief. "I was so bad I made Maddy look good."

"Nobody's that bad." Mike had watched a few hands the last time the game was held at Claire's, and he still couldn't believe anyone would fold with a pair of kings showing.

"Liv said to tell you hello."

"I was up. She could've told me herself." Like every other male in Paradise Point, Mike treasured face time with Olivia. His stature had increased considerably when it became known he had met Olivia years ago down in Florida.

"She still hasn't recovered from seeing you in your jockeys last month." She polished off her juice. "So what kept you up? Another John Wayne marathon on TNT?"

"*Sands of Iwo Jima*, *The Searchers*, and *Flying Leathernecks*. That Brad Pott couldn't hold a candle to The Duke."

"Pitt."

"Whatever. The Duke — now there was a movie star. You went to see a John Wayne movie, and you knew what you were going to get."

The Duke before dawn was more than she

262

could cope with. "What we both need is a shot of caffeine." She pushed her chair away from the table and stood up, stretching.

"What's this?" Corin's letter dangled between her father's fingers.

Damn. She had completely forgotten it was lying there on the table like a forgotten occasion of sin.

"Nothing." She grabbed it from him and stuffed it in the pocket of her jeans. No point reliving those thrilling days of yesteryear when she had taken a walk on the wild side at Del Mar Vista, Phase II.

"Looks like something to me. You don't see too many Afghanistan postmarks these days."

"It's Liv's," she said, which was factual if not entirely truthful. "She left it behind."

"It's from that brother of hers, right?"

There was no point in denying the obvious. "Corin signed a contract to photograph a companion book to the documentary. He sent me a courtesy note through Liv to let me know."

"Now you got me wishing I still smoked." Mike dragged a rough hand through what was left of his hair. "I wondered how long it would take him to show up after Billy died."

"So tell me how you really feel, Dad." As if she hadn't heard more than enough of his opinions when the interlude with Corin had been going on.

"I told you then, and I'm telling you now. He had no business making a play for you."

"It takes two," she reminded her father. "I'm every bit as much to blame for what happened between us as he is." Maybe more. Corin had been single at the time, while she was still a married woman. Separated, but married. They had never slept together but it was only the fear of God instilled by Claire's Catholic upbringing that had kept her out of Corin's bed.

"He's not right for you. He wasn't then, and he never will be."

"I think I'm old enough to decide who, if anyone, is right for me."

"He reminds me of Billy, God rest his soul."

"The Y chromosome is the only thing those two had in common." Billy had been a local boy who dug his roots deep into the town where he was born, while Corin had hit the road as soon as he was old enough to drive. Yet Billy was the one who couldn't keep his pants zipped, while Corin had been blindsided by his wife's infidelity.

"Mark my words, it's going to start up again. I don't want to see you get hurt."

"Aren't you reading too much into this, Pop?" All the same things she had been reading into his note since Olivia handed it to her eight long hours ago. "The photographer they had signed to handle the stills for the book was diagnosed with cancer last week and called in a favor. That's all there is to it."

"I wasn't born yesterday. One look at that postmark, and I knew trouble was brewing."

"All this because Liv left a letter behind." She threw in an eye roll for emphasis. "Good thing she didn't leave her diary. You'd be in CCU on life support."

"You always did have a smart mouth."

"It's genetic."

"You don't need that kind of problem," Mike said. "He's not for you. He never was."

"There's no problem. What happened between us is long over, Pop. A lot's happened since then. Believe me, we won't be picking up where we left off."

"Your mouth to God's ear. That's all I'm saying."

Outside, the faintest glimmer of dawn seeped through the curtained windows.

"I'm going to regret this in about three hours," she said with a groan. The days of tearing through a day on little or no sleep were long gone. She would look like her own grandmother before the day was through.

"I heard Tony Fenelli's son ask you out for pizza."

That woke her up. "I'd appreciate it if you'd quit listening in on private conversations." This was worse than when she was a teenager. At least then she had her four sisters on hand to share the parental scrutiny.

"You don't want somebody to hear, take it outside."

"This is my house. If I want to talk to somebody, I'll talk to them."

"So don't complain if I overhear."

"Now I understand why Mom wanted to put a cow bell around your neck."

"I like Fenelli. He got a bum deal from that wife of his. You should go out with him."

She couldn't help grinning. "Not that it's any of your business, but I saw him yesterday at the bar and told him to call me."

"Leave the kid home and have some fun. I'll take care of him."

"We'll see . . . maybe. Just don't ask Lilly over if I do. I don't want anyone ironing my magazines." She stifled yet another yawn. "I suppose you heard about my new job, too."

"You decided to sell Mary Kay with your sister Frankie?"

"Not even close," she said, delighted that she finally found a piece of information he hadn't finagled, eavesdropped, or lucked his way into. "Start the coffee, and I'll tell you about it over pancakes."

"PBS must starve those people," Maddy said as she and Rose finished clearing away the breakfast dishes later that morning. "When I told the sound guy we were out of cherry preserves, he started sobbing, and I had to look away."

"They have healthy appetites," her mother said, smiling even as she cast a cautious eye toward the doorway. "I like that in my guests."

Which was a kind way of saying they were both counting the days until Maddy was safely tucked away at Cuppa with her computer and her ledger books.

"I promised Olivia I would stop by this afternoon and look through some of the paperwork." She topped off the sugar bowl and eyeballed the salt and pepper shakers. "I figured on doing it after lunch, if it's okay with you."

"I was hoping you'd be around later. Lucy is bringing over some fabric samples. I thought we could —" She stopped. "You do what you need to do, honey. There's plenty of time to deal with the dress later."

"No, no. I can stop by Olivia's after I pick Hannah up at the bus stop. I'm dying to see what Lucy has in mind."

The two women looked at each other and burst into laughter.

"Bizarro world," Maddy said, shaking her head.

"Is that one of your Seinfeldisms?"

"Up is down, black is white, I'm having a big wedding." She grinned. "That's Bizarro world."

"I was surprised to see Kelly here last night," Rose said as they double-teamed unloading the dishwasher. "Did she say anything to you about the incident Hannah mentioned?"

"We did a little tap-dancing around it," Maddy said, "but I don't think we really got anywhere. I remember what it's like just before graduation. You don't have time to breathe, much less eat. And Kelly's ten times the achiever that I ever was."

Or ever would be, but that was a whole other story. Some women had big dreams. Some women made their big dreams come true. Maddy knew which camp she was in, and to her mother's eternal dismay, it was a pretty comfortable fit.

"It's probably just a springtime stomach cold or pregraduation jitters."

"That's possible," Rose said. "Of course you've talked to Aidan about it."

What was it about her mother's questions that always made her feel so inadequate? For years she had blamed Rose for using the wrong words or the wrong tone of voice or even choosing the wrong moment to ask the question in the first place, but lately she had come to realize a good portion of the problem began and ended on her own psychological doorstep.

Achievers very often raised slacker kids, and while Maddy wouldn't exactly call herself a slacker, she wasn't looking to conquer the world. Sometimes she looked at Hannah and wondered if she wasn't destined to watch her little girl become a Wall Street shark or CEO of a Fortune 500 company with a seven-figure income.

"Please tell me you've talked to him about what Hannah said, Maddy. Kelly's going to be your daughter in just a few months."

"And she'll be away at college, Ma, and after that, she'll probably marry Seth and become senator from the great state of New Jersey. Her days of needing an on-site mother are pretty much over."

Rose looked at her and laughed. "Tell me that when Hannah is seventeen and ready to leave home. Honey, the days of needing an on-site mother are never over. I still needed Fay right up until the end and . . ." She gestured toward Maddy, who had the decency to turn bright red at being outed. "Even the prodigal daughter comes home sooner or later."

"This is different," Maddy insisted. "Kelly and I are friends. We don't have that parent-child thing going. If she thinks of anyone as her mother, it's Claire."

"I think you're wrong."

Maddy felt her back stiffen. "I know I'm right."

"I see the way the girl looks at you, honey. It's changed over the last few months. She seems to hold you in very high esteem."

"I wish you wouldn't say things like that." It made her uneasy to think that Aidan's daughter would look to her as a positive example when she felt that so much of her life had been spent in varying stages of chaos and bewilderment. "If anything, she's *my* role model."

"If you won't try to get Kelly to open up to you, at least make sure you keep Aidan fully informed. This is the man you're going to build your life with, honey. Kelly's his only child. For your sake as well as for hers, don't keep secrets from him."

"Speaking of which, she almost passed out on the floor while we were setting up a tray for Lassiter and company."

Rose spun around to face her. "Did she hurt herself?"

Maddy shook her head. "Thank God I moved fast enough and caught her before her knees gave way completely."

"Did she lose consciousness?"

"No, but I never saw a human being go so completely white before in my life."

"Did you call Aidan?"

"No."

"Maddy —"

"Ma —"

"How would you feel if this was Hannah we were talking about, and somebody else knew an important fact about her health and welfare that you needed to know?"

She tossed a pair of whisks into the drawer with a tad too much force, and they bounced out again and snaked across the floor like hyperactive Slinkys. "Thanks for the advice, but I think I've said all I'm going to say. He knows Kelly much better than I do. He lives in the same house with her. If something's wrong, I'll bet he'll be the first to know."

Aidan looked up from the vat of dip he was mixing for the lunch crowd's Buffalo wings in time to see Claire close the kitchen door behind her.

270

"You look like hell," he said as she hung her shoulder bag from the peg near the pantry. "Bad night?"

"Thanks, pal." She shot him a look from dark-circled eyes. "Like you're a regular Pierce Brosnan yourself."

"I didn't sleep." He tossed in some more blue cheese for good measure. "What's your excuse?"

"More blue cheese," she said, eyeballing the vat of dip. "Don't skimp. It's bad for business."

He flung in some more crumbled cheese and stirred the whole mess with a stainless steel spoon longer than his arm. "We have an office party coming in at eleven-thirty. Billing department from Mo's Sporting Apparel."

"That's today?" Claire frowned. "I thought Winnie made it for next week."

"Looks like you got your signals crossed. They'll be here in an hour, and we still need to —"

She waved away his words. "Same old, same old. I know what we need to do."

There was a sharp edge to her words, sharper even than usual.

"You got a problem helping Tommy set the tables?"

She made a sound that might pass for a laugh in another galaxy. "I could set tables in my sleep, Aidan."

She was going to leave. He knew it in the time it took her to draw her next breath. It was there in her eyes, her posture, every goddamn thing, and it had probably been there for months now. Maybe years. And he never saw it coming until now.

Anger burned through his gut, running alongside bitter disappointment. And yeah, some resentment, too. You didn't walk out on family.

"Hand me the hot sauce, would you?" he asked. He wasn't going to make it easy for her to walk out that door.

She swiveled around, grabbed the bottle, then placed it next to the pile of chicken wings waiting to be lowered into the deep fryer.

"You really do make the best wings in the state," she said.

"Sucking up," he said. "Not a good sign."

She leaned against the worktable and crossed her arms over her chest in the stance he had come to recognize as her take-one-step-closer-and-you're-dead pose.

"You know, don't you?"

He pushed the vat of dip to one side and began feeding chicken wings one by one into the fryer. "I do now."

She sounded almost nervous as she began parroting facts and figures about the damn tea shop, outlining her responsibilities, her hours, every goddamn thing Olivia and Rose had told her regurgitated for his approval.

"Hostess and baker?" He met her eyes across the deep fryer. "Sounds like they got themselves a good deal. No wonder they pitched it to you."

"And what the hell is that supposed to mean?"

"You'll be working twice as hard there as you do here, and for what? A paycheck instead of a partnership."

"But I'll be doing it because I want to, not because I —" She stopped, and an ugly red stain moved its way up from the base of her throat. "Sorry. You deserve better than that."

"Won't get an argument from me."

"I'm not leaving you in the lurch, if that's what you're worried about. I spoke to Peggy Randall. She said she'd be glad to pick up my hours here and more."

"You plan on selling your half of O'Malley's to Peggy, too?"

"Do you want me to?" Her voice shook with emotion.

"No," he said, refusing to be moved by her distress, "but since when does my opinion count for shit in this discussion."

"I'm not quitting the family, Aidan. We'll still be partners. I just need to try something new."

"Sorry," he said, "but I don't see the big difference between pulling drafts and pouring tea."

"I do," she said. "For one thing, I won't see Billy every time I walk through the door."

"No, but you'll still see him every time you walk through your own front door."

Her smile faded. "Would it kill you to make this easy on me?"

"Yeah, it fucking well might." He slammed a

few more chicken wings into the hot oil, narrowly escaping a vicious splash. "I think this is going to be O'Malley's best summer ever. It wouldn't kill you to stick it out."

"Oh yeah?" she said, mimicking his tone of voice. "It fucking well might."

"They let you use that kind of language in a tea shop?"

"I'll let you know when I get there."

He lifted the basket of fried chicken wings from the deep fryer and set them to drain. "Is there anything I can say to change your mind?"

"I need to leave, Aidan. I need —" She stopped and shook her head. "Sometimes I think I'm drowning here." Her voice broke on the last word. "I might fall on my face and come crawling back next month, begging to pull some drafts, but at least I'll know I tried." She blinked back tears. "I have to know I tried."

"You fight dirty," he said, lowering another batch of wings into the fryer, but he was lying. She didn't fight dirty. She fought the way she did everything else, with a balls-out, in-your-face passion he admired more than he would ever be able to tell her. Right now, however, that passion was about to screw up his life.

"It's my only talent." She pushed her mop of auburn curls off her face. "I'll still be involved with things around here. We'll still be partners."

Yeah, they were partners, but it struck him that a good partner didn't walk out the door and leave the other partner juggling the workload.

274

His emotions ran the gamut from pissed off to hurt to deeply sympathetic, and damn it, sympathetic was winning out.

He had been where she was. He knew the toll it took on her to walk through those doors every day and immerse herself in Billy's old domain. Whatever Billy's faults, Claire had been there beside him every step of the way. Aidan had walked through that door with her on a daily basis since the accident, seen the same ghosts, ducked the same memories. He couldn't imagine the bar without Claire's laugh, her running commentary, her frequent flashes of temper, and he was afraid their many regulars wouldn't be able to either.

For the last seventeen years she had been the one person on earth he could count on. She had opened her heart and her home to Kelly and him without reservation when they needed it, and she had never asked for anything in return.

Until now.

"Give me Peggy's number. I'll call her and see what she has to say." Not particularly gracious, but it was the best he could manage.

She rounded the work counter and kissed him on the left cheek. "Thanks," she said. "You know I'll come in if you get in a pinch some night."

"So what are you standing here for?" he said gruffly. "Don't you have a new job to go to?"

She grabbed for a fresh apron on top of the

stack near the sink. "O'Malleys don't walk out without giving notice. You're stuck with me for at least another few weeks."

He was so filled with conflicting emotions that he turned away and pretended avid interest in a bag of onions on the counter. "Put the blue cheese dip in the fridge and start setting up the tables. Tommy thinks all you need is a cocktail napkin and a bowl of nuts, and you're good to go."

"Watch it, O'Malley. I was here a long time before you started pulling drafts. I'm still an equal partner. If you push, I'm gonna push back even harder."

"If we're equal, why am I always doing the grunt work? Let's get moving. We have a crowd of hungry sporting goods accountants to feed."

They fell back into their normal brother/sister banter, but everything was different between them, and they both knew it. The moment she made her decision, everything changed. She was the bar's connection to Billy and the old days, more so even than Aidan. Aidan's working connection with O'Malley's was only a few years old, while Claire's went back almost twenty years.

She was the one who greeted the old-timers by name when they walked through the door, the one who sent flowers when somebody died, bought Mass cards, visited hospital rooms, remembered who liked his burgers rare and whose life was in the toilet, and she did it with a smart-ass laugh, a sly wink, the sense that they were all in it together, always had been, always would be.

You could renovate the bar, add outdoor dining, spruce up the menu until it looked like something Emeril or Wolfgang would whip up, but you couldn't manufacture a soul. A place either had one or it didn't, and you knew it the second you walked through the door.

Claire was the soul of O'Malley's Bar and Grill, and when she left to start her new job, she would take the hearts of every regular with her. Aidan's included. She was the sister he never had. The O'Malley family connection he had always wanted. They didn't share DNA, but she was blood just the same.

He could've fought her on this. For one long moment he had considered calling in lawyers he couldn't afford and trying to block her from leaving, but when push came to shove, he couldn't do it. He wouldn't do it to her. He was making a new life for himself, and Claire deserved the same chance, even if it meant O'Malley's future hung in the balance. She'd earned it.

She was feisty, opinionated, a little rough around the edges, not always diplomatic, a survivor like everyone else who had ever walked through that door, and one damned tough act to follow.

Chapter Fourteen

Seth looked up from the computer screen when Kelly entered the room later that morning. They had both earned a free period to work on school projects as one of the many bonuses of scholarship and were alone in the newspaper office with a pair of file cabinets, a computer monitor, and their growing fears. "Anything?"

She shook her head. "Nothing."

"How do you feel?" he asked as she sat down at the worktable next to his.

"Pretty good."

"Really?"

"Yes, really. Definitely better than I felt the last few days."

"Maybe that's a good sign."

She wasn't sure if it was a sign of anything but wishful thinking, but she kept that thought to herself. One of them might as well hang on to hope. "I think I'm going to buy one of those home pregnancy tests this weekend. My dad and Maddy are going to Spring Lake on Saturday. I figure I'll drive over to the mall near

278

Bay Bridge where nobody knows me and pick one up after the graduating class's interview."

He reached for her hand and held it tight. "I'll call in sick and go with you."

"You promised Mrs. DiFalco you'd finish the carport this weekend."

"So I'll finish it Sunday."

"I'll be there and back in a half hour. Besides, I'll be working at the inn on Saturday, too."

She laced her fingers with his and let his warmth flow into her. Quiet came easily for them. It always had. They flowed from conversation to silence and back again as easily as breathing. She tried to imagine what this would be like with a boy who didn't care about her, who didn't love her the way Seth loved her, and the thought filled her with sadness.

"Did you know this is what happened to Maddy?"

He looked over at her. "I thought she was married to that gray-haired guy, and they split up."

"They never married. She got pregnant, and he didn't want to start over again with a family when he already had grandchildren, so they broke up."

"Bastard."

It wasn't that simple. She had seen the way Maddy spoke about him, with friendship and affection. "Remember how he was when he came to the hospital to see Hannah? He might not have wanted her, but he loves her."

"Then he should've stayed with them. You don't walk out on your kid."

"Maybe sometimes it's the only thing you can do." People wanted different things from life, at different times. You could love someone with your entire heart and soul and still not be able to make it all turn out all right in the end.

"Your father didn't walk out on you."

The statement brought her up short. "That was different. My mother died."

"Some men might've walked just the same."

A chill spiraled up her spine. "You wouldn't." *Would you?*

"No," he said, "and you wouldn't either."

She nodded, but she wasn't so sure. Lately she had found herself wishing she could just disappear. She wanted to leap behind the wheel of her car and drive until she ran out of money or gas or highway, drive to someplace where they didn't know her as the good girl, the perfect daughter, the model student, the one who never made mistakes, never said the wrong thing, never disappointed anyone, not even herself.

It was all coming at her so fast that she found it hard to arrange her thoughts into some kind of order. She had always known exactly where her life was headed, as if she had been born with a schedule hardwired into her brain that kept her on time and on track. Just a few more months, and she and Seth would be leaving for college, heading up to New York and Columbia and a whole wide world of experiences she could never enjoy in Paradise Point. Sometimes she looked at her old friends, at Aunt Claire, at her father, and felt like she was watching them from across a divide that grew wider every day.

They were happy with their lives. They liked it right there in the town where they'd been born, tending bar, raising families, having their hair styled at Upsweep or buying stationery at Le Papier or watching the tourists watching them from the front porch of The Candelight. Only Maddy had ever wanted something different. She had broken away from the pack when she was Kelly's age and headed to Seattle, where she made a life for herself. A life she might still be living if Hannah hadn't come along.

The thought made her uncomfortable. Hannah was an adorable little girl, funny and bright and dangerously perceptive, and in a few months she would be Kelly's sister. Someone who would look up to her for advice and friendship. Strange to think that little Hannah had been the catalyst for such big changes in her mother's life which, in turn, changed Kelly's and Aidan's lives as well.

But that was the way it happened, wasn't it? Babies changed everything. Sit one down in the heart of a family, and the aftershocks could be felt for years.

As bad as things had been after the warehouse accident, that was how good they were now. Her father was happy, really happy, for the first time in Kelly's life. The kind of happy that made people smile when he walked into the room. The kind of happy that would make it possible for Kelly to fling herself into her new life in September without feeling guilty and torn between her home and her future.

It was as if all the stars had finally slid into alignment just for her, and they were pointing her toward the path she had been working toward her whole life. She was so close she could reach out and touch it, grasp the stars and hold them in the palm of her hand.

As long as she wasn't pregnant.

Claire spent most of the day trying not to think about the fact that one morning she was going to wake up and discover that Corin Flynn was in town. He hadn't been specific in his note to Olivia. All he had said was that he was en route. She told herself that it didn't matter, that he had asked his sister to pass along the information as a courtesy, a social heads-up if you will, but that was a lie, and she knew it. There had never been anything casual between them. Right from the start they had both recognized the import of what was happening between them and where it might lead.

God, she didn't want to think about him. She had trained herself not to think about him, to consign those memories to a dark corner of her heart, the place where old dreams were buried.

When push came to shove, she had chosen her flawed husband. Their imperfect marriage. Their wounded family, and the home they had built together. She had known exactly what she was doing and why, and if she had any regrets, she would take them to her grave.

She was wiping down the bar after the lunch rush when she saw Peter Lassiter and his crew walk in. A second later, Gina Barone came racing in, all laughter and smiles, and joined them. What the hell was that all about?

"I'll do the bank run for you," she said to Aidan, who was counting out the main register.

"No problem," he said, not looking up from the count. "I'll drop it off on my way to deliver the signed building permits to town hall."

"I'll do it," she repeated as Lassiter acknowledged her stare with a pleasant nod of his head. He turned back to Gina and said something that made her sway toward him and toss her overprocessed hair. "Just give me the pouch, will you."

"For Christ's sake, Claire!" He pushed the stack away from him and reached for a bottle of water. "You made me lose count. Now I've got to start over."

"I'll do it."

"What the hell's the matter with you? You hate doing the bank."

"I've gotta get out of here," she said, aware of the rising note of hysteria in her voice.

"So go. Nobody's stopping you."

She liked a good brawl as much as the next person but not now. All she wanted was to escape.

"I owe you one," she said as she grabbed her purse from the rack beneath the register. "I'll be back after I pick up Billy."

"Whatever." He waved her off and resumed counting the half-day receipts.

She escaped into the kitchen and out the back door, almost knocking into poor Tommy, who was sitting on the top step.

"Sorry," she said, rubbing his shoulder where the door banged into him. "I should've looked first."

"Goddamn dangerous out here," Tommy muttered. "Safer sitting inside a smoke-filled bar."

Normally she would have offered up a wisecrack, some sarcastically funny comment meant as a combination apology and disclaimer, but all she could think about was putting as much distance between herself and O'Malley's as possible. If she had needed further proof that it was time to move on, this was it. Her entire body vibrated with the need for change, for new possibilities, new challenges, not the navel-gazing into the past that Lassiter and his crew were looking for.

And what was Gina doing with them, she wondered as she climbed behind the wheel of her car and started the engine. The woman looked all buddy-buddy with Lassiter, who didn't seem her type at all. Gina usually went for flashier men, guys with muscles and —

Now there was something she definitely didn't want to think about. Gina and her taste in men could be summed up in one word: Billy.

No, that wasn't something she wanted to think about at all. She had spent way too much time dwelling on that over the years, and all of that thinking had never brought her one step closer to understanding anything at all about the life she had shared with him.

She drove out to the lake and parked near the gazebo. A group of gray-haired model boat enthusiasts congregated near the shore while their radio-controlled schooners and cabin cruisers glided quietly along the still waters. Their laughter floated in through her open window and surrounded her, and she found herself choking back tears. She joked that her father had a better social life than she had, but there was nothing funny about it. Her family had been her entire world all these years, O'Malley's her only social outlet. By choice and by necessity, she had let her world shrink around her until it became both jailer and protector.

Leaving O'Malley's was the right thing to do.

So was taking David Fenelli up on his invitation.

She needed to prove to herself, and to anyone else who might be interested, anyone who might not have seen her in a long time, that the old Claire Meehan O'Malley had been replaced by —

Okay. So maybe she hadn't worked out all the problems yet, but it was a start.

Besides their bad luck with men, DiFalco women were known for their high energy levels which, in most cases, translated into nonstop talking. Gina was a perfect example. Maddy and her cousin were the first to show up at the bus stop that afternoon. Gina had stopped off for a late lunch at O'Malley's with the PBS crew, of all things, and so far she hadn't stopped for breath in the retelling.

". . . Lassiter is such a doll, and that Crystal — what a hoot! We're going out together Saturday night. I promised to show her some of the best spots on the shore."

"You and Crystal?" Maddy asked.

"Sure," Gina said with a shrug. "Why not? She's young, but I think she can keep up with me."

"Does she know you like Barry Manilow?"

Gina grinned and gave Maddy a soft punch in the shoulder. "I'll take her to the karaoke place near Wildwood. Her tattoos and piercings will fit right in."

"Will you?"

"I fit in everywhere," Gina said. "It's all in the attitude."

Gina talked. Maddy drifted. They had

reached that accommodation years ago, and it still worked for them.

"I don't believe it." Gina nudged Maddy and tilted her head in the general direction of the post office. "So how long has that been going on?"

Maddy turned to look.

Then she looked again.

Claire and David Fenelli were deep in conversation near the bank of mailboxes. David downright glowed with pleasure as something he said was greeted with a loud whoop of laughter from Claire.

"I've never heard her laugh like that," Maddy said. "Have you?"

It was a perfect straight line, a softball Gina would usually hit out of the park. "No," she said, surprising Maddy. "Not for a very long time."

"Isn't David the one whose wife —"

"Yep," said Gina. "She walked out and left him with three kids."

Maddy whistled softly. "Do you think they're dating?"

"You're the one who's almost an O'Malley. I was going to ask you."

"I'd be the last one she confided in."

They tried very hard not to stare, which meant that they couldn't take their eyes off the pair. Maddy had planned to ask Claire if she wanted to check out Cuppa with her after the school bus arrived, but she couldn't muster up the guts to walk over to where Claire and David were standing and insert herself into the conversation. Not too many months ago it had been Aidan and her laughing together on the corner while everyone watched and wondered.

Denise almost tripped over her baby's stroller as she wheeled past Claire and David. "So what's that all about?" she asked, gesturing toward the two — Maddy didn't dare call them a couple — who were still acting like they had invented laughter.

"Five dollars if you go over there and ask them," Gina said with a wink.

Pat didn't know either. Or Fran. Or any of the other mothers who joined them.

"She's been holding out on us," Fran said.

"Fenelli?" Pat sounded dubious. "I thought he was still carrying a torch for his ex."

"You're way behind the times," Vivi said. "He took Deby Bartok out to dinner twice last month."

Gina's jaw dropped. "He's seeing Deby Bartok?"

"Not anymore," Vivi said with a smug smile. "She said she still has some issues and maybe they could just be friends."

Gina rolled her eyes. "Yeah, and all of her issues have to do with chocolate cake."

"What good are you?" Denise said to Maddy. "She's almost your sister-in-law. The least you could do is get the scoop for us."

"You're all a bunch of wimps." Gina cupped

her hands around her mouth. "Hey! Are you too good for the likes of us?"

Claire said something to David, who nodded, and they joined the crowd at the corner.

"So what was so interesting you couldn't be bothered with us?" Denise asked in a playful tone of voice that made Maddy cringe inwardly.

David didn't bat an eyelash. "We're planning to overthrow the board of ed and replace them with the cast of *Friends*."

"They're unemployed now," Claire said with a straight face. "We figure they'd appreciate the work."

The cast of *Friends* couldn't have delivered their lines with better comic timing. Maddy burst into laughter and was joined, a beat later, by the rest of the gang of mothers, who most likely didn't find it half as funny.

Claire's eyes met hers for a second, but she wasn't sure if her expression said *Thanks* or *Go to hell*. In four months they would be family. She would give Claire the benefit of the doubt and assume the former.

"So what brings you to our corner today, David?" Maddy decided to ask him before Gina had a chance to ask something even more embarrassing. "You're usually over at Maple and Ocean."

"You know your corners." David gave her a slightly gap-toothed smile that was surprisingly appealing.

"Corners are very important around here,"

she said, smiling back. "Part of the social order."

"Actually I'd better motor over there," he said. "Claire and I started talking, and I lost track of time."

They were all over Claire before the poor guy rounded the corner, bombarding her with questions and one-liners that would make a censor blush.

"Clearly you all need psychiatric care," Claire said, shaking her head. "Get over it, ladies. We were talking about this week's soccer practice."

"A likely story," Denise said with a wag of her eyebrows. "That didn't look like soccer talk to me."

"Just because he wears glasses doesn't mean he isn't hot," Pat added to the mayhem. "He's got a great butt."

"I like his hands," Fran chimed in. "I never noticed how big they are."

"Big hands, huh?" Gina had a dangerous look in her eyes. "You know what they say about big hands."

Maddy had never been happier to see a school bus filled with screaming kids in her entire life. Claire's expression was unreadable, but then again, it usually was. She couldn't possibly know about Gina and Billy and stand there day after day cracking jokes and making small talk. And she couldn't possibly have any suspicions about Joey. No woman could be that forgiving. It simply wasn't possible.

Maybe Claire didn't know how serious it had been between Billy and Gina. Maybe that was how she was able to handle it. Gina was just one of many, no more important than the salesclerk at Super Fresh or the bank clerk one town over. Marriage seemed to be equal parts love and accommodation, and nobody on the outside looking in could understand the balance.

Before Gina had told her about the affair, Maddy had enjoyed the byplay at the corner, the freewheeling, easygoing give and take. But ever since learning the truth, she had found herself wishing Gina would take it down a notch or three, if not for Claire's sake then for her own. It wasn't funny any longer. She and Claire had their problems, but the woman deserved a hell of a lot better than she was getting from Gina. Claire was Billy's widow. Gina wasn't. That had to count for something, and the sooner her cousin got that fact through her head, the better off they would all be.

The kids exploded from the school bus on a wave of shrieks and giddy laughter. By the time the school year ended next month, they would need to meet the bus with tranquilizer guns. A slight exaggeration, to be sure, but not by much. The energy level was downright scary, like a sugar high taken to the tenth degree. Gina's dynamos were the first off. No surprise there. Fran's kids, Denise's, Pat's brood, Vivi's, Billy Jr., followed by Hannah, who was talking his ear off.

Hannah had developed a fascination for Claire's youngest and trailed after Billy, regaling him with stories of an imaginary dragon who lived behind her Grandpa Bill's house in Oregon.

"Billy has the patience of a saint," Maddy said to Claire as Hannah chattered away. "Even her grandmother occasionally asks for a time out."

"Hannah seems to be his one exception to the 'girls stink' rule."

Maddy laughed out loud. "He's that age, isn't he? I'd forgotten how it is."

"Believe me, these are the easy years. Just wait until Hannah decides you're too stupid to live. That's when the fun really starts."

"And you've gone through it four times already?" With a fifth on the horizon.

"Call me crazy," Claire said with a sigh. "I'm a regular glutton for punishment."

Of course she was anything but. Claire might be prickly at times, but no one would ever say she wouldn't lay down her life for her children.

"Sometimes I'm not sure I have what it takes to manage one," Maddy said. "I feel like I'm making it up as I go along."

"So does everybody," Claire said. "We all make it up as we go along and hope for the best."

That was the most Claire had said to her since she and Aidan got engaged. Maddy decided to take advantage of the crack in the ice. "I was thinking of walking over to Cuppa to check things out. Want to join me?"

"They're waiting for me at the bar. Tommy wants to leave early."

"Five minutes," Maddy urged. "I think we need to see what we're getting ourselves into."

"When you put it like that . . ." Claire turned toward Billy, who was still being talked into submission by Hannah. "We're walking over to see Olivia's new store, Billy. Hold Hannah's hand when we cross the street, okay?"

"You made her day," Maddy said as they waved good-bye to the others and set out down the block. "She'll be floating on air."

They chatted about the weather, the need for new school buses, the cost of auto insurance in the Garden State. Nothing important. Nothing memorable. But at least they were talking. Claire seemed a little preoccupied, but that was better than the thinly veiled dislike she had been exhibiting the last few weeks.

"Looks like they've got a full house," Claire said as they reached the old McClanahan place. "Liv must've hired every workman in town."

"And a few outlanders," Maddy said with a nod toward two well-known contractors from Cape May whose trucks were parked front and center.

"It must be nice to be able to hire the best and not worry about pinching pennies."

"Remember that when we negotiate compensation."

Claire's eyes widened. "You're good," she said. "I hadn't given that a thought."

"I was an accountant for nine years," Maddy reminded her. "I watched a lot of people make a lot of mistakes. I guess I learned something along the way."

"Have you talked about money yet?"

Maddy started to laugh. "Now here's where it gets embarrassing: I was so excited about the job that I didn't even think about money."

"No wonder they came to us," Claire said dryly. "We're the cheapest talent in town."

Maddy was about to point out that a woman who could afford the priciest painters and decorators between Paradise Point and Philadelphia could also afford to pay a fair wage to the two women who would be running the place. Fortunately, sanity returned moments before she opened her mouth to speak. Claire was close friends with Liv. Rose was Maddy's mother. Anything she said to Claire was likely to be repeated to Olivia at the speed of light and, if she was being honest, she wasn't above gossiping with her mother about her future sister-in-law.

Hannah tugged at Maddy's hand. "I don't like it here," she whispered. "I want to go home."

"We'll go home in a little while," Maddy said. "Claire and I are going to be working here this summer, Hannah. We need to look around."

"I don't like it," Hannah repeated, upping the decibel level while Billy watched, wide-eyed. "It looks like the witch's house."

"Hansel and Gretel," Maddy said to Claire, who nodded.

"It does look a little fairy tale–ish, doesn't it?"

"Hannah's a baby," Billy piped up. "A big fat baby."

Hannah swung her book bag at him. "Am not."

"Are, too. You're a big fat scaredy cat."

"Take that back!" She took another swing at him, clipping his shoulder with her bag.

"Scaredy cat! Scaredy cat! Scaredy —"

Hannah swung at him a third time, hitting him in the back, then burst into wild tears. She grabbed Maddy around the waist, crying as if her heart would break.

Claire, red-faced, whirled around and faced her son. "Apologize to Hannah this minute, mister."

Billy looked down at his sneakers, while Hannah sobbed loudly against Maddy's right hip. Maddy, however, wasn't fooled by this sudden transformation from street fighter to wounded fawn.

"Hannah, tell Billy you're sorry you hit him."

"Will not." She looked up midsob, and Maddy noted her precious daughter's eyes were bone dry.

"Hannah."

Claire nudged Billy forward. "William."

The two kids mumbled unrepentant apologies. Hannah glared at her somewhat fallen idol, while Billy pretended she wasn't there.

A pair of workmen toting a quartet of two-by-eights brushed past them with a brusque, "Watch out."

"Maybe this isn't such a good idea after all," Maddy said, gesturing first toward the workmen and then toward the kids. "I think we're an accident waiting to happen."

"I hear you," Claire said. "Why not tomorrow morning after the bus leaves?"

"Sounds great," Maddy said. "We'll take a look, then sit down and talk about it at Julie's."

"Deal." Claire flashed a quick, semidefrosted smile. "Sorry about Billy's smart mouth."

"I'm sorry Hannah hit him with her bag." At least the mothers were trying to play nice. "Don't look now, Claire, but I think Billy's about to go Dumpster diving."

Claire turned in time to see her son scaling the top of the dark blue Dumpster. "William Michael O'Malley, if you're not down here in the next four seconds, so help me, you're going to grow up thinking TV is an urban legend."

Hannah, alligator tears forgotten, watched transfixed as Billy pushed his luck as long as he dared. He balanced precariously on the edge of the Dumpster, a wicked grin on his face, and looked like he was about to take a dive into the remains of Old Man McClanahan's kitchen cabinets, when Claire took two giant steps in his direction, and he quickly clambered down, looking triumphant and sheepish as only an eight-year-old boy could do.

Maddy took Hannah's hand and turned to leave.

"By the way," Claire said, "in case you're wondering, there's nothing between David Fenelli and me."

"I would never have asked," Maddy said. *But I was wondering.*

"We're taking the kids for pizza Friday to celebrate the end of the season."

"Okay," Maddy said, feeling like Alice down the rabbit hole. Amazing what a girl could find out by not asking.

"So now you know."

Boy, do I.

Who would've guessed there really *was* something going on between Claire O'Malley and David Fenelli?

Chapter Fifteen

"Sorry I'm so late." Maddy burst into the room, hair flying, cheeks pink, radiant with youth and health and happiness. How many times during those long years of separation had Rose longed to see her daughter burst through a doorway just that way, filled with high spirits, trailing joy behind her. "You won't believe what's going on with Claire O'Malley! She's —" Her gaze fell onto the spill of silk and satin on the bed. "Oh!"

Rose's heart beat faster as her daughter bent low over the rum pink and pressed her cheek to the shimmering fabric.

"It's so — oh no!" Maddy blinked furiously. "I hope it's waterproof."

"Not to worry." Lucy blinked back tears of her own. "A few tears, a few crystals. Only we'll know the difference."

Rose was too filled with emotion to speak. There were so many things she wanted to say to her daughter, so many hopes and dreams to share with her. So many mistakes to own up to. So much lost time to make up for.

"Lucia brought a few sketches with her," she said instead, pointing toward the drawing pad lying facedown on her dressing table. "Take a look."

Maddy drew her right forearm across her eyes, then flashed a silly grin. For the briefest moment, an instant really, she saw her daughter as a little girl, all arms and legs and energy, and she saw her as a teenager, all tumbling hair and lovely curves and plans for a future that didn't include her mother or Paradise Point. It all went by so fast. If you looked away for a heartbeat you missed so much . . .

Hannah and Priscilla ran into the room, trailing beach sand and chocolate chip cookie crumbs. Lucy scooped up Priscilla before the puppy had the chance to jump up onto the bed and put paw prints on the luscious fabrics.

"Ohh!" Hannah reached out to touch the slippery rum pink satin. "A Barbie wedding dress!"

"That's a great idea, Hannah," Lucy said. "I'll make Barbie a wedding dress just like your mommy's. What would you think about that?"

Hannah beamed at her great-aunt. "She needs shoes, too."

Maddy tugged on her daughter's ponytail. "Honey, first you thank Aunt Lucy, then you hit her up for the Manolo Blahniks."

"She's definitely a DiFalco." Rose winked as she said it. "The shoes are the first sign."

The three women burst into laughter while Hannah, still a little young for Manolos, leaped onto the bed and did a somersault across some ivory duchesse that probably cost enough to fund her first semester at a decent college.

Nobody blinked.

"So which sketch do you like best, Maddy?" Lucy sat down on the edge of the bed across from Maddy and Hannah. "I'm partial to the one with the Grecian style drape in the back. With your height and your lovely shoulders, we can . . ."

Everything Rose had hoped for when she orchestrated that terrible trip to the bridal department at Saks suddenly materialized right there in her bedroom. Maddy, standing tall and lovely in a puddle of sunshine while Lucy draped her in satin and lace. Hannah and Priscilla, propped up on pillows near the headboard, watching everything with wide-eyed fascination. Her beloved sister Lucy, eyes shining with happiness, as she shaped a gown fit for a princess with straight pins and love.

There was only one thing wrong with the picture. Peter Lassiter and his tattooed assistant Crystal were standing in the bedroom doorway watching the whole thing.

"Do you need something?" Rose asked with perhaps a shade less friendliness than she usually displayed to her paying customers. "This is my bedroom suite." Didn't their mothers teach them to knock?

Crystal drifted into the room as if in a trance. "Ohhh," she breathed, running her hand down a column of silk draped across the slipper chair in the corner. "This is like something out of a fairy tale."

Maddy, glowing with happiness, beamed a smile. "If you think that's something, come over here and take a look at the lace Lucy brought with her."

Suddenly Crystal seemed every bit as young and innocent as Hannah. Her face lost that look of urban ennui and became the face of an average young woman who still believed in happy endings. Even Peter dropped his cool, professional demeanor and told a charming story about his own wedding that made the females in the room sigh out loud.

They were joined by the sound guy, one of the cameramen, and before Rose knew what was happening, her cozy family moment was being captured on film and audio for posterity, not to mention the entire NJTV viewership. Maddy, her charmingly self-conscious daughter, seemed to bloom under the shower of attention. She struck poses for a surprisingly demanding Lucy, who managed to drape one-dimensional fabric with so much style and flair that even Hannah could easily imagine the finished product.

"What does this remind you of, Rosie?" Lucy asked around a mouthful of dressmaker's pins.

"The night before my wedding," Rose said. "We ran out of those tiny little pearl buttons, and you had us draping silk over buttons we snipped from three pairs of pajamas."

"You covered buttons?" Crystal asked from the center of the bed where she sat cross-legged next to Hannah and Priscilla. Her ever-present notebook was open on her lap.

"Forty of them," Rose said with a groan.

"Don't tell me Toni and Connie helped," Maddy said, anchoring a swath of ivory lace against her chest with her right hand while Lucy measured the length of her left arm. "I can't imagine them doing anything that might ruin their manicures."

"Oh, they weren't quite so high maintenance yet," Lucy said with a laugh. "That was still a few years off."

Crystal was busy scribbling her notes. "How did you cover the pajama buttons?"

Lucy explained the process while Rose felt herself pulled back through the decades. She had waited a long time to marry. Until Bill Bainbridge walked into her life, no man had ever seemed worth the changes that marriage would bring to her world. They were going to be happy forever. They were going to join their very different, very demanding lives, and make it work. No sacrifice would be too great. No need would ever go unfulfilled. Like two starry-eyed teenagers, they had believed love would overcome any obstacle life — and life styles — threw their way.

She looked down at her hands, the hands of a much older and wiser woman, and waited for the sting of regret to subside. They had tried so hard to make it work, for their own sake as well as Maddy's, but the differences between them had been more than even love could handle. It had taken twenty-five years for them to find their way back to each other, and she couldn't hope but pray life would treat Maddy and Aidan with more kindness. Happiness shouldn't have to wait that long.

"Okay," her aunt Lucy said as she added one more pin to the bodice. "Now climb up on the footstool — careful! careful! — and slowly . . . slooowly . . . turn around so I can see what —"

"Aidan!" Maddy shrieked, clutching the pin-prickly satin to her chest. "How long have you been there?"

He was standing in the doorway, arms crossed over his chest, grinning like a canary-eating cat. "Long enough," he said. "I followed the laughter."

"Why didn't you say something?"

The grin widened. "I was enjoying the view."

She felt herself blush from the soles of her feet to the top of her head. She had been so lost in the excitement that she had forgotten she was standing there almost naked, swathed in fabric like a dressmaker's dummy, in front of God and PBS.

"Isn't this bad luck?" Crystal asked. "I mean, you're not supposed to see the bride in her dress before the wedding day, right?"

"This isn't my dress," Maddy said as she hurried toward the doorway. "This is just the suggestion of my dress."

"I don't know." Crystal didn't sound convinced. "It's going to be your dress pretty soon, isn't it?"

"Oh, we don't believe in that nonsense," Maddy said as Aidan held out his hand to her. "That's nothing but a superstition."

"Crystal's right," Lucy said to Maddy's surprise. "It might be a silly superstition, but it wouldn't hurt, would it?" She motioned for Aidan to disappear.

"Oh, don't be ridiculous, Lucia." Rose sounded mildly exasperated and more than a little amused. "Every single one of us honored that ridiculous superstition, and look what happened. This is a new world we're living in. Let's make some new traditions."

"Whoa!" Crystal fumbled through the bed covers for her pen, then started scribbling in her notebook. "That's deep."

Maddy curled into Aidan for a pin-pricked hug. "So what brings you here in the middle of the afternoon?" He smelled of soap and shampoo and liniment, the way he always did after an encounter with Nina and the monster machines of physical therapy.

"I wanted to drop this off," Aidan said, pulling a brochure from the back pocket of his jeans and handing it to Maddy. "This is where we're staying in Spring Lake. I circled the suite."

"A suite?" Maddy's eyes widened. "Isn't that kind of pricey?"

"Third floor, tower, with a balcony and fireplace."

"Any neighbors?"

"Not a single one."

Maddy lowered her voice. "I wish it were Saturday already."

He brushed a quick kiss against her temple and breathed, "Me, too."

"Nobody told me you were going to Spring Lake!" Lucy sighed. "One of my favorite towns."

"They're going away on Saturday for a romantic weekend getaway," Crystal said. "Aidan arranged the whole thing himself."

Maddy's jaw dropped in surprise. Was nothing sacred these days?

"You people are scary as hell." Aidan fixed Crystal with a look. "How do you know what I arranged?"

"We know everything," Crystal said happily. "It's our job."

Maddy looked at Aidan and winked. "And it's our job to make sure you don't."

TO: jerseygirl@njshore.net
FROM: ClaireOM@njshore.net
TIME: 9:15 P.M.
SUBJECT: Tomorrow

Maddy:

I spoke to Olivia. She said the workmen don't start until noon tomorrow so we'll have to pick up the key. She'll leave it tucked behind the left shutter on the front window at Le Papier. First one to the bus stop picks it up.

Yours,
Claire

TO: Olivia@lepapier.com
FROM: jerseygirl@njshore.net
TIME: 10:01 P.M.
SUBJECT: Interview Fri A.M.

Olivia, would you consider being my interview subject Friday 8 A.M. at O'Malley's? Great drive-time publicity for Le Papier and Cuppa and I promise it won't take more than an hour of your time.

I'll even throw in free coffee and Claire's great cranberry-orange muffins if you'll say yes.

Thanks,
Maddy

TO: ClaireOM@njshore.net
FROM: Olivia@lepapier.com
TIME: 10:42 P.M.
SUBJECT: FW: Interview Fri A.M.

Don't you people =ever= get off the phone? I've been trying to ring you but I keep getting that abominable voice mail of yours. (You really should think about losing that outgoing msg — all I hear is Bruno barking.)

Take a look at the attached msg from Maddy. I think it's a natural for you. How about it?

(And don't make me pull rank because I will. Just because the shop isn't open yet doesn't mean we can't start promoting it. It's time you got to work.)

God didn't put me on this earth to type.

PHONE ME! Maddy needs an answer ASAP. (I think that mystery writer, the one with the bad hair, backed out.)

— Liv

TO: Olivia@lepapier.com
FROM: ClaireOM@njshore.net
TIME: 11:03 P.M.
SUBJECT: Re: FW: Interview Fri A.M.

Who does she think she is, waltzing into O'Malley's like she owns the place?

NOBODY gives away my muffins without asking me.

And no, I'm not getting off the phone so you can browbeat me into doing what you want. I'm IMing with David Fenelli about the soccer team's luncheon next month and that's more important than her radio show.

Besides, if she wanted to interview me, she would've asked me. You own the place. You do the interview.

— Claire

TO: jerseygirl@njshore.net
FROM: Olivia@lepapier.com
TIME: 11:22 P.M.
SUBJECT: Re: FW: Interview Fri A.M.

Now I hope you don't get all DiFalco on me, Maddy, but I asked Claire if she would do the interview with you on Friday instead of me. I want to keep Cuppa and Le Papier separate — what could be better than our manager inter-viewing our hostess/baker?

Of course she's being a wee bit stubborn but never fear. I'll win her over before

Friday morning.

— Liv

TO: ClaireOM@njshore.net
FROM: Olivia@lepapier.com
TIME: 11:42 P.M.
SUBJECT: Blatant Bribery

I'll watch Billy Jr. four Friday nights in a row if you'll do the interview.

Liv

TO: Olivia@lepapier.com
FROM: ClaireOM@njshore.net
TIME: 11:50 P.M.
SUBJECT: Re: Blatant Bribery

Too bad I don't go out on Friday nights.

Try again, Liv.

— Claire

TO: ClaireOM@njshore.net
FROM: Olivia@lepapier.com
TIME: 11:54 P.M.
SUBJECT: Re: Blatant Bribery

See attached

TO: Olivia@lepapier.com
FROM: ClaireOM@njshore.net
TIME: 11:58 P.M.
SUBJECT: Re: Blatant Bribery

<<you can drive my Jag for a whole weekend>>

Nope. Can't drive a stick.

<<a Day of Beauty up in Short Hills>>

I'd rather be tied naked to an anthill.

<<Six months' free rentals at Blockbuster.>>

Will you pay the late fees?

Sorry, Liv. You'll have to do a whole lot better.

— Claire, who can be bought if the price is right

TO: ClaireOM@njshore.net
FROM: Olivia@lepapier.com
TIME: 11:58 P.M.
SUBJECT: Blatant Bribery: final offer

No red-blooded Jersey girl can refuse this offer:

2 front row tickets for Tom Jones at Caesars in A.C. next month if you do the interview.

TOM JONES!

— Liv

TO: Olivia@lepapier.com
FROM: ClaireOM@njshore.net
TIME: 11:59 P.M.
SUBJECT: Re: Blatant Bribery

See? I can be bought.

It's a deal.

— Claire

TO: jerseygirl@njshore.net
CC: ClaireOM@njshore.net
FROM: Olivia@lepapier.com
TIME: 12:02 A.M.
SUBJECT: radio interview

Maddy, Claire said she would be de-lighted to do the interview with you on

Friday morning. You can work out the details together. It'll be great team-building practice for the two of you for when Cuppa opens in July.

Break a leg, ladies!

— Liv

Chapter Sixteen

"Julie's talking to herself," Maddy said from behind her coffee cup.

Claire swiveled around to take a look. "I don't see anything."

"Look again. Her lips are moving, and she's the only one at the register."

"Big deal." Claire swiveled back to face Maddy. "I talk to myself all the time. Until my father moved in, it was the only adult conversation I had during the day."

Maddy burst into laughter. "I haven't reached that point yet, but there are days when I'm pretty close."

"Just wait until you have two or three of them home at the same time. It's an occupational hazard. You either start talking to yourself or end up fantasizing about Big Bird and a hot tub."

The table was strewn with sheets of scribbled-on notepaper, Maddy's Day Runner, and a big fat blue vinyl loose-leaf binder stuffed full of recipes. A stack of lists rested to the right of

Maddy's pancakes, while Claire had adorned a half-dozen paper napkins with notes, diagrams, and lists of her own.

All things considered, it had gone far better than Maddy had anticipated, and they had Olivia's decorator to thank. Their uncomfortable discussion of the upcoming radio interview was forgotten the second they unlocked the door to the old McClanahan place. Maddy had been expecting a roomful of two-by-fours, Sheetrock, and empty paint cans, not the magnificent replica of a cozy English country drawing room complete with chintz-covered overstuffed chairs, mismatched antique end tables, two working fireplaces, and a score of lamps that would do Louis Comfort Tiffany proud.

"I'll need a whole new wardrobe," Claire had breathed as they stood in the doorway.

"I'll need a whole new personality," Maddy had answered, grateful once again that she would work primarily behind the scenes.

It wasn't smoke-filled O'Malley's or the apple pie and a cup of joe atmosphere found at Julie's Coffee Shop. This was upscale, exclusive, expensive — a lot like Le Papier and The Candlelight, come to think about it. And it had *Success* stamped all over it. Ideas popped between them like corn in a movie theater as they wandered through the small space, inspected the under-construction kitchen, projected themselves two months down the road on opening day. Maddy hated to admit it, but most of the ideas were Claire's. Good ones, too. She had never really thought of Claire beyond the woman at the bar and Billy's mother. This side of her came as a complete surprise.

The ideas were still popping as they walked down the street toward Julie's, and now, two hours later, the fruits of their labor lay scattered in front of them on scraps of paper, napkins, in notebooks, and on place mats.

"So we've agreed on a severely limited menu," Maddy said, glancing down at her notes.

"Definitely," Claire said, glancing around the room for what seemed like the hundredth time since they got there. Every time the front door squeaked open, she seemed to forget Maddy was there and zero in on the newcomer until Maddy was tempted to send up a flare to remind Claire of her presence. "Classic Brit tea fare: scones, lots of cream, intricate little sandwiches and pastries. I have two books on classic English tea service. I'll use them as my references."

"What about soups? We could do soup."

"No soup. We're not a luncheonette."

"But we'll be open during lunch hour."

"You can't eat soup gracefully in a wing chair."

"I can eat soup in a moving vehicle."

"No soup," Claire repeated. "We want a simple, clear-cut culinary identity."

Sorry, Claire, you can't impress me. I watch the

315

Food Channel, too. "That will make menu planning and shopping for supplies a snap, but where will the variety come from?"

"There's a lot you can do with those little sandwiches," Claire said, "not to mention the pastries."

"I'm a pretty decent baker," Maddy said in a gesture of solidarity. "I can help with some of the baking."

"I can count," Claire shot back, "if you need some help crunching numbers."

"Hey," Maddy said, raising her hands in the air between them. "I'm trying to help."

"I don't need any help, thanks."

Maybe we could serve soup if you accepted a little. But she didn't say it, even though the words were bubbling up like a pot of Manhattan clam.

"Hey, girls." Julie's timing saved them from a possible Alexis v. Krystle moment. "I just pulled out a fresh batch of blueberry muffins. How about I top off your coffee and bring out a couple."

"You're being awfully nice today, Jules." Maddy grinned up at the older woman. "Buttering up the competition?"

"Competition?" Julie twirled her pencil between index and middle fingers. "Your frou-frou tea shop won't be any competition for me."

"Thanks a lot." Claire bristled with righteous indignation. "I think we'll do —"

"Claire, she was joking," Maddy broke in before her future sister-in-law went too far. "Right, Julie?"

"Yeah," said Julie with a puzzled expression on her face. "What the hell else would I be doing? You'll get the watercress sandwich set, and I'll pull in the BLTs on white toast. Not much overlap, if you ask me."

"You didn't need to apologize for me," Claire snapped when Julie went off to get the muffins.

"I didn't," Maddy said, struggling to rein in her rising temper. "I was trying to keep things from going too far."

"Listen." Claire leaned forward, nervous energy practically jumping from her body. "I really don't need you to intercede for me with Julie or anyone else for that matter."

"Don't worry," Maddy said. "It won't happen again."

Julie dropped a platter of warm blueberry muffins down on the table between them, topped off their coffees.

"Thanks, Jules." Maddy reached for a muffin.

"The muffins look great," Claire said with a forced smile. "Thanks."

Julie shot her a look, then walked away without a word.

Maddy knew a well-placed "I told you so" wouldn't help familial relations, but the temptation was almost overwhelming.

Claire jumped in surprise when a dark-haired man walked into the café and took a seat at the counter.

"Are you okay?" Maddy asked. "You jump every time somebody walks through the door."

"Fifth of the day." Claire raised her coffee cup by way of explanation.

"You might want to consider decaf," Maddy said. "You're practically coming out of your skin."

The front door squeaked yet again — clearly Julie was having herself a great morning — and Kelly, arms piled high with books, walked in and headed for a booth in the back.

"Kelly!" Claire called out. "Over here, honey."

Kelly looked around. Her gaze landed on Claire, then slid to Maddy, and she smiled. It wasn't quite the thousand-megawatt smile Maddy knew and loved, but who could blame her. She probably hadn't expected to find her aunt and future stepmother lying in wait. The girl was seventeen. At that age you would rather pretend you'd been raised by wolves than ac-knowledge any of your relatives.

But Aidan had done his job well. Her smile never wavered as she walked over to their table. "Hi," she said, holding her books close to her chest. "What're you guys doing here?"

Maddy opened her mouth to answer, but Claire was too quick for her. "You first, Kelly Ann. Shouldn't you be in school?"

"Free period," Kelly said with a glance in Maddy's direction. She was probably looking for a kindred spirit.

Or the nearest exit.

So am I, Kel. So am I.

Maddy made a show of checking her watch. "Rosie's going to have my head on a platter," she said, gathering up her papers into an untidy bundle. "I'm on latrine duty this afternoon." The PBS crew was moving out, and a group of seniors from Long Island were moving in, which meant major housekeeping chores were on tap. Lucy expected her to drop by for a fitting that afternoon, as well, but that was looking a little dicey.

"Are you excited about Saturday?" Kelly asked. "My father showed me an on-line brochure — wow!"

Claire gave her one of those speculative, borderline paranoid glances that seemed to be her trademark. "What's going on Saturday, and why is it in a brochure?"

"My dad and Maddy are going up to Spring Lake for the night. He found this great tower suite with a working fireplace and a balcony and an ocean view."

"That's the way you live at The Candlelight," Claire remarked. "Sounds like a busman's holiday to me."

"Except this busman doesn't have to clean the johns," Maddy said, as good-naturedly as she could manage. She smiled up at Kelly, who was taking in the byplay, spoken and unspoken, between her aunt and future stepmother. "I told Hannah you were coming over on Saturday. She's so excited."

"I thought you were coming over for supper on Saturday," Claire said to her niece.

"I said I'd try, Aunt Claire. I didn't say for sure."

"You could have told me you'd changed your mind."

"I didn't change my mind. I never said yes in the first place."

"I don't like the way you've been acting lately, miss." Claire was in full mother-as-general mode. "We need to sit down and have a long talk."

To Maddy's horror, Kelly's big blue eyes swam with tears. "I'm doing the best I can," she snapped at her aunt. "I don't know what else you want from me."

The door wasn't more than fifteen feet away from where Maddy sat, pinned between Claire's anger and Kelly's hurt. Would they hate her if she jumped up, grabbed her papers, and made a run for it? They both were staring at her like they expected her to add something to the mix, but what on earth could she say that would make the slightest difference? She wasn't part of the family, not yet at least, and she wasn't sure if her natural tendency to take Kelly's side was the right or wrong thing to do.

Claire was the one with experience. She knew what worked with kids and what didn't. Better to leave it to a woman who knew what she was doing, not to a woman who hadn't a clue.

She slid out of the booth and scooped up her

papers and Day Runner. "Claire, try to be there by eight ten on Friday, if you can. We'll go live at eight thirty-two. You'll be our last drive-time segment." She beamed a smile in Kelly's general direction. "Grab one of those blueberry muffins while they're warm, Kel. Jules outdid herself."

Cleaning johns at The Candlelight had never looked so good.

The door had barely closed behind Maddy when Aunt Claire unleashed one of her snarky comments.

"You and your father better get used to that," she snapped as Maddy moved swiftly past the front window with a wave good-bye. "Leaving seems to be what she does best."

"That's a rotten thing to say. You heard her. She has to get back to work."

"A word to the wise," her aunt said, not backing down. "That one ducks the tough questions better than the White House. It's a family trait."

It scared her the way her aunt always managed to zero in on exactly what she was thinking. Maddy was funny and warm and very understanding, but somehow every time Kelly was ready to spill her problems to her future stepmother, Maddy managed to put up an invisible barrier that made her stop short. Which was okay. It wasn't like Kelly was Hannah's age and really needed a mother to talk to.

After all, wasn't she the one other people

came to when they needed help? Her father. Her aunt. Her friends. Everyone knew they could always rely on Kelly.

Her aunt didn't stop for breath. She leaped from complaining about Maddy to grilling Kelly about why she wasn't in school, why she was there in the coffee shop in the middle of the morning, why nobody had told her about her dad and Maddy's Spring Lake weekend.

"I thought you knew," Kelly said, hoping her aunt would forget she wasn't answering any of her other questions. "It's just one night. What's the big deal?"

"The big deal is that there's a bar to run. I wasn't planning to work Saturday night, and now I'll have to."

"So don't work. It's not like you're going to be there much longer, right?"

"I don't like that tone of voice, Kel."

And maybe I don't like being treated like a four-year-old. "If you have a problem with Maddy, why don't you talk to her about it? I don't see why I should be put in the middle."

"Nobody's putting you in the middle. I was simply —"

"Just because you're unhappy doesn't mean everyone else has to be unhappy, too." The words spilled out before Kelly could stop them. She hadn't meant to say them, but once they were out, she couldn't pull them back. "Why can't you just let things change without making everyone feel guilty about it?"

She had seen her aunt angry before, and she had seen her hurt. But she had never seen her defeated. She looked like her world was about to come crashing down around her shoulders as she gathered up her notebooks and random sheets of paper, then slid out of the booth.

"Aunt Claire, don't go! I'm so sorry. I didn't mean to —" She reached out, but it was too late. Maddy wasn't the only one with a talent for making an exit.

"What's with her this morning?" Julie asked as she deposited Kelly's hot tea and dry toast in front of her. "She was jumping out of her skin every time the door opened."

"I don't know," she said. "She did seem kind of frazzled, didn't she?" Which was putting it mildly. And why would her aunt care who came and went from the coffee shop?

"That's one way to put it. She walked out without paying her bill."

Kelly reached for her tote bag. "I'll take care of it."

"You keep your money, sweetie. I'll start a tab for her. That's one woman I wouldn't mind having something on."

So far, this wasn't turning out to be one of her better mornings. After puking her guts out in the bathroom during gym class, all she had wanted to do was get as far away from the curious looks as possible. The last thing she'd expected was to walk into Julie's and find Claire and Maddy sitting there, shooting eye daggers at each other. Aunt Claire's radar was starting to pick up signs of trouble on the horizon, and it wouldn't be long before she confronted Kelly head-on with her suspicions.

Her father sensed something was wrong, too. He kept setting up opportunities for her to run to him and dump her problems in his lap the way she used to do when she was a little girl. He loved her. He wanted to help her. How could she tell him that she had moved beyond his reach?

I'm pregnant.

The words rattled around her brain like pebbles in a tin can, like random words — *diesel, peony* — tossed together by chance.

I'm pregnant.

She couldn't run away from it any longer, couldn't pretend it wasn't happening, that it was nothing but cold ice cream on an empty stomach or a low-grade flu that would disappear in a couple of days.

I'm pregnant.

She was almost three weeks late.

She threw up almost every single day.

Her breasts were so sore it hurt to put on her bra.

Last night she had stayed up until almost four, searching the Web for everything she could find about pregnancy, symptoms, alternatives. The amount of information out there was staggering, and no matter how she tried to spin it, she couldn't run away from the truth.

Okay, so she hadn't run a home test yet, but that would just be confirming what she already knew inside her heart.

I'm pregnant.

She waited for the flood of emotion she had always believed would follow that realization, but nothing happened. Shouldn't she be feeling something? Last week the idea that she might be carrying a baby inside her had sent her into a near meltdown, but now she felt nothing. No terror. No joy.

Nothing but a huge, yawning emptiness where her future used to be.

She opened a notebook to a blank page and uncapped her pen. Making lists always helped her to clarify her thoughts. Somehow seeing the problem laid out in black and white, the components neatly numbered and in order, made anything seem manageable. Grandma Irene had taught her the value of list-making when she first started grade school. All you had to do was capture the problem, and the solution would follow.

Maybe Grandma Irene was watching over her right now, nudging her toward the path she was meant to follow. It was a nice thought, even if she really didn't believe it.

She was in this alone.

She drew a vertical line down the center of the page. That seemed a logical way to begin. On the left she would put all the reasons why she should keep the baby. On the right she would list the reasons why she shouldn't.

The right side filled up quickly.

She was too young.

She had no money and Seth had even less.

They both had full scholarships to Columbia and a world opening up before them that most definitely did not include a baby.

She and Seth had planned out their life together years ago. They shared the same goals, the same ambitions, the same dreams. First school, then the fun of seeing all of that schooling, all of that hard work, channeled into the challenge of launching their careers. They were going to do great things. They dreamed big, and they knew how to make those dreams come true. Together they could make a difference in the world.

One day, in the shadowy far-off future, there would be babies but not yet. Not for a very long time. She didn't want to end up like her Aunt Claire, angry and trapped and so jealous of everyone she could barely see straight.

Once again Grandma Irene was right. All she had to do was look at the list, and her path was clear.

Eleven reasons why this wasn't the time to have a baby.

Not one single reason why it was.

She stared down at the expanse of white space and the pale blue horizontal lines on the left side and waited for something, anything, to materialize, but nothing did.

Only one decision made any sense at all, no

matter how you twisted or spun the facts. Saturday morning she would drive over to the CVS at the mall and buy a home pregnancy test, just to be sure, and then she would do what she had to do before too much more time elapsed.

She had to talk to Seth. He had the right to know what she was thinking, how she was feeling. She also knew that he would support whatever decision she made. He had sworn to be with her every step of the way, and she believed in him. She had always believed in him. He would understand and be there for her, just as he had promised.

"Need more tea?" Julie paused, coffeepot in hand, next to her table.

"I'm okay."

"Eat the toast," Julie urged. "Don't make me give it to the gulls. Those greedy beggars scrounge enough off me as it is."

Kelly nodded and pretended to take a bite of toast, but the second Julie moved away, she put it back on the plate. Her stomach had finally settled down. There was no point in pressing her luck.

She had done enough of that already.

"Hey, watch where you're going with that thing, Claire!" Frankie, the produce manager, leaped aside as Claire's shopping cart barely missed his left hip. "I don't have collision on my ass."

"I'm sorry, Frankie." She spiked a bunch of

celery into her cart. Nothing like taking out your aggressions on innocent vegetables. "I didn't see you standing there."

Frankie glanced down at his aproned bulk. "Didn't see me? I weigh two hundred eighty pounds. They can see me on Mars."

"Everyone's a comedian," she said with a shake of her head. "Are you out of string beans?"

"We're out of everything. The farm truck's behind schedule. Come back around four."

"Like I have nothing better to do than make a second run to Super Fresh."

"Whaddya want from me, Claire? We're out of string beans. You want 'em, you come back. We're not Ray's Pizza. We don't make deliveries."

By the time she pulled into her driveway, she had managed to alienate the checkout clerk, the pharmacist, and every driver who had the misfortune to be on the road with her. That sparring contest with Maddy had gotten under her skin more than she had realized. The sight of that small diamond sparkling on her left ring finger had seemed to awaken every ugly emotion she had spent a lifetime tamping down and send them spilling out across the table.

It wasn't that she wished for Aidan to be alone, because she didn't. He deserved happiness. God knows, so did she, but happiness showed up where and when it wanted, and this time it was Aidan's turn. But she wasn't convinced Maddy Bainbridge would be around for the long haul. There was something about her, an impermanence, that irked Claire, as if the woman always knew the exact distance between herself and the nearest exit.

Just look at the way she had acted at the coffee shop. She couldn't get away from there fast enough when Claire and Kelly tangled. The woman had almost left skid marks on Julie's freshly waxed floor as she sprinted toward freedom. That wasn't the kind of wife Aidan needed, and it sure as hell wasn't the kind of stepmother who could steer Kelly through her college years. The first sign of trouble, real trouble, would send her running for her life.

Not that it was any of her business. Aidan could marry whomever he wanted to marry. There was nothing she could do about it. She was there to advise him if he wanted her advice. She was there to help Kelly if she wanted her help. If they didn't want her — well, that was their mistake. She would still be there when they finally came to their senses.

Her father was sitting at the kitchen table eating a tuna sandwich when she came in through the back door schlepping a trio of grocery bags.

"You look like a sherpa," he observed, looking up from his paperback Spenser mystery.

"An old sherpa," she said as she dropped the bags on the counter near the sink. "I could use a hand unloading the trunk."

"Why do you think your mother and I had so many kids," he said, folding down the corner of a page. "No more trunks to unload, lawns to mow, or sidewalks to shovel."

She couldn't help laughing. "It didn't work for me either, Pop. Finish your sandwich first. The cat litter can wait."

"Guess who's home for the weekend?"

She quickly ran through the possibilities. "It can't be Kathleen. I didn't see her car."

"She bummed a ride with one of her friends."

"Where is she?"

"Sacked out in her old room." Her father took a gulp of Pepsi.

"Is she all right? Why did she come down for the weekend? She isn't —"

"She's fine," he said. "She needed a quiet place to finish writing her school paper."

Claire's knees went weak with relief, and she sank down onto a chair opposite her father.

"You've got to lighten up," he said, observing her trembling hands. "She's doing great now."

"I know, but —"

"She's all grown, Claire. You've done everything you can do. Now it's up to her."

"You weren't here when she was in trouble, Pop. You don't know what it was like."

"I'm old, but I'm not stupid. You think I don't know what addiction's all about?"

If you weren't there for the visits to the ER, the near misses, the screaming fights, the terror of almost losing your firstborn, you didn't have a clue. But there was no point to saying any of it. He loved Kathleen, and his belief in her had never wavered, not even when Claire and Billy had feared the worst. What were facts and figures compared with that kind of unconditional support?

"You're right," she said, patting him on the arm. "I worry too much."

"So what else is new?" He pushed half of his sandwich toward her. "I'm saving room for those brownies you made last night."

She reached for the sandwich and took a bite. "I thought you were laying off desserts for a while."

"Next week." He finished off his Pepsi. "So how did it go this morning at Olivia's place?"

"Don't ask."

"You and Rosie's girl had a problem?"

"Can you believe she tried to undermine my position at Cuppa by trying to take over some of the baking?"

"She's a lousy cook?"

"I don't know," she said. "And besides, that's not the point."

"So what is? You want to bust your behind working two jobs for one salary?"

"It's only temporary. We'll be hiring somebody to help out with the baking once we get up and running." Olivia didn't want to miss the high tourist season, which meant an accelerated and possibly somewhat rocky start-up. She knew that when she agreed to come aboard.

"Since when are any of your kids afraid of hard work?"

"Work smart," he said, "not hard. You don't have to do it all yourself, Claire. Do what all the big shots do: learn to delegate. That's the ticket."

"You really have to stop watching *The Apprentice*, Pop. We're talking tea and cookies, not multimillion dollar mergers."

"Listen to your old man on this. You gotta give a little to get a lot, kiddo. That's the real secret to getting along in this world."

"A disaster?" Rose asked as she scoured the commode. "How so?"

Maddy looked up from the tub she had been scrubbing. "I took off from Julie's like I had a rocket in my pocket. You're looking at a gold-medal-winning escape artist."

"I'm sure it wasn't that bad."

"It was worse. The second they started arguing, all I could think about was how fast I could get out of there." She dried off the soap holder and placed a wrapped and fragrant bar of French-milled soap on the ledge. "I'm a coward."

"You did what any sane woman would do in a similar situation. You excused yourself from a family argument."

"I bailed out on Kelly."

"Is that how it seemed to you?" Rose wiped down the lid with disinfectant.

"Every time she looks to me for advice, I start looking for ways to change the subject. What's wrong with me?" She arranged minibottles of shampoo and conditioner in the amenities basket, then piled it high with beribboned packets of sweet herbal bath salts. "I'm thirty-three years old. I'm a mother. Why do I want to run every time Kelly looks like she's about to confide in me?" Worse yet, was she going to feel the same way when Hannah was seventeen and in trouble?

"You're a lot like I was."

"Very funny."

"I'm serious." She motioned for Maddy to add one more packet of bath salts. "I can't count the times I did the same thing when you were growing up."

"Maybe in an alternate universe," Maddy said with a laugh. "The Rose DiFalco I grew up with had the answer for everything, including the whereabouts of Jimmy Hoffa."

"I did a pretty good job of faking it, didn't I? Half the time I felt like I was only a half step ahead of you and losing ground fast."

Maddy wiped the mirror clean with long, vertical strokes. "There's no softness in Claire. She wants Kelly to adhere to some arbitrary rules that were set up a long time ago. Her words were whizzing right over the girl's head, and she didn't even know it."

"It's hard to let go, honey, no matter how many times you've done it."

"So why do I feel so guilty? None of this has anything to do with me. What difference is it to me if Claire and Kelly have a spat?"

Rose sat back on her heels and brushed a lock of hair off her forehead. "If you really feel that way, maybe it's time you did some thinking about your future with Aidan."

"That's a hell of a thing to say."

"You're not just marrying a man, honey, you're marrying a family, same as Aidan is. He has every right to expect the same commitment to his daughter that you expect him to feel for yours."

"I'm very fond of Kelly."

"She has enough friends. She needs a mother."

"We've been down this road, Ma. She has Claire."

"Claire isn't her mother."

"Neither am I."

"You can only turn her away so many times, Madelyn. God willing, you and Aidan have a long life together ahead of you, and Kelly is going to be part of it. The decisions you make now are going to influence the future in ways you can't even begin to imagine."

"Geez, Ma, we're beginning to sound like a *Lifetime* movie. All we need is for your long-lost secret child to show up at the door."

"Excuse me." Crystal rapped on the doorframe, and both women burst into gales of laughter. "Was it something I said?"

That, of course, generated more laughter.

"Your timing was perfect," Maddy said when she regained at least a little bit of her composure. "We had just conjured up my mother's long-lost secret child."

The poor girl looked totally confused. "Whatever. I just wanted to tell you we're leaving now."

"I thought you were going to film check-in." Rose was the only woman Maddy had ever seen who could look elegant policing a bathroom.

"We'll be back. Beep Peter's cell when the bus rolls in, and we'll come right over."

"We're not going to hold things up," Rose warned her. "If you're here, you're here. I don't inconvenience my guests for anyone."

"Gotcha, Mrs. D. You do what you have to do. We'll work around you." Suddenly she seemed to take in the scene in front of her: scrub brushes, pails filled with soapy water, toilet brush, and industrial-strength, environmentally friendly cleaning products, all wielded by two women on their knees. "Wow! You mean you guys clean your own bathrooms?"

"Who on earth did she think did the cleaning around here anyway?" Rose demanded after Crystal disappeared. "House elves?"

"Let's face it, Ma: you don't exactly look like a charwoman." She gestured toward her own grubby jeans and faded T-shirt from a long-ago Rolling Stones concert at the Meadowlands. "Whereas your daughter . . ."

"Please don't tell me that's the same shirt you wore in high school."

"You won't hear it from me."

"You always did get emotionally attached to your clothing."

"Remember my favorite pair of Jordache jeans?"

"The ones you insisted had to be dry-cleaned."

"At thirteen it made sense to me."

"Remember that when Hannah turns thirteen, and you can't pry her favorite pair out of her hands."

They fell into companionable silence, punctuated only by the swish of water over tile or the soft sound of fresh, fluffy towels sliding into position in the built-in cabinet.

"We make a great team," Rose said as they lugged cleaning paraphernalia downstairs to the utility room.

"We do, don't we?" The realization caught Maddy by surprise. "When did that happen?"

"About two decades later than I had hoped," Rose said with her characteristic honesty.

"It better not take Claire and me that long at Cuppa. As it is, our acting skills are going to be stretched to the max tomorrow." Maddy's optimism for the success of their business relationship was fading fast. "At least conflict is good for the ratings."

"Conflict might be good for ratings," her mother said, "but it doesn't wear well on a daily basis."

"Tell me something I don't know." The first thirty-something years of Maddy's life as a daughter were proof of that.

"Lucy called while you were out," Rose said as they settled down in the kitchen over a pitcher of iced tea. "She asked if you could postpone the fitting until next week. Her arthritis is acting up, and her hands won't behave."

"No problem," Maddy said. "I'll call her, and we'll reschedule."

"And you'd better check your messages. Fred from the radio station was trying to find you. He said he called your cell, but there was no answer."

Maddy made a small gesture of resigned embarrassment. "Guess I forgot to recharge it again."

"Madelyn, what on earth is the point to having a cell phone if you don't keep the battery charged?"

"I like the way it looks dangling uselessly from my belt loop."

"Go check your voice mail."

"Later."

"He called a few hours ago."

"Ma, enough. I'll check for messages in a little while, okay?"

"You're being irresponsible."

"Why? Because I don't think a cell phone has to be an electronic leash?" She conveniently chose to ignore the many times that electronic leash had made life a whole lot easier when it was tugging at someone else.

"You're just like your father. God forbid he should check for messages when he's out driving around like a teenager with a brand-new license. The two of you are like peas in a pod."

Maddy kissed her mother on the cheek. "Thanks," she said. "That's one of the nicest things you've ever said to me."

Rose tried to look stern, but the twinkle in her eye — a twinkle that just might have been there many other times when Maddy was too busy or too angry to notice — gave her away.

"I think so, too," she said. "Now check for your messages, and let's get back to work."

Chapter Seventeen

Corin Flynn had faced down snipers in Sarajevo, survived the rocky mountains of Afghanistan, and the terror-filled streets of Baghdad, without flinching. He had known fear, known it intimately, and he knew how to use that fear to propel himself deeper into situations a sane man would run from. Fear was a good thing, a motivator. Fear taught you to trust your gut instincts, even though reason was pulling you in the opposite direction.

But nothing he had ever experienced staring up at a Kalashnikov held by a terrified sixteen-year-old boy with nothing left to lose came close to what he felt when he pulled into the Joyce Kilmer Rest Stop on the New Jersey Turnpike and finally lost his nerve.

He broke into a cold sweat eight miles away from Newark Liberty Airport as the land gradually lost its urban-industrial edge and grew greener, more suburban.

The twitch beneath his left eye kicked in south of The Oranges.

By the time he climbed from behind the wheel of his rented Ford and headed for the low brick building that housed public bathrooms, two fast-food restaurants, and an information center, the adrenaline was flowing so hard and fast he felt like it was morning in Kabul where the sound of machine gun fire and rocket explosions took the place of a snooze alarm.

A man couldn't stay angry forever. He knew that. The deep, gut-twisting anger he had felt the last time he saw her had been replaced by an emptiness that nothing could fill. He had traveled the world in search of the one thing that would make him forget her, plugging in danger for love, and still coming up empty. In the last eight years he had gained a reputation for being a risk-taker, the guy with the camera who walked where sane men feared to tread. Somewhere along the way he had acquired a career, a damn good one at that, and made a name for himself, but that emptiness inside just kept on growing bigger.

He bought a large black coffee from Mickey D's — more caffeine, yeah that was what he needed — and stepped back outside to breathe in the mingled scents of new trees and old petroleum and found himself thrown back through time to the day he learned there were ways to kill a man that had nothing to do with bullets.

He finished his coffee, fantasized a cigarette, then tossed the empty cup into a trash bin a few feet away. The sun was beginning to rise over a stand of wobbly pine trees across the highway. With a little luck he'd reach Paradise Point in time for breakfast.

He had asked Olivia to tell Claire he was coming and why. She had been through hell these last few years, and he wouldn't do anything to complicate her life any more than her husband's death already had. He wanted to see her just one more time, hear the sound of her voice. He wanted to make sure that the life she had chosen was still the one she needed to be happy. He would do what he was being paid to do — capture images of a town and its people — and then he would forget Claire O'Malley had ever existed.

And maybe one day he might even stop loving her.

Maddy and her crew were already at O'Malley's when Claire arrived. She had set her alarm for five-thirty so she would have time to shower, wash her hair, try to tame it with a whip and chair, and obsess over her pathetic excuse for a grown-up wardrobe.

"It's a radio show," her father had pointed out as she gratefully accepted a cup of coffee from him just before she spun out the door. "You look fine."

There were two ways of looking at that statement. *You look fine . . . for radio,* or *You look fine, and yes, I know other adults are actually going to see you.* She had the sinking feeling the former came closer to the truth than the latter ever would, but she didn't have time for an extreme makeover. A swipe of lipstick, a handful of Tic Tacs, and a quick Hail Mary, and she was out the door.

"Hey, Claire!" Maddy hailed her from across the bar. "Help yourself to some coffee. I'll be with you in a sec."

Help yourself to some coffee? Like Claire wasn't the one who usually made the coffee 365 days a year at O'Malley's.

"She didn't mean it that way." Aidan startled her out of her surly train of thought. "You've watched her run interviews here before. That's what she says to all her guests."

It was, but Claire refused to be mollified.

"Got the jitters?"

She shook her head. "Why should I? It's just local radio."

He gave her a look she didn't feel like analyzing, then rejoined the crowd of half-asleep regulars at the bar, one of whom was a sparklingly wide-awake Olivia.

"Took you long enough," Claire complained when the woman finally joined her in exile halfway between the crowd at the bar and Maddy's crew near the window. "I was beginning to think there was something going on between you and Mel Perry."

"And when there is, you'll be the first to know, I promise you." She lowered her voice.

342

"No word from Corin, but Peter says he's scheduled for a shoot on the dock tomorrow morning so . . ."

"It doesn't make any difference to me, Liv. Our moment came and went a long time ago."

"Really?" Olivia arched a brow. "I hear you've been jumping out of your skin around here every time the door opens."

The door squeaked open on cue, but Claire steadfastly kept her gaze locked and loaded on her friend.

Olivia waggled her fingers over Claire's left shoulder. "Good morning, Mr. Fenelli. Aren't you looking well this fine day!"

Strange how relief and disappointment could feel so much alike. She turned around and smiled as David joined them.

"Don't you ever work?" she teased him.

"One of the bennies of self-employment," he said. "You can take a morning off to cheer on a friend."

He was right. They had become friends somewhere along the way. She wondered when it had happened.

"Thanks," she said, aware of Olivia's curious gaze. "I need all the support I can get."

"You'll knock 'em dead." He gave her one of those endearingly goofy smiles. "How about I take you to breakfast when you're through?"

Olivia gave one of those theatrical coughs favored by sitcom actresses and women who will not be ignored.

"You, too, Olivia," David said. "I'd love it if you joined us."

"Sure you would," Olivia drawled as she patted his arm lightly, "but I'm afraid I have to say no. I have a store to run and employees to badger."

David was too polite to look relieved as he met Claire's eyes again. "So how about it?"

There were a million reasons not to, but a civilized breakfast with an ordinary, everyday, run-of-the-mill nice guy sounded like exactly what she needed. "Sounds great," she said, "provided we don't go to Julie's."

"Paula's Pancake Palace," he said. "It's in —"

"Bayport," she said. "The blueberry pecan silver dollars are to die for."

"Interesting," Olivia said when he excused himself to grab some coffee at the bar. "Since when are you two breakfast buddies?"

"Since right now."

"He's smitten."

"Will you keep your voice down?"

"The signs are all there." Olivia was nothing if not relentless. "Goofy smile. Sweaty palms. A twinkle in his —"

"Sorry to interrupt." It was Maddy's assistant Angie. "I need to do a sound check." She smiled up at Claire. "It's painless. I promise."

Easy for her to say. She was on the other side of the microphone.

"You're looking a tad green about the gills," Olivia observed when Angie walked away.

"I don't think I can do it. You're the one who should be giving the interview, not me."

"Of course you can do it." Olivia placed her hands on Claire's shoulders and turned her away from the door. "Maddy gave you a list of questions she might ask. All you have to do is stay focused and remember to plug Cuppa every chance you get. How hard is that?"

She sucked in her stomach and glanced at her reflection in the mirrored wall behind the bar. "I should've worn the black pants with the silk blazer. I look like a blimp in this skirt."

Olivia looked queasy. "You mean those hideous pants with the elastic waistband? Over my dead body."

"I look six months pregnant in this sweater. I should never have quit smoking."

"You look smashing. My wrists are bigger than your thighs. Go near one cigarette, and you'll answer to me. Besides, this is a radio interview. You could be stark naked for all anyone will know."

Claire laughed despite herself. "Believe me, if you saw my stretch marks —"

"No excuses," Olivia cut her off. "We're in this together. I did an interview with Maddy two weeks ago. Rosie is on next month. Now it's your turn. I warned you there would be a lot of publicity events involved in launching the tea shop."

"I thought that meant you wanted me to bake cookies for reporters. If you'd told me it meant panty hose and lipstick, I might've thought twice."

When Olivia laughed, men dropped to their knees and thanked their Maker. Like right now. The same old goats who had barely grunted at Claire ten minutes ago looked up in Rockette unison from their copies of the *Racing Form* at the sound of Olivia's laughter. To a man, they sat up a little straighter, smoothed down the memory of hair, and flashed removable smiles 1-800-Dentist would be proud of.

"How do you do that?" Claire wondered as Olivia waggled her beringed fingers in the direction of her adoring geriatric fan club. "When I laugh, they turn up the volume on the TV."

"Of course they do. You're family." Olivia upped the wattage on her smile. "I, however, am still the mysterious stranger."

Claire felt an eye roll coming on. "You've been here over two years."

"That doesn't matter. I didn't grow up here. They never saw me in braces or a training bra —"

"You wore a training bra?" She clapped her hands over her ears. "Please! Leave me with my illusions."

"See what I mean? A touch of mystery is a powerful tool for a woman. You should try it."

"I'm almost forty. If I was going to be mysterious, I should've started sooner." Claire glanced pointedly in the general direction of

Olivia's spectacular cleavage. "Maybe I'll buy a Wonder Bra instead."

"You don't need a Wonder Bra. You just need to start going out more."

"I go out plenty," Claire said. "I go to Super Fresh. I go to meet Billy Jr. at the bus stop. I go to the dentist and to church and —"

"You know what I'm talking about."

"The same thing you're always talking about, and I'm still not interested."

"Of course you're interested. You just can't bring yourself to admit it."

She had to hand it to Olivia. Five minutes ago she wouldn't have believed anybody could manage to take her mind off her stage fright. Nothing like an old argument to help a woman refocus.

"I'm having breakfast with David. That should —"

"Thirty seconds," Angie called out. "Let's go! We need a mike check."

"Break a leg, Claire." Olivia gave her a push, and Claire found herself hurtling toward either certain death or public humiliation. At that moment, she wasn't sure which option was worse.

Maddy, her future almost sister-in-law, gave her an encouraging smile as Angie, who didn't look old enough to be out without her mother, pushed a chair under her rear end.

"Count one to ten one more time," Maddy told her, "so they can be sure you're miked properly."

"One . . . two . . . three . . . four . . ."

"Got it." Angie checked her watch. "Back on in three seconds."

"I think I'm going to be sick," Claire said, grabbing Maddy's hands. "Maybe you should —"

Too late.

Angie pointed to Maddy.

Maddy smiled, then leaned forward toward the microphone.

And that was the moment when Claire's brain shut down.

"This is Maddy Bainbridge. We're live at O'Malley's on The Pier in historic Paradise Point on the beautiful Jersey Shore with co-owner Claire O'Malley, who is about to join forces with Olivia Westmore, Rose DiFalco, and yours truly at . . ."

Olivia, cleavage billowing, beamed encouragement from the sidelines while she sipped a latte from the new cappuccino machine they had installed to entice the more upscale market. So far, none of the regulars wanted anything but suds or a plain old cup of joe but —

Oh God. Stop daydreaming! Maddy was winding up the introduction, and any second she would expect Claire to say something halfway entertaining, and her mind was nothing but dead air space. *You're the mother of five . . . you've changed diapers in the back of a VW . . . you can make a Halloween costume in three minutes flat while waiting for the school bus — a measly radio interview should be a piece of —*

Cake! Was that it? She was supposed to be talking about all the cakes and petit fours and buttery, expensive cookies bursting with chocolate that she would be baking and serving up at Cuppa on a daily basis, about how her fairy godmothers, in the form of Olivia Westmore and Rose DiFalco, had offered her the chance of a lifetime. Who would have guessed those years of producing chocolate chip cookies for the school bake fair would be her way out of what had become a safe and comfortable place to hide.

She sucked in a gulp of oxygen, squared her shoulders, and pulled herself together on behalf of overworked, underslept mothers everywhere and let it rip.

She was loose. She was funny. And, God help her, she was even sincere. She wanted Cuppa to be a success, and she wanted to be one of the main reasons. She had never been particularly ambitious. Her focus for the last twenty years had been her children and family, and O'Malley's got whatever part of her was left over. This was different. She knew exactly what Cuppa needed, knew what women would be looking for in a tea shop and how to provide it, and that gut-level intensity powered her interview with Maddy, who, Claire couldn't help but notice, started looking a tad shell-shocked as the minutes passed.

But everyone else seemed to be enjoying the show. Aidan grinned at her from behind the bar. The old guys managed to stay awake. And

David Fenelli, aka Ryan's father, flashed her a thumbs-up.

"You were great," Maddy said during a commercial break after the interview ended. "My producer said phone lines at the station are popping. I think everyone loves the idea that a woman raising five kids alone can take on so many challenges and make them all work."

"Better not ask me to take a polygraph on that last one." Claire reached for a glass of water. "I can't remember anything I said."

"Most of my guests say the same thing. There's a kind of self-inflicted amnesia that —" Maddy glanced over Claire's left shoulder and whistled softly. "Would somebody tell me how Olivia does it? A second ago there wasn't a man under sixty-five in the place, and now she has a major hunk draped across her shoulders like a pashmina wrap."

"I think she grows them in her basement," Claire said as she turned around to see who Maddy was talking about. "A little peat moss, some Bud Light, Three Stooges reruns, and —"

He smiled at her. Or maybe it was only the memory of his smile that she saw. Her first thought was that God was playing another one of his little jokes on her, like cellulite and freckles and the inability to not say exactly what she was thinking.

Her second thought was that time hadn't been kind to either one of them. He was leaner, tougher in ways she couldn't imagine. His thick, dark hair had gone completely silver. His deep brown eyes were almost lost in a network of lines and creases. His life was in his eyes. The anger, the mistakes, those lost days . . .

". . . God forbid he should call first," Olivia said, her words fighting to be heard against the rush of memory inside Claire's head. She could feel the heat of his body warming the fabric of his shirt . . . smell the clean, salty tang of his skin —

"Maddy, I want you to meet my baby brother, Corin Flynn."

Maddy extended her hand. "Corin Flynn, the photographer?"

"Guilty."

"Corin's notorious for not answering his phone calls," Olivia said, sounding like an over-indulgent big sister. "He'd rather fly halfway around the world to say hello than pick up a phone."

He called me every night for weeks, Livvy . . . the sound of his voice was my lullaby. . . .

"You should give him lessons, Claire," Maddy said. "Nobody knows how to organize the way you do."

You asked me to come away with you that last night . . . you said they didn't need me the way you did, but you were wrong. This is my home, Corin. You don't belong here.

"Nice to see you again, Claire."

"It's good to see you, too." *Go away. Please, if you ever felt anything at all for me, you'll leave.*

"You two know each other?" Maddy asked.

351

"Fifteen seconds," Angie called out.

"The Meehans and the Flynns were next-door neighbors down in Boca," Olivia explained, hanging on to her baby brother's arm. "We're all old friends."

I owe you big time, Liv.

"Ten seconds, Maddy!" Poor Angie sounded frantic.

"Gotta go," Maddy apologized. "I'll catch you guys later." She had an extra smile for Corin. "I'd love to interview you about your time in Afghan—"

"Maddy!" Angie's voice rang out.

Seconds later Maddy was back behind the microphone, interviewing Peter Lassiter and his assistant Crystal about the Paradise Point documentary. Claire listened for a few seconds, then her gut-level dislike of Lassiter and his crew took over, and she moved toward the crowd of regulars at the bar where Corin and Olivia quickly joined her.

"She's good," Corin said about Maddy. "Very easy and natural."

"Isn't she?" Olivia agreed. "One day somebody's going to hear one of her broadcasts and snap her right up."

They waited for Claire to add her compliments into the mix, but a nasty, jealous demon had control of her tongue. "And here I thought Cuppa was her holy calling."

"Meow," Olivia said. "Is there a problem brewing?"

"Just being a wiseass," Claire said, painfully aware of Corin's nearness . . . and the intensity of his scrutiny. "You know my creed: no straight lines left behind."

She waved at David Fenelli, who took that as encouragement and crossed the room to join them. He said hello to Olivia, who introduced him to Corin. The two men exchanged reasonably pleasant greetings and a handshake.

"You were great," David said as he turned to Claire. "You knocked 'em dead."

She preened a little bit more than she might have without an audience. "You really think so?"

"I really think so."

"Oh, Claire!" Olivia gave her forearm an affectionate squeeze. "In all the commotion about seeing Corin again, I forgot to tell you: you were fan-tas-tic! You and Maddy sounded like a comedy tag team."

"Swell," Claire said. "That'll sell a lot of tea."

"Don't underestimate the power of humor," David said. "Who said tea and laughter don't go together?"

Corin said nothing. He observed the byplay between Claire and David, the byplay between Claire and Olivia, and she knew he was trying to calculate the relationships, trying to fit them into the viewfinder he carried around inside his head.

David checked his watch. "Still time to catch the blueberry pecan, if you're ready to go."

"Let me tell Aidan I'm leaving, and we're out of here."

She spoke quickly to Aidan, who was so focused on Maddy that he barely paid attention, then ducked into the bathroom and ran her fingers through her mop of red curls and tried not to notice the lines on her forehead and the shadows beneath her eyes.

"Relax," she told her reflection. The worst was over. They had made it past the first awkward hellos, past the initial shock of discovering time hadn't exactly stood still for either one of them. The earth didn't stop spinning on its axis. There were no hearts and flowers. No sweet love songs. When their eyes met, she had seen nothing more than polite interest, which she returned in kind.

They were just a middle-aged woman and a middle-aged man who had known each other once a very long time ago and lived to tell the tale.

Olivia put her hand on Corin's arm as Claire and the guy with glasses headed for the door. "Let her go," she said quietly. "You'll only end up with a broken heart."

"I wasn't going anywhere," he lied as Claire walked past the window, laughing.

Olivia linked her arm through Corin's and drew him toward the crowd of regulars clustered at the other end of the bar. "Let me introduce you to my friends," she said. "They'll have lots of ideas about who and what you should photograph."

That wasn't the way he worked as a rule. His photos were spontaneous, born of the moment, a quick flicker of time captured before it slid into the past and disappeared. Only for an old friend like Dean would he get himself trapped in a Jersey Shore town, snapping picture postcards of renovated diners and the corner church.

Only to see Claire again.

Her sorrows showed clearly on her face. In the way she carried herself. The look in her eyes when she saw him again. There had always been something fragile beneath her sharp-edged, competent exterior. A tender vulnerability she worked very hard to hide from the world.

"Come here, little Brother." Olivia tugged at his arm. "If you don't want to photograph Barney's tattoo, I'll eat my Jimmy Choos."

Barney was a burly firefighter on the dark side of fifty, one of the crew who had been on duty the day Billy O'Malley died. The tattoo was an intricate depiction of a stretch of beach overlaid with flames and the year 2001. Every man who had been on duty that day bore the same indelible badge of honor.

"Liv's right," he said to Barney. "How would you feel about letting me snap a few pictures later today?"

"Come by the firehouse after four," Barney Kurkowski said. "I'll show you around."

He was Olivia's brother, and that seemed to

be good enough reason for them to let him into their lives.

Olivia's new friends were a varied lot. Grocery clerks. Bank tellers. Doctors. Lawyers. Retired cops and firefighters. Teachers. Insurance salespeople. Unemployed dock workers, down-on-their-luck fishermen, and a few six-figure entrepreneurs thrown in for good measure. No caste system there on the Jersey Shore. His sister might love fancy cars, fine wines, and big diamonds, but she wasn't a snob. Paradise Point was a good fit for her. She dazzled the old guys, charmed the young ones, and was a good friend to them all. Even better, that friendship seemed to be returned in full measure. He was glad to see she had found a place to call home at last. One of the Flynn kids was bound to get it right sooner or later, and he was glad it was Olivia.

A young woman walked through the front door and was greeted with a storm of greetings. Tall, slender, with freckles and curls the color of a newly minted penny — she seemed familiar. The owner of the bar, Claire's brother-in-law Aidan, moved toward her as fast as his pronounced limp would allow and enveloped the girl in a bear hug.

". . . studying for finals . . ." he heard Aidan say.

She had a clear, sweet laugh that made you feel like smiling. One of those happy girls the gods loved. "It's too noisy in the dorm," she said, waving at some of the old guys standing next to Corin. "I figured I'd come home, hole up in my old room, and pig out on Ma's —" Her clear-eyed gaze brushed over him, hesitated, then returned. Her brows slid downward, then quickly relaxed into their normal position. "— macadamia nut cookies," she continued smoothly.

"You could use a few pounds," Aidan said. "You're as skinny as your mother."

"Not to hear her tell it. Since she quit smoking . . ."

The words all blurred together until they were white noise deep inside his head. Kathleen. It had to be. The only one of Claire's girls who had kept her distance from him during that magical time, watching the progress of their romance with eyes that had seen far too much already.

"Toss me your keys," he said to Olivia, who was batting her eyelashes at a man old enough to be their grandfather. "I need to crash."

She pulled a pair of keys on a leather fob from her enormous handbag. "Here," she said, pressing them into his hand. "I made up a room for you, and there's plenty to eat in the fridge. Help yourself."

He gave her a quick one-arm hug.

"It'll get easier," she whispered in his ear. "I promise."

Sure it would. But with luck he'd be long gone when it did.

"You're not eating your pancakes." Claire gestured toward David's plate with her fork. "Come on, David. They're getting cold."

He made a halfhearted attempt at downing a few bites, then pushed his plate away from him. "I'm no good at games, Claire."

She poured more butter pecan syrup over her short stack. "Too bad," she said, mustering up a smile. "I happen to be the world's greatest armchair *Wheel of Fortune* player in Paradise Point."

He didn't smile back at her. "That's not what I'm talking about."

"Then maybe you'd better tell me what you are talking about." Billy Jr. and Ryan hadn't had a falling out. At least not one she knew about. "I know I haven't been carrying my share of the load the last few days. I promise I'll fax you a copy of the catering menu for the soccer dinner —"

"Was it serious?"

She had never felt more clueless in her life. "I don't know. Maybe you'd better tell me what 'it' is before I answer."

"Olivia's brother."

She couldn't speak. She didn't want to lie, and she couldn't tell the truth.

"Okay," he said after a long, uncomfortable silence. "It's not my business. I know that."

"So why did you ask?"

"I like you, Claire. A hell of a lot. But if

there's someone else in the picture, I want to know."

"David, I —"

"I'm asking a lot. I know it. But I spent a long time in second place when I didn't know there was another man in first, and it's not something I want to do again."

Her throat tightened. She knew all about second place. "You're a nice guy, David."

"But — ?"

"But we don't know each other."

"We've known each other for years."

"As parents, but not as people."

"There's an easy fix for that. Let's go out for dinner tomorrow night. I won't mention kids if you don't."

"I'm really not such a great bet these days, David. Between the kids, my father, the bar, and now working for Olivia and Rose at Cuppa, I —"

"That's bullshit."

"What?"

"You heard me. We're both busy. That's a given. I find time for tennis. You find time for poker."

"That's different."

"If there's something between you and that guy, tell me, and we'll go back to being PTA buddies. I like you, Claire. I like sitting here with you. I'd like to see where this could go, but I want to know the rules."

"There's nothing between Corin and me." *Not anymore. Not after seeing that look in his eyes.*

He didn't try to hide his relief. "So take a chance, Claire Meehan O'Malley. Why not try a nice guy this time around. Forget pizza with the kids and let me take you to Chadwick's tomorrow night for lobster. What do you say?"

Billy was almost three years gone, and Corin had never been anything but a wonderful dream. She could have been anyone this morning, Maddy or Barney Kurkowski or Aidan, for all he seemed to care. There hadn't been a flicker of anything beyond polite recognition when he said hello.

That's what you wanted, isn't it? The last thing you needed was for him to sweep you into an embrace and set the whole town talking.

She had spent the last few days with her gut twisted into a series of sailor's knots, worrying about what kind of scene he might cause when he finally showed up. He had every right to be angry. She had been less than kind to him in the past, completely blind to the pain her actions caused him. She had done as much damage, in her own way, as Billy had.

Corin knew her secrets. He knew her family's secrets. He had been dangerously angry when they parted on the Boardwalk eight years ago. He could have easily taken that information and used it to hurt her the way she had hurt him. He still could. There was no statute of limitations on the damage he could cause if he wanted to, but she doubted now if he even remembered. She should be grateful there wasn't the slightest degree of warmth in his eyes when he saw her this morning, not the slightest hint of what they had shared.

Thank God they had both moved on. He deserved to be happy, even though she doubted he would ever stop moving long enough to give happiness a chance to find him. He had a restless nature, a questing soul that took him to places even the map makers had yet to find. The thought of him living out his days in Paradise Point with her was as funny as the thought of her hitting the road with him in search of adventure.

Clearly some things were not meant to be.

She was okay with that. More than okay.

Across the table David Fenelli was waiting for an answer. It wasn't a proposal of marriage. Just a dinner invitation from a nice guy she had known forever. She could spend the rest of her life trapped in the past, or she could begin the slow process of accepting the fact that the future might never arrive. All she really had, all anyone had, was now.

David was smart and funny and bone-deep kind. She could do a hell of a lot worse and probably not a whole lot better. Everyone liked him, from her father to Olivia to her kids. She wouldn't have to introduce him, explain him, or apologize for him. David would fit right into her life as if he had always been there.

And Corin had already seen them together. This would only be further proof, as if he needed or wanted any, that her life was rich and full and happy. Let him think she was busy every night of the week, too busy to wonder about what might have been.

Let him see her with David everywhere he looked. At Chadwick's, or waiting for the school bus on Main Street, or laughing together at O'Malley's. Let him know she had made the right choice, the only choice, and that she had no regrets.

"Dinner sounds great," she said finally, trying to look past the expression of relief and anticipation in his eyes. "I love lobster."

He would pick her up at seven at the house. Maybe they would catch a movie later on. Maybe not. They agreed to follow the evening wherever it led.

David would never hurt her or ask more of her than she had to give. He was a good man with a good heart, and he deserved better than being any woman's second best.

It might not have been the most romantically flattering thing she had ever thought about a man, but it was probably the most honest. That had to count for something.

Chapter Eighteen

The interview with the officers of the seventy-fifth graduating class of Paradise Point High School began at eight in the morning and was scheduled to end no later than ten, but by ten-thirty, Kelly was beginning to think they would be trapped in the library listening to Andrea Portnow prattle on about past proms until it was time for the one hundredth graduating class to receive their diplomas.

Peter Lassiter had begun the interview, even though his assistant Crystal still hadn't shown up for work. A half-asleep cameraman and one sound guy recorded the conversations for posterity when they weren't catching a quick forty winks when the boss wasn't looking. She had had to excuse herself twice for bathroom runs, something that hadn't gone unnoticed by her assembled classmates.

Seth caught her eye across the table, and it was almost as good as a hug. He would be heading over to work at The Candlelight as soon as the meeting broke up, while she planned to race up to the mall at Bay Bridge to purchase a home pregnancy kit. By this time tomorrow they would know what the future had in store for them.

The real future, not the fantasy they had been constructing since they were seven years old, not the orderly, well-thought-out future they spouted for Lassiter and his tape recorder. The one they were going to have to deal with every day for the rest of their lives.

"Kelly, wake up! I asked you a question." Andrea Portnow's braying laugh snapped Kelly back to attention.

"Sorry." Kelly's smile was automatic. "I was thinking about —"

"We need the folder with the pictures." Andrea, the class historian, was all angles and eyes, a Disney animation come to life.

"Pictures?"

Andrea sighed loudly. "The ones from the last reunion. You took them home to scan them, re-member?"

No, she didn't remember. Not even a little.

Andrea shrieked and pretended to fall back into her chair in a dead faint. "Are you telling me that the *perfect* Kelly O'Malley actually *forgot* something?"

Everyone around the table burst into laughter. Everyone, that was, except Kelly and Seth.

"I left the folder home," she said, her voice painfully tight. "If you want, I'll go get it."

Peter Lassiter gave her one of his comforting smiles. "It's not like we need it today," he said. "You can drop the photos off tomorrow."

"You don't know how totally *weird* this is," Andrea went on. "I mean, Kelly is the one who *never* makes mistakes."

"Drop it, Andrea." Seth was clearly struggling to rein in his anger. "Everyone makes mistakes."

"Not Kelly," Tino DeSantis said. "The rest of us screw up all the time and depend on Kel to keep it all together."

"Guess there's a first time for everything," Brian Gomez, a gifted musician headed for Juilliard, said with a shake of his head. "My idol lies broken at my feet."

Any other time that might have seemed funny to Kelly, albeit in an ironic kind of way, but today it cut through her like a well-honed blade.

"I'm sorry." She stood up, hands shaking. "I'll be back in a sec."

"Geez, Kel!" Andrea rolled her eyes. "Maybe if you quit downing those water bottles you wouldn't have to go so much."

"You don't have to explain anything to us, Kelly." Peter Lassiter gave her an easy smile. "We'll still be here when you get back."

Kelly almost cried with relief when Crystal chose that moment to burst into the room, waving dark blue and silver fingertips as she called out, "Anyone want to see Uranus?"

She used the resulting laughter and commotion to make a dash to the bathroom one more time as her stomach launched another revolt against the rest of her body.

Afterward she washed her face at the sink and rinsed out her mouth. She had to get out of there. She couldn't keep her mind focused on the interview, no matter how hard she tried. First they had given an overview of the school and its place in the town's history. Then they had spent at least thirty minutes arguing over when the school's colors changed from cranberry and navy to navy and white. Finally she had managed to present her material about past valedictorians and the proud history of scholarship and achievement of the alumni. Seth and Brian Gomez still had to detail the laundry list of accomplishments garnered by the sports teams over the years, and after that Andrea and Tino would launch themselves headfirst into a glowing review of the theater department and then it would be too late.

She had to get out of there. For a moment Andrea's teasing had almost brought her to tears. Her emotions were ragged and raw, and it wouldn't take much to send her spinning out of control. Not to mention the fact that there had to be a limit to how many times you could excuse yourself to use the bathroom before somebody called the doctor. Andrea had been shooting quizzical looks in her direction for at least an hour now, and there was no way she wanted to be on her radar screen for any longer than necessary.

Besides, it was almost eleven o'clock, and she still had to drive over to the drugstore at the Bay Bridge mall so she could buy the pregnancy test without everyone in Paradise Point knowing she was late. Mrs. DiFalco expected her at The Candlelight around three o'clock, and time was running out.

She pulled out her phone and pressed in Kathleen's cell number.

"Wake up and call me back on my cell in five minutes," she whispered to her puzzled and sleepy cousin.

"Why?"

"If I don't get out of here, I'm going to go crazy."

"Where are you?"

"Remember Andrea Portnow?"

"Tim Portnow's snotty little sister?"

"I'm stuck here at school with her, and if you don't help me get out of here, I'm going to pull her hair extensions out with my bare hands. Call me and pretend your car stalled and you need a lift."

"Are you okay, Kel? This isn't like you."

Saint Kelly. The world's only living perfect teen-ager. The one who never lied, never made mistakes, never had a bad hair day . . . the one who would never find herself knocked up a few weeks before graduation.

"Are you going to help me or not?"

"Hang up. I'll count to two hundred and call you back."

O'Malley power to the rescue. Five minutes later, her cell phone rang, and ten seconds after that she was on her way to the mall.

Lying was easy once you got the hang of it.

It seemed like everyone in South Jersey had all decided to converge on the Bay Bridge mall that morning. The parking lots were jammed, and Maddy had to drive up and down the rows like a circling shark waiting to pounce on the first defenseless spot that opened up. She managed to beat out a Lexus for a spot near Bloomingdale's and raced into the mall toward Lorelei's, the lingerie store Gina had recommended.

She hadn't been in the store more than two minutes when she found out that Gina hadn't lied. When you saw the right one, you knew. Boy, did you know. The second Maddy's gaze landed on the icy blue satin and lace confection, she went giddy with excitement. Her cousin was clearly an erotic genius. The tap pants and camisole were sexy without being obvious. They didn't shine a spotlight on your natural charms; instead, they invited a man closer to discover those charms for himself.

And they even hid stretch marks and cellulite.

What more could a woman ask for?

She gathered up tap pants, camisole, flirty satin slides in the same shade of icy blue, and a matching satin robe that tied at the waist and stopped midthigh.

"Somebody's going to have a great weekend," said the salesclerk with a broad wink. "Lucky girl!"

"I really am," Maddy said as she handed over her credit card. After all the months of bad timing and missed opportunities, they were finally going to —

Ripe, juicy images rose up in front of her and sent pleasurable ripples of anticipation up her spine. Just a few hours from now they would be alone together in that beautiful tower suite in Spring Lake, with nothing but their imaginations and a bottle of champagne for company.

She floated out of Lorelei's and was halfway to her car when she remembered one more very important item and doubled back to CVS. She had stopped taking the Pill when she found out she was pregnant with Hannah, and there hadn't been any reason to start taking it again since total abstinence had proved itself to be a highly effective form of birth control. Aidan struck her as the kind of man who would make sure they were both protected, but she was a modern woman, after all, and — well, better safe than sorry.

Condoms were located in the back of the store near the pharmacy, tucked away with contraceptive foams, jellies, creams, and cigarettes for afterward. The positioning struck her as odd but not half as odd as the limitless varieties of condoms available. Large. Extra Large. (No mention of small or medium in deference to the sensitive male ego.) Ribbed. Smooth. Natural. Every color of the rainbow. Reservoir tip. Lubricated. Flavored. Whatever happened to plain old condoms, the kind that minded their own business but got the job done? She chose a box with the least number of bells and whistles, metaphorically speaking, and was about to take it up to the register when she heard a familiar female voice.

". . . and this is the most reliable?"

"That's what I said." The pharmacist had clearly answered that question many times before.

Maddy prayed the purchase was a box of condoms and not an EPT.

"I'll take it."

"That'll be twelve seventy-five."

She had only seconds to make a decision. Did she preserve Kelly's privacy and duck behind the display until the girl left the store or did she —

"Can I help you, ma'am?" an eager sales clerk asked.

She almost jumped out of her shoes. "No, no thanks. That's okay."

"If you're looking for something in particular, I can —"

"Really, I'm fine. I'm just —"

"Maddy!" Kelly popped up behind the eager salesclerk. "What are you doing here?" Her eyes drifted down to the box of condoms, and her cheeks reddened. "Oh!"

It could have been worse. She might have been wearing the tap pants and camisole, but it was still pretty embarrassing for both of them. "I didn't know you shopped this mall."

"I — uh, I don't usually but . . ."

Kelly clutched a paper bag like it was all that stood between her and disaster. Every maternal instinct Maddy possessed screamed for her to grab that bag and see exactly what the girl had purchased. Maybe there was a reason why their paths kept crossing this way. Nobody else in Kelly's family seemed to see the clues, but Maddy did, and they all added up to just one thing.

It's none of your business. She's almost eighteen. If she wants to talk to you, she will. It's not like you're doing anything to stop her.

Kelly dropped the paper bag into her canvas backpack. "I guess I'd better get going. I have to work at the library before I show up at The Candlelight."

Here's your chance, Maddy. You're standing there with a box of condoms in your hand. You'll never get a better opening line than that. Say something . . . just get her talking . . . maybe there's really nothing going on . . . you're not going to know if you don't reach out to her.

But did it have to be today? She wasn't a mother today. She wasn't an almost-stepmother. Today she was a woman who was eager to be with the man she loved for the very first time. Twenty-four hours. That was all she asked for.

Kelly had done just fine without her for almost eighteen years. Surely one more day wasn't too much to ask for.

Maddy glanced at her watch. "I have to run, too. Aidan's picking me up in ninety-seven minutes."

They were both parked near Bloomie's, so they headed toward the store exit.

"Miss!" The eager clerk darted into Maddy's path. "I think you forgot something."

Another ten steps, and she might have been arrested for shoplifting a box of condoms. Wouldn't that have put a nice spin on a romantic weekend?

"You don't have to hang around," she said to Kelly, who was far too polite to even think about leaving Maddy. "You have a full day ahead of you."

"You sure?"

"Positive." She placed a hand on the girl's shoulder and gave her a gentle push toward the door. "Go!"

Kelly gave her a grateful smile and was gone before Maddy drew her next breath.

"Close call," the pharmacist said with a laugh as he rang up her purchase. "Those alarms were ready to start ringing."

"Closer than you know," Maddy said.

Seth was waiting for Kelly at the far end of the lake where they always went when they wanted to be alone. He had been sitting on the fender of his brother's car and jumped off the second she wheeled into the parking lot.

"Did you get it?" he asked as she ran into his arms.

"Better than that," she said as he enveloped her in a hug. She took a deep, steadying breath. "I ran the test. I'm not pregnant."

He seemed to freeze at the words. His entire body went still, and for a second she thought he had stopped breathing.

"Seth, did you hear me? I'm not pregnant."

Her heart turned over at the mix of relief mingled with a touch of disappointment on his face.

"It's okay to be a little sad," she said, touching his mouth gently with hers. "I am, too."

"I thought I'd be happy," he said, "and I am, but —"

"We're young and healthy. We'll have other chances."

He met her eyes. "We would have made it work, Kel. I wouldn't have walked out on you. I would have taken care of you and the baby."

"I know that," she said, "but I'm glad you won't have to."

And, if she was being completely truthful, she was glad for herself as well.

Seth had to get back to work by one o'clock. She waved good-bye to him, smiling broadly as she did, and managed to hold it together until his brother's Honda rounded the south side of the lake and disappeared.

She had never lied to Seth before. Not ever.

They prided themselves on always telling each other the truth, no matter how difficult the truth might be, but this time she couldn't bring herself to do it.

The difference between thinking she might be pregnant and actually knowing it was true turned out to be much greater than she had imagined it would be. She had been reasonably certain that the results of the pregnancy test would be positive, but she hadn't come close to understanding how she would feel when she actually saw the black plus sign looking up at her.

"Okay," she whispered as she slid behind the wheel of her car. "You did it."

She had set the wheels in motion, and now she had to follow through.

The decisions she made in the next few days would have consequences that followed her for the rest of her life, but what other choice was there? She closed her eyes and saw her family as a line of dominoes falling one by one by one if she gave them the slightest push. They had all been through so much for so long and were only now — finally! — beginning to push sorrow aside and learn how to be happy. Her father had found Maddy, and in a few months they would marry and probably start a family of their own. Her cousins were all doing okay, including Kathleen, whose troubles had seemed insurmountable just a few short years ago. Kathleen was pulling As at Rutgers. And what about Aunt Claire? Not only was she going to leave O'Malley's to manage Cuppa, she was actually going out on a date with Jason Fenelli's dad.

It wouldn't take much at all to bring it all crashing down around their shoulders. They all expected so much from her, and it had been so easy to make them happy. She liked doing the right thing. She liked being the one you could depend on. She liked knowing that the things she did, the goals she achieved, made them proud of her and, in a way, of themselves as well.

And, oh God, there was Seth. She loved him more than she loved life itself. He was her past, her present, and her future. They shared the same memories. They wanted the same things from life. They even dreamed the same dreams at night. He was kind and smart and funny and blessed with the most generous heart she had ever encountered. He was going to do great things with his life, wonderful things that would make a difference in the lives of children who needed a helping hand. He knew where he was going — he always had — and he needed an education to help him get there.

She rested her forehead against the steering wheel and wondered what would happen if she stayed there in her car forever. She was tired right into her bones, tired in a way she'd never known before. One mistake over the course of a lifetime, and suddenly the futures of the ones she loved most were thrown into doubt.

Why tell any of them, if one week from today

there would be nothing left but a memory? She knew what she needed to do, and she would do it. She didn't need their anger or their tears, and she definitely didn't need their disappointment. She was disappointed enough in herself for the entire population of Paradise Point. But there was a way out of this mess, a way that wouldn't take the ones she loved down with it. All she had to do was stay strong a little bit longer, and it would be like none of this had ever happened.

Chapter Nineteen

Maybe it was his mood, but the silence in the car as they rolled up the shore toward Spring Lake was making Aidan uncomfortable. Maddy seemed distant, remote almost, deep in thoughts that he had the feeling didn't include him.

"You're quiet today," he said as they slowed to pay a toll.

"So are you," she said, leaning over and quickly kissing his right shoulder. "I thought we were enjoying the scenery."

"There's something you don't hear every day in New Jersey."

She laughed, that warm, real laugh he loved. "Good," she said. "That means we'll keep it a secret from the rest of the country."

He knew her face the way he knew his own, which was amazing if you stopped to think about it. He had spent almost forty years learning his own and less than six months loving hers, and yet the curves and planes of jaw and cheekbone on her beautiful face were burned into his consciousness. The vertical pleat between her brows that meant she was worried. The slight twitch beneath her lower lid when she was under stress. The half smile that meant she was amused against her better judgment. The flash of fire in her eyes when she was gearing up for battle — usually with her family. They were all a part of his emotional vocabulary now.

Right now it was the vertical pleat that commanded his attention.

"Everything okay?"

"Why wouldn't it be?"

"That's not an answer."

She swiveled around in her seat and looked at him. "You're serious."

Now he felt paranoid as well as uncomfortable. "I sprang this on you without warning. Maybe I should have —"

"I love you," she said. "I love that you thought of this, that you made all the arrangements yourself, and all I had to do was shop for sexy lingerie and jump into the car."

What more do you want from her, O'Malley? A declaration written in blood? She bought sexy underwear. Be happy already.

She said she loved him, and he had no reason not to believe her. During the worst of it earlier this year, she hadn't faltered. Not even once. When he asked her to marry him, to make a family with him, she had said yes without hesitation, without stopping even for a second to wonder what she might be getting into. She was willing to make a life with him, spend the next forty or fifty years with him, and it still wasn't enough to erase the feeling that something was wrong.

There was a restlessness about her, a quality of movement that made him uneasy. She was quicksilver, ready to slip just out of reach. Funny how the qualities that drew you to a person were often the same qualities that scared you the most. He had no idea what she was thinking about. For all he knew, she could have been planning their wedding or a way to over-throw the government. It was anyone's guess. Still, it seemed to him that things between them had changed in the few weeks since their en-gagement. She was more preoccupied, more distant, more likely to wake up tomorrow morning and realize the whole thing had been a mistake and — sorry, O'Malley — maybe it was better to call it off now before it was too late.

She was still looking at him, waiting for him to say something. *I don't want to disappoint you, Maddy. I don't want you to wake up tomorrow looking for a way out of your promise.*

He wished she had known him the way he had been before the warehouse accident. He wished he had had the chance to love her when he still had a body he could trust. Too bad that man was a long time gone. His body wasn't the same powerful instrument it used to be. His faith in it had been shattered, same as his bones. Things that had come naturally to him a few years ago were now accomplished through an act of will and a hell of a lot of luck. She didn't know that, but he did, and that made all the difference.

Maddy had promised herself that she would leave work and family worries back in Paradise Point for the next twenty-four hours, but that was proving to be more difficult than she had anticipated. To her surprise, it wasn't Hannah or Rose or the uneasy situation developing with Claire that clamored for her attention.

It was Kelly.

She couldn't shake the memory of their awkward meeting at the mall or her overwhelming certainty that Aidan's daughter was pregnant. The defenseless look in Kelly's eyes had said it all, and she wondered why she was the only one who seemed able to see it so clearly. Maybe it was because she had been where Kelly was not that long ago. Okay, she had been older and in what she had believed to be a stable relationship, but that sense of being on a runaway train was as fresh to her today as it had been when she first found out about Hannah.

It hurt to remember how much she had longed for her mother during her pregnancy, how deep the loneliness went as the months passed and Rose never once made the trip across country to see the miracle that was happening to her only child. Of course now she knew the truth — her mother had been undergoing chemotherapy in her battle against breast cancer — but at the time all Maddy had understood was that Rose simply didn't care.

Kelly had never even had the luxury of anger. Her mother died when Kelly was a baby, leaving her with nothing but photos and other people's memories to hold on to. How she must wish she had a woman she could talk to, somebody who loved her unconditionally.

There was Aidan, of course, but Maddy was beginning to understand what he meant when he said in many ways Kelly had raised herself. Good kids rarely got the time and effort their more rebellious peers demanded. They seemed to be guided by some kind of inner gyroscope that kept them balanced, no matter what life threw at them. Who could blame a parent for letting down his guard after sixteen or seventeen years of perfect behavior?

This wasn't something Kelly could share with her father, no matter how strong the bond. Aidan liked Seth, but he was still Kelly's father, and the intensity of their relationship got under his skin, which, in turn, made Kelly defensive and guarded.

She knew Kelly and Seth had been together since childhood and that everyone in town expected they would spend the rest of their lives together as well, but things didn't always go the way you planned. Babies changed everything, as Maddy had learned firsthand. The girl needed support. She needed somebody to talk to, somebody who understood. And, God knew, she needed guidance. If Maddy's guess was right and there was a baby on the way, Kelly would have to make some hard choices beginning now, choices that would affect the glittering future she had been working toward for so long.

Her head ached with wondering what she should do next. She knew what her mother would say: "Tell Aidan. Don't keep secrets from the man you're going to marry." And there was a lot to recommend Rose's perspective. Aidan was Kelly's father. Kelly was still a minor. Legally, if not ethically, Maddy wasn't even part of the equation. She should turn to him right now and lay out the information as she knew it, detail her fears and suspicions, and let him decide what to do next.

That was what her mother would do. It was what Claire would do. It was what any sane woman who was about to be married in a little more than four months would do. But was it the right thing for Kelly?

Oh God, she wished she knew the answer.

They reached Spring Lake a little after five o'clock. The town was every bit as charming as she had remembered, and Maddy winced as they drove past the spot where Aidan had taken his tumble that fateful winter night.

The inn Aidan had chosen was named the Sea Breeze, a requisite Victorian-era structure as wide and deep as the sandy beach that beckoned on the other side of the boardwalk. Where Paradise Point had a smaller, more intimate feel, Spring Lake was more expansive. B and Bs in her hometown were renovated Victorian-era houses, not renovated hotels the way they were here. You could fit the entire first floor of The Candlelight into the center hall of the Sea Breeze.

"Your room is ready," the owner of the inn said as she handed over two keys and rang for someone to carry their bags. "Dinner will be served at eight p.m., just as you requested."

Neither Maddy nor Aidan said a word as they followed a young man up the twisting staircase to their third-floor suite. He fiddled with his master key for a second, then pushed open the door and motioned them inside. He deposited their bags near the foot of the bed, showed them how to operate the Jacuzzi and the fireplace, then quickly disappeared.

"So now I know how Dorothy felt when she woke up in Oz," Maddy breathed.

Where The Candlelight was all soft, romantic elegance, this room was full-on sensuality. The bed seemed to float in the center of the room, angled slightly so you could watch the waves crashing against the shore while you lay cradled in each other's arms. The Jacuzzi was nestled in a curve of wall between the sitting room and the bedroom, with a perfect view of either the fireplace or the moon over the ocean, depending upon your preference. Candles, chunky ones and long skinny ones and tiny votives in burgundy crystal holders, were situated on every available surface. They lined the edge of the tub, surrounded the bed, and shimmered from mirrored shelves built into the wall.

Even the air seemed to have been fine-tuned to mount the ultimate assault on their unwary senses. The clean springtime smell of freesia mingled with the unmistakable bite of the sea and blended with the faintest overtone of spice.

The effect was intoxicating and extremely seductive, exactly as it was intended to be.

In Maddy's fantasies, they had been naked and in each other's arms before the door closed behind the bell man. In reality they were painfully awkward with each other, making polite conversation about the room temperature, the view, and whether or not tips were inclusive. She made a prolonged show of unpacking, something that should have taken forty-five seconds on any other day. And Aidan spent an unconscionable amount of time fiddling with the thermostat and checking the drain on the Jacuzzi.

For two people who would be married in a little more than four months, they were as uncomfortable as strangers. Back home in Paradise Point where they had no time to be alone and even less privacy, they couldn't keep their hands off each other. Heat snaked through her body as she thought about the things they had done and the things they had talked about doing when the moment was finally right.

This was supposed to be that moment, and yet there they were on opposite sides of a room created for lovers who knew how to make the most of it.

She wanted to say something, anything, but the words wouldn't come. Her throat was locked tight against them. He stood near the door that opened onto the balcony, arms crossed over his chest, looking out toward the ocean. His cane rested against the lamp table in the corner. She thought she had never seen a more beautiful man — or a lonelier one — in her life. He was so strong in so many ways, so confident in situations that would make another man crumble, and yet, there in that room with her, he suddenly looked vulnerable.

Love did that to you. It stripped you bare in ways that had nothing to do with the flesh. It left you exposed to wind and rain and storms that would send a sane person running for cover. You had to be crazy or crazy in love to stand there naked in a hurricane and ask for more.

He must have sensed her watching him because he turned away from the window. Their gazes caught and held, suspended in that midway point between them.

"It's a beautiful day," she said, finding her voice at last. "Why don't we take a walk on the beach before dinner."

"Come here," he said, and her heart almost stopped beating.

"Why don't I go change into that beautiful lingerie I bought," she suggested. She couldn't possibly feel more exposed in her lacy undergarments than she felt right now, fully dressed. "It's way too expensive to just sit in my suitcase."

"Come here," he said again, more softly this time.

She sighed as she moved into his embrace. His chest was broad and hard-muscled, warm against her cheek. His arms were bands of steel holding her close. Everything about him was big and powerful, the textbook definition of all things masculine. But his hands — oh God, his hands. Big gentle hands that knew how to touch a woman the way she needed to be touched. All she had to do was touch him, breathe in the smell of his skin, and the jumbled pieces of her world fell into place.

Everything she thought she knew about making love, about what defined physical pleasure — none of it came close to what she felt when he began to unbutton her sweater. A simple action, the stuff of backseats and high school Saturday nights, and yet she began to tremble when he slid the first pearl button out. Heat pooled low in her belly as he released the second button with sure fingers. Three buttons, four, five. *Don't stop . . . please don't stop.*

He didn't. She should have known better. He seemed to read her body as if she had drawn him an erotic map, some wonderful dark magic guiding his hands and mouth to all the right places at precisely the right moment. His hands skimmed the curve of her breasts, her rib cage, her belly. She sucked in her breath as he slid one hand under the waistband of her jeans as all the ways in which she was less than perfect threatened to extinguish that lovely flame. She wasn't a girl any longer, she wasn't twenty-one and perfect. She was a woman. She had given birth. This body of hers with all of its perfect and imperfect parts was made to give and to receive pleasure, and oh God, it did that so well. . . .

Her fingers fought with his shirt buttons, struggling to push them through the button-holes and failing, and finally she gave a tug that sent them bouncing across the floor. The sound he made — surprised delight — moved through her like music. His chest was bare, gloriously bare, and she placed her mouth against the midpoint and drank in his heat and his smell, gloried in the soft mat of curls, his warm flesh, the rapid thunder of his heartbeat beneath her lips.

He cupped her bottom with his hands, fingers sliding between her thighs, touching her in a way that made her bones melt.

"The bed," she whispered, and seconds later they sank together into the mountain of satin and down.

Magic . . . more than magic . . . the way he

touched her . . . the heat of his mouth as he ran his tongue over her breasts, her nipples, down over her soft belly, lower and then lower still, and she cried out his name as he tasted her, deeply, intimately, and made her believe she was beautiful and this could go on forever and ever . . . the two of them . . . this wonderful bed . . . all the time in the world to learn all there was to know . . . every secret inch. . . .

"Now don't make a big deal out of this," Claire said to her family as she dug through the back closet for shoes an adult woman might actually wear on a night out. "We're going out for dinner, not eloping to Vegas."

Her father, daughter, and son exchanged glances.

"I saw that," she said as she plucked a Payless special from under a stack of forgotten winter boots and broken umbrellas. "This is David Fenelli we're talking about, guys. Not Armand Assante."

"Armand Assante?" Kathleen made a face. "Who's that?"

"Beats hell out of me," Mike said. He looked down at his grandson. "You got any ideas?"

"He's not a Met," Billy said, which pretty much consigned Armand to the recycle bin.

"We'll be fine," Kathleen said as Claire sat on the bottom step and tried to slide her feet into the very high heels. "I'm going to make tofu in szechuan sauce. I found some bok choy at the market and some snow peas. I was thinking of asking Kelly if she wanted to join us."

"She's working at The Candlelight tonight," Claire said automatically.

"I want meat," Mike said. "It's suppertime. You have meat at supper."

"I thought we were getting a pizza," Billy chimed in. "Kelly could pick it up at Ray's and bring it over."

The household chatter buzzed around her head like summer bees. Pizza talk. Her father complaining about Fritzie the cat. The general pandemonium that seemed to be part and parcel of the Meehan-O'Malley clan's daily life. It was all white noise to Claire.

"These can't be my shoes." She looked down at her feet. "I can't even slide my toes into them."

"Sure you can." Kathleen crouched down in front of her. "It won't be pretty, but you can do it." She took Claire's foot in her left hand and the impossible shoe in her right and tried to bring them together.

"Then these aren't my feet."

"You're getting older, Mom," Kathleen said with all the annoying wisdom of the young. "Your feet are spreading."

"I still wear the same size shoe I wore when I was your age."

"I . . . don't . . . think . . . so," Kathleen grunted as she tried to jam Claire's toes far enough forward to accommodate the rest of her foot, but it was like parking an eighteen-wheeler in a garage built for a minivan.

"Kath, that's enough. It's not going to happen. My heels days are over."

"No, don't give up. These shoes are so amazing! Maybe if we ice your feet for a couple of minutes they'll shrink and —"

They locked eyes and started to laugh. Big loud gales of raucous laughter that sent men and beasts scurrying from the room in search of safety. Claire rolled sideways on the top step, helpless with laughter, while Kathleen sat on the floor with her head on her mother's knees, laughing until she cried.

It felt good to laugh, but it felt even better to hear her daughter's laughter fill the room. She couldn't remember the last time that had happened. Maybe it never had. The last ten years had been filled with so much pain, so much trouble, that laughter had always been in short supply. She had always loved her kids, protected them, tried to guide them, but she had never laughed with them, and it struck her now as a terrible shame.

She had always envied Aidan his easy relationship with Kelly and wondered why she found it so hard to achieve with her own children. But then her niece made everything easy. She had glided effortlessly between childhood and adolescence, then floated without so much as a ripple through her teens. Aidan hadn't a clue what parenting was really about. He had never been forced to check his own child into a rehab center or spend sleepless nights praying she would be found after she ran off.

She placed a hand on her daughter's mass of shiny-penny curls. They were cool and silky and sweet against her fingers, so different, so very different, from those lost days when even basic hygiene had been abandoned in favor of scoring more of whatever would keep her highest longest. God help her, but she hadn't always believed Kathleen would win the battle, but somehow Billy — her heart twisted at his memory, so clear, so vital — had always believed Kathleen would find her way back to them. He had given her hope when hers was long gone.

"Be careful, Mom," Kathleen said after their laughter faded. "I don't want you to get hurt."

Claire frowned and looked down at the spiky shoes she had pulled from the closet. "I know I haven't worn heels in years, but I think I can still keep my balance."

"That's not what I'm talking about."

Claire started to laugh again. "Oh, honey, if you're worried about David Fenelli, you don't have to be. My heart isn't in any danger."

"I saw him this morning at the bar, Mom. I know he's here in town."

Kathleen, that's no way to talk to Corin. Apologize this instant for being so rude!

I don't know what got into her, Corin. She's never like that. I'm so sorry.

Her oldest. Her most troubled. The child who

saw the most and said the least. The lightning rod for pain and trouble.

The only one who had known Corin was much more to her mother than just the brother of a new friend.

She took her daughter's hand and squeezed it. "You don't have to worry about me," she said. "He's here as a favor to a friend. He'll be gone by the end of next week."

"I don't want him to hurt you again."

"He never hurt me, honey."

"I was there, Mom. I remember what happened."

"He never did anything to hurt me, Kathleen. I was the one who hurt him."

"I don't believe you. I used to stand outside your door after we came back to New Jersey and hear you crying yourself to sleep."

"I'm sorry," she said, still holding her daughter's hand. "I never wanted to worry you."

"Don't patronize me. I'm almost twenty-one. I think I can handle the truth. It's not like I'm going to go out there and challenge him to a duel." Kathleen met her eyes head on with an intensity Claire was all too familiar with. "I know about Dad. We all do. I know how hard it must've been for you."

You wait and you worry and you wonder if your kids are going to make it through their adolescence, and then you hold your breath while they crash through their teens, and just when you're ready to throw in the towel and admit defeat, they surprise you by growing up to be someone very special.

But why you had to find this out five minutes before a nice guy named David Fenelli knocked on your door was a question for the ages.

"We'll sit down tomorrow, Kath, and I'll tell you the story, but the short version is that I hurt him very much. I didn't mean to. I had left your father for what I assumed would be for good, but when he showed up that day and I saw how much he wanted us to come home, I found I couldn't do it."

"Because you loved Dad more than you loved Olivia's brother?"

"Because I loved our family."

"That's not what I asked."

"You're asking a black-and-white question, Kathleen. Marriage is shades of gray."

"You loved Dad. You wouldn't have gone back with him if you didn't."

People stay together for all sorts of reasons, Kathleen, reasons you're too young to understand.

"Your father loved our family as much as I did. We were committed to the five of you."

"Which means you must have loved each other."

"What a question, Kath. Where did that come from?"

"Because I have the right to know." Her voice broke on the last word. "Because I *need* to know."

"Oh God, don't go telling me you've been

talking to Lassiter and his crew." Suddenly everyone in town had been bitten by the need to tell all, damn the consequences.

"So what if I did. Why shouldn't I talk to them?"

"You know how I feel about people poking around in other people's business."

"You're afraid someone will talk about Dad and his . . ." She didn't finish the sentence, which was probably for the best.

"That was nobody's business but your father's and mine."

"And ours," Kathleen said quietly. "Oh don't look at me like that, Mom. It was hardly a secret."

"I know it wasn't a secret," Claire said, "but —"

"But what? You want me to go on pretending he wasn't out sleeping with other women because that makes everything sound better?"

"That's family business, and it should stay within the family."

Kathleen laughed out loud. "I think you're twenty years too late for that, Mom. You don't really believe nobody will bring up his extracurricular activities, do you?"

She had been hoping exactly that. "I don't see why anyone would be interested."

"Neither do I," Kathleen admitted, "but this is a small town. Small towns love gossip, and television feeds off the stuff."

"Even PBS," Claire noted wryly.

"Does it still hurt?"

Claire didn't pretend to misunderstand the question. "Sometimes," she said honestly, "but much less than it used to."

"I would have left him the first time," Kathleen said with the certainty of the young. "The minute he stepped out of line, he would've been history."

Her beautiful young warrior child hadn't a clue. "I hope you never have to make that decision."

"None of it makes sense to me. I mean, when you love each other, you're supposed to be happy. I don't remember many times when you and Dad seemed really happy."

"You're right," she said. "We didn't seem to do happy as well as other families, did we?"

"Do you ever wish you'd stayed down in Florida with that guy?"

"I made my choice, and I didn't look back," she said, and it was almost true. She didn't look back because she couldn't. It hurt too much. "Besides, how could I ever regret a decision that brought Billy Jr. to us?"

They had been happy, really happy, for a while, and the memory of those months had sustained her through some tough times.

Kathleen's eyes never left hers. She needed to know that despite everything there had been love, but Claire couldn't seem to find the right words to make her daughter understand what she didn't really understand herself. There had been love. Maybe not the kind of love either she or Billy had dreamed about, that once-in-a-lifetime kind of magic, but there had been love and always would be.

"Did you love each other?" she asked again, a note of need in her voice that hadn't been there before.

He had given them a home, and she had given him a family, and in the end they had each chosen to protect what they had built together. If that wasn't love, what was?

"Of course we did," she said as she held her daughter close. "We might not have been Ozzie and Harriet, but we loved each other."

"Really?"

"Really."

"I knew it." Kathleen's smile was just a tiny bit smug. "I just wanted to make sure you knew it, too."

Her daughter's relief almost broke Claire's heart.

"Son of a bitch!" Mike Meehan bellowed from somewhere down the hallway. "This damn cat's going to end up killing someone."

"Is Fritzie okay?" Claire called out. "She's old. We have to watch out for her."

"I'm old, too," her father yelled back. "I don't see anybody worrying about me."

Claire and Kathleen exchanged looks as they tried very hard not to burst into laughter.

"How long you gonna make this poor guy wait?"

God forbid her father should actually walk down the hallway to deliver a message.

"He'll be able to use a senior discount by the time you get your shoes on."

"You should've said David was here," Claire bellowed back. "I'll be right there."

"Uh-oh," Kathleen said, pointing toward her mother's bare feet. "Speaking of shoes . . ."

Claire looked down at her big feet and the little shoes.

"Better get the ice," she said.

And then, just like before, just like they had been doing it all their lives, they started to laugh.

The twelve senior citizens from Long Island were a lively group who weren't content to nod off around a roaring fire after dinner. Instead, they climbed into their van for the trip up to the bright lights of Atlantic City.

"And where are those PBS cameras when we really need them?" Rose murmured as she and Kelly waved good-bye to the group as they headed north to that mecca of slot machines on the Jersey Shore. "The last time I heard so many kind words about my cooking, I was talking to myself."

Kelly covered her mouth with her hand and yawned. "Sorry," she said with an apologetic grin. "You should ask them to write some of that down for you, Mrs. DiFalco. It would make great ad copy."

Rose gave her one of those looks that used to make Kelly's knees knock before she got to know that Maddy's mother was really a softie. "We're going to be family," she said, placing a beautifully manicured hand on Kelly's forearm. "I think we can dispense with the formalities, don't you?" Her smile was warm and genuine. "I don't suppose either one of us would feel comfortable with Grandma, but I think we could manage if you called me Rose, don't you?"

Kelly nodded. "Thanks," she said. "I'd like that."

Rose draped a companionable arm across her shoulders as they headed back into the house. "You did a wonderful job with Mr. Benedetto and his missing medicine."

"No big deal," Kelly said. "All I had to do was make a few phone calls."

"And drive over to the pharmacy."

"Hannah loved the ride. She said everything is more exciting after dark." She liked keeping busy. It gave her less time to think.

Rose rolled her eyes. "Words to strike terror in a grandmother's heart. Maddy was the same way at her age, a born night owl."

"Not me," said Kelly.

"Nor I," Rose said. "I may burn the midnight oil, but I'm a lark through and through."

They scanned the kitchen for anything that might need doing, but it was as clean and neat as a picture in a magazine.

"Gramma!" Hannah, Priscilla in tow, appeared in the doorway to the kitchen. "I thought we were going to play scrapbook."

"We are." Rose's voice always took on a certain indulgent tone when she spoke to her granddaughter. "Kelly and I were just making sure the kitchen was shipshape."

Hannah pulled on the sleeve of Rose's soft blue sweater. "*Now,* Gramma! I wanna see pictures of Mommy when she was little."

"You're welcome to join us," Rose said, ruffling Hannah's bangs with an affectionate hand. "I found boxes of old photos in the attic when I started searching around for items to share with Peter Lassiter. I set aside some wonderful snapshots of Irene and Michael and your father's parents for you."

The family parlor in the rear of the house was Kelly's favorite room. The walls were lined floor to ceiling with books on every subject imaginable from art to zoology and everything in between. The lower shelves were stocked with picture books for Hannah, pop-up books, books with sound effects, all of the wonderful old kids' classics Kelly had known and loved when she was Hannah's age. An enormous flat-screen television was hidden inside an enormous antique oak breakfront that had been reworked to serve as an entertainment center. The big, cushy leather couches were strewn with dozens of needlework pillows and draped with hand-knit cashmere and mohair throws in jewel tones that took her breath away.

Best of all was the huge old library table set up near the bay window that overlooked the garden. Made of rosewood, it was scarred from decades of use, but those years of living had also given the wood a patina that made Kelly want to rest her head on its surface and listen to its secrets. Rose called it their "workbench," and it usually was home to any number of crafts projects in progress. It wasn't unusual to find Hannah's finger paints and Barbies sharing table space with Maddy's knitting and Rose's jigsaw puzzles or watercolor supplies.

Tonight, however, the table had been cleared of Barbies and knitting needles to make room for at least two dozen boxes of photos, a three-foot-high stack of scrapbooks, and enough decorative paper, shears, fancy glues, stickers, archival quality papers, and pens to stock a branch of Staples.

"Wow!" she said, turning to Rose. "And you're going to put every single photo into a scrapbook?"

"Not even I'm that ambitious," Rose said with a laugh. "We'd end up needing a room at the Library of Congress to hold our family history." She explained that the first step was to sort through the boxes and cull duplicates, underexposures, and the downright unacceptable. From there she would begin a more rigorous winnowing process with an eye toward a cohesive theme or chronology in each scrapbook.

Hannah climbed up onto one of the chairs

and reached for a stack of paper and a fistful of brightly colored markers. She uncapped the top of a cherry-red pen and was soon lost in her own world. Rose motioned for Kelly to take a seat, then withdrew a manila envelope from the top drawer of the secretary in the corner.

"There are some wonderful shots of your grandparents here," Rose said as she handed her the envelope, "and a few of your dad and your uncle Billy when they were kids."

"This is *so* cool!" Kelly said as she spilled the mix of black-and-white and color prints on the table in front of her. Familiar, well-loved faces smiled up at her across the years. She laughed at the sight of her father and her uncle Billy dressed in cowboy outfits one long-ago Halloween and blinked away tears at one of Irene cradling a newborn Kelly in her arms in front of O'Malley's. She couldn't remember ever seeing her great-grandmother Irene so happy.

"Oh God!" Kelly breathed. "Is that my mom standing next to Grandma Irene?"

"That's a great shot," Rose said, peering over her shoulder. "I think that was the day your parents brought you home to Paradise Point for your christening." She leaned closer. "Flip it over, Kelly. There might be a date on it."

Scribbled in pencil were the words *"Kelly's Baptism — July 5, 1986,"* and *"Irene O'Malley/Kelly Ann O'Malley/Sandy O'Malley (Aidan and Sandy's first)"* across the back in Rose's distinctive script.

Her throat tightened as she saw another newborn and another christening —

She couldn't think about it. She *wouldn't* think about it. Someday the time would be right, but not now. Definitely not now.

"You look very much like your mother," Rose said in a matter-of-fact tone of voice. "She was a beautiful girl."

Kelly tried to say thank you, but she couldn't seem to make the words come out, no matter how hard she tried. It seemed like she couldn't do anything at all, much less make sense of her own life. Her mother wasn't real to her. She existed only in other people's memories, in flat, one-dimensional photographs and a handful of old greeting cards tucked away in her father's top drawer. Whatever it was that had made her Sandy O'Malley had died with her, and no snapshot could ever bring it back.

Very little escaped Rose's notice, but she didn't remark on the tears streaming down Kelly's cheeks. Instead, she took the top box from the corner stack and slid it toward Kelly.

"I only went through a portion of this box. I thought you might like to go through the rest. My mother loved taking snapshots," she said with a small chuckle. "I think she documented just about every family in town."

Kelly pointed toward the bottom left-hand corner of the box. "Someone scribbled *'O'Malleys'* right there."

Rose gave her shoulder an affectionate

squeeze. "Maybe she had a feeling those pictures would be important someday."

Hannah looked up from her artwork. "Why are you crying?" she asked Kelly. "Are you sad?"

"Kelly was looking at a picture of her mother and Grandma Irene," Rose said with enormous tact. "She misses her grandma very much."

Hannah thought about that for a moment. "Kelly can borrow you sometimes, Grandma. I won't mind."

"Anytime she wants," Rose said with a wink for Kelly. "She's part of the family, right?"

Kelly's left hand slipped to her belly in a gesture as old as time itself. She quickly caught herself and pretended to adjust the hem of her sweater, but not before she caught the look of curiosity in Rose's eyes.

"Look at this," she said, pointing to an almost invisible snag in the knitted material. "I caught it on the car door this morning." Her stupid eyes started to fill with tears, and she made a face. "It's my favorite sweater." *Lame, Kel, really lame. Who cries about a snagged sweater?*

Rose met Kelly's eyes over the top of her reading glasses. Curiosity was still there, only this time there was sadness threaded through it as well, and Kelly looked away.

"Maddy is wonderful at fixing things," Rose said gently. "I'm sure she could help you."

"It's just a sweater," she said, reaching into the box for a stack of photos. "It can wait."

403

"Sometimes even the best of us have to ask for help."

She didn't say anything, just looked down at the stack of photos.

"Ask her," Rose said, pressing a kiss to the top of her head. "Trust me. She'll be glad you did."

Chapter Twenty

Nothing Aidan had imagined or dreamed or wished for came close to the reality of Maddy, warm and satisfied, asleep in his arms.

The room was bathed in starshine. The only sounds were her soft breathing, the beat of their hearts. There was nothing else the world could show him that would ever compare to what they had shared in that bed, naked in every way a man and woman could be.

No more secrets. She knew him now the way he really was. She knew the scars, the limitations, the frustrations, the pain, and she hadn't run for the door. The ring was still on her finger. She was there in the bed beside him. He had everything he had ever wanted within the span of his arms, and yet the feeling that he was losing her lingered.

It wasn't anything he could put his finger on, no particular incident or conversation that led him to think that she was slipping beyond his grasp, but the sense of impending loss was there just the same, and he didn't know why.

She sighed softly and looked up at him. "I fell asleep." Her laugh was apologetic. "I'm sorry."

"Don't be." He pulled her closer. "You earned it."

She pressed her lips to his shoulder. "I did, didn't I."

He grasped her by the waist and rolled her on top of him.

"Nice upper body strength you've got there, fella."

He liked the view. She had a beautiful, lush body. A woman's body. Full breasts, tiny waist, hips that cradled a man and reminded him why he had been born.

"You're going to get tired of doing all the work," he said.

"Try me."

She moved against him, and he was instantly hard.

"I'm impressed," she said, reaching for protection. She ripped open the packet, and he grew harder still.

"I aim to please," he said as she unrolled a condom down the length of his shaft.

She leaned forward and kissed him deeply. "So I see."

He slid his hands down from her waist to her hips and positioned her over him. She caught his rhythm and, taking control, lowered herself slowly, painfully slowly, until he was lost in her heat. She made him feel young. She made him feel strong. She made him believe good things were possible, that happiness was there for the taking. Most of all, she made him feel loved, and for a little while the uneasy feeling that this taste of heaven wouldn't last forever receded like a bad dream forgotten in the morning light.

She cried out when she came, a low, guttural cry of almost unbearable pleasure that sent him tumbling right over the edge with her.

Instead of curling up against him and sleeping afterward, this time she seemed energized. Once their heartbeats had returned to something approximating normal, she leaned over him, her breasts grazing his chest and sending pleasurable ripples of sensation along tired but resourceful nerve endings.

"It's almost eight," she said, peering at the tiny clock on the night shelf next to the bed. "No wonder I'm starving."

"I can think of a few other reasons," he said, and she laughed.

"They're going to be bringing our dinner any minute. We really should —"

"They've probably figured out what's going on in here."

She gave him a wonderfully wicked smile. "Well, we don't need to confirm their suspicions, do we? Put on one of those gorgeous silk robes that are hanging in the closet."

"I'm not wearing a silk robe."

"Just to answer the door."

"Especially not to answer the door."

"Then I'll put one on and answer the door."

"No."

Her smile widened. "Aidan, somebody's going to have to put on something in the next two minutes or —"

Two quick taps on the door were followed by a cheery, "Your dinner is served!"

Maddy dashed for the bathroom, leaving Aidan to fend for himself. No way he was putting on a red silk robe. He couldn't find his pants, and naked wasn't an option. So he grabbed for the bed sheet and hoped for the best.

The room service waiter was personable and clearly accustomed to being greeted by guests in varying stages of undress. He set up a small table near the open French doors and quickly turned it into a work of art with intricately folded napkins, candles, fresh flowers, and enough china and silverware to host a family of twelve.

"You're good," Aidan said as the guy settled a bottle of Veuve Clicquot into the wine bucket.

"I try."

He gave him a great tip, promised to call if they needed anything else, then locked the door behind him.

"The coast is clear," he called out to Maddy.

She popped out of the bathroom wearing a short, pale blue robe that clung to her curves and stopped midthigh, leaving her long legs bare and inviting. She looked like every man's idea of a goddess. Whoever had designed that outfit had his undying gratitude.

She took one look at him and burst into laughter. "You look like you're on your way to a toga party!"

"It was good enough for Caesar."

She eyed him up and down, then let loose with an ear-splitting wolf whistle. "If Caesar'd had legs like yours, O'Malley, we'd still be speaking Latin."

"You flirting with me, Bainbridge?"

"You bet I am," she said. "What does a girl have to do around here to get some dinner?"

He made a few suggestions, and Maddy decided they should try one of the juicier ones between the lobster and the crème brûlée.

"Room service," he said with a shake of his head. "Is it great or what?"

Claire devoured her last bite of lobster and sank back in her chair a happy woman. "Tell me the truth, David: is this how real grown-ups live?"

"Beats me," he said, polishing off his prime rib. "I've heard rumors, but I can't prove anything."

"Look around," Claire said with a wave of her hand. "Nobody in this room has school Monday morning."

"Sara Ogilvie over there has school Monday morning."

Claire made a face. "She teaches math. You techie types are way too literal."

"It's a failing," he said, "but at least we know how to balance the family checkbook."

"Just don't tell me you use coupons."

"I'm not saying anything."

Look at you, Claire Meehan O'Malley: you're not only out on a date, you're having a good time.

David Fenelli was great company. He liked to listen, he liked to talk, and she didn't have to cut his food for him. What more could a woman ask for?

How about Corin for starters?

Now there was a stupid idea. Want a recipe for disaster? Try wanting someone who had stopped wanting you a long, long time ago. No, she wasn't going down that particular patch of bad road ever again. Not for anybody.

So what if she jumped every time the front door opened. That was nothing but some weird kind of biochemical response to stimuli, a reflex reaction to the contradictory messages bombarding her poor, overworked synapses. Funny how you could want something and not want it simultaneously and with the same degree of intensity. The last thing on earth that she wanted was for Corin Flynn to show up at Chadwick's for lobster . . . and damned if she wasn't disappointed every time the door opened and he didn't.

David was watching her. "If you're worried, call them."

He thought she was worrying about her family. The guy was too nice to live. She pulled

410

herself back into the moment and rolled her eyes. "If they can't manage without me one Saturday night every twenty years, there's no hope for the lot of 'em."

His serious expression melted into an easy smile that triggered a smile in response. "So if you're not that worried, how about we take in a movie?"

"Movie?" Claire feigned puzzlement. "You mean, where you go and sit in a big room with a lot of other people and watch moving pictures on a giant screen?"

"Right," said David, deadpan. "And they have sound, too."

"Do they give you a remote control so you can fast-forward through the dull patches?"

"No, but the stale popcorn with fake butter makes up for it."

Their waitress popped up with dessert menus, and they ordered cappuccinos and an enormous slice of chocolate mousse cake to share.

"I'd recommend a brandy, but you two seem to be having enough fun without it."

"She's right," David said as the waitress headed back to the kitchen with their order. "I'm glad you said yes, Claire."

So was she.

The movie didn't begin for another hour and twenty minutes, so they made short work of the chocolate mousse cake and lingered over their coffee, and by the time he motioned for the waitress to bring over their check, Claire had put thoughts of home, family, and Corin Flynn from her mind and relaxed into the moment. It wasn't something she usually did well. She was better at worrying, obsessing, wondering what disaster was lurking around the next corner waiting to pounce.

Which was why she didn't see it coming when it finally did.

They were halfway to his car when her cell phone chimed.

"Don't freak out," Kathleen said, "but Grandpa's in the emergency room."

"Jesus Mary and Joseph!" Claire stopped walking dead in her tracks and cupped her hand over her ear. "Say that again." Better yet, don't say it again and let it all be one god-awful bad joke.

"Grandpa tripped over Fritzie in the back hallway," Kathleen said. "I think he broke his ankle."

"Where are you?"

"The waiting room. He threw me out."

"I mean, what hospital?"

"Good Sam."

"Billy's with you, right?"

"I sent him to the coffee shop for sandwiches." A short pause. "The Szechuan tofu wasn't exactly a success."

No surprise there. "I'll be right over."

"Something happened to your father?" David asked as he opened the car door for her.

"He's at Good Sam."

"His heart?"

412

"No," she said. "The cat."

He gave her a blank stare, and she quickly explained the situation. "I've warned him a thousand times about watching out for Fritzie, but does he listen?" Her hands were shaking, and she clutched her purse tightly to control them. The last time she saw her husband alive was in the emergency room at Good Sam. It wasn't a place she wanted to revisit. "Why didn't I have a light installed in the back hallway?"

"I put one in for my father last year, but he'd rather bitch and stumble around in the dark than replace the lightbulb."

He kept up an easygoing, low-key monologue as he drove them to the hospital, and that initial burst of panic began to subside. A broken ankle was an inconvenience, but it wasn't life-threatening. She wasn't going to lose him.

David let her off at the entrance to the ER, then went to park his car. Claire dashed through the automatic doors and bumped straight into Kathleen, who had been waiting for her.

"He's back there," Kathleen said, pointing toward the area beyond the information desk. "Cubicle three."

Claire's hands started to shake again, and she plunged them into the pockets of her jacket. "Did you eat?"

Kathleen nodded. "Tuna sandwiches." She grinned at her mother. "Billy's request. The tofu sucked."

She glanced around. "Where is he?"

"Donna Leitz is upstairs visiting her grandfather. She brought her youngest daughter with her. Billy's showing her the cafeteria."

"David's parking the car. Keep him company, would you, while I go see how Grandpa's doing."

Kathleen gave her a hug. "You got it."

Years ago one of the counselors they had gone to see in an effort to save their family, to save Kathleen, had told them that if they kept working at it, if they managed to keep their focus and never give up, they would be rewarded. She was right. This wonderful, caring young woman standing in front of her was living proof.

She pushed through the double doors and walked straight toward cubicle 3, averting her eyes as she passed the spot where she had said good-bye to her husband. Mike Meehan's booming voice had the curtain rippling.

"Get my clothes," he demanded the second he saw her. "I'm not staying in this dump waiting for them to scratch their —"

"Shut up, Dad!" She marched over to the examining table and kicked the step stool out of his reach. "You're not going anywhere."

"The hell I'm not. Help me off this damn table. They're not going to keep me prisoner here while they take a coffee break."

"I'm not helping you go anywhere until they examine your ankle."

He screwed up his face into a mass of angry

wrinkles. "I've had hangnails that hurt more than this. Gimme a couple of aspirin and call it a night."

She knew testosterone poisoning when she saw it. A man could walk ten miles through a blizzard with a broken leg while a common cold would send him to bed, whining, for a week.

"I called Lilly," he said. "She'll get me out of here."

"You called Lilly?"

"Left a message on her cell. If you don't spring me, she will."

"She springs you over my dead body." The woman would iron his wrinkles and treble his fiber content before he knew what hit him.

A young, fresh-faced nurse popped into the cubicle. "How are we doing in here?"

"He wants out," Claire said with a roll of her eyes.

"I know," said the nurse. "Everyone in the hospital knows."

"One X ray," her father bellowed. "How the hell long does it take to take one X ray?"

"You're not the only one in the hospital who needs an X ray, Mr. Meehan," the nurse explained with more patience than Claire had at her command. "We haven't forgotten about you. You'll be taken as soon as possible."

"I'm old," Mike Meehan said. "I'll probably be dead before you get to me."

"Dad!" Claire wanted to throw herself in front of a runaway gurney.

"Let me see what I can do," the nurse — clearly a woman with a heart of gold as well as the patience of a saint — offered. "Be right back."

"You're worse than Billy," Claire said as soon as the nurse left the cube, "and he's only eight."

"A lot of fuss about nothing," her father said. "Take a picture, wrap it up, send me home. They're acting like it's brain surgery. Go fuss over Barney Kurkowski."

"Barney? What's he doing here?"

"Smoke inhalation. He waved when they brought him through."

"Don't move a muscle," she warned him. "I'll be right back." The only good thing about that broken ankle was it lessened the chances of a jailbreak.

"Bring my clothes with you," he called after her, "or I'm leaving here in my skivvies."

Kathleen and David were chatting in the waiting room while a Larry King rerun blared from the television suspended overhead. They both jumped up when they saw her.

"How is he?" David asked.

"A pain in the ass," she said, and Kathleen laughed.

"Good," her daughter said. "That means he'll be okay."

"The nurse went to see if she could move him up to the head of the line," she said to Kathleen. "Would you go keep an eye on him for a second?"

416

Kathleen pretended she was gearing up for battle, then marched down the hallway.

"Great kid, that daughter of yours," David said.

Claire crossed herself. "From your mouth to God's ear." She glanced around the waiting room. "Have you seen Billy anywhere?"

"You just missed him. He raced through with one of Donna Leitz's kids."

"Go home, David Fenelli," she said. "It's going to be a long night. At least let me spare you the sight of my father breaking out of the hospital in his underwear."

"I don't scare easy."

Maybe he didn't, but she did. She needed a larger buffer zone between family and friends. It was a lesson she had learned during her marriage.

"I'd love a rain check on that movie," she said, hoping he would take the hint.

"I'm glad to hear it."

"Dinner was terrific. Chadwick's was even better than I remembered."

"So was the company."

"Thanks for inviting me."

He gave her a look she couldn't decipher, a combination of affection, curiosity, and maybe a touch of irritation. She didn't know him well enough to be sure. "You have a way to get home?"

"Kathleen brought my car."

"Okay then." He hesitated, and this time she

knew exactly what he was thinking and she took a step backward.

"Drive carefully," she said.

That was the thing about nice guys. They played by the rules. "I'll call you," he said, and she had no doubt that he meant it.

She waved good-bye and dashed through the double doors like a maiden hell-bent on preserving her innocence, which, considering her stretch marks, was pretty funny.

Kathleen was flirting with a strapping young intern near the nurses' desk. Cubicle 3 was empty except for her father's copies of *Sports Illustrated* and the *Racing Form*. This seemed as good a time as any to hunt down her youngest before he turned the hospital on its ear. Her father was more than enough trouble for the nice men and women of Good Sam.

"We can't let you in right now," the attending physician told Corin as he tried to sneak into the ICU.

"I'm sure Kurkowski wouldn't mind."

"You're probably right," the attending physician said, "but the rest of the patients and their families might have something to say about that."

"Fair enough." There were some boundaries that deserved respect. "Did you see where the rest of the film crew went?"

"Surgical waiting. They're following the Morantz kidney transplant."

"The sisters?"

"Good story," the doctor said. "Reminds you that the world is more than assholes and bastards."

"Hey, Doc, watch it, will you?" He gestured toward the kid who had been following him up and down the corridors for almost an hour now.

"Yours?"

"No. I was hoping you knew where he belonged."

"Take him down to patient services. They'll track down the parents."

The doctor's pager went off, and he disappeared down the hallway.

"Where's he going?" the kid asked, turning away from his inspection of the inner workings of an empty water cooler.

"His pager went off."

"Did he have an emergency?"

"He didn't hang around long enough to tell me."

"Wow! Bet there was a big crash on the turnpike, and they brought all the dead bodies here."

"There's a happy thought." Blood, gore, twisted metal. The stuff of dreams for a whole lot of little boys in a country where it wasn't business as usual.

"Where you going now?"

"Up to surgical waiting."

"They don't let kids up there."

"Then I guess we'll shake hands and say good-bye."

The kid had one of those faces that got under your skin. "But I don't know where my mom is."

Great. Now he was bringing out the heavy artillery. Next thing he'd whip out a puppy and a baseball mitt.

"Where did you last see her?"

"Home. She went out with some guy and left me there."

Shit.

"So how'd you end up here?" It was obvious there was nothing physically wrong with the kid. No broken bones. No blood.

"My grandpa broke his ankle."

"So why aren't you with him?"

"I don't know where he is."

"Why don't I take you to the patient information center, and they'll tell us where your grandpa is."

"I'm hungry. Can we go to the cafeteria first?"

He had the suspicion that he was being worked over by a master manipulator.

"Are you sure there's nobody waiting for you?"

"Nope."

"I'm thinking maybe you're a short doctor."

"I'm not old enough."

"I've seen those interns," Corin said. "They're not much older than you are."

"I'm eight. You can't be a doctor when you're only eight."

"I was making a joke, kid," he said, holding

open the door for the literal little rug rat. "I know you have to be at least thirteen."

A tired nurse looked up from her knitting, as they walked in, and glared at his cameras.

"Take one picture of me," she warned, "and you'll be on life support."

"I hear you, Florence Nightingale."

She had a great bawdy laugh, and he was smiling as he slung his gear onto a tabletop and claimed a chair. The kid took a chair across from him.

He pulled out two singles from his back pocket and pushed them toward the kid. "Why don't you get us something from the vending machine?"

"Get what?"

"Surprise me."

"Cool!" He was off like a shot.

The kid was worse than the barnacles he'd watched the fishermen scraping from the hulls of their boats that morning. He reminded Corin of the way he had been at the same age, sparking with curiosity, a dry sponge ready to soak up everything the world had to offer, even if he took out a phalanx of adults in the process.

The kid darted from the sandwich machine in the corner to the candy and snack machines near the door then back again. He had one of those great all-American faces: a sprinkling of freckles, huge dark blue eyes, straight nose, what they used to call an impish grin. He'd love to take a few shots of him, but you didn't photograph kids without express — and preferably written — permission from a parent or guardian. With a face like that on the cover, the companion book to the Paradise Point documentary would hit the *Times* list the first week on the stands.

His gaze drifted from the kid, to the refrigerated case, to the knitting nurse with the bawdy laugh, and he let his mind drift with it. They'd asked him to zero in on the firefighting and fishing parts of the community. He'd spent the day on the docks, photographing the different families who made their living from the sea, then headed over to the firehouse in time to join the crew for an early supper that was interrupted three times by emergency calls that were easily brought under control.

The fourth one, however, was the real thing. A grease fire at one of the local fast-food drive-throughs had quickly grown serious, and he watched through his viewfinder as a well-trained crew walked straight into hell and tamed it. He'd seen a lot of brave men and women do a lot of brave things in his lifetime, but this ranked high on the short list.

This was what Billy O'Malley had been doing when he died. He had heard a lot about Claire's late husband, and there wasn't much he had found to admire about the guy, but this was something nobody could take away from him. He didn't much like finding anything good about O'Malley, but a man who would walk through fire to save somebody else — hell, it was more than he had ever done with his life.

The kid ran back to the table with two packs of Oreos and a bag of Goldfish.

"We need milk," the kid said, "but it costs another dollar for a container."

"You're a hustler," Corin said. "A midget hustler."

"You can't say midget," the kid told him sternly. "My mom says they want to be called little people, and that's what we should do."

So liberal sensibilities were alive and well on the Jersey Shore. He wondered how political correctness managed to coexist with the more conservative mom and apple pie values he had encountered on the docks and in the firehouse.

"The milk," the kid prodded him. "We've gotta have milk, or we can't eat the cookies."

He slid two more singles toward the blue-eyed bandit. "That's it," he warned. "The bank's closed."

Did all kids move that fast, or was this one turbocharged? Wait until he sucked up those cookies and the sugar rush hit. He would be doing wheelies on the ceiling. He watched as the kid slid a single into the machine, punched a button, then waited for the thunk as a carton of milk hit the tray. He slid in another single, punched a button, collected the second container of milk, then brought everything back to the table.

"We each get a pack of Oreos," the kid said. "We can flip for the Goldfish."

The kid really was a little hustler. He would go far in life.

"I have a better idea. We can split the Goldfish."

They each tore into a pack of Oreos and jammed the cookies into their mouths like a pair of four-year-olds. Which wasn't that big a stretch for the kid but wasn't something Corin wanted captured on film for posterity.

He was about to rip into the bag of Goldfish and start doling them out when the kid looked past him.

"Uh-oh," he said. "It's my mom."

"If she wants Oreos, she's on her own," he said. "You took my last single."

He heard footsteps behind him and then a familiar voice. "Thanks for keeping your eye on him, Corin."

She sounded tired, a little puzzled, definitely wary. The second the words hit the air, it all fell into place, and he wondered how the hell he had missed it. The kid was his father all over again. He'd spent enough time looking through photos of Billy O'Malley at the firehouse that afternoon, studying the face of the dead man who had been Claire's husband. The dark hair. The straight nose. The dark blue eyes. That off-center grin. There it was, right in front of him, in miniature.

He must have been blind.

"Don't you feed this kid?" he asked as he turned to look at her, opting for the easy joke to get them past this moment. He stood up, instinctively knowing he would need every advantage he could get.

Too bad she didn't see the humor in the remark. "I'll reimburse you. How much did he take you for?"

"I was making a joke."

She plunged her hand deep into her purse and pulled out a fistful of singles and put them down in front of him. "That should cover it."

"I don't want your money."

"Please," she said. "You don't have to pay for my son's cookie habit."

"Claire —"

Billy jumped up in a flurry of cookie crumbs. "I'm going to go see Grandpa."

"He's getting his ankle X-rayed right now."

"I'll wait for him," Billy said.

"You don't know where they took him."

"Yes, I do. The nurse showed me."

"Take Kathleen with you," Claire said. "You'll find her outside of Grandpa's cubicle."

Billy started to make his escape, but Claire stopped him with some kind of invisible maternal force field. "Thank Corin for the cookies."

"Thanks," the kid said, then tore out of the coffee shop at warp speed.

"He's eight," she said, patches of color staining her cheeks and throat. "They're not known for their manners."

"He's better than the camera crew filming upstairs."

She tried to smile, but the results weren't very impressive. "I hope he wasn't too big a pain in the ass."

"He asks a lot of questions."

"Like I said, he's eight. They eat, and they ask questions."

"Your father's here?"

She grimaced and ran a hand across her face in a concealing gesture he remembered very well. "Broken ankle," she said. "He tripped over one of our cats and took a header in the hallway."

"How's he doing?"

"Bitching up a storm, so I don't think it's too serious."

"I was about to split a bag of Goldfish with your kid. Want some?"

"No thanks. I'd better get back upstairs and see what's going on."

"Claire, I —"

"Don't." She raised her hand between them. "There's no point. I know how you feel. I even understand it. Why don't we just leave it at that?"

"He's a great kid." *You made the right choice, Claire. There was nothing I could offer you that would have equaled a son like that.*

"I know." She softened a little. "He's the one I was —"

"— pregnant with the last time we saw each

other." He had never seen a woman look more tired, or more lovely, in his life. He had spent eight years hating the existence of a child he had never met, only to have it all turned inside out over Oreos and Goldfish. "He looks a lot like his father."

She was instantly on alert. "How do you know that?"

He told her about the afternoon in the firehouse.

"You probably heard a lot of stories while you were there."

"Nothing you hadn't told me already."

"I doubt that." The look in her eyes was unreadable. "It's been a long time, and a lot has happened since then."

He wanted to say something profound, something so wise and comforting that it would erase the mistakes, the longing, the years that had separated them, but all he could do was reach for her hand. She had long, strong fingers. Her nails were short and unpolished. The cold metal of her wedding ring bit into his palm.

She gave nothing. No encouragement. No censure. Anger he could have dealt with. Tears he could understand. But indifference — there was nothing a man could do if a woman just didn't give a damn.

They were standing only inches apart, and he caught the faint scent of perfume on her skin, felt the heat of her anger.

"You deserve an apology. I acted like a shit the last time I saw you."

"I should have told you I was pregnant. I was afraid if I —"

"Nothing would have kept me away, Claire."

"That would have."

The fight went out of him. She was right. The sight of her big with Billy O'Malley's child had put an end to his dreams of a future for them. She was carrying the future in her belly, and it didn't belong to him.

He nodded, and she closed her eyes for an instant.

"See?" Her glance drifted toward the cafeteria entrance and skimmed the knitting nurse. "I wanted those last few hours with you so badly that I didn't care how it made you feel." The old Claire would have wept with remorse or breathed fire. The one who stood in front of him had her emotions under lock and key. "I just want you to know that I'm sorry."

"It didn't go the way either one of us expected."

Wishful thinking, or was that a flash of something close to fire sparking behind the cool facade?

"What did you expect?" she asked him. "We never really got that far."

Not even close. Eight years ago on that sunswept Boardwalk in Atlantic City, he had responded to the sight of her with an eruption of outrage and betrayal that still shocked him with its ferocity. He had no right to those emotions, but that hadn't stopped him from spilling anger like gasoline on a fire neither one of them had known how to control.

A pair of doctors drifted into the cafeteria and shot a quick look in their direction. Claire pulled her hand away.

"I have to go," she said. "I want to stop in and see how Barney's doing."

"I'll go with you."

"Not a great idea. You're not on my father's top-ten list," she said. "Or my daughter's, either."

"I saw her yesterday at O'Malley's," he said. "She looks just like you."

Her expression softened, and again he saw through the wall of self-defense she had constructed and caught a glimpse of the woman he remembered.

"She warned me about you."

"She remembers me? She was just a kid."

"Kids remember more than we give them credit for."

"What did she say?"

"She's afraid you'll hurt me again." She didn't break the look passing between them. "I told her it was the other way around."

"She didn't believe you."

"No, she didn't. She's had too much experience with the other side of that coin."

A trio of nonknitting nurses joined the one with the bawdy laugh, followed quickly by a pair of doctors who nodded at them.

"That's my father's oncologist," she said, pointing toward the younger of the pair.

"I shot a roll of film watching the other one prep for the delivery room," he said.

"I'd better go," she repeated. "I have to phone my sisters, try to track down my brother —"

"I'll be at the lighthouse Monday afternoon around three o'clock. The Coast Guard is going to let me spend an hour photographing it from the inside. I want you to join me."

She opened her mouth to tell him all the reasons why she wouldn't show up, but he stopped her before she started.

"Don't say anything. It's up to you. Either way, I'll be there at three."

She looked at him for a long moment, and again he saw through the layers of defenses, through the pain, through the years that separated them, and for an instant he saw the woman he fell in love with. She could say what she wanted, but that woman still existed.

And if she didn't, maybe he would get to know the woman who did.

"Not you, Gramma," Hannah said when Rose stood up and declared it was time for the child's bedtime bath. "I want Kelly."

Rose turned to her. "It's a dirty job," she said with a wink. "Feel like tackling it?"

Kelly pushed away from the table and stretched. "Only if there are bubbles involved."

"Can Barbie take a bath, too?" Hannah asked.

"Only if she takes off her astronaut outfit before she gets into the tub," Rose warned her granddaughter. "The last time Barbie took a bath, the plumber found a picture hat and a winter coat stuck in the pipes."

"We'll be careful," Kelly promised.

Rose stood up and took off her glasses. "Poor Priscilla. She's probably ready to burst. I think I'll take a break from scrapbooking while you two are upstairs and take our girl for a walk."

Rose went off in search of Maddy and Hannah's toy poodle puppy while Hannah raced Kelly upstairs to one of the luxurious family bathrooms that would bring out the inner mermaid in even the most die-hard landlubber.

Hannah was a talker, and she chatted happily while Kelly ran the bath, adjusted the temperature, then added the kid-friendly bubbles and waited for them to froth up into a fragrant white mountain. Finally the little girl, Barbie, and an aging Jasmine action figure from Disney's Aladdin were settled in the tub. Kelly pulled the dressing table chair closer and sat down to supervise.

The room was steamy and fragrant from the gardenia-scented bubbles, and the combination of the warmth and the soothingly sweet sound of Hannah's happy chatter soon had Kelly drifting. The frothy bubble bath was strangely fitting, because all evening she had felt like she was in a bubble herself, safe and protected. That was part of The Candlelight's charm.

Warmth and comfort were programmed into every overstuffed chair, every crackling fireplace, every slice of chocolate mousse cake. The second she crossed the threshold that afternoon, everything else had dropped away, and she had felt less alone, less frightened of what lay ahead. Nothing beyond The Candlelight seemed real. Not that manic run to the mall. Not the big fat plus sign that confirmed her fears. Not lying to Seth and telling him they were in the clear, that there was no problem, no baby, no end to their dreams.

It was easy to just let go and drift, to pretend that she was exactly the same girl she had been this time last month or the month before and that her future was still golden.

And it would be golden again. She would do what she had to do and then pick up right where she had left off before this detour.

She loved her father, and she loved her Aunt Claire, but there was something special about being part of this family of women who had already welcomed her into their midst. Rose no longer scared her into silence. Sitting around that wonderful table piled high with their combined memories, Kelly had experienced a feeling of kinship that startled her. Rose's sister Lucy treated her like one of her own nieces. Hannah charmed her out of her shoes. Even the colorful cousins felt like extended family.

Only Maddy seemed to remain just out of reach. Oh, she was warm and friendly and funny, but that was as far as it went with them. Sometimes Kelly had the feeling that they were standing on opposite sides of a very wide river, waiting for someone to come along and build a bridge between them. She had held her breath this morning when Maddy caught her buying the testing kit, sure that Maddy would confront her the way her Aunt Claire or any of her friends' mothers would have done. But not Maddy. She had chatted on just like Hannah in the bathtub, like nothing unusual was going on.

Which was okay. Really. It wasn't like Kelly blamed her or anything. Maddy wasn't her mother. She wasn't even her stepmother, not yet. She was just a really nice woman who didn't want to take on the problems of a girl she barely knew. She had her own daughter to worry about, her own mother, a wedding to plan, her radio show, Cuppa, a million other things besides Kelly and her problems. If she didn't want to get involved, she didn't have to.

A mother had to listen to her daughter's problems. A mother had to be there when her children needed her. A mother —

Look at her getting all sentimental and weepy just because she had spent the evening sorting through some faded photographs of people who were dead and gone.

You look very much like your mother . . . she was a beautiful girl.

"Are you crying?" Hannah's voice cut into her thoughts.

433

"No, I'm not crying. I was resting my eyes." Wasn't that what older people always said to cover up everything from tears to catnaps?

"You're supposed to be watching me."

"I am watching you."

"You can't watch me with your eyes closed."

"You're right," she said, forcing her lids into the upright position. "I'm sorry, Hannah."

"My mommy wouldn't close her eyes."

She was probably right about that, too. There seemed to be a list somewhere out there in the universe of all the things mommies would and wouldn't do, and every little girl had it memorized.

"Then I promise I won't take my eyes off you, Hannah." She made a silly bug-eyed face that propelled the little girl into a fit of bubble-fueled giggles but not before she saw the look of relief in her eyes.

"Okay," Hannah said, once again restored to her rightful position as empress of all she surveyed. "That's what my mommy would do."

A lump formed in the back of her throat, hard and painful. At barely five years of age, Hannah already knew more about the secret world of mothers and daughters than Kelly ever would.

Chapter Twenty-one

Courtship, of course, was the easy part. Both Maddy and Aidan knew that the magical spell that had embraced them for the last twenty-four hours in that room overlooking the ocean would vanish in the face of real life. That was a given. But they couldn't help wishing they could delay the inevitable just a little bit longer.

Checkout time was noon. Maddy was sure she could hear the clock ticking down the minutes as she and Aidan toweled off after one last interlude in that wondrous Jacuzzi.

"We really should get ourselves one of those," Maddy said as she slipped into her jeans and zipped them up.

"You've seen my place. The bathrooms are the size of coat closets."

"Then let's move."

"I thought we decided we were going to live in my house."

"We also decided we were going to have ten kids and send them all to Princeton." She wrapped her arms around him and pressed a kiss to his back. "This is called fantasy, O'Malley. Get with it."

"I don't need fantasies anymore," he said. "Not since I found you."

Pretty speeches didn't come easily for the man she was going to marry. Those ten words were all of Shakespeare's love sonnets rolled into one.

"I feel married to you now," she whispered against his back. "I feel like last night was our wedding night." The commitment to him, to their future together, was that strong.

He turned around and gathered her into his arms, and she had the sense of being exactly where she was meant to be, the one safe place in a world that shifted and changed beneath your feet. She knew his secrets now. She knew the effort it took for him to do things she took for granted. Anything she thought she'd known about the level of pain he dealt with on a daily basis had fallen far short of the truth. He had been afraid she would find him less of a man when she saw him as he was, but the truth was he was so much more than even she had dreamed.

She could see him with Hannah, helping to guide her toward adolescence, helping them all navigate the choppy waters of her teenage years, and she thanked God that she had found a man who valued the same things she valued, a man whose heart would expand to include everyone she loved. This wasn't love the way she had envisioned it when she was in her twenties. When she first met Hannah's father Tom, love had been an adventure. Watching the sunset from the balcony of Tom's penthouse. Weekend trips to Vancouver. An uncertain future that seemed more like playing house than building a real life together.

What she had found with Aidan went far beyond what she had known with Tom, almost as if the experiences belonged to two different women.

Maybe they had. She had changed since returning home to New Jersey and her family. The urge to run when the going got tough was slowly being replaced by the need to stay where she was, to dig her roots a little deeper, to admit there was something wonderful about being part of a family, even when the family in question sometimes made you crazy.

She had finally decided what to do about Kelly, and she had Rose to thank. Her mother was right. She wasn't doing anyone a favor by keeping her suspicions and worries to herself. Tomorrow evening she would sit down with Aidan and tell him what she knew, the plain facts without embellishment, and pray that she had been worried for nothing.

They checked out of their suite with just two minutes to spare, both of them reluctant to leave their secret hideaway but feeling the pull of home and children.

"Go ahead," he said as they merged onto the Parkway headed south. "You know you want to."

"You want to just as much as I do."

"Yeah, but I can't. I'm driving."

"I know it's ridiculous. Rosie would have called if there was anything we needed to know, but I can't help myself."

"If you didn't do it, I would," he said, and she burst into laughter.

She reached into her tote bag, pulled out her cell phone, then punched in her mother's number. All she had to do was say hello. Rose took care of the rest.

"Our kids are okay," she said to Aidan after she disconnected, "but Mike Meehan is in the hospital."

She relayed the tale about Fritzie, the broken ankle, the minor surgery, the chemotherapy-connected complication.

"Sounds like Mike isn't exactly being a model patient. Rosie said Claire's having a tough time keeping him there. She called two of her sisters, but they're not sure they can break free to help her out."

"Her sisters only show up when there's a will to be read," Aidan said. Then, "Damn. That means she's probably not going to work this afternoon."

"And Barney Kurkowski was checked in. Smoke inhalation."

Aidan flinched. When a firefighter got close to

438

retirement, nobody rested easily until the day he hung up his gear and said good-bye.

This led to a flurry of phone calls to O'Malley's that ended up with Aidan saying he'd take over Claire's four o'clock spot.

"I forgot to tell you the juicy gossip Rose heard at Mass this morning. Gina took Crystal to that karaoke bar down near Wildwood and ended up getting herself tattooed."

"What did she get, and where did she get it?"

"A triton's horn, and it's someplace you're never going to see and live to talk about."

"Sounds like they had a few too many margaritas. How the hell did they drive home?"

"Crystal panicked when Gee passed out on the way back to the bar. She called Peter Lassiter, and he drove down to get them."

"That'll look good on tape."

"That's exactly what I was thinking. She's had a rough time of it lately with Joey being sick and all that trouble with her ex. She was just blowing off steam. I really hope they don't use it in the documentary." God knew her family had already provided them with enough material to run a weekly series for the next ten years. "Crystal swore it was an off-the-record night out but . . ."

"She's not a kid, Maddy. She knew what she was doing when she went off with Crystal."

"I know you're right but —" She stopped midsentence and shook her head. Gina's problems were better saved for another time. "Let's declare a moratorium on the real world until we see the Welcome to Paradise Point sign bearing down on us. What do you say?"

"I say I like the way you think." She felt the heat of his look in every secret part of her body. "Almost as much as I liked the way you —"

Now that was the kind of talk that made the miles fly by.

It was all beginning to seem real to her in a way it hadn't before this weekend. Up until now it had all been about the wedding — what to wear, who to invite, where to hold it — and very little about the marriage, but that had all changed overnight. Suddenly she saw them not just as the giddy bride and groom on top of a spun-sugar wedding cake, but as a husband and wife with children to protect and a future to build, and it was as exhilarating as it was terrifying.

"What do you think Rosie will say when you tell her?"

"Shh," Maddy said, holding her index finger to her lips. "I don't want to think about it."

"She's not going to be happy."

"No, she's not. She thought a September wedding was too short notice. Late July is going to push her right over the edge."

"Good thing we didn't elope this morning."

They had come very close, and only the fact that their daughters deserved an easier entry into living as a blended family had held them back. Waiting until September suddenly made no sense at all. They loved each other. They were well past the age of consent. They understood exactly what they were getting into and wanted to do it just the same. They also both knew that life came with no guarantees, and sometimes the smartest thing you could do was to follow your heart.

They had talked late into the night about anything and everything, and now, speeding down the Parkway, they picked up the threads and began to weave them into something real. Major issues like where they would live (Aidan's house) and how many children they wanted to have together (they finally talked the number down to two) and whether or not they would raise them as practicing Catholics (to be determined) came together effortlessly in seamless agreement.

They talked about O'Malley's. They talked about The Candlelight. They talked about her radio gig. He told her about his plans to go back to school and pursue the degree he had abandoned years ago. She told him that she wasn't sure it was going to work out for her at Cuppa, that it was painfully clear she and his brother's widow didn't see the world through the same lens.

"You don't have to like each other to work together," he said. "All you have to do is stick around and make it work."

"You make it sound like I've spent my life running away from things." She let out a loud, theatrical sigh. "A girl runs away for ten or fif-

441

teen years and — boom! — she finds herself with a reputation."

His silence went on a beat too long.

"Laugh," she said. "You were supposed to laugh."

"Stick around, no matter what," he said. "You can run away from anyone else, but don't run away from me."

An odd little chill rippled up her spine at his words.

"As if that could happen," she said, but she couldn't help thinking about Kelly as she did.

Aidan asked if she wanted to stop in at the hospital with him and see how Mike Meehan was doing, but she begged off. She didn't know Claire's father well at all, and she was eager to get home and see Hannah.

"I'll stop by tomorrow," she said. "I'm sure he won't miss me."

Mike Meehan was one of those men who gathered friends the way squirrels gathered nuts in the fall. His room was probably crowded wall-to-wall with enough visitors to constitute a fire hazard.

Aidan pulled into the driveway behind the house and unloaded her bag. They laughed at the sound of Priscilla's excited yapping as she scratched at the back door with insistent puppy claws.

"Rosie's car is gone," Maddy observed as he carried her bag into the house. The ever-watchful Priscilla greeted them with much tail-wagging, then galloped out to the yard to take care of business. "She and Hannah must have gone over to the hospital to see Mike."

"There's a note on the table," Aidan said as he placed her bag near the doorway. He picked it up. "Hospital first, Gina's second. She'll be back around six."

She wrapped her arms around him. "You mean we actually have the house to ourselves?"

He pretended to peer under the kitchen table. "Unless Lassiter and his crew bugged the joint."

She shuddered. "Don't even say that! They've learned enough about the lot of us as it is."

He tilted her chin up for his kiss. "So you're going to tell Rosie tonight?"

"Yep," she said, her lips moving against his. "No point delaying the inevitable."

"July twenty-first." A full eight weeks earlier than originally planned.

"You'll hear her scream of horror all the way at O'Malley's."

"You're sure?"

"Positive."

He whispered something in her ear that made her melt into him and want to never let go. She was going to suggest something illicit and highly erotic when Priscilla came charging back into the house, trailing what looked like a small bramble bush behind her.

"Coward," she said as Aidan made for the door.

She could hear him laughing as he drove away. So much for her graceful reentry back into everyday life.

Priscilla looked up at her with those big brown eyes of hers, and Maddy sighed. "I know, I know," she said. "My hair's curly, too. It's a pain in the neck, isn't it?"

She hunted down the grooming comb and a small pair of blunt-tip scissors, then sat down on the back porch to untangle the poor puppy from the forest of brambles and thorns she had somehow stumbled into. A steady breeze was blowing in off the water, turning the late after-noon noticeably chilly. Priscilla didn't think too much of standing still while Maddy tried to work through the mats and burrs, so Maddy had to gather the puppy up in a bear hug with her left arm while she carefully wielded the scissors with her right.

"You look like you need some help."

Maddy jumped, almost pitching Priscilla to the ground, at the sound of Kelly's voice. "Where did you come from?"

"Sorry if I scared you," Kelly said. "I rang the front doorbell. When nobody answered, I fig-ured I'd come around and let myself in with the back door key." She laughed as Priscilla wrig-gled free and bounded down the steps toward her, tail at full mast. "When did you guys get home?"

The words were innocent enough, but Maddy felt herself go instantly into red alert.

"About fifteen minutes ago. Your dad went on to the hospital to see Mike Meehan."

"I suppose he'll be working tonight."

Maddy nodded as she gathered Priscilla back up onto her lap and prepared to try again.

"So what brings you here?" Maddy asked as she gently eased the wire comb through some nasty knots on the dog's coat.

"I left an envelope of photos on the dining room table this morning."

"Sounds like Rosie had you and Hannah scrapbooking last night."

"It was fun," Kelly said in her usual easygoing manner. "Between your Grandma Fay and my Grandma Irene, they must have known everything there was to know about everyone."

"Did she show you the box labeled O'Malley?"

"Yeah, and it was pretty amazing. I didn't realize our families were that close way back then."

Way back then was probably around the time of Maddy's birth.

"Door's open," she said, "if you want to get them."

Kelly hesitated a second, then hurried up the three steps and let herself in through the kitchen door.

A moment later she let herself back out again. She had a thick brown envelope tucked under her arm.

"You found everything you were looking for?"

"No problem. Mrs. D left them on the sideboard for me."

There was a natural rhythm to conversations between friends and family, and Maddy waited for the *good-bye* and *see you later,* but Kelly didn't say a word. She didn't leave. She didn't talk. She just stood there, looking down at her running shoes.

"Kelly?" Maddy slid Priscilla from her lap and stood up. "I was just about to splurge on some of Lucy's Black Forest cake and a pot of tea. Why don't you join me?"

"I shouldn't. I have a lot to do. I'd better go."

"One piece," Maddy urged, like one of those food pushers whose main goal in life was to make sure you couldn't squeeze your thighs into your jeans.

"Next time, okay? I have to give my cousin Kathleen a lift to the train station and —"

She couldn't hold back the question. It had been there between them all week, and it wasn't going away.

"Did you run the test, Kelly?" Oh God, what was she doing? It sounded so harsh, so stark. So not her business.

"Test?" The girl tried to look puzzled, but the expression in her lovely eyes gave her away.

"The home pregnancy test you bought at the mall yesterday."

Kelly's face turned dead white, and Maddy pulled in a breath. Her muscles tensed, and she felt an almost irresistible urge to race down the steps, dash across the yard, then jump into her car and drive as far away from this whole thing as her battered old Mustang could carry her.

Aidan was right. They were all right. She did want to run. Her mother and her aunts and her cousins, even Claire. All of them. She didn't need this. God knew she didn't want any part of it. It would be easy to turn away from Kelly's troubles, let them flow through her fingers like grains of sand. But she knew too much about what Kelly was going through, felt too much and too deeply for the young woman to take the easy way out. Not this time.

She put her arm gently around Kelly's shoulder and led her back inside the kitchen. All of Kelly's natural ebullience and self-confidence had drained away. The girl sank into a chair, shoulders slumped, her lovely face a mask of sadness.

"How far along are you?" Maddy asked as she knelt down beside the girl.

Kelly's whole body recoiled at the question. "Maybe five or six weeks." Her words were little more than a whisper, and Maddy had to lean close in order to hear them.

"You're sure?" Maddy pressed. "You ran the test and it was positive."

"Positively positive," she said with a small, hollow laugh. "I ran it twice."

"So did I when I first found out Hannah was on the way."

"I thought I was being anal about it."

"So did I."

One of the things Maddy had always found disconcerting about her future stepdaughter was the very adult way she carried herself. Aidan called her an old soul, and the more Maddy saw of her, the more she had come to believe that was true. Her self-possession and maturity were so far beyond where Maddy had been at that age — or now, for that matter — that Maddy had always been mildly in awe of the girl, more than a little uncomfortable.

But suddenly she was just a seventeen-year-old girl, a girl in terrible trouble, and Maddy's maternal instinct kicked into high gear. She saw herself in Kelly, and she saw Hannah not that many years from now, and the thought of her little girl facing such a life-changing situation made her wish she could stop time. She opened her arms to the girl, and Kelly clung to her like a terrified child. She whispered that it would be okay, that everything would be okay, that she wasn't alone, that she didn't have to face her future by herself, that she was loved and cared for . . . powerful incantations against a terrifying and uncertain future.

Kelly was trembling in her arms. She felt painfully fragile, as if a harsh word, the wrong look, might snap her in two. No matter how hard Maddy tried, she couldn't warm the girl's hands.

"You're freezing. I'll make you some tea."

Kelly shook her head. "No, thanks. I can't keep anything down today."

How well she remembered. "I promise once you get past the first trimester it vanishes like a bad dream." She started to say more about the miraculous changes that happen almost the day after you finish the twelfth week when Kelly started to cry.

Not just gentle tears streaming down her cheeks, but ugly sobs that rose up from the depths of a despair Maddy prayed Hannah would never know.

"I know it all seems terribly overwhelming right now, Kel, but you're not alone. You have your entire family behind you. We'll all help you. And there's Seth." Oh God, how would Seth handle this? Kelly and Seth were very close — Rose joked that at times they seemed like an old married couple — but Maddy knew all too well what an unplanned pregnancy could do to a relationship. If two reasonably mature adults couldn't make it work, what hope was there for a pair of teenagers? "Have you told Seth?" she asked gently.

"He knew I was late," Kelly choked out between sobs, "but —" She shook her head, then buried her face in her hands. "I told him it was a false alarm."

She stroked Kelly's hair and tried desperately to make light of the remark. "Well, honey, the truth is going to have to come out pretty soon. In another two or three months, he'll be able to see it for himself."

"No, he won't." Kelly looked up at her, face streaked with tears, anguish plainly visible in her eyes. "After tomorrow there won't be a baby."

Maddy felt like she had been leveled by a bulldozer. So this was how it felt when your convictions slammed headfirst into the real world. It was one thing to say a woman had the right to choose, but looking at Aidan's daughter, she found herself unable to speak over the deep, aching sense of loss that suddenly filled her heart at the thought of the choice she had made.

"Don't look at me like that," Kelly begged her. "I've thought it all through, and there's no other way."

"I'm not looking at you any way, honey. I'm just . . . surprised by your decision. You should talk to Seth before —"

"No! It's better this way. You know Seth. You know what he's like. He'll toss away his scholarship and say he wants us to get married, and then where will we be? His whole future —" She shook her head. "Do you see why I can't tell him? My way is better. By tomorrow night it will be all over, and everything will be back to normal."

"Not for you."

"Sure it will," Kelly tried to smile. "It's not like I've had time to get attached to the idea or anything. It's not even real to me yet. I can handle this myself, but I couldn't handle seeing everyone —" She broke down again, those terrible

450

racking sobs that tore Maddy's heart out. "Things are just starting to go right, you know? Seth has the scholarship . . . Daddy has you . . . Aunt Claire has the new job, and Mr. Fenelli seems interested in her, and —" She stopped and sucked in a loud, shaky gulp of air. "If I decided to have the baby, everything would change. I know it would. Everybody's dreams would be put on hold and — I mean, this isn't what they expect from me, you know? I'm the one they depend on. I don't get into trouble. I do what I'm supposed to do. I'm the one who's supposed to make them all proud." Her hands cupped her flat belly, then quickly slid away. "Not get knocked up two months before graduation."

"You need to talk to Seth, honey. This is his responsibility, too." She wiped away some of the tears with one of Rose's pale yellow linen napkins. "And you need to talk to your dad. He's a good man. He'll stand by you." Aidan would support his daughter in every way he could — she didn't doubt that for a second — but she also knew the news would break his heart. This wasn't the future he had wanted for his daughter. *All I ever had to do was point Kelly in the right direction, and she did the rest.* How many times had she heard him use that sentence to deflect praise for his parenting skills as his daughter claimed one award after another, added one more achievement to her lengthy list of triumphs.

"It's too late. I have an appointment for tomorrow at five. They had a cancellation, and I was l-lucky enough to get it."

"You don't have to do this, honey. There are other alternatives."

She met Maddy's eyes. "Once you held Hannah, would you have been able to give her up for adoption?"

"No," she said, wishing just once for the easy, forgivable lie. "I wouldn't have."

"You can't tell anyone," Kelly begged. "I don't even know why I told you."

"You didn't tell me anything, honey," she reminded the girl. "It wasn't hard to figure out."

"Oh God." The color drained from Kelly's face. "You don't think anyone else has figured anything out, do you?"

"I don't know," she said carefully. "Sometimes we see what we want to see and manage to block out everything else." God knew she had done that many times in her life and would probably do so again. "Your father has been worried about you. I can tell you that."

"See!" Kelly sounded triumphant. "That's what I don't want. If he knew anything about this, it would kill him."

"Kelly, your father is a very strong man. Yes, he'll be upset, very upset, to find out you're pregnant, but it won't kill him. He'll be there to support you, same as he always has."

"I've thought it all out," Kelly said, "and my mind is made up. This is the right thing for me to do. I know it is."

"You're a minor. You can't undergo a surgical procedure without parental permission."

"Yes, I can. I searched the Internet for the information. New Jersey doesn't require parental permission or notification."

"Are you sure? Laws can change without you realizing it."

"I'm sure."

"You sound like you've researched this pretty well."

"I have." Her smile was grim. "You should see the lists I made."

"Some decisions defy logic."

Kelly shook her head. "I can't afford to think that way. This is the best decision for everyone concerned."

"Please tell your father," Maddy begged her one more time. "I know they call it a minor procedure, but I'd feel better if he knew where you were." Surgery was minor only when it was happening to somebody you hadn't grown to love dearly.

"You know where I'll be. Isn't that good enough?"

"I know why you're going, but I don't know where you'll actually be."

"Please don't do this," Kelly whispered. "You're not going to get me to change my mind, so why don't you just let me do what I have to do?"

"Would it hurt to take a week or so to really think about it? You still have time."

Kelly leaped to her feet, startling Priscilla, who had been sleeping beneath the table. "I've done nothing *but* think about it for weeks now. If I think about it anymore, I'll go crazy."

She looked exhausted, terrified, frightened, and painfully young.

"You're asking a lot of yourself, honey. You think it will be easy to keep a secret like this, but it won't be. It's going to change the way you see the world and yourself."

"I can handle it."

"You think you can, but —"

"Now I get it. You're going to tell him, aren't you?" Kelly's voice rose in accusation. "That's what all this is about. The second I walk out, you're going to call my father and tell him."

She didn't deny the accusation. Of course she had to tell Aidan. She loved him. He was the girl's father. He had to know. "I'm in a terrible position, Kelly. Your father and I are going to be married. He deserves my loyalty." And that meant telling him everything.

"And I'm going to be your daughter. Don't I deserve your loyalty?"

"You're the reason I'm doing this," Maddy said. "It's your welfare I'm concerned about. I can't let you go off to God knows where without telling your father about what's going on. You both deserve better than that from me."

"He'll try to talk me out of it."

"You don't know what he'll do, honey. Nei-

454

ther do I. In the end it will still be your choice. That much I'm sure of."

Kelly grew very quiet, and Maddy matched her silence with silence of her own. If she walked out that door, there was nothing Maddy could do to stop her. They both knew Kelly held all the cards. Which one she would play was anybody's guess.

Kelly was the first to speak. "What if I tell you exactly where I'm going? I'll give you the name of the clinic, the address, what time I'm supposed to check in. If I do that, will you promise to keep my secret?"

Maddy felt like she was free-falling from a burning plane straight into a forest fire. No matter what she did she was bound to crash and burn.

"And if I say no?"

"Then I'll drive up to New York tonight. I know of two clinics where I could find help."

Kelly was shaking so violently she had to hold on to the back of the kitchen chair for support. *Please, God, if this ever happens to Hannah, help me to find the right words to say.* Clearly she hadn't been able to find the right ones to reach Kelly. Her mind was clearly made up, and Maddy knew that nothing she said or did would make a bit of difference. She wasn't her mother. They didn't share a history, a richness of mutual experience a mother could draw upon to sway her daughter over to her side. The truth was, they barely knew each other, and no matter how well Kelly's experience mirrored Maddy's, the bond between them was tenuous, at best.

The girl was on the edge of making a life-changing decision, one she would live with every day for the rest of her life. There were no easy answers in a situation like this. Maddy knew that firsthand. No matter what Kelly decided to do, she would pay a price. But she shouldn't have to pay that price alone.

"I'll keep your secret," Maddy said at last. "I still feel Seth and your father should know what you've decided, but I'm willing to keep your secret if you'll let me come with you tomorrow."

"You want to go with me to the clinic?"

"Yes."

She stared at Maddy as if she had never seen her before. "Why?"

"Because you need me there."

"I already told you I —"

"You need me there with you," she continued, "but not half as much as I need to be there with you."

Relief and suspicion played themselves out across Kelly's face. "You'll come with me, and you won't tell anyone?"

"If that's the only way I can make sure you're not alone, then yes, I will."

Kelly wrote down the name and address of the clinic and handed it to Maddy. "I have to be there at five."

"I'll drive you."

Kelly opened her mouth to protest, but

Maddy was in charge, and she quickly shot down all arguments.

They arranged to meet at the high school parking lot near the football field at two o'clock. The clinic was two towns over, in the small office building a half-mile before the turnoff for the lighthouse.

She walked Kelly around front to her car.

"Please think about the things I said," she begged Kelly as the two women hugged. "You're allowed to change your mind."

"I won't," Kelly said. "I know what I have to do."

So did Maddy, and she had less than twenty-four hours to make it happen.

Chapter Twenty-two

It was after six when the fishing boat docked back at Paradise Point. The captain, a clean-cut young man who looked more like an accountant, eased the vessel up to its berth, and minutes later, Corin and the PBS crew were back on dry land.

"This was *so* not a good idea," Peter Lassiter's pierced and tattooed assistant Cyrstal declared as they walked toward the parking area behind O'Malley's Bar and Grill. "I feel sick."

"A bit of advice, kid," Harry the sound man said with a grin. "Don't drink a pitcherful of margaritas the night before you head out to sea. Not unless you know what you're doing."

Crystal hadn't exactly been a happy camper out there on the bounding main. She had spent the first two hours of their trip with her head over the railing, begging God to end it all before she ended it herself. Her colleagues had been merciless, ragging her about her low tolerance for drink, urging Corin to snap candid photos of her in the throes of major digestive disturbances. Yeah, that and colonoscopies. Great idea.

The day had been a waste. He made a living finding beauty in the ordinary, and today he had come up empty. The pictures he had taken were run-of-the-mill, picture-postcard compositions that didn't intrigue or illuminate. The brilliant glitter of sunlight on the ocean was flat and muddy. The incongruity of the young fishing boat captain barking orders to his grizzled crew looked staged and false through his viewfinder.

He found himself longing for the weathered beauty of Claire's face, the fine lines that fanned out from the corners of her eyes, the narrow nose with the smattering of freckles, the elegant Katharine Hepburnesque cheekbones. Her mouth. He could spend a lifetime photographing her mouth. Big wide smile. The tiny gap between her front teeth. The surprising fullness of her lower lip when he caught it between his teeth and —

"Hey!" Crystal tapped him on the shoulder. "We're going out to Antonio's for clams. You're coming, right?"

"Sure," he said as they reached their cars. "As long as one of you guys knows where the hell Antonio's is."

Lassiter had the On Star system, so he climbed into his Lexus and headed out like a high-tech Magellan, followed by the sound and film crew in a rented van. Crystal, still a bit hungover and more than a little put out over the endless teasing, hitched a ride with him.

"You think you're up to garlic and wine?" Corin asked as they fell in line behind the van. "You might be better off with a bowl of cereal and an early night."

She looked up at him with enormous, dark-circled eyes. "Is that an offer?"

He laughed out loud. "No, it's a suggestion. You were in pretty bad shape out there this afternoon."

She groaned and rested her forehead against the closed window. "You know what really pisses me off is that my horoscope said this was supposed to be a great day for travel."

"Did your horoscope mention anything about chugging a gallon of margaritas the night before?"

She forced a laugh. "I must have missed that part."

"I hope it was worth it." Most of his mornings-after had followed less than memorable nights-before.

"Oh yeah. It was a fab place." She gave him a sly grin. "If you think I was bad, you should've seen Gina DiFalco. She got a tattoo, then passed out cold on the sidewalk."

Want proof you're getting older? There it was. Crystal might as well have been talking about life on Mars.

"Did she get hurt?"

"She was too wasted to feel much of anything.

When you're that old, you really shouldn't drink so much, you know? Peter drove down to bring us back." She made a face. "He wasn't too thrilled with me, but I think I'll be able to get back in his good graces when he hears the tape."

"You taped singers at a karaoke bar?"

"That's how it started, but I ended up hitting the jackpot."

"You found the next American idol in Wildwood, New Jersey."

"Better." She lowered her voice to a conspiratorial whisper, even though they were the only two people in the car. "I found the hook for the Paradise Point segment."

"I thought they already had a hook." O'Malleys and DiFalcos. Ten decades. Two families. One big fat Jersey wedding.

"Nope," she said. "I'm not going to tell you. You'll just have to wait like the rest of them."

Fine, he thought. *Whatever.* He'd rather think about Claire.

The odds were probably 60-40 that she wouldn't show up tomorrow at the lighthouse. Just because he hadn't been able to shake off the memories didn't mean she hadn't moved on. She was the one who broke it off. She was the one with the husband who showed up one day like a romance novel hero and carried her back to the shore. She was the one who showed up pregnant by the man she'd married, the same guy who had taken her trust and —

The same guy they worshiped at the firehouse.

461

The same guy who went into that fire to save his brother. The same guy who must have done some fucking things right along the way to have won her heart and kept it all those years.

Martyrdom wasn't her natural state. His Claire was a fighter. A survivor. She wouldn't just lie down and let the guy stomp all over her. Not the woman he knew and loved. There had to be something more to the story, some bond that was invisible to the rest of the world — or at least to him — that had kept them together all those years, but damned if he knew what it was.

He wasn't a fool. He knew going in that there wouldn't be a Hollywood ending to their story. She wasn't going to leave her home and family and fly off to Malaysia with him, no matter how he fine-tuned the fantasy. That kind of thing happened in movies where nobody had to worry about where the kids would go to school or who would take care of an aging father. Seeing her at O'Malley's yesterday morning, he had been struck by the fact that she was exactly where she belonged. It wasn't something he had wanted to see, but only a blind man could have missed the signs. Her neighbors had come out in droves to cheer her on at that interview. They had gathered around her afterward to offer their congratulations . . . and their critiques. She laughed with some of them, chided others, and hugged a lucky few, all while she fielded congratulations on joining his sister's team at the tea shop.

The confused, uncertain, sharp-tongued

woman he had fallen in love with down in Florida years ago had been replaced by a confident, decisive, sharp-tongued woman he could easily fall in love with all over again.

If she would let him.

Once again Claire found herself grateful for her big, loud, chaotic family. They made it impossible for her to spend more than thirty consecutive seconds replaying those minutes with Corin in the hospital cafeteria last night. Every time she found herself reconstructing the dialogue or conjuring up the way her hand felt in his, her father yelled for a bedpan or one of her sisters phoned with a new excuse why they couldn't drive down to Paradise Point and lend a hand.

Friday morning at O'Malley's, Corin had seemed like a pleasant stranger, Olivia's younger brother, a talented photographer she had met once a long time ago. His smile had been bland and meaningless. The look in his eyes had revealed nothing at all. She had felt relieved, hurt, angry, and everything in between. David Fenelli's obvious admiration had been a balm to her bruised ego, and she had greedily basked in his attentions.

Her motives for accepting his dinner invitation might not have been as pure as they should have been, but life was nothing if not surprising. David had been funny, attentive, and very appealing in his rumpled nice-guy way, and by the time the meal was over, she had relaxed and started to have a wonderful time.

He fit into her life the same way she fit into his. Their kids liked each other. He was the kind of man any woman would love to have as a friend and maybe, just maybe, something more. Sane. Dependable. Kind. The more they talked over their dinner, the more she liked him and the guiltier she felt for seeing him initially as second best. He wasn't second best to anybody. Unless he had a secret Jekyll-Hyde thing going on behind closed doors, he was the kind of man any woman would happily rank number one.

It had been going great. Conversation never flagged. They got each other's jokes. When he suggested extending the evening by taking in a movie, she had been honestly delighted. She liked his slightly offbeat take on all things pop culture, and she'd been looking forward to dissecting the film with him later on, when *POW!* Her father fell down and broke his ankle, and she ended up in a hospital cafeteria in the middle of the night holding on to the hand of the man she had dreamed about almost every night for eight long years, and it felt like they were starting over again, picking up the pieces of something neither one of them had been able to control or even understand.

So now what? She hadn't a clue. Where did two middle-aged adults go with these feelings when neither one of them was exactly an expert when it came to love?

The sound of her father's laughter rang out through the open door to his room.

"Sounds like a party in there," one of the nurses commented as she hurried by.

"The man knows how to have a good time," Claire said, and it was true. He had worked hard all his life, suffered through the long and painful death of his wife, battled heart problems, cancer, and now this broken ankle, and he kept on going. Sure, he could be cranky and irascible at times, but he never gave up. He expected good things from life, and as a result, more times than not, life usually delivered.

There was a lesson in there somewhere, and maybe one day she would have time to figure it out.

More laughter spilled out of her father's room. She had stepped out to give him some privacy while the nurse's aide helped him with some personal issues, but nobody could be having that much fun with Jell-O and a sponge bath.

She tapped on the doorjamb. "You decent, Pop?"

"Come on in, dear." Lilly Fairstein smiled up at her from her perch on the edge of Mike's bed. "We were just sharing a cup of soup."

"Pull up a chair," her father said. "Lilly made plenty."

"You made the soup?" Claire asked. "From scratch?"

"I made the phone call," Lilly said with a wink. "The Catered Affair did the rest." She pointed toward the containers lined up along the windowsill. "Help yourself. I brought chicken noodle, minestrone, and a truly wonderful Manhattan clam. They use fresh thyme. It's to die for."

"You're right," Claire said a few minutes later as the room filled up with Mike's pals. Their instincts were unerring when it came to free food. "The Manhattan clam is definitely to die for."

"Tell me about it." Mel Perry smacked his lips from the corner of the room. "That minestrone's better than Mama used to make."

"You're not Italian," Tommy Kennedy shot back. "Your mama was making corned beef and cabbage, same as mine."

"My great-grandmother was from the Old Country."

"She was from Newark," Mike chimed in. "I remember her."

They were off and running. Her father's cronies were a laughing, jovial bunch who didn't think twice about having a party in a hospital room. They had all spent a lot of time in rooms just like this one, and they had learned the hard way to make the most of what you had for as long as you had it.

A lesson she was still learning.

"Did you hear from your sisters?" Mike asked her between arguments.

"Frankie's in her third trimester, so she's not going anywhere. The others said they'll get back to me tomorrow."

"Your brother?"

"I left a voice mail, Pop. You know Tim. He's not the greatest when it comes to call-backs. But they all send their love."

"Same in every family," Lilly said, as she bustled around the room tidying up. "It doesn't matter how many children you have, there's usually just one you can count on."

"Claire's the one," her father said. "Ever since she was a little girl, she was the one her mother and I could count on."

"See?" Lilly tossed the empty containers into the trash. "A big family like yours and it's always one child who comes to the rescue."

"I wish I'd known this when I was a teenager," Claire said with a roll of her eyes. "I would've asked for a raise in my allowance."

The crowd burst into laughter.

"Okay," she said. "I know an exit line when I hear one." She gathered up her stuff and kissed the top of her father's head. "I'm going home to see what we need. The social worker gave me a list of things I need to check on before they release you."

"Beer and a satellite dish pretty much does it for me."

"Yeah, well, I'm talking about special equipment for the bathroom, making sure the pathways are unobstructed —"

"Hanging a light over that damn cat," Mike said to more laughter.

"I'll see what I can do about that." She said good-bye to everyone, then glanced around. "Anybody know where my son disappeared to?"

Mel Perry looked up from the *Racing Form*. "I saw him down at the nurse's station. They set him up with a jigsaw puzzle or something."

"Something that doesn't require batteries? This I have to see for myself."

"Claire?" Lilly approached her at the doorway. "May I speak with you for a second?"

"Sure." The two women stepped out into the hall. "What's up?" She had been given a different view of the uber-perfect Lilly that afternoon, and she liked what she saw. She also would have had to be blind to miss the affection between Lilly and Mike.

"You have a lot on your plate," Lilly said. "The bar, your new job at Olivia's tea shop, your children." She paused for a second, worrying her strand of pearls with a flawlessly manicured hand. "How would you feel if I asked your father to stay with me for a few weeks while he recovers from his fall?"

"You want my father to come live with you?" Her recliner-and-remote-control father living with a woman who ironed her magazines? She couldn't bring the picture into focus.

Lilly looked charmingly nervous, and Claire's heart unexpectedly started to melt. "As you know, I live in a retirement community. My

468

home was constructed with certain realities in mind." Her bathroom had the necessary safety rails, removable bath chair, nonslip flooring already in place. "The hallways were built to accommodate wheelchairs. No steps to worry about." She gave Claire an uncertain smile. "And no cats for Michael to tangle with."

Good thing she was already in a hospital. A few more surprises like this, and she'd need a defibrillator. "Have you talked with him about your idea?"

"No, I thought I should speak with you first."

Her own family wasn't this considerate of her feelings. She felt instantly guilty for all the terrible things she had thought about Lilly Fairstein in the past. "I don't know what to say, Lilly. That's an incredible offer but —"

"I'm not being entirely altruistic, Claire. My place is very big and very empty. I would enjoy having a man to fuss over for a few weeks, but the last thing I want to do is step on your toes in any way. Family comes first."

Claire was surprised by the conflicting emotions Lilly's offer stirred up.

"It's really up to my father," she said finally and was rewarded with the biggest smile she had ever seen on anyone past her fifth birthday.

"So you wouldn't mind if I broached the subject with him tonight?"

"Not at all, Lilly. I'm fine with whatever he decides."

The woman threw her slender arms around

Claire and gave her a warm hug. "I'm delighted!" she declared, her bracelets jingling merrily. "Absolutely delighted!"

And I'm amazed, Claire thought as she and Billy drove home. Absolutely amazed.

"There's Kathleen!" Billy pointed toward a figure dragging a backpack behind her as they rounded the corner of their block.

Claire beeped the horn and pulled over to the curb. Kathleen's face lit up when she saw them, and she dashed over to the car and jumped into the backseat.

"I thought you were catching the six-twenty-two back to Manhattan," Claire said as her daughter buckled her seat belt.

"Kelly promised me last night that she'd drive me to the station. She was supposed to pick me up at five-fifteen, but she never showed up."

"You called her?"

"I tried. I got the machine at home and her cell just rang through."

"You should have called me. I would've come right back."

"I did," Kathleen said. "Your phone was switched off."

"I turned it off at the hospital and forgot to turn it back on." She shifted into gear and made a quick U-turn. "We have fourteen minutes, guys. Think we can do it?"

"Yeah!" Billy pumped the air. "Hit it, Ma!"

"I'm really pissed," Kathleen grumbled as they raced along Main Street toward the train station two towns away. "I can't believe she screwed me like this."

"Do you think you might be overreacting just a bit?" Claire asked over her shoulder.

"It's just that it's Kelly, you know what I mean? You expect other people to screw up, but not her."

There was something about the statement that struck a nerve with Claire, but it vanished before she could examine it. She smiled at her daughter in the rearview mirror.

"Pull that seat belt tighter, honey, because I have some news you are not going to believe."

"Mike's going to shack up with Mrs. Fairstein?" Aidan looked suitably shocked when Claire and Billy dropped by to grab some take-out chili for their supper and share the latest news. "When the hell did that happen?"

Claire glanced at her watch. "About two hours ago. Lilly phoned to tell me he said yes." She laughed. "Actually, he said, 'Hell, yes!' "

"Lot of changes going on around here," he said, loading some corn chips into a container for Billy. "You need a scorecard to keep up with them."

"Is that a dig? Because if you're talking about Cuppa, you can just —"

"Down, Red," he said. "I was talking about myself. Maddy and I decided to move up the wedding date."

She did a good job of faking happiness. He

471

had to give her that. "So when's the new Big Day going to be?"

"July twenty-first. She's going to run it by Rose tonight."

"That'll register at least a five on the Richter scale," Claire said.

"What's the Richter scale?" Billy asked, looking up from Aidan's computer, where he had been playing something that involved street-fighting dinosaurs.

"It measures earthquakes," Aidan told him and laughed when the kid's eyes almost bugged out of his head.

"We're going to have an earthquake?" Billy asked. "Cool!"

Claire launched into an explanation of sarcasm, irony, and metaphor that Aidan saw whizzing over his nephew's head like a convoy of paper airplanes.

"What your mother's trying to say is that when Rose hears about this, she's going to yell loud enough to rock the town."

"You're good at this," Claire said dryly. "Ever think of trying parenthood?"

"Now that's the sister-in-law I know and love: never met a zinger she didn't like."

"I don't think Olivia's going to be too thrilled when she hears the news. That means Maddy will be useless the first month Cuppa's open."

"Women have been known to work and plan a wedding," he said.

"You two are going on a honeymoon, aren't you?"

He nodded.

"Well, unless you're staying in beautiful downtown Paradise Point, that'll leave me holding the tea bag until she gets back."

"So you're saying July isn't a good idea?"

"I'm not saying anything. I'm just pointing out a few things you might've missed."

"Don't blame Maddy for this. It was my idea."

"I'm not blaming anyone, Aidan. It's just that it's typical of —" She clamped her lips together in a tight line.

"Typical of what?" Like he didn't know what she had been about to say. Flighty, unpredictable Maddy Bainbridge . . .

She shook her head and changed the subject. "Speaking of parenthood, what's with Kelly? She said she'd take Kathleen to the train station, and she never showed up."

"I haven't seen her since we got back. She stayed at The Candlelight last night. I suppose she's still there."

Claire gave him one of those raised-eyebrow looks. "Didn't you try to call her?"

"I swung by home to see if she was there and left a note. She knows where to find me."

Claire tapped her front teeth with the nail on her right index finger. "It's not like her to just drop out like this."

"Drop out? She blew a trip to the train station. What's the big deal?"

"I don't know that it is a big deal," she said. "All I know is it's not like her, and it worries me."

It worried him, too. The nagging sense that something was wrong had been with him for weeks now. "She's been a little edgy lately. I tried to get her to talk to me this week."

"Any luck?"

"She burst into tears and ran from the room."

"Kelly did that?" Claire sounded shocked.

"She was crying like it was the end of the world."

"Maybe she and Seth are having troubles."

"Nope. Sorry to say they're tight as ever."

"School?"

"Still pulling *A*s." He frowned. "She hasn't been feeling too great. Some kind of stomach thing. That's probably what it is."

"Maybe she's pregnant."

Claire's words hit him like rocket mortar. "What the hell are you trying to say?"

"I'm not trying to say anything. I said it. I'm worried about her, too, Aidan. Something isn't right, and the signs are pointing one way."

"Bullshit."

"Lower your voice. The kid's listening."

"Like you haven't said worse."

"I've reformed." She had the grace to look embarrassed. "At least around home."

"Why would you think she's —" He had trouble getting the word out.

"Gut instinct. Mother's intuition." She

shrugged. "The fact that she puked her guts out Monday afternoon at the mall."

"What?"

"I thought I told you that night."

"You told me she didn't feel well."

"It was more than that. Hannah was with her. Apparently she had a major encounter with the porcelain receptacle."

"Jesus." This was worse than rocket mortar. He didn't want to think about his daughter and Seth. She was still only five years old, wasn't she? The sweet, innocent baby girl who thought he was a hero. "Kelly's too smart for that."

"I was too smart for that, too," she reminded him. "And so was Maddy. Even smart people make mistakes."

"I'm not buying it. This is a kid who makes lists of lists. She brings back her library books a day early. She rewinds tapes before she returns them to the video store. That's not the type of kid who ends up pregnant."

She gave him a look that was too close to pity for his liking, and for the first time he was scared.

"I'll close up," Aidan said to Owen hours later as the last of the regulars waved good-bye.

"I don't mind doing it."

"Go home and get some sleep. You did double duty all weekend. You deserve it."

Owen didn't even try to stifle his yawn. "Is Tommy opening in the morning?"

"Last I heard. If he doesn't, I have his back. We won't need you until four."

Owen thanked him and took off, leaving Aidan alone with his increasingly troubled thoughts.

It was too late to phone Maddy, but he needed to touch base with her, to reassure himself that he hadn't dreamed last night, hadn't imagined the things they did or the promises they had made to each other. He sent her an X-rated E-mail, then followed it quickly with a mushy, sentimental poem meant to make her laugh. She hadn't responded yet, but he imagined things were pretty chaotic at The Candlelight, especially if she had broken the news of the new wedding date to Rose.

He had spoken briefly to Kelly around ten o'clock. She was home and fine, hunkered down over some schoolwork. A normal Sunday night. He asked her about Kathleen and the train station, and she said she'd been so busy at The Candlelight that she totally forgot.

Last week he wouldn't have thought twice about any of it, but tonight it only added to the growing sense that something wasn't right.

He locked up the place a little before midnight and headed for home. As he pulled into the driveway, he noted that the porch light needed to be replaced and added it to his mental to-do list. Kelly's room was dark, but the small table lamp on the desk in the living room was lit, and that was where he found his daughter, asleep over a stack of photographs.

She looked incredibly young with her head resting on her arms and her buttery yellow curls tumbling this way and that. She wore his moth-eaten old black sweater, the one with the hole in the right elbow, and sweatpants. Her feet were bare and propped up on a stack of books. For a second he was a young and terrified father, alone with a squalling, needy infant with feet so tiny they could both fit in the palm of his hand with room left over. Where had the years gone? In a few months she would be out of his house forever. Had he taught her everything she would need to walk this world? Had he taught her anything at all, or had she always been far ahead of him in the things that really mattered?

His gaze fell on the stacks of photos scattered across the tabletop, and his heart seemed to stop beating for an instant as the ghosts of his family filled the room. Grandma Irene and Grandpa Michael, smiling up at him from the front door of the original O'Malley's before the Hurricane of '52 tore it apart. His parents in their Sunday best at his First Communion. Billy Jr. — but wait, that wasn't his nephew grinning at him in black and white, that was his brother Billy on his ninth birthday, all freckles and scabbed knees and enough energy to power most of New Jersey.

They were all there. Aunts and uncles he

barely remembered. Favorite dogs. The cat Billy had rescued from the creek behind the church.

And Sandy.

There she was, his first love, cradling their newborn baby daughter. She was only a kid herself at the time, young and wide-eyed and in love. Same as he had been. The head-over-heels, forever kind of love people prayed for but rarely found. Everybody had said the odds were against them, but for a little while they had proved them all wrong. Sure they were too young and too poor and too unprepared for what it meant to be parents when they were still kids themselves, but somehow they'd managed. Or they would have managed if fate had been kinder to them and —

"Dad?" Kelly's voice was soft, almost apologetic. "You're looking at Mom's picture?"

"Hey, sleepyhead, where did you find this? I don't think I've ever seen it before."

She yawned and wiped the sleep from her eyes. "Mrs. DiFalco gave me a box of photos from her attic. Can you believe how amazing they are?"

He picked up the photo of Sandy and looked at it under the lamplight. "This was taken just before you were baptized. It had been raining on and off all day, and your mother was fussing over you, worrying you were going to catch cold, even though it was ninety degrees outside."

"I wish —" She stopped and lowered her head. "You know."

"Yeah, I know." He had wished it, too, over the years. "I'm lucky, though. I see your mother every time you smile."

She looked at him with those old-soul eyes of hers. He had always joked she had been born knowing everything she needed to know and had been teaching him ever since. "Doesn't that make you sad?"

"Knowing that your mother lives on through you? No, that doesn't make me sad, Kel. It makes me —" He struggled for the right word to convey a concept so profound it humbled him. "Grateful," he said at last. "It makes me feel grateful."

She made a small noise and looked away.

"Don't go crying on me, Kel. These are good memories."

Her arms were wrapped tightly across her chest in classic defensive posture.

"Kel, you haven't been yourself all week. Claire —"

She spun around and flashed him her mother's smile, derailing his train of thought. "Wow, I completely forgot! Did you and Maddy have a great time?"

"Great enough that we're moving up the wedding to July."

"July? Wow!"

"You're okay with that?"

"Sure. Why wouldn't I be? I really like Maddy, and Hannah's a doll."

He started to laugh.

"What's so funny?"

"You never disappoint me, Kel. I must've done something damn good in another life to rate a daughter like you."

"I wish you wouldn't say things like that."

"You've earned them. A man couldn't ask for a better daughter."

She shook her head. "You're wrong. I've made lots of mistakes, really bad mistakes."

His gut twisted into a sailor's knot.

"I'm listening," he said. "You know you can tell me anything." *God, if you're listening, if you remember my name, help me know the right thing to say.*

The look in her eyes was very old and very sad. "I'm not a little girl anymore," she said. "I can't run to Daddy with every problem."

"You have a problem?"

"I didn't say that."

"Claire's worried about you, sweetheart. She said you were sick to your stomach last week at Short Hills." *She's a great kid, God. She deserves all the good luck you can send her way.*

"Great," she exploded. "I suppose she told you I was . . . bulimic or something."

"Are you?"

"No!" She pulled a childish face. "Yuk!"

"So what happened?"

Silence had never sounded so loud as he waited for her answer.

"Sometimes I get sick when my period starts. That's all."

He held her gaze. *You've never lied to me before, Kelly. Tell me the truth, and I swear to you everything will be okay.* "You're telling me the truth?"

"Yeah," she said, shooting a fiercely indignant look his way. "Not that it's any of your business." She started tossing photos back into the box marked *O'Malley.* "And you can tell Aunt Claire the same thing."

Relief almost brought him to his knees. "I'll tell her."

"Good." She stomped out of the room. Seconds later, her bedroom door slammed shut behind her.

She was pissed off, but she wasn't pregnant. Apparently God hadn't entirely forgotten his name.

Chapter Twenty-three

"The Celtic cross?" Gina demanded Monday morning as she flashed her upper left hip to the mothers crowding around her and to her little Joey's delight. "I'm Italian! What the hell was I thinking?"

"How many margaritas did you have anyway?" Gina's sister Denise grabbed her youngest by the back of his collar before he skittered away. "You pass out at the sight of a sewing needle."

Everyone laughed but Maddy. She lingered at the edge of the crowd, mimicking their responses while her thoughts remained with Kelly. She had gone through the motions with Hannah and her mother, the usual morning routine, but she hadn't really been present. All she could think about was Aidan's daughter, what she was doing, how she was feeling, what the future would hold for them all.

Anything could happen between now and late afternoon when they had arranged to meet up in the parking lot. She might decide trusting

Maddy was a big mistake and take matters back into her own hands. The entire issue might be resolved before Maddy had a chance to make a difference. It wasn't that she wanted to bend the girl to her will. This was Kelly's life and future, not hers. She understood that. She also understood that she had never needed her own mother more than the day she had discovered Hannah was on her way.

She had longed for her mother, a Rose she had really never known, during those first few weeks, and had never felt the emotional distance between them more keenly. Her father Bill had been enormously supportive and understanding, but it was her beloved stepmother Irma who had provided the maternal warmth and unconditional love she had desperately needed.

She saw all that and more, maybe too much more, in Kelly's eyes, and she couldn't turn away.

Maybe she was crazy to be taking this risk for Kelly. She was crawling out on a very shaky limb, one that could send her future with Aidan crashing down at the slightest breeze, but the girl had no one else to turn to. Kelly was the quintessential golden girl, the good girl who solved her family's problems rather than made problems of her own. There was no room in that perspective, at least not that Kelly could see, for mistakes. She had to be perfect, or her entire family would collapse.

It wasn't fair. Not to Seth or Aidan. Not to

Claire. Certainly not to Kelly herself. Families pulled together in times of trouble. At least that was what they were supposed to do, and neither Seth nor the O'Malleys would have that chance if Kelly followed through with her plans.

Since when do families do what they're supposed to do? You can't guarantee it will work out the way you hope it will. Kelly knows them better than you do.

It was a chance Kelly needed to take, no matter what her ultimate decision turned out to be. All Maddy wanted to do was open up a window of time for Kelly to think about her options, to consider all possibilities, before she made a truly irrevocable decision.

She says her mind is made up. She's going through with it tomorrow. What then, Bainbridge? Will you be able to keep her secret from the man you love?

Kelly wasn't the only one in trouble. Aidan might never forgive her for what she was doing, but she couldn't see any other way. She believed Kelly when she said she would run off to a clinic in New York if Maddy broke her promise and told him. She knew the odds were against it, but if anything happened to Kelly and she hadn't at least tried —

". . . really think we were going to let you off that easy, did you, Maddy?"

The Great Tattoo Unveiling was over, and they had turned their attentions to Maddy and her romantic weekend.

"Was it wonderful?" Denise asked with a big fake romantic sigh.

"The hell with that," Gina said. "Was *he* wonderful?"

They all laughed, even Claire, who up until that moment had looked like she was undergoing root canal.

"So wonderful they moved up the wedding date," she said before Maddy could open her mouth.

"Get *out!*" Gina gave Maddy a Seinfeldian shove that almost knocked Maddy on her butt. "I still have five pounds to lose before Lucy measures me for my bridesmaid dress."

"July twenty-first," Claire said. "Better get moving."

"You're well informed," Maddy said to her future sort of sister-in-law. Aidan must have spread the word last night at the bar.

"Have you mentioned it to Olivia yet? It'll be interesting to hear her take on it."

Gina let loose with a loud *meow* that made everyone except Maddy and Claire laugh again.

"Why would Olivia care when I get married?" Maddy asked, her temper sparking dangerously. "She knows Aidan and I are — oh." She had completely forgotten about Cuppa. "Oh God. That's going to be a problem, isn't it?"

Claire's look said it all.

"That went well," Maddy said to Gina after the school bus left and the other mothers scattered. "I think I managed to confirm every awful thing she ever thought about me." Flighty. Unreliable. A terrible candidate for wife and mother.

"Forget it," Gina said. "I've got real problems."

"Please don't tell me you did something even dumber than that tattoo."

Gina could do innocent indignation better than anyone. "That photographer is coming to Upsweep later to take my picture for the book, and I look like the Before poster child."

"I think he's coming to The Candlelight tomorrow."

"Hey," Gina said, "this is about me, remember? I look like hell. I'm not supposed to look like hell. I own a salon. This is going to be terrible for business."

"I don't think they're looking at this as a promo opportunity for Upsweep, Gee."

Gina bent down and retrieved Joey's stuffed dinosaur for the stroller-bound toddler. "You know what, cuz? I liked you a hell of a lot more before you got yourself engaged."

"And what does that mean?"

"Don't mind me," Gina said as she straightened back up. "I'm in a lousy mood."

"Still hungover?"

"Do you ever have the feeling something awful is about to happen, but you don't know what it is and you don't know how to stop it?"

"I wish you wouldn't say things like that."

That horrible someone-walked-over-my-grave feeling ran up her spine.

"I know, I know. I sound like my mother, don't I? Next thing you know, I'll be telling you somebody gave me the evil eye."

Maddy crossed herself. "Now you have me acting like *my* mother. Don't say things like that, Gee. Don't even think them."

"I almost went to Mass with Lucy this morning," Gina said. "*That's* how strong this feeling is."

Maddy, who had gone to Mass with Lucy that morning, said nothing at all.

Corin followed Olivia over to Cuppa a little after eight to shoot a roll of his sister at the incredibly kitschy cottage she was turning into an English tea shop. It wasn't exactly his cup of tea, so to speak, but he had no doubt that her instincts were right on the money, and she would have another huge success on her hands. She walked him through the place, pointing out architectural details that he might otherwise have gone to his grave without recognizing, and he dutifully took a few shots of wainscoting. Whatever the hell that was.

He also managed to grab a few candid shots of Olivia as she scrutinized the new wallpaper and checked out the window treatments.

"Enough," she said, laughing as he circled her like a paparazzo. "That's my bad side."

"You don't have a bad side, Livvy. Never had, never will."

"Good genes, brother mine. We were both born lucky."

They locked eyes, and the irony of the statement hit them both at the same time. Great parents. Great childhood. Great genes. Yet there they were, charging fearlessly into early middle age with no kids, no spouses, not even a cat to give a shit if they came home early, late, or not at all.

Somewhere along the way they had stopped being lucky, but he would be damned if he could figure out when or why.

He was saved from a morose trip down angst lane by the noisy arrival of Lassiter and his crew.

"I'm finished here," he said, grabbing for his camera bag. "I'll get out of your way."

"Don't leave on our account," Lassiter said after a jovial good morning. "A few stills of the process in motion might be a good addition."

Corin checked his watch. He was due at Upsweep in a half hour, but that was only two blocks away. *What the hell,* he thought and popped off the lens cap.

"Act natural," he ordered everyone to great laughter. They had been saying that to the citizens of Paradise Point for the last month with varying degrees of success.

Crystal was setting up her recording equipment on one of the enormous work surfaces in what would be the kitchen in another day or two. He liked the way the morning sunshine glittered off her quintet of eyebrow piercings. He crouched down a few feet away from her and started snapping as she fiddled with dials, ran a mike check, and pretended she wasn't being photographed.

"Forget I'm here," he said as he aimed the camera up her nose. "I'm part of the scenery."

"I hate being photographed," she said. "I end up looking like a baked potato."

"Baked potatoes are good," he said, trying to put her at ease. "But you're no plain old baked potato . . . no, don't look at me . . . just do what you're doing . . . you're baked potato with cheddar cheese and bacon bits and green onions and maybe some really hot salsa —"

She started to laugh, and the sun zeroed in on the stud fastened through her tongue.

"You must drive the metal detectors nuts at the airport," he said as he paused to change rolls.

"I'm an agent for social change," she said, clicking the stud against her bottom teeth. "The day will come when body piercings are as common as makeup and hair color."

He decided to leave that one alone. "So what did the PTB think about your hook for the documentary?"

"Shh!" She placed her index finger to her lips. "I haven't had a chance to transcribe the tape yet, but it's going to blow them away!"

"The guys at *60 Minutes* are getting pretty

long in the tooth. You should walk your skills up to Fifty-second Street and see if there's an opening."

"Yeah, I can just see me sitting next to Mike Wallace." Crystal pulled her notepad from her backpack and uncapped her pen with her teeth. "That would be one for the Emmy reel."

"Listen, kid, if you managed to score a story in the middle of a Jersey Shore karaoke bar, you could blast the rest of 'em off the screen."

"I'm going to try to transcribe it tonight. I have the tape all set up and ready to go as soon as I get back to the rooms." She winked at him. "Get a good picture of Gina Barone. It might come in very handy."

"Miss O'Malley, would you care to rejoin the rest of us and answer the question?"

Kelly struggled to swim up to the surface of consciousness. "I-I'm sorry, Mr. Alfredi. Would you repeat the question?"

He dismissed her with a look and turned toward Carol Mortensen. "Miss Mortensen, please enlighten the rest of us with an answer."

"Yalta, Mr. Alfredi."

"Thank you, Miss Mortensen. Perhaps Miss O'Malley is proficient enough at *Jeopardy* that she can reconstruct the original question using that answer as her clue."

The class laughed. She didn't even blame them. She might have laughed, too, if the situation had been reversed. She hoped she wouldn't have, but lately she was beginning to think just about anything was possible.

Seth was waiting for her in the hallway, and her heart twisted into a sailor's knot at the sight of his familiar, beloved face. She wished she didn't have to smile and lie to that face, but she was in so deep now there was no turning back.

"What was that all about?" he asked as they walked to the cafeteria for lunch.

"I fell asleep," she said with a self-deprecating laugh. "I was up until four working on that paper, and when he started droning on about Stalin and FDR, I drifted off." Which was another total lie. She had stayed up all night staring at the six photos Rose DiFalco had given to her. Sandy O'Malley had lived nineteen years, and a handful of photos, her husband's memories, and a daughter named Kelly were all that remained to prove she had walked the earth.

Seth lowered his voice to a whisper. "Maybe you should run that test again."

"Oh, shut up!" she snapped, pulling her hand away from his. "I told you the results on Saturday. What more do you want from me?"

She wished he would get mad, maybe tell her to go to hell, or call her a bitch and leave her standing there alone in the entrance to the cafeteria. That was what she deserved for lying to him.

But he didn't do any of those things, which

was why she loved him so much. Instead, he looked at her closely for what seemed like forever, then he fell back into step with her, and they walked into the cafeteria together like it was just another day.

Gina Barone loved the camera, and unless Corin badly missed his guess, the camera loved her right back. She reigned over staff and clientele at Upsweep like a benevolent despot in leather. She flirted, she cajoled, she laughed, and when she thought nobody was looking, she looked sad enough to break a man's heart.

Most of all, though, Gina Barone loved to talk. By the time he had been in the shop an hour, he knew the social and sexual histories of just about everyone in town.

"Glad I don't live here," he said as he snapped a shot of Gina as she mainlined espresso between customers. "A man's gotta have a few secrets."

"Oh, honey," Gina said with a dangerously sexy laugh, "secrets are highly overrated."

The sentence resonated with him. She had been disarmingly honest about her many and varied romantic adventures, and those adventures seemed to be part of what drew the women of Paradise Point to her shop. Gina was her very own reality show, and she was in no danger of being voted off the island any time soon. Not if the crowd of women waiting in the lounge for hair treatments or massages or manicures was any indication. They had reveled over her tale of the tattoo parlor visit after a pitcher of margaritas down the shore. He had already heard Crystal's version of the outing, and Gina pretty much corroborated the whole thing with the exception of the mystery tape Crystal had alluded to. It wasn't hard to imagine Gina talking first and thinking a year or two later.

Gina's talking points bounced all over the place. She changed gears with the ease of a Ferrari, shifting from talk of Manolo Blahnik stilettos to Pilates classes to the sale on roasters at Super Fresh without missing a beat. She kept her customers chuckling during bizarre beauty rites that would have terrified the bravest warriors. Watching her work with squeeze bottles of color, folding strands of unsuspecting hair into aluminum foil packets, seeing her wield her shears with the artistry and precision of a da Vinci — he was impressed as hell, and he let her know it.

"So put your dermis where your mouth is," she said with a sly wink. "You look like you could use a facial and some moisturizer."

He laughed out loud. "And some highlights?"

"Low lights," she corrected him. "Although I'm not altogether sure I'd touch that gorgeous gray of yours."

"Look who's awake and looking for his mommy." Amber, one of the nail technicians, stood in the doorway. She held the hand of a toddler with thick dark hair and dark blue eyes. Something tugged at Corin, a feeling of familiarity that came and went in the space of a breath.

"Mr. Joey!" Gina opened her arms, and the little boy flew across the room and into her embrace. "Boy, did we miss you!" She met Corin's eyes over the child's silky head. "Nap time just finished. He likes to make an entrance."

Everything about her changed with the little boy's appearance in the doorway. She glowed the way women glowed in an Impressionist painting, that golden inner light that existed only in the imaginations of men and lunatics. Clearly that little boy held the key to her heart in his chubby hands.

"Joey, this is Corin. Why don't you shake hands with him, and maybe he'll take your picture."

Corin bent down to eye level and held out his right hand. "Good to meet you, Joey."

Joey considered him for a moment, then gave him a surprisingly strong handshake for somebody who weighed maybe thirty pounds. His attention was focused on the Hasselblad hanging around Corin's neck, and he made a quick grab for it.

"I should've warned you," Gina said as she scooped the kid up into her arms. "My boy has the quickest hands in South Jersey."

Joey was the baby of the family, and he knew

how to work it. There wasn't a female in the place who wasn't crazy about him, and if he hung around much longer, the kid would have Corin in his back pocket, too.

". . . he's had a tough few months," Gina was saying as he clicked back into the conversation, "but I think we're finally out of the woods." She pretended to knock wood against her left temple, which made the little boy laugh.

"You'd never know he had any problems," Corin said.

She gave his arm a squeeze. "Your mouth to God's ear and back again."

Joey had the same all-American-boy quality he had spotted in Claire's youngest, the kind of face you saw in 1950s commercials for peanut butter or breakfast cereal, right down to the freckles that peppered the bridge of his nose.

"How about I take a picture of the two of you?" he asked, popping off the lens cap once again. "I like the way the light's coming through that window."

Gina made a joke about bad hair days, but she seemed pleased, so he sat the two of them down near the window and snapped a quick series of shots that felt right to him. Better than right. The viewfinder found something in Gina, a depth of sadness, a measure of kindness, that were easily lost in the heat and volume of her personality.

Okay, so maybe he was a sucker for mother-and-child shots. They could be corny as hell, sentimental to the point of triggering the viewer's gag reflex, but when they worked, they could crack the ice around anyone's heart.

He just might have his cover shot for the book.

"I wish you had told me sooner that you were planning to be gone this afternoon, Madelyn." Rose was using what Maddy thought of as her I Am Queen voice.

For once Maddy didn't blame her mother one bit. "I forgot, okay?" she said, feigning daughterly annoyance. "I promised Kelly I'd go shopping with her for a prom dress. We're going over to Bay Bridge and if we don't luck out, I might drive up to Short Hills." *Too much information.* Any good liar would know you keep your cover story simple.

"We're expecting three couples from Virginia this evening. I was counting on you."

"Maybe Aunt Lucy could stop by and lend a hand."

"Your aunt is almost eighty." A wry smile broke through the displeasure. "Besides, I believe she has a date tonight."

"Ma, I wish I could help you, but I promised Kelly I would help her."

"And it has to be today. This is the only opening on your respective calendars."

"I'm sorry," she said. "It has to be today."

She could see the wheels spinning as her mother considered the situation. Unfortunately,

Rose was no fool. "This isn't about a prom dress, is it, honey?"

Tears filled her eyes, but she refused to acknowledge them. "No, it isn't."

Rose touched her arm. "If you need to talk —"

She shook her head. "We'll be okay." She gave her mother a hug. "But thanks for being here for me."

"Always," Rose said, hugging her back. "That's one thing you can count on."

Chapter Twenty-four

"I'm out of here." Claire untied her apron and hung it on the hook behind the door. "I have to go over to the hospital and see if the social worker has been in to see Dad yet."

Aidan didn't look up from the carrots he was chopping for the soup pot simmering on the stove. "You'll be back after you pick up Billy, right?"

Her stomach dropped to her feet. "Jesus Mary and Joseph," she said. "I completely forgot about Billy. He has a dentist appointment at four-thirty." Or was it five? Her mind was total mush.

Now, that got Aidan's attention. "So what's the big deal? Go to the hospital. Come back and get the kid. It's not like you haven't done it before."

True enough, except she had planned to go straight to the lighthouse the second she was finished at the hospital.

"Would you pick him up for me?"

He gestured toward the bar with his knife.

"Tommy's going home at two-thirty. I'll be the only one here."

"No, you won't. Owen's taking over the rest of my shift."

"Thought of everything, didn't you, Red?"

"I try." She was beginning to wonder how he was going to get along without her. "Is Kelly working at The Candlelight tonight or the library?"

"She's not working at all. Maddy's taking her shopping for a prom dress."

She felt a nasty little pinch of jealousy. "Why didn't she ask me? I found dresses for four daughters. Hannah's barely out of training pants."

His poker face wasn't any better than hers. "Look, I'm sorry. She probably knows how busy you are with work and Billy and your father and —"

"Stick it," she said as she turned and started for the exit. "I wasn't born yesterday, Aidan. I know things change. Just do me a favor next time and don't bullshit me. I can take anything but that."

Kelly was waiting for Maddy in the high school parking lot, just as they had planned.

"Do you have everything?" Maddy asked as the girl fastened her seat belt.

Kelly nodded. "ID, money, extra sanitary pads."

"Okay," Maddy said. "Then we're on our way."

Maddy told her about Hannah's latest escapade as they made a left on Main Street then headed toward the intersection with Route 582. She added a few extra details about Priscilla's part in the drama, hoping to elicit at least a chuckle from the girl, but nothing. She sat there looking out the windshield, hands folded tightly in her lap, face pale and drawn. Even in profile Maddy could see the deep shadows under her eyes.

"We're running ahead of schedule," she said as they stopped for a traffic light. "Would you like to take a walk around the lake or something?"

"Maybe they can take us early," Kelly said.

What she really wanted to do was pull over to the side of the road, lock the doors, and beg Kelly to tell Seth and Aidan about her pregnancy before she took this final and irreversible step. The afternoon suddenly seemed to have a momentum of its own, pulling them deeper into a tangle of lies neither one of them was prepared to handle.

They had slowed to a crawl behind a road repair crew when Kelly turned to her and said, "Did you know my mom?"

"Sure I did," Maddy said. "Well, sort of. Sandy was six or seven years older than I was, so we weren't friends or anything, but I knew her."

"Did you like her?"

Maddy smiled. "Everyone did. She had a

part-time job at the ice cream shop one summer, and she always gave me extra sprinkles on my cone."

"What did she sound like?"

"Oh, Kelly, I'm not sure I can remember. It was a very long time ago and —" A memory, half-formed but vibrant, began to surface. "Musical! That's how she sounded: musical. She did the reading of 'The Night Before Christmas' one year at the tree-lighting ceremony, and I remember everyone saying that she had a very musical quality to her voice." She almost cried at the look of pure gratitude Kelly gave her. She and Rose had had their problems over the years, but those problems seemed very minor compared to not having those years at all. She tried to imagine a world where she had never known her mother's voice, or her touch, or the smell of her perfume, but the thought was too bleak, too terrifying to contemplate for long.

"I spent all night looking at the photos Mrs. DiFalco gave me."

Maddy suddenly realized Kelly's hands were folded over a tiny stack of snapshots. "Sandy was a very pretty girl," she said carefully. "You look a lot like her."

"Mrs. D said the same thing last night, and so did my dad. I want to see it, but when I look in the mirror, I just see myself looking back."

Maddy reached across and pulled down the sun visor on the passenger side. "Your nose, for one thing," she said. "And your smile . . . and there's something about your eyes when you laugh that makes me think of your mom."

"It's scary, you know?" She leaned forward, examining her reflection for hints of Sandy O'Malley, who would be forever nineteen. "She was an only child, just like me, and now that both my grandparents are dead, I'm all that's left of her." Tears streamed down her face faster than she could brush them away. "If I vanished right this second, it would be like she'd never existed at all."

"She exists in the hearts of many people," Maddy said carefully. "She's remembered and loved."

But that wasn't what Kelly was talking about, and they both knew it. She was talking about those connections of blood that link the generations. She had felt that way when Hannah came into the world, blessed that something of herself and of Rose and Bill and her Grandma Fay and all the others who had come before would live on into future generations. It wasn't something you could convey with words; it ran far too deep for that. It was visceral, primal in its intensity, life doing what it did best: renewing itself once again.

"Honey, maybe we should stop at a diner or something and have a cup of tea." *You need time, Kelly. You need to take a deep breath and let the people who love you best help you.*

"No." She flipped the mirror up and pulled

herself together. "I just want it all over with. Once it's finished I'll be fine."

She would give it just one more try before she admitted defeat. "You've given a lot of thought to what you think is best for Seth and for your father and for everyone else, but not once have I heard you say what you think might be best for you. It's your body and your decision, Kelly, but more than that, it's your life we're talking about. You're going to live with whatever you decide every day for the rest of your life. Make sure it's what you want, not what you think you should want."

Kelly nodded, and Maddy had the sense that she might as well have been speaking to Priscilla.

"He's all yours," Claire said as Lilly opened the front door to her Lincoln Town Car so Mike could slide in. "And may God grant you patience and fortitude."

Lilly laughed out loud. "Oh, he's just an old teddy bear," she said. "Once I get him set up with his cable and his remote control, he won't be any problem at all."

"Are you two going to stand there gassing all afternoon, or can we blow this joint? *Judge Judy*'s on in twenty minutes."

The two women looked at each other and shared an eye roll.

"You have his chemo schedule?" Claire asked. "He's been on a Tuesday/Thursday rotation but —"

"I have it right here." Lilly patted her Kelly bag. "Along with his meds, his scripts, and his Dentu-Creme."

"Jesus H. Christ, can't a man keep anything private in this world?" Mike bellowed from the front seat.

"Dad, your teeth were sitting in a glass on your nightstand for the last two days. I think Lilly's figured it out."

A florist delivery van beeped and motioned for them to move. Claire quickly leaned into the car and kissed her father, then gave Lilly an impulsive hug.

"Take good care of him," she said. "He's a pain, but I love him."

Lilly promised she would, and Claire stood there on the curb, sniveling like a baby as they drove away. *It's only for a few weeks,* she told herself. *And it's for the best.* Mike would be much happier being fussed over by Lilly and more likely to make a quicker recovery. Never underestimate the power of trying to make a good impression. Besides, Olivia had E-mailed both Claire and Maddy last night to say the workmen would be finished by Thursday or Friday, and then the fun would begin in earnest. There were menus to plan, recipes to test, suppliers to locate, advertising to worry about; the list went on and on. Maddy didn't look all that thrilled when she mentioned it to her at the bus stop, but Claire couldn't wait to get started.

Maybe she wouldn't go over to the lighthouse

after all. Suddenly in the clear, uncompromising light of midday, it didn't seem like that terrific an idea. She had already changed her mind at least two dozen times since she awoke that morning, which was almost as many times as she had changed her outfit.

She wasn't a foolish woman. She knew he was looking for closure, not commitment. They had hurt each other badly that long ago afternoon in Atlantic City. That was undeniable. She had been thinking only of herself when she told him she would be there. She could have told him on the phone that the calls and letters had to end, that she believed her husband had really changed, and that their marriage had a chance to succeed, but she didn't. She had wanted to see him one more time, breathe the same air, see the way his dark eyes lit up when he saw her.

Why else would she have conveniently forgotten to tell him she was eight months pregnant with her husband's child? They had both said things — ugly things that had a greater half-life than uranium — and while forgiveness was possible, forgetting was so much harder.

Maybe closure wasn't such a bad thing. She hadn't been able to achieve it with Billy, and she would go to her grave wishing she had told him what the last few years of their life together had meant to her. But life didn't come with a schedule that warned you when your time was running out. You went to bed at night and awoke in the morning confident that you would do the same thing tomorrow and tomorrow and tomorrow and that the people you loved would always be there.

She slid behind the wheel of her car and drove on autopilot past the senior center, the site for the new church, through Paradise Point, past the lake, down the main streets of Port Pleasant and Breezy Beach, around the arboretum, past the women's health center —

What was Maddy's car doing in the parking lot of the women's health center? She knew for a fact that she and Maddy shared the same gynecologist. Why would she go to a clinic when she had a perfectly fine doctor of her own? And it had to be Maddy. There weren't too many Mustangs of that vintage in the state, much less within a three-town radius. Besides, wasn't she supposed to be out hunting down prom dresses with Kelly? At least that was the story Aidan had told her.

Idiot! The truth smacked her right between the eyes. Kelly must have asked Maddy to go with her to the center for birth control, and Maddy hadn't been able to figure a way out of it. She knew Aidan had been frank with his daughter about the facts of life right from the beginning — and she had tried to treat Kelly with the same commonsense approach she had used with her own girls — but there came a time when your children quit confiding in you and looked outside the old family circle for advice and support.

Maddy was the perfect choice. She was still new and exotic to Kelly, a local girl who had been away long enough to carry the scent of far-away places, even if in Maddy's case she had only gotten as far away as Seattle. Almost family but not entrenched in old battles and expectations.

Besides, Maddy hadn't been a mother long enough to have developed the same finely tuned sense of paranoia that was part of parenthood. She wouldn't automatically leap to worst-case scenarios every time Kelly said she had a problem.

It made sense, but it still hurt. Like Aidan, she had been a little distracted over the last few years since the warehouse fire, but she had tried very hard to be there for Kelly, to make sure she didn't veer off track. Even good kids could find themselves in bad trouble. If she had learned nothing from Kathleen's problems, she had learned that. She wished her niece had felt comfortable enough to ask her for advice, but more than that, she wished Aidan hadn't lied to her. That hurt more than anything else could. They were family. Their lives had been intertwined for more than twenty years. She deserved better than an easy lie. She had zero tolerance for bullshit, especially from O'Malley men, and she intended to read him the riot act as soon as she got back.

The Women's Health Cooperative was located in a one-story white brick building a few hundred feet off the main road. The parking lot was small, and Maddy wasn't sure if she was relieved or disappointed when they found the last spot near a towering maple tree in full bloom.

"We don't have to go in if you don't want to," she said as she turned off the ignition. "You're allowed to change your mind." She knew she was beginning to sound like an endless loop, but she was willing to risk embarrassment if it meant making sure Kelly understood.

"I'm okay." She flashed Maddy a shaky smile. "I just want to get this over with."

"You could take another day or two," Maddy went on. "A week. You still have time to think it through."

Kelly shook her head. "I'm going in now," she said. "If you don't want to, I understand."

Kelly had no idea how much Maddy didn't want to, but that was beside the point. Somebody had to be there with her, and like it or not, Maddy was that somebody.

The parking lot was unpaved, and the crushed shells and stones crunched and shifted beneath their feet as they walked to the side entrance. Kelly took a long, deep breath when they reached the door, then held it open for Maddy. A discreet bell sounded in the reception room where three teenage girls and four women around Maddy's age thumbed through magazines or looked off into space. Faint strains of Enya wafted through the room, lending a soft, unthreatening quality to the atmosphere. Stacks of reading material graced a refectory table against the wall.

Maddy followed Kelly over to the window where a middle-aged woman with snowy white hair smiled at them.

"Can I help you?"

"I — my name is Kelly O'Malley. I have an appointment."

The woman's eyes flicked to the computer screen off to her left. "You're early," she said. "We like that." She slid a sheaf of papers toward Kelly. "I know you did the presurgical phone interview, but we need a bit more info and some signatures." She looked up at Maddy. "Are you her mother?"

Maddy shook her head. "Stepmother."

"I'm glad you came along. We were a bit concerned that Kelly wasn't bringing anyone with her." The phone rang, and she shrugged apologetically. "Just fill everything out, Kelly, and bring it back to me when you're done."

The sliding window clicked shut.

They found two seats together near the refectory table. Kelly balanced the forms on a copy of *Time* and started filling in bits and pieces of information where required. Maddy had never felt more useless in her life. She was sitting not two feet away from Aidan's daughter, but she might as well be on the moon for all it mattered. She couldn't promise her that life would be rosy and happily-ever-after if she chose to keep the baby. She couldn't promise that Seth would step up to the plate and shoulder his half of the responsibility. She hoped and believed that Aidan would find a way to get past his shock and disappointment and be there for Kelly the way he always had been, but once again, she couldn't promise anything at all.

Kelly finished filling out the various forms, signed what needed to be signed, then returned the papers to the white-haired nurse at the window. She was handed a paper cup and directed to leave a urine sample in the patients' bathroom off the hallway. They would repeat the pregnancy test and then, assuming it was positive, when her turn came, Kelly would be prepped for the eight-minute procedure. She would be groggy afterward and would rest in one of the recovery rooms for a few hours until she was ready to be sent home with Maddy.

And after that, all they would have to do was figure out a way to live with the consequences of their decisions.

Corin had begged the owner of the one-hour photo shop on Main Street to let him use the darkroom for a half-hour. The owner, one of the many DiFalco cousins, drove a hard bargain, and he was fifty dollars poorer when he closed the door behind him and started processing the roll of film he had taken at Upsweep that morning.

Something had been bugging him ever since

he left Gina's shop, but he couldn't put his finger on what it was. He had the feeling he was looking at a puzzle with one piece missing, but damned if he knew what kind of puzzle it was or what that one piece could possibly be.

His booking agent had tracked him down that morning to tell him he had to be on site in Malaysia twenty-four hours earlier than originally planned if he expected to link up with the three embedded journalists he would be accompanying deeper into the region. He considered telling his agent to stick it, but he had signed the contract and already spent the money.

Lassiter, Crystal, and the rest of the crew had detoured up to Surf City on Long Beach Island for the day. One of the problems with doing the kind of work they did was the fact that they had to be willing to bend their schedule to meet the demands of the people whose lives they were chronicling. The head of the LBI historical society had just been offered a treasure trove of memorabilia found in a Surf City attic, and they were driving up there to film the story for the documentary.

"If you could finish up with the churches and the hospital before you go, we'll be in good shape," Lassiter had said over coffee that morning.

Corin agreed. "If Dean decides to take the summer to recuperate, I might be able to fly back in August or September to tie up loose ends."

"We wanted wedding photos, but they kept changing the damn date."

The ever-changing wedding plans of Maddy Bainbridge and Aidan O'Malley had become a running joke for the crew. Big wedding. Small wedding. Hotel reception. Clambake on the beach.

They were all staying at a second-rate B and B on the other side of town, the kind of place that made a Motel 6 look upscale. The crew talked longingly about the first-class accommodations they had enjoyed at The Candlelight, with special emphasis on the great coffee. Crystal had set up her laptop and transcription machine on a folding table in the library, but she hadn't managed more than the introduction by the time they left for Long Beach Island.

"We're leaving now," Lassiter called out from the front hallway. "Come on, Crystal, let's go!"

"Damn." She pressed a series of buttons, then smacked the heel of her hand against the side of the laptop.

"That's a piece of prime electronic equipment," Corin said. "You can't smack it around like a vending machine."

She pressed more buttons, then thumped the wrist rest with the heel of her hand. "Damn damn damn. I need to do a reboot."

"Crystal, we're out of here now with or without you."

"Would you do it?" she begged Corin. "If I

512

don't get my ass out there, he really will leave without me."

"Go." He wasn't a computer expert, but even he could manage a reboot. "I'll take care of it."

"Don't peek," she ordered him. "That's proprietary information. I'll know if you peek. This is blockbuster stuff. Don't screw around with it, okay?"

He couldn't help it.

He peeked.

GINA BARONE — Transcript — 8 May Unauthorized — signatures TK (Peter Lassiter, creator — NJTV)

(Transcribed by Crystal W.)

GINA BARONE: [audible: music; misc. ambient noise] . . . told you this was a great place, didn't I, Crystal . . . wait! What's that? You drinking a cosmo . . . very Sex and the City, girl . . . no, no . . . gimme a margarita . . . big margarita, okay? . . . yeah, a pitcher sounds good . . . thanks. . . .

This is so great here . . . you're gonna love it . . . the only place I know that's worth paying for a baby-sitter . . . I haven't been anywhere since Joey — hell, no! Not tonight! No sad stories tonight . . . no way. . . .

Not a hell of a lot to go on there. To his surprise, he had felt a surge of relief that there had been no justification for the uncomfortable feeling he had every time he saw that look of triumph in Crystal's eyes as she spoke about "The Gina Tape." He had read the transcript of the official preinterview and interview with Gina before he went to Upsweep to take some pictures and was surprised how much he liked her. She was brash, blunt, and seemingly fearless when it came to the truth, but something continued to tug at him, and he'd be damned if he could figure out what it was.

Maybe seeing the contact sheet in front of him would help. He was a visual person. The way a person's face reflected light told him more than their words ever could, and he was sure the photos of Gina would reveal a bottomless well of sorrow that ran counter to the way she presented herself to the world.

The darkroom was set up for maximum efficiency, and he finished quickly. The pictures were good but not great, and he was disappointed. He had expected to see more in Gina's face through the camera lens, but instead he saw less. It happened sometimes. Over time you get a feeling for who the camera would love and who would disappear beneath its one-eyed stare, and usually you were right. But every now and then, like right now, you got it dead wrong.

He was marking the ones he wanted to enlarge when he hit the ones of her with her son Joey, and it all changed in an instant.

"Jesus," he breathed. Everything he had

hoped for was there in those pictures. He'd been right after all. This was cover material. The kind of evocative portrait that pulled an emotional response from everyone who saw it. Sorrow rose up from the flat image and sucked the air from his lungs. That beautiful shot of a mother and child was drenched in it. He knew from the transcripts, the authorized ones, that Joey had been hospitalized a few times over the winter, but even that didn't explain the haunted expression in her eyes or the feeling that the answers were right there in front of him if he only knew how to look.

Think, he told himself. *Think harder.* The pieces were all there, but what did they add up to?

Gina. The expression in her eyes. The tape Crystal made. Joey with the straight nose and freckles, the dark blue eyes and thick black lashes, the cleft in his chin —

That was it. He had noticed it the first time he saw Joey, but it hadn't held any real significance at all for him. A random coincidence in a world filled with them. But this was a hell of a lot more than a coincidence. Gina's kid was a dead ringer for Claire's son . . . and Claire's son was a dead ringer for his father, Billy O'Malley.

Shit.

The guard at the lighthouse shook his head. "Nope, he never showed up. He was supposed

515

to be here at two, but —" he looked at his watch "— it's two forty-five now, and no sign of him."

Claire had been nursing a pretty healthy head of steam since seeing Maddy's car parked in front of the Women's Health Cooperative, and this pushed her temper into the red zone.

"He didn't call to cancel?"

"Nobody does," the man said. "They figure what else do we have to do out here?" He gave her a friendly smile. "I have fifteen minutes until it's time to lock up. If you want the *Reader's Digest* tour, I'd be glad to oblige."

She wanted the tour about as much as she wanted another round of root canal, but the man was being very gracious, and she was probably too angry to get behind the wheel of a car. She needed to cool off, both physically and emotionally, before she set off for home, or else she might force some poor unsuspecting motorist into a ditch if he so much as looked in his rearview mirror.

The guy walked her around the outside of the old lighthouse keeper's cottage, a plain, one-story shingled cottage with double-hung windows and shutters that had been functional rather than decorative.

"The keepers must have had small families," she said, peering into the tiny structure. "No room for a brood like mine."

She admired the small garden behind the house and the stone pathway that led down to the beach then followed the guard across the lawn to the lighthouse itself.

"This isn't the original," he was saying. "The original was erected in 1834, but a storm took it out ten years later. They didn't manage to find the money for a new one until after the Civil War. This lighthouse was in continuous use from 1871 until 1946 when it was shut down permanently and . . ."

How much useless information was he going to spout? Why didn't he shut up before she did something really terrible then buried his body under the azalea bushes? *You're losing it. The guy's giving you a guided tour. What the hell is your problem?* The poor man wasn't doing anything wrong. His only misfortune was being in the wrong place at the wrong time when the person she really wanted to stuff under the azaleas was the son of a bitch who hadn't bothered to show up.

Maybe that had been his plan all along. Maybe he had waited eight years for the chance to let her know exactly how he had felt on the Board-walk in Atlantic City. She understood all about revenge and retribution. Over the years she had plotted all manner of grisly scenarios that usually involved her husband and half of the female population of Paradise Point. For all she knew, Corin was parked somewhere up the road, laughing his ass off while she toured the outside of a locked lighthouse with a guy who didn't even know she hadn't heard a word he said.

Oh damn. She was going to cry. Right there in front of a perfect stranger who had already figured her for the loser she was. She hated women who cried over men. Anger was better. Anger didn't smack of martyrdom, and she had had enough of being viewed as Poor St. Claire, patron saint of wronged wives, to last a lifetime.

The tour limped to a close. The de facto guide had taken a long lunch in order to show Corin around, and now he had to get back to his office doing whatever it was he did to earn a living. He invited her to enjoy the grounds or maybe walk the beach, then said good-bye.

They shook hands, and she barely managed to control the wild desire to lay waste to everything in her path. The lighthouse. The keeper's cottage. Every tree and plant and shrub. If she could grab the ocean with her bare hands and wring it dry, she would. She had spent too much time waiting for a husband who didn't come home when he should to ever wait for another man again as long as she lived. He set her up, and she walked right into the trap like the pathetic fool she had always been.

She was in her car and about to turn the ignition key when she saw him turn into the driveway. He beeped his horn twice and gestured for her to wait, but she started the engine and threw the car into reverse.

"Fuck you," she said out loud as she started backing out of her parking spot. She wasn't going to be played for a fool by any man over the age of reason. Never again.

She slammed on her brakes as he angled his rental car behind her to block her exit. Two could play that game. She leaned on the horn, a long, loud, angry blare that she hoped could be heard in Philadelphia, but he refused to move.

Her car was old and battered. Another ding would just get lost in the shuffle. She threw the gears into reverse again and backed into his passenger door just hard enough to make her presence known.

"You better move that thing," she yelled out her open window, "because I'll drive right over it if I have to."

He didn't move. What did he care? It was a rental.

She nudged the car again, harder this time.

He still didn't move.

He wanted closure? She'd give him closure. She leaped out of her car and thumped the hood of his rental with a closed fist.

"Move!" she yelled in the voice of a crazy woman. "I swear to God if you don't move in the next ten seconds, I'll push you and that car straight into the ocean."

Clearly she had lost her mind. She hadn't a clue how you pushed a car into the Atlantic, but she was more than willing to figure it out on the fly. She didn't care how she looked, how she sounded, what he thought of her. She just wanted him to move that damn piece of junk so she could escape.

"Move!" she yelled again. The last time she had felt anything close to this kind of blind rage was on the steps of the church on the day of Billy's funeral when she had torn into his grandmother Irene like she had set the fire that took her husband's life.

"Claire." She hadn't even seen him get out of his car. The man had balls, she'd give him that. A sane person would have kept a zip code of distance between them. "Let me explain."

"I don't give a damn about your explanations. Just move that car so I can get out of here."

"I'm sorry." He didn't back away. He moved closer. The man was certifiable. "I got hung up. I called Liv for your cell number. You didn't answer, so I left a voice mail —"

"I have five kids. I always answer."

What was the matter with him? She had caught him flat-out lying, and he still didn't back down. "Check for messages. I didn't even know if you'd be here, but I called anyway."

"If you're such a Good Samaritan, why didn't you phone the poor guy who left work to show you around?"

"I tried, but the choice finally came down to standing there making phone calls or getting here as fast as I could."

"Shut up. I don't want to hear your excuses. Just get out of my way so I can go home and pick up my son."

"Check your messages, Claire. I wouldn't lie to you."

So he wanted to prolong the charade a little longer? Okay, why not? It wouldn't kill her to humor him. It might even be fun. She stormed back to her car, fumbled through her bag, then yanked out her cell phone.

"It's off," she said, astonished. "It's never off."

He didn't say *I told you so,* but he might as well have. She could hear his words just the same.

"I wouldn't do that to you, Claire." He was standing so close she could smell the residue of soap on his skin. "You deserve better."

She did deserve better. She knew that. Her anger deflated like a punctured balloon.

"I'm sorry," she managed, clutching the cell phone in trembling hands. "It's just that —"

"I know." His voice was soft, so tender, the voice she had heard in her dreams. "I know. . . ."

He *did* know. That was the amazing thing. He always had. From the very beginning he had seen her the way she really was, stripped of the titles *daughter* and *mother* and *wife.* Nobody else had ever seen her that way or known her so intimately and probably never would. She was far too good now at camouflage.

"I'm dreaming," she breathed as they moved into each other's arms. "You're not real."

"I'm real." His lips brushed hers lightly, and she gasped at the forgotten power of a kiss.

"You're very real." His lips found hers again, quickly, sweetly, and all the pain, all the sadness, all the anger that had flooded her just moments ago washed away like words written in sand.

He pulled her closer, and her body seemed to melt into his. *Be careful,* a small voice warned. *You're lonely, and it's been a very long time. Don't read too much into a man's touch just because you need to feel his body against yours, smell the familiar scent of his skin, savor the sweet, remembered taste of his mouth.*

It all came rushing back to her, all the things she had wanted to believe were figments of a lonely woman's imagination, the product of a specific time and place and of an emptiness so deep she had been afraid she would die of it.

"Nothing's changed," he said when they broke apart, gasping for breath.

"Everything has."

"Not the way I feel about you."

"You don't even know me," she said. "Not anymore. I'm not the same woman you met in Florida."

He brushed her hair away from her eyes. "I'm Corin," he said. "Who are you?" A silly, slightly mocking request that carried more weight than either one had expected.

"I don't know," she said softly. "I used to be so sure about everything, but now . . ." Her words trailed off into the sweet afternoon breeze.

"Don't move." He sprinted back to his rental,

leaned through the open driver's-side window, and pulled out an armful of yellow roses.

"Yellow roses!" She buried her face in the fragrant mass. "I can't believe you remembered."

"Yellow roses not red, mocha ice cream sodas, champagne cocktails, hamburgers medium rare with pickles and red onions, *Frasier* but not *Friends*, yes to rock, no to rap, anything but basketball, and a happy ending whenever possible."

Her own family wouldn't have been able to come up with that list.

"How long do we have?" he asked as she gently laid the flowers on the front seat of her car.

She checked her watch. "Sixty minutes, and then Cinderella turns back into a soccer mom."

He took her hand, and they ran down the path to the beach. She had the surprising sense that they had somehow picked up where they had left off, resuming a conversation interrupted almost nine years ago on another beach.

"I've lived near the ocean my whole life," she said as they strolled along the water's edge, "but somehow I never get tired of it."

"I'm that way about mountains," he said, stopping to snap a lone sandpiper standing ankle deep in foam.

"You once said you were going to do a book on mountain ranges. No captions. Just photos."

"I said a lot of things but didn't get around to too many of them."

"You've done more than most people."

"Easy to mistake action for accomplishment."

"What happened to the brash young man I met in Florida?"

"He turned forty. An album of pretty pictures isn't a hell of a lot to show for a man's life."

"Depends on the man and what he's looking for."

"I found what I was looking for a long time ago, Claire."

She shook her head. "You think you did, but —"

"I'm not a kid. What I felt for you was real, Claire." He paused. "It *is* real."

"I never meant to hurt you."

"That's the hell of it, isn't it." He leaned against an outcropping of rock and pulled her close to him. "You never meant to hurt me, and I never meant to fall in love."

"We were a family," she said. "That meant much more to both Billy and to me than either one of us had realized."

"You made the right choice."

She looked into his eyes. "You mean that?"

It was always hard for a man to make the connection between a woman's pregnant belly and a real live child who walked and talked and brought chaos wherever he went. She could almost see him connecting the dots.

"He's a great kid, Claire. I hope his father knew how lucky he was."

"We were both lucky," she said. "I don't know

if he had a premonition that he didn't have much time left, but everything was different after we got back from Florida." She laughed softly at the look on his face. "I didn't say perfect, I said different. At least I know I wasn't sharing him with anyone else at the end. I don't think I could have handled that."

He didn't say anything. His expression didn't change. But she had the sense that he didn't quite believe her.

"I would have known," she persisted, a lioness protecting her memories from harm. "I always knew."

"I'm glad for you," he said after a moment. "If I had to lose you to him, I'm glad he finally realized what he had."

He told her about his brief marriage and how much he regretted hurting an innocent bystander with the wreckage of his dreams of a life with Claire. "I married her in Paris not long after I saw you on the Boardwalk."

"How long did it last?"

"Less than a year. She had one major flaw: she wasn't you."

"Maybe you should have tried harder. My father always said the first ten years of marriage were like a shakedown cruise. You couldn't fix the problems until you figured out where they were hiding."

"We did the right thing. She's remarried and the mother of three. She sends me a thank-you note every Christmas."

She looked at her watch. "Damn. I have to leave in ten minutes. Billy has a dentist appointment, and I have to swing by the bar and pick him up."

"How does it feel having just one kid at home these days?"

"Strange," she admitted. He had known her as the mother of four kids under the age of twelve. "The house seems very empty."

"Show me your brood," he said as they walked back to their cars. "They must be pretty grown up now."

"You wouldn't recognize the little ones. The twins are both five-ten," she said, "and Maire's closing in on them fast."

"You have pictures with you, don't you?"

"You must be kidding." Her organizer bulged with them. They leaned against her car as she showed him a sampling, complete with narration. "That's Maire . . . she's in Ireland right now . . . she'll be back home in a few weeks . . . Courtney and Willow are in the military . . . that picture was taken the day they left for basic training . . . you saw Kathleen . . . here's one of her at the beach last year . . . she had a rough go of it, but look how amazing she is . . . and of course you know Billy Jr."

He reached for the photo and looked at it closely. "That kid has a great face."

She beamed with pride. "Doesn't he?"

"Cleft chin," Corin noted. "You don't see that very often."

"I told him he had a Kirk Douglas chin, and he looked at me and said, 'Who's Kirk Douglas?' Talk about feeling like a dinosaur." She gathered up the photos and stuffed them back into the organizer. "I wish I didn't have to leave."

"Then don't. We could get some takeout and have a picnic on the beach."

"I have to. He has a dentist appointment."

It all goes by so quickly, Corin. Until he's on his own, I have to put him first.

Given a choice, it would always be family. She was made that way, and nothing, not even the way he made her feel, could change that. But that didn't diminish the power of her emotions where he was concerned. *Tell him what you're thinking. Don't let him leave without hearing you say the words.*

She touched his hand in a tentative, uncertain gesture. "I've missed you." His phone calls. His letters. The sound of his voice. "Your friendship meant so much to me."

"Past tense?" His expression was rueful.

"You know what I'm saying." The sexual chemistry between them had been undeniable, but it was the unexpected gift of friendship that had stolen her heart. "Soul mates don't come back into your life every day of the week. We have some catching up to do."

He had a way of looking at her that made her feel loved, safe in the way a woman needed to feel safe in order to blossom and grow.

He took her hand and brought it to his lips. "I won't ask you to go steady with me until I come back from Malaysia."

She started to laugh, the kind of laugh she had lost many years ago. "Do I get to wear your class ring?"

"Depends what your boyfriend has to say about that."

"I don't have a boyfriend."

"What about that guy I saw you with Friday morning?"

"That was our first date."

"Will there be a second?"

"He took me to dinner Saturday night."

"You like him."

"He's very likable."

"Any plans for a third?"

"I don't know," she said. "Part of that is up to him, isn't it?"

"I'm not afraid of competition." He turned her hand over and kissed the palm, making her shiver. "This is only the beginning, Claire," he said. "Are you willing to see where the road takes us?"

Claire drove back into town in a state of elation, confusion, and almost giddy excitement.

He had asked if she was willing to see where the road took them. There were no guarantees. They both knew life didn't come with any. He lived out of a backpack. Her roots grew deep in a sleepy Jersey Shore town. Family life was a mystery to him. Living without the support of her own blood was even more of a mystery to her.

She didn't care. Change was in the air, and she wanted to embrace it wherever she found it. Deciding to leave the safe cocoon of O'Malley's for the uncertainty of Cuppa was the first of many steps toward some big, unknowable future that had the chance to be disastrous or wonderful or something in between.

They made no promises. They told no lies. They had seen too much, been hurt too often, for anything but the clear-eyed truth. Hopeful romantics, that was what they were. Old enough to know better but young enough to still believe happiness was possible.

She even looked different. She kept stealing glances at her reflection in the rearview mirror. She looked happy, like a woman with a delicious secret she wasn't quite ready to share with the world. Corin was leaving tonight for Malaysia, but even that wasn't enough to dim her sense of optimism and hope. If what they had was real, it would still be there when he returned at the end of the summer. No matter how it played out, where that road he talked about led them, nobody could take away the unexpected gift of this single hour together on a strip of Jersey Shore.

She whipped into the parking lot behind O'Malley's just shy of five-thirty. The place was packed for a Monday afternoon, and she was glad. She wanted the bar to take off like a sky-rocket on the Fourth of July. It was long past time for the O'Malley luck to change.

Aidan and Billy Jr. were in the back. Billy was washing down a plate of brownies with milk from his favorite beer stein, while Aidan chopped onions for the ubiquitous vat of chili.

"Hey, guys," she said then turned to her son. "Better go brush your teeth, Billy. Dr. Danzig isn't going to be very happy with all that choco-late."

"Can't," her offspring said. "I don't have a toothbrush."

She reached into her tote bag and withdrew a toothbrush and a tube of Colgate. "Nice try," she said as she handed them over to him. "Now get going. Your appointment's in twenty min-utes."

"You're in a better mood than you were when you left," Aidan observed as Billy grumbled his way into the bathroom. "Did Mike get settled in at Lilly's place?"

She stared at him for a second, struggling to figure out what he was talking about. "Yeah," she said finally, "but he was seriously pissed when I handed over his Dentu-Creme to Lilly. He actually thought she didn't know."

"His teeth were in a glass on his nightstand," Aidan said, laughing. "How the hell was he planning to explain that?"

"Love is blind." She grabbed a chunk of green pepper from the bowl on the work counter.

"Toss me another onion from the basket, would you?"

"Big or small?"

"Big."

She chose one the size of a softball and lobbed it to him. "Speaking of being pissed, I wish to hell you hadn't lied to me about Kelly."

"I thought we went through that before. She asked Maddy to look for a dress with her. Don't go reading more into it than there is, Red."

"Cut the bull, Aidan. I know where they went. I saw Maddy's car."

He narrowed his eyes in the same way his brother used to do when he had the feeling he wasn't going to like what he was about to hear. "Where did you see her car?"

"The women's health center out past the bridge. Did you think I was going to freak out because she wanted birth control? Okay, so maybe I'm a little hurt that she turned to Maddy, but I'm not stupid. I know she's practically grown now. I know she and Seth —" She stopped at the look on his face. "You really did think they were out shopping for a dress, didn't you?"

His expression said it all.

Oh God, she thought as Billy Jr. raced back into the room. *What on earth have I done?*

Chapter Twenty-five

"More tea, anyone?" The waitress tried hard not to look in Kelly's direction, which probably wasn't easy since she was crying loud enough to be heard in Philly.

"Just the chicken rice soup, please," Maddy said, "as soon as it's ready."

The waitress nodded and hurried off to the kitchen.

"I don't want the soup," Kelly managed between bouts of tears. "I hate chicken rice soup."

"It's medicinal," Maddy said. "And I'm not taking no for an answer."

Maddy sounded the way Kelly had imagined her own mother would sound, firm but loving, her voice more healing than any soup could possibly be.

Which, of course, only made her cry harder.

"Drink some water," Maddy said. "You'll dehydrate."

Kelly obediently did what she was told. She took two big sips of icy water, then put the glass back down on the paper place mat.

"I can't believe I did it," she said. "I just can't believe it."

Maddy reached across the table and took her hand. "Don't be so hard on yourself. You did what you thought was right."

"But what if I'm wrong? What if —"

"Here we go, ladies." The waitress deposited steaming bowls of chicken and rice soup in front of them. "If you need me, let out a yell."

"I hate chicken and rice soup," Kelly said again, peering down at the bowl.

"So do I," Maddy said, "but I'm my mother's daughter. The medicinal value of chicken soup was too strong for me to resist."

Kelly started to laugh but quickly dissolved back into tears. She had started crying within moments of leaving the Women's Health Cooperative over an hour ago, and so far she hadn't been able to stem the tide.

"Come on," Maddy urged. "Eat. You need your strength."

"Those little ricey bits are disgusting."

"You sound just like Hannah."

She took a spoonful then pushed the bowl away. "Will you tell my father?"

Maddy looked up, eyes wide with surprise. "I promised you I wouldn't say anything, and I meant it, honey. That's your decision to make, not mine."

She shook her head. "You don't understand. I *want* you to tell Daddy."

For a second she was afraid Maddy was going

to get up and head for the door, and she held her breath. *Please don't go . . . please don't leave me here.*

"Kelly, do you really think that's the right thing to do?"

"Please! You have to help me. He's going to be so hurt, Maddy!" She was crying so hard she could barely manage to push out her words. "He's always been so proud of me, and now I've ruined everything." She struggled to pull her emotions back from the edge. "All you have to do is tell him, and I'll do everything else. Just break the news to him, and I swear I'll never ask you for anything ever again."

Lassiter and his crew were still up in Surf City when Corin got back to the B and B. He walked straight over to the tape recorder Crystal had been using and pressed the Play button.

Gina's voice was instantly identifiable through the raucous laughter and loud music of the karaoke bar, but her words were difficult to decipher. He raised the volume and leaned closer. Crystal was a clever woman, and she saved tape by clicking on and off when Gina wandered away from the table in search of another margarita. Neither one of them was much of a singer. He winced as Gina's throaty alto attempted to scale Whitney Houston heights in a painful rendition of "I Will Always Love You."

There had to be more to the tape than this. His mind started to drift toward Claire, when

Gina's voice pulled him back. *Shit.* He rewound, then hit the Play button again, listening carefully. Her words were slurred, but he had no trouble understanding her. His suspicions were right. The resemblance between Claire's son and Gina's boy wasn't coincidental.

Gina and Billy O'Malley had stayed away from each other for a few years, when they slipped and made love one afternoon. He didn't know if it had been lust or boredom driving them, but this time their luck ran out, and Gina became pregnant.

"I asked him to come over that last morning. I had just found out I was pregnant, and I knew it was his because — well, figure it out for yourself, okay? Anyway, I told him, and he was . . . he came apart . . . all he kept talking about was Claire and his kids . . . what this would do to them . . . and I said you never gave a shit before . . . why do you suddenly give a damn how they feel . . . I was angry and hurt . . . we had been together off and on for almost twenty years, and this was our baby I was carrying . . . anyway we had a fight . . . the worst one ever, and I knew . . . and it was still going on when we heard the fire alarms going off . . . he had to go . . . it scared me, he was so out of his head with anger . . . be careful I told him right after I said he should go fuck himself . . . don't drive like a maniac . . . do you know he actually hit my mailbox when he was pulling out of my driveway . . . sometimes I think that's why . . . you

535

know . . . that's why he got trapped in the warehouse . . . he wasn't thinking . . . couldn't concentrate . . . I wish . . . shit . . . I wish —"

Her anguish was unmistakable, and he felt a sudden and surprising flash of remorse for all the lives that had been irrevocably changed by Billy's fatal weakness.

Claire's words from earlier that afternoon came back to him.

At least I know I wasn't sharing him with anyone else at the end. I don't think I could have handled that . . . I would have known . . . I always knew.

Did she know? He found it hard to believe she could look at Gina's son Joey and not see her own son, her own dead husband, looking back at her. He hadn't been in town more than twenty-four hours before he had nailed down the resemblance and begun to wonder about it. Probably half the town had figured it out by now, whispering behind their hands when Claire or Gina walked by.

He couldn't change that. He couldn't reach back through time and beat some sense into the bastard, make him see what he was doing to his wife, his family, any more than he could understand her need to protect her memory of their marriage. Sooner or later the truth would come out. This was a small town. Secrets didn't stay secret forever. One day Gina would have one margarita too many and slip again, or maybe Claire would want to put the final ghost to rest once and for all.

But he would be damned if she found out in a televised documentary along with everybody else.

"Sorry, Crystal," he said as he replaced Gina's tape with a blank one from the box on the table.

This was one of those times when he was reasonably certain God looked the other way and maybe, just maybe, smiled.

Maddy waited in the high school parking lot while Kelly started up her car. The plan was simple. They would drive back to O'Malley's, where Maddy would break the news to Aidan while Kelly drummed up her courage to face her father.

It wasn't much of a plan, but it was all they had. Clearly the girl was hanging on by an emotional thread. There wasn't time to prepare Aidan, to ease him toward the truth. His daughter needed him, and she needed him now. Her tears had finally stopped, but Maddy wasn't fooled. The young woman was overwhelmed by the enormity of her decision, and she desperately needed the support of her family to see her through.

Which left Maddy wondering exactly where she would figure in the equation once Aidan was told about the part she had played in Kelly's decision.

But it was too late now. She made a right into the parking lot behind O'Malley's and claimed one of the employee spots. Kelly came to a stop right behind her.

She turned off the ignition and sat there staring ahead into the gathering dusk. There was no way she could put a pretty face on the ugly truth. She had betrayed Aidan's trust. When the dust cleared, she knew he would be there for his daughter, but whether or not he would be able to forgive Maddy was anybody's guess.

She paused by Kelly's car before she went inside. "Give us fifteen minutes," she said. *And say a prayer.*

Kelly looked up at Maddy. Her eyes were swollen from her crying jag, red-rimmed and still weepy, but Maddy saw the faintest beginnings of acceptance. *I love you, Kel,* she thought. She wasn't sure when it had happened, when respect and reserve had been replaced with love, but there was no denying the very real emotion that filled her heart. She wasn't quite ready to say it, not with the future up in the air, but there it was, just the same.

"He won't blame you," Kelly said. "I won't let him."

She reached through the window and gave the girl's shoulder a quick squeeze. "Try to relax, honey. He loves you more than anything in this world. It's going to be okay."

The bar kitchen blazed with lights. Laughter rose in waves from the building and mingled with strains of vintage Springsteen. The spicy smells of chili and cheeseburgers wafted toward her. He made great chili. She had always said that. No store-bought chili powder for him, he always blended his own from —

His voice seemed to come from nowhere. "I wondered when you'd show up."

Her heart lurched against her rib cage as he stepped out of the shadows near the kitchen door.

"You scared me!" She could hear her pulse pounding in her ears. "I didn't see you there."

His gaze shifted toward the parking lot. "Why is Kelly still in her car?" She shrugged. "I need a cup of coffee," she said, falling far short of the light tone she was aiming for. "Let's go inside."

He didn't budge. "Why is Kelly sitting in her car?"

The hairs on the back of her neck lifted in response. She wasn't sure exactly what he knew or how he knew it, but there was no mistaking his tone of voice or the charged atmosphere between them.

She had never been good at confrontation. Even during those years of endless arguing with her mother, she had hated the loud voices and slammed doors, the siege mentality that had plagued their relationship. Running away was what she did best. Her fifteen years in Seattle were proof of that. This time, however, there was no place left to go. She was where she was meant to be, the place she had longed for all her life.

"Please," she said as she reached for the latch on the back door. "We need to talk."

He was bigger and heavier than she was, so physical intimidation was out. If he wanted to storm across the yard and confront his daughter, there was nothing she could do to stop him. She held her breath and prayed as she stepped into the kitchen. Thank God, he followed her inside.

The kitchen looked the way it always looked: cluttered, chaotic, but weirdly effective. Aidan had a system that not even Claire had been able to figure out. Chili bubbled on the stove next to a pot of pasta e fagiole. The grill gave testament to years of burgers and Philly cheese steaks. His laptop graced the top of the fridge.

"Okay," he said, leaning his cane against the side of the work counter, "why the hell didn't you tell me?"

She should have known better. They had never been very good at anything but the truth. Right from the start they had been open and honest with each other, and she had blown it all to bits. Her intentions had been good, her motives pure, but that didn't mean a thing when it came to the damage she had caused.

"It all happened so fast," she said, aware of how lame the excuse sounded. "I'd had my suspicions, but I kept looking the other way. She tried to talk to me. I knew she wanted to tell me something, but I was so afraid of what she had to say that I kept pushing her away." She paused to drag in a shaky breath.

"Why didn't you tell me?" he repeated.

If only she could erase that look in his eyes, a combination of anger and pain, and she had no one but herself to blame. "Aidan, I didn't mean to hurt you. I wanted to tell you more than anything. I tried to convince Kelly to tell you, but she threatened to drive up to New York alone if I did. If anything had happened to her, I —"

"Why the hell would she drive up to New York?"

She felt like somebody had dropped a two-ton block of ice on her chest as she realized they had been talking at cross purposes. *God, if you're paying any attention at all, help me know what to say.* "I'm sorry," she said, "but I'm not following you."

"Claire saw your car at that women's health center near the bridge. She figured out what was going on and tore a strip off me for not telling her."

The real story? Oh God. It was almost laughable. He and Claire thought they had gone to the center for birth control. Abortion would never have crossed their minds.

"Sit down," she said. "I have to tell you something."

"How about telling me why you lied. She's my daughter. You're going to be my wife. I thought we were all on the same team. I don't get it. She never hid things from me before. Why the hell would she start now?"

541

She took a long breath and plunged headfirst into the deep end of the pool. "Because she's never been pregnant before, Aidan."

Everything stopped for Aidan with those seven words. His world shrank in on itself, squeezing out sight and sound, until there was nothing left but a dark emptiness deep inside his heart where a lifetime of dreams once lived.

She might as well have lobbed a live hand grenade into the room. Not even a bomb could have done as much damage as those seven words.

"I'm sorry," she whispered. "I know this is hard for you."

How could she? He could barely grasp the meaning of it all himself. "How long have you known?" He sounded old, as if he had lived two lifetimes in a matter of moments.

"Since yesterday," she said, watching him with eyes filled with pain that matched his own.

"And you didn't tell me."

She shook her head. "I couldn't. I wanted to, you have to believe that, but she had options, Aidan, legal options. The choices all belonged to her. We made a deal, and I had to keep my part of the bargain."

"That's bullshit."

"It's the truth. She didn't want any of you to know. She was going to have an abortion, and it would all be over and forgotten. She even lied to Seth and told him she'd gotten her period."

"She wouldn't do that. Kelly's never lied to anyone in her life."

A flash of something close to pity moved quickly across her face. "Don't you get it, Aidan? She was so afraid of disappointing all of you, of not living up to expectation, of disrupting our wedding plans, that she was going to sneak off and have an abortion and live with the secret. You don't know how much —" She cut off her words abruptly, her attention focused on the back door.

He turned around, and time stopped. His baby girl, his beloved daughter, his one great achievement stood there in the doorway with her lovely face — so much like her mother's — bathed in tears. He looked at her and thought it couldn't be true. This was Kelly O'Malley, a beautiful young girl with the kind of future ahead of her that every parent dreamed of for their child.

He wanted to reach out and make it all better, but pain grabbed his gut and twisted hard. She had it all, the brains and the talent and the drive to do anything she wanted, to become anything she wanted to be, and now, in an instant, it was all gone. One moment, one mistake, and her life, her future, would never be the same.

"Aidan." He heard Maddy's voice from a great distance. "She needs you. Please don't lock her out."

The last thing he wanted to do was lock her

out, but a terrible sense of loss overwhelmed him, robbing him of movement and speech.

"Daddy?"

Da . . . da . . .

Daddy, can I have a new Barbie for my birthday?

Was my mommy pretty, Daddy?

Everyone else gets to stay out until eleven, Daddy. Why can't I?

I got it, Daddy! A full scholarship to Columbia.

She was a whisper of love in her mother's eyes. A baby cradled in his arms. A little girl with strawberry blond curls and a laugh that made him cry with joy. A teenager whose future could have taken her anywhere she wanted to go. A young woman with a baby of her own growing inside her belly.

He wasn't sure how it happened. Maybe he took a step toward Kelly or she took one toward him. It didn't matter. Suddenly his beloved child was in his arms, her tears wetting the front of his shirt, while he struggled with the death of one set of dreams and the birth of new ones.

"I'm sorry," she said through her sobs. "I'm so sorry."

"Shh." He stroked her hair the way he had when she was a little girl and her biggest problem was what to have for dessert. "It's going to be okay. Everything's going to be okay."

He said it because it was what she needed to hear, but at that moment, with his pregnant teenage daughter crying on his shoulder, he didn't think there was a chance in hell.

Claire tapped Tommy Kennedy on the shoulder. "Give me a cigarette."

"The hell I will," Tommy said as he pulled a draft for Mel Perry. "I thought you quit smoking."

"Maybe I'm starting again. Just one, Tommy. I'm jumping out of my skin."

He slid the draft down the length of the bar and was rewarded with a round of weary applause from the regulars. "What's going on?"

"Aidan and I tangled a few hours ago." She drummed her nails on the side of the cash register. "I think it's a good thing I'm leaving, TK. We both need a change."

"I'm not giving you a cigarette. Go out and take a walk around the parking lot. That'll clear your head better than a Camel."

"I might not come back."

"Sure you will. You didn't finish that piece of chocolate cake yet."

"You I'll miss," she said, kissing him on the cheek. "My brother-in-law I can do without."

She threaded her way through the clusters of neighbors and friends and slipped out the front door. People made their jokes about New Jersey — and some of them were even true — but there was nothing more beautiful than the sweet smell of a spring night by the shore. A heady combination of sea air and lilacs that made her feel hopeful about the future.

She tilted her head back and looked up at the

darkening sky. Corin was probably halfway to Newark Liberty by now and from there the long trip to Malaysia and whatever lay beyond. She touched the yellow rose she had pinned to the pocket of her shirt. He said he would come back, and she believed him. Anything was possible in this world, even happiness, or so they said.

She walked slowly down the front steps and followed the flagstone path that led to the parking lot in the back. She had told Aidan a thousand times that they should do something about the unlighted lot before O'Malley's got hit with a slip-and-fall, but there had never been enough money to take care of everything that needed their attention. Maybe someday, she thought. Maybe this was the year when all of their fortunes changed for the better.

Corin had stopped in at O'Malley's to say good-bye an hour ago. Her heart had almost torn through her chest when she looked up and saw him walking toward her. The regulars had welcomed him into their midst because he was Olivia's brother, but it was clear they had quickly come to like him for himself. She wasn't quite sure why that pleased her so much, but it did.

"Look at him," Tommy had said with a laugh as Corin chucked a McDonald's bag into the trash behind the bar. "Guy stops by so he can clean out his rental car."

"Hey, I drove around for ten minutes looking

for a trash basket. Don't you people believe in garbage?" Corin returned the teasing with the same kind of easy charm that had endeared his sister to everyone in town.

"Don't be a stranger," Mel Perry had boomed as Corin got ready to leave for Newark Liberty. "Remember, you've got family here."

After he left, she found one last yellow rose propped up near the old cash register.

She couldn't remember the last time she had looked forward to spring with a sense of renewal and — was it possible? — passion, but suddenly she was flooded with hope. Better than hope. She was flooded with the certainty that at long last life was going to treat her right.

She wasn't exactly afraid of the dark, but the parking lot at night wasn't her favorite place. She was about to turn around and return to the front when a voice reached out to her from the shadows.

"Hi, Claire."

She peered into the darkness and saw Maddy sitting on the trunk of Kelly's car. "What are you doing out here?"

"Kelly's got me pinned in. I'm waiting for her to come out and move her car so I can go home."

"Is she off somewhere with Seth?"

"She's in the kitchen talking to Aidan."

"So go in and ask her to move it."

She shook her head. "Not a good idea right now."

A deep silence fell between them, and Claire shivered as someone walked across her grave. "Is there a problem?"

The moodiness . . . that episode in the bathroom at the mall . . . oh God . . . it couldn't be . . . please . . .

"Yes, there is." Maddy reached out and touched her forearm. "Kelly is pregnant."

Her mind went blank. She could actually hear wind rushing through her brain, bits and pieces of memory, words and images all jumbled together in one giant sensory mass.

I wish your cousins were like you, Kelly . . . you're the one we don't have to worry about . . . this is Kelly, the O'Malley who is going to really go places . . . you know what your father always says: all he ever had to do was point you in the right direction, and you did the rest. All said with love and admiration and more than a touch of awe, but it was so much — too much — for any young woman to live up to.

She tried to concentrate as Maddy told her the story, ending up with a chance encounter at a mall drugstore and a trip to the women's health center.

"Why didn't you tell Aidan?" she asked as she tried to make sense of it all. "He's her father."

"She said she would drive up to an abortion clinic in Manhattan if I did. All I could think of was Hannah in the same position and how terrified she would be all alone in the city. If anything had happened to Kelly —" She shook her head. "So I made a bargain with her. I would respect her decision if she would let me be there with her."

Claire felt the stirrings of admiration building up inside her.

"So what made Kelly change her mind?"

"A snapshot Rose found in the attic." Maddy's smile was wistful. "A little three-by-five of Sandy and Kelly on the day of her baptism."

"I remember that day. They drove in from Pennsylvania with the baby, and the way Irene fussed over her you would've thought she was the new Messiah." Had they ever been that young, that happy? She wanted to think so, that it hadn't all been smoke and mirrors.

Sandy was little more than a baby herself, a tiny little blond with big blue eyes and a smile that could light up the world. She had been so proud of her beautiful baby girl, so filled with joy that just being in the same room with her made you feel good for the rest of the week.

Maddy's eyes grew soft with memories of her own. "You know how it is when you first hold your baby daughter in your arms and you see your mother and grandmother and aunts and your sisters in that tiny little face, and then you blink and she's holding a baby daughter of her own."

Claire nodded, unable to speak.

"That's exactly how it happened," Maddy continued. "She realized that this baby wasn't just part of her and Seth, it was part of her mother, too, and suddenly there was only one thing she could do."

They looked at each other, and just like that their differences disappeared. Kelly was all that mattered. She was one of them now, part of their tribe, and the child she was carrying would propel their dreams forward into another generation.

Claire gestured toward the brightly lit kitchen behind the bar. "You should be in there with the two of them, working things out."

A week ago she would have fought loud and hard to be there in the middle of everything, hungry for the future but too afraid to let go of the past to reach out and grab for it. She wouldn't have missed these years with Kelly and Aidan for anything, but it was Maddy's turn now. She had earned that right when she risked her future with Aidan to keep his daughter safe from harm.

Maddy slid off the car and brushed off the back of her jeans. "Can I borrow your keys? I need to get home."

"You can't leave."

"Yeah," she said. "I can. I need to see Hannah."

"Go in there and talk to him."

"It won't change anything. He's right. I should have gone to him the second I found out Kelly was pregnant."

"This isn't 1953," Claire shot back. "I know

my niece. If she said she would head to a clinic in New York if you told Aidan, then that's exactly what she would do." The thought of Kelly alone in some impersonal clinic in God knows what kind of neighborhood made her feel physically ill. "You did the right thing. I hope I would have had the guts to do the same."

"Thanks," Maddy said, "but that doesn't change things. I'll come back for my car in the morning."

"Don't go," Claire pleaded. "He can be a jackass sometimes, but that doesn't mean he doesn't love you."

Aidan's voice cut through the soft spring air. "She's right."

If there ever was a time to call in a favor from God, this was it.

Claire quickly excused herself and disappeared into the kitchen, leaving Maddy alone in the parking lot. Maddy was exhausted in every atom of her body. The simple act of standing upright was almost beyond her ability.

"It's been a long day," she said as Aidan made his way slowly across the rutted ground toward her. "I'm going home."

"This can't wait."

"It will have to," she said. "I want to go home and see my daughter."

He wasn't using his cane, and her breath

caught as he maneuvered his way around the potholes and branches that littered the ground like land mines.

"Where's your cane?" she asked. "You shouldn't be out here without it."

"Fuck the cane," he said. "This is more important."

"I'll come back tomorrow for my car," she said over her shoulder as she turned to leave. "Tell Kelly I'll call her."

"She's asleep at the kitchen table. If you wait a few minutes, you can tell her yourself."

"Nice try, but I already told you I'm out of here." Two steps, three, five, the distance between them grew, but he kept walking toward her.

His voice cut through the sounds of music and laughter that spilled from O'Malley's. "Kelly told me everything."

"So did I, but you weren't listening."

"I wasn't listening to anything at that moment, Maddy. I had just found out my daughter was pregnant."

He was right. Of course he was right. But she was too exhausted and angry and scared to admit it. "I betrayed your trust, Aidan. I didn't think about you at all." She flung the words at him like a challenge. "I was only thinking of how to protect Kelly."

"I know," he said. "You were thinking like her mother."

The truth of his words struck her like a blow

and her throat tightened. "Occupational hazard, I guess."

"But it's more than that, isn't it?" He sounded hopeful, scared, everything in between.

"I love her," she said simply. "I don't know exactly how or when it happened, but I love her the way I love Hannah. All I could think about was making sure she wasn't alone."

"Thank you," he said, and in his words she heard seventeen years of love and worry and bittersweet triumph.

She lowered her head and started to cry softly. She wasn't sure if she was happy, sad, exhausted, relieved, or some potent combination of all those emotions and more, but it didn't matter. The tears spilled down her cheeks and left wet splotches on her cotton sweater just the same.

"I didn't mean to make you cry."

"I know," she said, but she cried anyway, as he closed the distance between them. She had always been a sucker for big men, for broad chests and wide shoulders, for powerful arms and muscular thighs . . . for stubborn, imperfect men with big imperfect hearts who knew how to love. She had recognized his goodness the first moment they met, recognized her future in his eyes even if that future wasn't turning out exactly the way she had imagined it.

"I know I should have told you everything right away," she said, "but I was terrified we might lose her if I did. She would have gone up to New York, Aidan, I know she would have, and if anything —"

The thought was more than either one of them could handle.

He pulled her close, and she settled into the familiar thrill of his embrace. His smell, his warmth, his love. "I don't know what's going to happen," he said, his mouth warm against the side of her throat. "We won't be your normal everyday newlyweds."

"Hannah would have made sure we never had a chance to be normal everyday newlyweds."

"I want you to know what you're getting into. Anything's possible. We could end up raising Kelly's baby."

She dropped her guard and let him see into her soul. "I know what I'm getting into," she said, as well as anyone could possibly know what the future held for them. "If Kelly needs us, we'll be there for her."

"This is a hell of a lot more than you were bargaining on when you said you'd marry me."

"You're right. It is."

"If you want to postpone the wedding until we see —"

She raised up on her toes and kissed him. "No."

"What was that?"

She kissed him again. "That was a no."

"Last chance to change your mind."

"Not now," she said. "Not ever."

"This is a hell of a lot to ask of you," he said.

"We were supposed to be talking about our own babies, not grandbabies."

"Is there a law that says we can't do both?"

The look in his eyes made her heart soar.

"We'll find out soon enough," he said, and then he kissed her and sealed their fate.

Whatever happened, they were in this together.

They were family.

Epilogue

Late September — Paradise Point

"This is a very important job," Kelly said as she fastened the last tiny hook on Hannah's dress. "The flower girl brings all of the magic to the wedding."

Hannah eyed her reflection in the full-length mirror. "I know," she said, lifting up her skirts so she could admire her ruffled petticoat. "Mommy told me."

She looked like an angel in her cotton candy–pink dress, and Kelly had to blink back sentimental tears as the little girl twirled around the room with Priscilla yapping at her heels. It seemed all she did these days was cry. Happy tears, sentimental tears, tears for no reason at all. Morning sickness had been replaced by an excess of emotion that had kept her in a constant state of hormonal weepiness.

There had been a July wedding after all, but not her Dad's and Maddy's. She and Seth had planned to marry eventually, but Mother Nature had her own ideas, and they were both old-fashioned enough to want to be married before the baby was born. Everyone said they were too young, that they should wait a little longer, see where their lives took them, but they had held fast to their plan and finally won their families over. Life didn't come with guarantees. It didn't care if you were seventeen or forty-five. Sometimes you just had to follow your heart and trust God would send an extra blessing or two your way.

She had made the right decision, the only decision possible for her and Seth, and she knew they would find a way to make it work. She believed in them. She had believed in them from the first moment she met him all those years ago in first grade. When you had love on your side, you were already halfway there.

Aunt Claire had asked Olivia if she and Maddy could hold the reception at Cuppa, and Olivia had not only let them open the doors wide to family and friends, she had found a house-sit for them near Columbia, a tiny studio apartment that had become the center of their universe. Seth worked nights in a Harlem bakery and attended classes during the day, while Kelly tutored and typed between classes for extra money. Her academic adviser was an understanding woman who promised her they would find a way for her to keep up her grades and maintain her scholarship after the baby arrived, and Kelly hoped she was right.

If she wasn't, she would just have to find another way to make those dreams come true.

Her life didn't look anything like she had thought it would, but that was okay. It was bigger, scarier, more wonderful, more precious than she had ever imagined.

Aunt Claire knocked on the doorjamb and poked her head inside. "How are we doing, girls?"

Kelly grinned at her aunt as Hannah did a lopsided pirouette and tumbled onto the bed, giggling. "I think Hannah's going to be a spectacular flower girl."

"I think so, too," her aunt said as Hannah giggled even louder. "I think she's going to be the best flower girl ever."

"Can I see Mommy now?" Hannah asked. "I want to show her my new shoes."

Aunt Claire made a show of admiring the little girl's satin ballet flats. "That's why I'm here, Miss Lawler. It's time for us to have our pictures taken with the bride."

"No pictures of me," Kelly said as they walked down the hall to Maddy's room. "I look like a blimp."

Her aunt's eyes misted over as she glanced down at Kelly's barely visible bump. "You look beautiful."

"Poor Lucy had to let out the seams three times."

"Do you remember when I was carrying Billy? I looked like I was carrying a giraffe."

"Don't make me laugh," Kelly protested. "I'm peeing every five minutes as it is."

Hannah darted past them and burst into Maddy's room. "Mommy, look!" she shrieked. "I'm a fairy princess!"

"The dress!" Lucy shrieked as Hannah flung herself into Maddy's arms.

"Don't worry about the dress," Rose said, dabbing her eyes with a pale blue handkerchief. "We can fix the dress."

"Speak for yourself," Lucy said, looking up from a quick repair of Gina's bridesmaid gown. "These poor old fingers are ready for retirement."

Corin Flynn quietly moved from corner to corner, snapping photos as he went. Kelly couldn't help but notice he took more than his fair share of her Aunt Claire. He had been in town for a week, and everyone had noticed that he spent most of his time at Cuppa. Sure, the tea shop was a rousing success, but he wasn't fooling anybody when he said he was simply trying to document the birth of a new business. She hadn't quite figured out what was going on, but clearly there was some kind of attraction between them. Her aunt glowed whenever she looked at him, something that hadn't escaped Mr. Fenelli's notice. Aunt Claire said she and Ryan's dad were just good friends, but Mr. Fenelli seemed to have other ideas, and it would be a lot of fun to watch what fate had in store for all of them.

Her aunt looked younger and happier than Kelly had ever seen her, and much of the credit went to the successful launch of the tea shop.

Claire and Maddy had turned out to be a terrific team, and they were already talking to Olivia Westmore and Rose about building an enclosed patio garden onto the cottage. Her aunt had quickly become the driving force behind the tea shop, and it wouldn't be long before she gave Rose and The Candlelight a run for their money.

No doubt about it. The O'Malley luck had finally changed for the better.

Crystal was downstairs taping interviews with the out-of-town relatives. She had stormed off the job a few months back, claiming somebody had sabotaged a "blockbuster" interview, but Peter Lassiter soon lured her back into the fold. In fact, the entire PBS crew was on site, capturing the sights and sounds of the big wedding for the documentary. Lassiter was talking to Maddy about doing the narration for the series, and everyone hoped the contracts would be signed, sealed, and delivered after she returned from the honeymoon.

"Oh Maddy," Kelly breathed as she looked at the woman she already thought of as her mother. "You look so beautiful."

"I hope your father thinks so," Maddy said, and everyone laughed. It was no secret that Kelly's father thought Maddy Bainbridge was the most beautiful woman on the planet. She could walk down the aisle in faded jeans and a T-shirt, and he would be mesmerized.

Just wait until he saw Maddy in this dress! Lucy DiFalco had poured all of her love and talent into creating a work of art. Yards and yards of ivory satin, the color of candlelight, heavily embroidered with crystals and fine gold thread that caught and reflected the light like diamonds. An elbow-length veil of spider's nest lace. Jewel-encrusted shoes with heels so high they made her dizzy just looking at them.

"You have a waist," Kelly said with a groan of envy. "I used to have a waist."

"And you'll have one again in January," Maddy said. "I promise you."

"Stan from the limo service just called," Denise bellowed up the stairs. "Ten minutes, ladies!"

Rose turned to Corin Flynn. "Would it be a terrible imposition to ask you to take a photo just for me?"

He gave her a smile that made Kelly immediately think of his sister Olivia. "I'll take as many as you want, Rosie. Just tell me what you're looking for."

"I want a photo with my girls," she said, dabbing her eyes again with the edge of her handkerchief. "All three generations."

He sat Rose in a slipper chair near the window and positioned Hannah on her lap. Maddy stood to Rose's right, backlit by the sun streaming through the window. Corin Flynn aimed his camera and clicked as Kelly watched. One day, many years from now, Hannah would find the picture tucked away in her grandmother's attic, and the whole day would come rushing back to her, and she would remember how it felt to be loved. Maybe Hannah's daughter would be there, too, a curious little girl with big blue eyes who loved to listen to stories about all the women who had come before.

Kelly looked up and saw Maddy watching her.

"You're part of the family, too," Maddy said, holding out her hand.

Kelly hesitated but only for a second. She took her place next to Maddy, then laughed when Rose motioned for Claire to join them, too. She could feel the circle expanding to welcome them all inside its embrace. She was where she belonged, at the heart of a family of strong and loving women who would be there for her every step of the way.

She placed her hands over her bump and felt the first stirrings of life beneath her fingertips. Faint, fluttery, unmistakable.

A daughter, she thought as Corin Flynn began to snap pictures of her tribe.

It just had to be.

About the Author

Barbara Bretton is the *USA Today* bestselling award-winning author of more than forty books. She currently has more than ten million copies in print around the world. Her works have been translated into twelve languages in more than twenty countries.

Barbara lives in New Jersey but loves to spend as much time as possible in Maine with her husband, walking the rocky beaches and dreaming up plots for upcoming books.

You can write to Barbara at barbara@barbarabretton.com or visit her Web site at www.barbarabretton.com.